The
Last of the
Honky-tonk Angels

ALSO BY MARSHA MOYER

❧

The Second Coming of Lucy Hatch

WILLIAM MORROW

An Imprint of HarperCollins*Publishers*

The
Last of the
Honky-tonk Angels

Marsha Moyer

Grateful acknowledgment is made for permission to reprint the
following copyrighted materials: Lyrics from "If You Were a
Bluebird" by Butch Hancock, © 1991 Rainlight Music
(ASCAP), adm. by Bug Music.

HarperCollins books may be purchased for educational,
business, or sales promotional use. For information please write:
Special Markets Department, HarperCollins Publishers Inc.,
10 East 53rd Street, New York, NY 10022.

FIRST EDITION

Designed by Stephanie Huntwork

Printed on acid-free paper.

Library of Congress Cataloging-in-Publication Data has been applied for.

ISBN 0-06-008163-5

03 04 05 06 07 WBC/QW 10 9 8 7 6 5 4 3 2 1

ACKNOWLEDGMENTS

I would like to recognize Jay Poth, author of *The Last Cowman*, for his assistance, however inadvertent, in helping me come up with a title, as well as our mutual friend Richard Willis, who introduced me to Jay and who gave freely of his time and expertise with regard to firearms, power tools, and arboreal incineration. Although few of Richard's contributions survived the final draft of the manuscript, fortunately our friendship did. Thanks, guys, and Hook 'Em.

I am grateful to Carrie Rossenfeld and Ginny Bernal for generously sharing with me some of their early obstetrical experiences; to Mark Akin, M.D., for explaining the science of prenatal sonograms; to Christopher Lueck for holding the torch in one hand while mixing margaritas with the other; and to my writing compadrés Cynthia Burdick, Court Sansom, and Stephanie Smith for moral support, computer savvy, and breakfast burritos.

Two Barbaras, Moyer (mom) and Braun (agent), deserve a big "thank you" this time out for their forbearance and wise counsel.

The version of Butch Hancock's song "If You Were a Bluebird" on the tape deck in Ash's truck in chapter eight is Miss Toni Price's exquisite rendition from her 1995 recording, *Hey*.

❧

I come loose sometimes, torn free of the bindings of my lives: before and after, then and now. It happens most often in the cleft between sleep and waking, that blurred purple place where we float unanchored, not knowing what's real and what's dreamed, where the dead walk hand in hand alongside us and the unborn have forms and faces, whole histories of loss and expectation. I lie in the dove-colored dawn, struggling to name the wrinkle of the sheet under my hip, the dark jut of the pines taking shape beyond the window, feeling my heart beat, cupped in the hands of two men. They take turns holding it, delicately, reverentially; the heat of their work-scarred palms rises up through the membrane, and when one of them passes it to the other, the transition is so tender I barely feel it. I see their faces, and there is a shining, some shared comprehension, that passes from one dark gaze to another.

Here, the first one says wordlessly; this is yours now.

Yes, says the second. I know.

In the gathering light, the ceiling fan circles lazily overhead. On the far wall, the bureau emerges from the gloom, another day in its same old spot. Out front, in the yard, one of the dogs beats its tail against the steps. Behind me the sheet rustles, shifts. A knee, brash and wiry-haired, inserts itself between mine; a brown arm circles my waist. Against my ear then, a voice sandpapered with sleep: Mmm.

Yes. I'm awake now. Present. No longer a foot in each life, but tethered to this sharp, specific earth.

And my heart, homeless until now, settles itself in Ash's palm, and rests there.

Lucy

 Looking back, it seems like there wasn't anything remarkable about that morning, just one of what till then had been an unbroken chain of mornings like it, a long fever spell of green and summertime and damp sheets and bare skin and Ash at the center, at the heart, of everything. We'd slept late, him spooned up tight behind me and, in the dreamlike way of those mornings, came awake with him, almost by accident, fitting himself inside me; there was no urgency to it, only something sweet and congenial, and we lay like that, joined but motionless, for a long time before his fingers traced their way over my hipbone and I started squirming and things shifted into the next gear, as such things are wont to do. I knew he had work to do that morning—building kitchen cabinets for old Mrs. Crouch at her house in town—but there was nothing rushed in his attentions, nothing that suggested there was anywhere in the world he had to be but there with me, his belly sweating against my back, breathing into the uncombed tangle of my hair, the two of us straining gently, then not so gently, toward some mutually agreeable conclusion.

He got up, finally, and switched on the air conditioner; even in June, Ash liked to sleep with the windows open and the warm night breeze drifting in through the screens, nothing but the blades of the ceiling fan slapping their tranquil rhythm overhead, but by ten A.M. the house was starting to stifle. He got into the shower, and I lay back against the sheets, positioning myself under the vent and allowing the cold jets of air to play across my warm, moist skin, turning it to goose-flesh. The sun through the curtains stippled my torso and thighs with bands of lemony light, and I recall very plainly that I loved my body, marveled not just at its health and vitality, its ability to serve and to please me, but at the round symmetry of my breasts, gently swelled belly, taut-muscled thighs, the pure expanse of my creamy, pink-tipped skin. I looked, I decided happily, juicy. It was no wonder Ash Farrell had been late for work every day for a month.

The shower stopped, and a cloud of steam drifted in from the bath-room, and in a few seconds I heard him humming, which meant he was shaving. A few minutes later he emerged, naked, his wet hair combed off his forehead. I smiled and preened at him from the bed, and he smiled back absently as he crossed to the walk-in closet.

"Ash?"

He came out stuffing the tail of a faded gray T-shirt into the waist-band of his Levi's. "Where are my boots?" he asked, and knelt and peered under the bed.

"*Ash*," I said again, and he lifted his head and said, "What?"

"Do you think I'm beautiful?"

He gave me an indulgent half smile, the kind men give their women when the women say or do something goofy or knuckleheaded. "I can't believe you have to ask me that," he said. But I had his attention now; I arched my back, rearranging myself among the disheveled sheets. "Do you mean beautiful in general, or now, in particular?" He sat down carefully at the foot of the mattress. Looking, but not touching.

"Either one," I said, stretching a bare foot toward him. "Now, in particular, I guess."

"It's a tempting display, I admit." He looked interested but wary, like I might be trying to dupe him.

"Don't you think I look juicy?" I pushed myself up on my elbows, nipples peaked and rosy in the stream of refrigerated air. A final assault, I let my right knee fall gently open, giving him the brunt of what, I hoped, I was talking about.

Ash laughed, and stretched out his hand and wrapped it around my nearest ankle. "Juicy Lucy," he said, and bent and kissed my instep. "That would be you."

"Don't go," I said, and I think we both were surprised by the edge in my voice, that what had been playful seconds before now sounded pinched and a little desperate.

He bent and nuzzled my cheek with his, freshly scraped and still smelling of shaving cream. "Mrs. Crouch is gonna fire my sorry ass," he whispered, his breath against my mouth making me shiver. Like the search for his boots under the bed, the remark was rhetorical. How many days like this in your life do you get to count, you and another soul reaching out across the wide, dark universe and in a single point of brightness finding each other? Ash knelt in his beat-up Levi's over me, and I pulled him into my arms so hard I could feel the precise arrangement of bone beneath muscle, so hard I could feel our two hearts beating, chest to chest.

He raised his face and looked into my eyes. "My Lord, Luce," he said. "What are you trying to do to me?" But I couldn't answer him. How was I supposed to put a name to what I felt? Why were all the words so frail and insubstantial? As long as I knew Ash, I would be looking for words to match the sensations, to declare myself with something approaching the scope of what our bodies learned to do.

I let him go, and he sat up and pulled on a pair of socks, and brought his boots out from under the bed. He lifted his pager off the dresser and squinted at it. "Uh-oh," he said. I listened to him pad down the hall in his sock feet and lift the phone out of its cradle. "Good morning, Mrs. Crouch, this is Ash Farrell. Yes, ma'am, I know I said nine o'clock and it's ten-thirty. Yes, ma'am, but you see, those fellows down at the True Value, the ones who were supposed to order the hinges for your kitchen cupboards . . ." He wandered out of earshot and I decided it was just as well, that one thing I didn't need was a lesson in what a

skillful fibber Ash was, not while I lay naked and spent in a puddle of
our combined fluids. Juicy Lucy, indeed.

"Mrs. Crouch is not a happy camper," Ash said, sitting down in the
rocker in the corner to pull on his scuffed old work boots as the image
of my husband, Mitchell, the last morning of his life, glanced across my
memory and then ricocheted off, into the shadows.

"Are you fired?" I asked, pulling the sheet over me.

"Nah." Ash placed his feet side by side on the floor and pushed himself out of the rocker. "Where else is she gonna find somebody like me?
Somebody with my unique skills." He grinned. "My attention to
detail."

He bent over and planted his hands on either side of my shoulders
and kissed me lightly on the lips. "Thanks for a memorable morning,
Miss Hatch," he said, turning to scoop his wallet and keys off the
dresser. "Maybe if you're not doing anything we could get together
later." I nodded, pressing the sheet against my breasts, trying to imagine that I looked like the heroine on the cover of a romance novel, rav-
ished and wanton, and not sweaty and bedraggled, like I felt.

"Ash?" I said, as he turned to leave.

"Yeah?"

But the only phrase that would come into my head was: *world without
end, amen*. It stuck there and went around and around, crazily, like a
record on an out-of-control turntable. I shook my head. "Nothing.
Never mind."

He considered me solemnly from the threshold. After several seconds, he smiled. "Me, too," he said softly, and I listened to him walk
down the hall and out the front door. His old truck sputtered and
roared; Ash gunned it a couple of times, then wrested it into reverse
and into his customary wild backwards arc across the yard, and finally
forward, down the road to town.

❧

Ash and I had been together less than three months then, and I still had
to stop sometimes in the middle of things and get my bearings, remind
myself where I was and how I'd come to land there. Not six months

before, I'd been Mrs. Mitchell Breward, the wife of a farmer going on fifteen years. Then Mitchell was killed, quickly and horribly, in an accident with a mowing machine; and I, deep in the shock that follows a sudden loss, had allowed my family to pack me up and bring me back to Mooney, my hometown. I hadn't realized how much I'd missed this patch of northeast Texas, where pine trees scraped the sky so high they shaded green to black against the blue, where the air was clear enough some mornings it hurt, in a good way, to draw breath; where twelve hundred citizens went about their days in the same old ways I remembered from childhood, everybody's nose in everybody else's business. I'd started to think I might be able to live out my life there, headstrong and alone, like my mama's sister, Dove; and then my brother Bailey and his wife, Geneva, insisted on taking me out to a local dance hall, and when the lights came up and the music started, there was Ash Farrell.

It wasn't love at first sight — not on my part, anyway, though Ash might beg to differ — but there was something from the beginning, a quiver of recognition, a voice that said, *I know this.* We dodged and parried around each other for two weeks; or rather, I dodged and parried while Ash just kept coming at me, waving bouquets of flowers, serenading me in the driveway at midnight, until something crusted over at the center of me began to yield. At thirty-three, I'd never been in love, not with the husband I'd lost or anyone before him, and to accept what Ash was offering — the gestures, the courtship, that delicious, menacing dance of sex — was terrifying, and irresistible. I wore myself out, resisting; I shorted out all my defenses, so that when Ash drove twelve hours across the state in a twenty-year flood to claim me, I was nothing anymore but a quivering heap of pure longing.

I don't recall when I knew I was in love with him. Maybe sex was a means for bringing down the battlements and letting it in; or maybe, like with the roses and the lullabies, it simply allowed me to receive something that was already present. But I was amazed by how deeply familiar it felt, how I slipped it around me like a downy old quilt, warm and welcome against my skin. I moved into his house the second night we spent together, although I kept up the rent on my own place a few miles down the road, lame little badge of my independence. We didn't talk much about it: about our feelings, about the future. We used the word "love" like it was some rare and ancient spice, something kept in a jeweled box under lock and key, a pinch or so doled out every few days, too precious to squander. I remembered the first time Ash said it to me, how I'd closed my eyes like his face was too bright, how all I could say in reply was, *Yes. Yes.* It was all new, untried. I was happy; and I thought that to examine happiness too closely was, like the loaf that won't rise, a sure invitation to trouble.

This was Tuesday, my day off from my part-time job at Faye's Flowers. The day, what was left of it, seemed to stretch before me like a roll of sparkly gift paper, waiting for me to pick what I wanted to wrap in it. I thought I might call my sister-in-law Geneva and see if she wanted to have lunch, or maybe drive over and help my aunt Dove in her garden. I even considered dropping by to visit my mama before I remembered she'd taken off for two months for Greece and Turkey, with a Bible Land tour group from Dallas, to walk in the footsteps of the Apostle Paul. I lay there for a while in the moist, tangled sheets beneath the frosty air-conditioning, in a contented wash of satisfaction and indecision, thinking about Ash, and in a few minutes, I was asleep.

⚭

I woke to the sound of tires coming up the unpaved road. The air conditioner had cycled off and I was lying in a pool of sun, the sheets sticking to me, and I blinked at the bedside clock as the sound of the vehicle drew closer. A quarter till noon; not likely Ash would be back so soon. Unless, of course, Mrs. Crouch *had* fired his sorry ass, after all. I rolled off the bed, peeling the sheets away from my skin, and looked out the window.

A red Chrysler sedan, a lot shinier and more formidable-looking than anything any of Ash's neighbors owned, slowed in front of the house. The car rolled to a halt, and after a minute the driver's door opened and a woman got out. It was immediately obvious that this person was not from Mooney or, for that matter, from rural East Texas. She had a sleek helmet of dyed-black hair, and was wearing a pricey-looking pantsuit, royal blue, with a flowered scarf and heels. Perched on her nose were sunglasses, which she lifted in order to squint at the house. She had on so much gold jewelry she looked like she'd raided a Sarah Coventry party.

The woman turned and leaned into the car, and presently the passenger-side door opened and someone else got out, a short, stocky girl dressed, in spite of the heat, in corduroy pants and a hooded sweatshirt. She stared over the roof of the car from behind lank brown bangs like she expected the house to sprout wings and take off through the ozone like a spaceship.

They seemed to be arguing. I was relieved when I saw that; I thought it was proof that they had the wrong address, that they'd stumbled into my life by mistake and in a couple of minutes I'd set them straight and they'd be on their way. I yanked the top sheet off the bed and draped it around me and pattered up the hallway just as the woman stepped onto the porch and raised her fist to knock.

"Hi," I said, jerking open the door, startling the woman on the other side of the screen with her mouth all agape and her curled hand frozen shoulder high, like a carved drugstore Indian. "You all must be lost."

Slowly she lowered her arm, studying me through the lenses of her dark glasses. "I'm sorry to bother you. We're looking for the home of Ash Farrell."

I'd spent more time than I cared to admit worrying about the kind of women who might one day show up on Ash's doorstep: the jilted girlfriends, the banished flirtations, the crushed crushes, to whom the current woman in Ash's bed—me—would be nothing but a minor inconvenience, a blip on the radar. But the woman standing there now looked so prim and officious, I didn't see how she could be any kind of real threat, and somehow the presence of the girl failed to register. I was such a fool.

"Well, you found it," I said. "Ash isn't here right now, though. He won't be home till this evening," I added. "Is there something I can do for you?"

The woman glanced back at the girl, who was scuffing the toes of her sneakers in the dirt, then let out her breath in an exasperated little huff.

"I am Marlene Farrell," she announced. "Ash's former wife. And this is our daughter, Denise."

I tried not to let my jaw drop. Ash kept an old photo of his ex-wife and baby in a drawer in the bedroom bureau; but the woman standing now on his porch, stiff and overdressed, her lacquered mouth zippered into a straight line, bore so little resemblance to the young beauty in the photo, I could not have picked her out of a lineup. I knew of Ash's brief early marriage, the daughter in Dallas he hadn't seen in seven years; but in the sweet lassitude of our new relationship, I'd come to think of it as happening in some bygone era, in a tall castle surrounded by a moat, where they would reside forever in a state of permanent amnesia, forgetting they'd ever heard Ash Farrell's name. Ash had told me the book was closed, and I'd been all too eager to believe him.

I pushed open the screen door and stepped out onto the porch. My sheet caught on the doorjamb and slipped a little, but I retrieved it in the nick of time, grasping it between my breasts. Marlene had dropped her dark glasses into place again, and without the feedback of her eyes, her expression was open to limitless interpretation.

"How do you do," I said. "I'm Lucy Hatch. I'm Ash's—"

Ash's what? Buddy? Roommate? Concubine? I realized I had never given this—my official designation—a single thought, and now it was too late; my silence damned me as surely as my stained and sweaty bedsheet.

"Yes, I see." Marlene raised her glasses to take me in, from my bare toes to the top of my sleep-tousled head and every inch between. Her eyes were the brilliant, unnatural turquoise you see at the bottom of swimming pools. "How far along are you?" she asked, in a tone that was almost conversational. Her eyes focused on my hand, gripping the sheet.

"Excuse me?" I thought she was asking if I'd been in the process of something: getting dressed, going out.

"I'm sorry to speak so intimately. It's just that, I knew the minute I saw you. I looked just like that myself, a couple of months gone."

"Ma!" the girl said then, shifting her weight from one foot to the other. "C'mon, he isn't here. Let's just get in the car and go home."

"Denise, if I've told you once, I've told you a thousand times. We are not *going* home. I am going to Chicago, and you are—" She cut her gaze at me. "You are staying here."

I blinked several times to clear the spots that danced before my eyes. Incredible to believe that five minutes before I'd been tucked between Ash's sheets, sound asleep, untroubled as a lamb. Now, with a handful of words, a few choice sentences, my life had changed in so many directions I barely knew which way to let my mind run.

"I do apologize for putting you in the middle of this, ah—Lacey, was it?" Her earlier question flashed across my memory—*How far along?*—and for a second I thought I was going to hyperventilate, but I didn't. I didn't bother to correct her, either. "I tried to call Ash from Dallas, several times," Marlene said, her voice rushed and defensive. "But he never seems to be home. Or always too busy to pick up the phone." Her eyes bore straight through my wrinkled sheet, straight into my soul.

She began to fuss with a clasp on one of her bracelets. "Look, I hate to be rude, but I've got a plane to catch in Little Rock. Tomorrow morning I'm starting an internship at PaineWebber, in Chicago. I wish there were time for us all to sit down and chat about this, but there isn't. Denise is a good girl, and it's time she got to know her father, that he . . ." She paused, turning to consider the girl who was circling aimlessly in the dusty patch of the front yard, a mystery child who from all appearances bore no genetic link to either of her parents; she looked as much like Ash as the man in the moon. "That he sees what she's become," Marlene said. "I hope you'll explain it to him for me."

"Explain what?" I asked. "What am I supposed to—"

"Tell him I'll call him in a few days and we'll talk. Tell him he *owes* this to me," she said, and there was a flat and bitter note in her voice that scared me a little. "Get your bag, sugar," she said to the girl, who looked at me helplessly over the roof of the car, then reached into the backseat and pulled out a beat-up duffel bag and slung it over her shoulder.

With a jerk of her chin, Marlene motioned the girl forward, and slowly she came, her eyes fastened to the ground. "Look at you," Marlene said, tugging briskly at the shoulders of her daughter's sweatshirt, brushing the long bangs out of her eyes. "Couldn't you have at least combed your hair?" she said. "Was that too much to ask you to do?" I thought I could hear every one of the words that hung unspoken on the girl's lips, choked off by the tears that swam in her eyes.

"I've got to hit the road, sweetie," Marlene said. "I'll call you in a day or two, when I get settled. Meanwhile, you know where to find me, right? Remember how to spell Kent's last name?" The girl nodded mutely. "You be sweet for these people, will you? Remind your daddy what it's like to have a kid around the house. It looks like he could use a refresher course."

Marlene kissed her daughter quickly on the forehead and then smiled tight-lipped at me, her turquoise eyes glittering like a snake's over the rims of her glasses. Then she climbed into her snazzy red car, executed a neat three-point turn in the front yard, and sped away, leaving nothing behind her as it had been before.

2

Denny

 So there I am, standing in the yard, a patch of dirt in a circle of pine trees, with my duffel in my hand, watching Ma head down the driveway in a cloud of dust, like if she didn't break the speed limit getting out of there somebody'd catch her and turn her around, put me in the front seat, and point us back toward Dallas. Good riddance, is what I was thinking, or trying to think, acting like it was the dust that put tears in my eyes, acting like I was as glad to be done with her as she was with me. We hadn't been getting along too good lately, Ma and me, ever since she took up with this Kent guy. He put ideas in her head, made her lose her funky old dresses and get that stupid haircut, told her what to read and eat and think till I couldn't even see the old Ma anymore under all the paint and hardware. I hadn't seen my dad since I was seven years old, didn't know much about him except that he'd built this house in the country near the little town where he was born and did some kind of carpentry work for a living and sang in a honky-tonk on the weekends.

That interested me, the singing. The rest of it sounded deadly as hell. I was used to the city, born there, lived there all my life. Not that I loved it, exactly—the freeways and the malls and all that stuff. I guess I felt like I could get lost there, just kind of be invisible. Aside from Ma, no one in Dallas paid the slightest bit of attention to me. I liked that just fine. I knew I'd make my mark, in time. I had a secret.

When the dust settled, Ma was a little red dot in the road, then just a sound like a bee makes buzzing around your head, then nothing. I couldn't get over the quiet; it was spooky, the way I felt when Ma went out in the evenings with Kent and left me alone in the condo, and I'd sit in the living room, and before long I could hear my own heart beating till I thought it would explode. There was a story in a book Miss Johns, my English teacher, gave me last year, about a guy who killed this old man and then cut him up into pieces and buried them under the floor, but when the cops came around, the dead guy's heart was still beating, louder and louder, and gave the killer away. He'd have gotten away with it otherwise. I always got to thinking about that buried heart until I'd have to run for the stereo and crank it up, just for the noise. I've never been fond of quiet. I patted the side of my duffel until I found the lump I knew was my Walkman, and it made me feel better. Not completely, but some.

Meanwhile, this girl, Lucy—or woman, I guess she was, even though she was real little and had all this wild, red-brown hair—was still standing on the porch wrapped in her sheet, staring at me like I'd just landed on a rocket from Mars. Which I guess, come to think of it, as far as she was concerned I had. The sheet had slipped a little, but I don't think she knew it. Most of a titty was showing, and one leg clear to the hip, so I knew for a fact she was naked as a jaybird under there. Her face was kind of puffy and her hair was a mess, but I could see, even all sleepy and confused and unsure, how pretty she was. I guessed Ma's stories about my dad were true, at least what I'd seen so far. She said he never could keep his eyes to himself or his pants zipped, either one. I wondered if Lucy really was knocked up, like Ma said. I wondered if she even knew.

After a minute she opened her mouth. "Denise?" she said. She looked like she was just learning to talk, like my name was her very first word.

"It's Denny," I told her right off. "Nobody calls me Denise except my mother." I switched my duffel to the other arm. It was heavy; everything I cared about was in there.

"Denny," she repeated, slow and thick, foreign-sounding. "Let me see if I can figure this out. Does Ash—did your father know you were coming?"

"Nope. Ma said she tried to call him a couple of times, but I'm pretty sure that's bullshit. He'd have said no way and she knew it."

I looked at the toe of my Converse high-tops, wondering if I should be embarrassed for cussing, but Lucy didn't even seem to notice. She was backing toward the screen door, trying to reach for the handle without losing the sheet. A couple of dogs—one big and black, one short and spotted—nosed their way out from under the porch and circled a couple of times, sniffing the dusty yard, then scooted back under the steps again. "Come on inside," she said. "I'll give Ash a call, try to find out what's going on."

I knew what was going on, and so did she; it was exactly what it looked like, no more and no less. My mother had dumped me on my dad's doorstep and left—no number, no forwarding address. Whatever was happening in this house, whatever made it possible for this woman to be lolling around naked in bed at almost noon on a Tuesday, that thing was about to change. Neither of us was too thrilled about it, and I was pretty sure my dad wouldn't be, either.

I set my duffel in the front hall. The house, in contrast to the day outside, was dark and cool. "Go on in," Lucy said, waving an arm in the direction of what turned out to be the kitchen. "Help yourself to something to drink. I'll call Ash." She padded down the hall and picked up a telephone that sat on a little table and turned her back to me, a fistful of sheet gathered on one hip.

The kitchen was big and bright, pottery on the windowsill, tall white cabinets, shiny, new-looking appliances. I opened the double-doored Frigidaire and examined the contents. They weren't too much into nutrition, apparently. Mustard, grape jelly, soy sauce. A shriveled head of iceberg lettuce. A Pizza Hut carry-out box, grease-stained but empty. An unopened twelve-pack of Budweiser and half a plastic-ringed six-pack of Coke.

I pulled loose a Coke and popped the tab and sat down at the table, keeping an ear peeled for what was going on out in the hallway. I heard her punch some numbers, then replace the receiver with a click. Digital pager, I guessed; Kent had one. Sure enough, after a couple of minutes, the phone rang, and she snatched it up. I couldn't hear what she was saying at first, only the low, tight pitch of her voice. After a minute she said clearly, "No, I'm *not* joking! Do you really think I'd joke about this?" Then, "Yes, I think you'd better. Uh-huh. Right away." She hung up.

I took a sip of Coke. I wondered if I would get to know this kitchen, if I would ever eat a meal off the blue-rimmed plates I saw in the drainer, if I would get to take a shower or spend a night in one of the beds. I wondered if I would get to unpack my duffel, or if they'd ship me off before Ma's tire tracks had disappeared in the driveway.

Lucy stuck her head around the doorjamb. "I called your father," she said. I guess she thought I was completely deaf. "He'll be right home. He'll straighten all this out, don't you worry." I nodded, even though I knew it was herself she was talking to. What did I have to worry about? She was the one whose love shack was being invaded by Martians. "Could you excuse me a minute?" she said. "I'm just going to get dressed."

"Good idea," I said. It made me sort of happy to see her turn red.

I sat at the table for a while, looking around the sunny kitchen and drinking Coke and trying to imagine my dad, what his life was like. In the past five minutes, I'd seen his dogs, his girlfriend, his front porch, and the inside of his refrigerator. Beyond that, I didn't have a clue. He and Ma split up when I was two. I'd seen him a handful of times since, the last on my seventh birthday. He'd come to our apartment shiny-eyed and smelling of beer, with a big talking doll in a paper Kmart bag, no bow or card or anything. I'd sat on the floor pulling that doll's string over and over, running it through its whole dumb routine until I knew it by heart, while out in the kitchen my parents talked in low voices, then, for about ten seconds, in a normal conversational tone, then finally at the top of their lungs. I remember a glass breaking, and my dad coming out of the kitchen with his eyes on fire, and Ma running after him with tears rolling down her face, screaming, "Son of a bitch! Son of a bitch!" He was supposed to take me to Burger King, but instead he'd grabbed me and given me a quick, rough kiss and told me to be a good girl and mind my mama. My last memory of him was the back of his head, slamming the door. Ma had cried, off and on, for two days. This was before Kent and all that, way before. Since then there'd only been cards on my birthday. I blamed Ma, and tried not to take it personal.

Now, all of a sudden, sitting at his table drinking his Coke and listening to his girlfriend running water in the bathroom, my insides started to fish-flop. The whole way from Dallas, a three-and-a-half-hour drive, I don't think it really hit me that I was actually going to come face-to-face with my father. Ma and I had been on our own so long, most times it was easy to forget I even had one. Some kids whose parents are divorced say that when they picture their father—let's face it, it's almost always the father who split—he's like this larger-than-life figure. But my dad, in my mind, was the opposite of that: smaller than life, a tiny little dot on the map of all the things that had happened to me. I couldn't remember much of anything about him except beer breath and one little kiss and that doll—whose string broke about two hours later, incidentally, and she never talked again—so when I tried to paint a picture of him in my head it was hopeless, there was nothing there but a man-shaped outline, blank inside. Knowing that outline was about to be filled in, I have to admit, made me a little nervous. I started chewing my fingernails, even though there wasn't much to chew on, just a few jagged edges and pieces of raw skin. It's a disgusting habit, I know, even if Ma didn't constantly remind me. Right then I didn't care; it made me feel better, and anyway I figured my dad better just see me right off for what I was. I didn't want him to get the wrong image of me, to think I was some kind of fairy princess.

It was a pretty long time—fifteen, maybe twenty minutes—before I heard a truck come rattling up the road and stop out front. The water had been running in the bathroom all that time, so I guessed I was going to meet him alone, which was fine by me, I didn't need her complicating it.

The front door opened and shut. "Hello?" a voice called, then, "Lucy?" I didn't say anything, just listened to footsteps coming up the hall. I pulled my fingers out of my mouth and sat up a little straighter. I should at least have brushed my hair. Too late. He was in the kitchen doorway. Exactly life-size.

"Denise?"

All my life I'd been hearing stories about my father, most of them bad ones—all his failings, what he'd said and done wrong. But every now and then, when Ma had been drinking wine or had a fight with Kent or both, she'd talk about what it was like when she met him, how she'd taken one look at him and been swept off her feet. Straightaway, the minute I saw him, I knew what she meant. He wasn't real big or anything, and he had on a grubby T-shirt and some old paint-splattered Levi's and beat-up work boots, and he was kind of sweaty, with his hair plastered back, but still. The dark hair I remembered was full of gray, but his eyebrows were furry and black as a pair of caterpillars, and his eyes almost as black below, staring at me with what looked like amazement. If it was, it was mutual. He looked a little like he should be selling something on TV, to tell you the truth, a little bit too good to be true. He didn't look like anybody's father I knew. He sure didn't look like he could be *mine*.

"Denise?" he said again, and this time I managed to get my mouth open.

"It's Denny. Nobody calls me Denise except Ma."

"Where *is* your mother?" he wanted to know. Rightly so; it didn't hurt my feelings any.

"Who knows? Probably halfway to Chicago by now."

"Chicago?"

I'd gotten real interested in a hangnail on my left thumb. "She's got a boyfriend there. He found her some kind of job. Training to be a stockbroker. She says she needs the summer to herself. To, you know. Concentrate."

"And she just left you here? Without talking to me about it or anything?"

"Well, she said she tried to call you a couple of times. I don't think she did, though. She wasn't taking any chances on anything messing up her big plan." I gave up and put the hangnail between my teeth. I didn't care how it looked. He was making me nervous as hell.

"This is crazy," he said. I wished he'd do something—yell, storm out, throw his arms around me, anything. "This is some kind of mistake." I didn't know what to say to that. I could imagine how it looked to him. He hadn't laid eyes on me for seven, almost eight, years, and I knew I wasn't exactly anybody's idea of a little dream girl. Then there was this woman, Lucy. I could see it was complicated.

"Where is Lucy?" he said then, like he'd read my mind.

"Bathroom." I picked up the Coke can and jiggled it. "I think we woke her up or something."

I cut my eyes at him, and damned if he didn't go as red as she had, from his collar to the roots of his hair. I wondered what time *he'd* gotten out of bed that morning. I was never having sex, I swore right then. All it did was make people crazy—make them cut off their hair, move halfway across the country, dump their kids with strangers. Make them drink, and cry by themselves in the middle of the night. In fact, I was thinking I might decide to become a nun. I'd have to turn Catholic first. I remembered Ma saying Dad used to be one, before he'd run off to Dallas and met her and lost it.

"Did she leave any way of getting in touch with her?" he asked. "A phone number or anything?"

"Nope. Her boyfriend's name is Kent Grizzatti, though. He moved up there last year. He's probably in the book."

"I can't believe it," he said, like to himself. "I just can't believe she's done this."

"Well, you know Ma," I said. "She's always been kind of a flake."

To my surprise, that made him smile—a big, loose, open smile, showing all his teeth. I saw they were exactly like mine, the front two just the slightest bit uneven, so you'd barely notice. How did that happen, I wondered? Was this the proof I needed, that he really was my father and not the glamorous stranger he seemed? And how did it turn out that what was maybe my best feature was the only one of his that wasn't practically perfect?

He stepped into the room. "Stand up, now," he said. "Let me have a look at you."

It was my turn to get red, but I did what he said. I was self-conscious about my looks, to the extent that I cared. Ma said I was a uniquely gifted child, that that, and not the standards of our superficial, physically fixated society, would carry me in the world. The rest of the time she was picking on me about what I ate, or begging me to do something with my hair, or telling me to get my fingers out of my mouth. I'm not a fairy princess, like I said.

Still, I felt funny with him looking at me that way, checking me out. I wished, for his sake, I had more to offer, wished I was sweet and curvy like his Barbie doll girlfriend, and not chunky and ratty-haired and nail-bitten, like I was. Wished, even, that I'd taken the time to do something with what I did have. It wouldn't have killed me to put on a clean shirt or yank a brush through my hair. I thought I'd show Ma, acting like a slob. I hadn't been thinking about this part, about being put under the microscope, hadn't known about those black eyes. I couldn't tell what he was thinking. To be honest, he still looked more or less stunned. I'd have given anything to tell him my secret.

Just then Lucy showed up in the doorway. She had on shorts and a light blue T-shirt and sneakers and some lip gloss, and her hair was in a long, loose braid. There was a big canvas purse over her arm. She was one of those people who look just as good when they don't make much effort as when they knock themselves out. I made up my mind that, if I got to stay there any amount of time at all, I was going to hate her.

"Oh, good," she said, seeing Dad, "you're here."

"Lucy," he said, "this is my daughter, Denise. Denny."

"We've met." She and I both said it, real fast. "Ash," she said, "I've got to run into town."

He turned around and stared at her. "What for?"

"Just an errand." I could tell she was freaking out. Her cheeks were bright pink, and she wasn't looking him in the eye. He probably figured it was because of me, but I knew better.

"Can't it wait a little bit? I was hoping you could help me figure out what to do here." He meant me.

But she was already backing into the hallway, toward the front door. "I'm sorry. I can't — I'll tell you later," she said, and left him standing there with his mouth hanging open.

In a minute we heard an engine start up. He and I watched, together, an old green car pull past the window and speed off down the road, kicking up as much dust as Ma, in just as big a hurry. I thought about asking him, *By the way, how many kids have you got? Do you even know?* But something stopped me, I don't know what. Except, when you got right down to it, I really hardly knew him. Then the dust died down, and he sighed and got a beer out of the refrigerator and went to call directory assistance in Chicago.

3

Lucy

I got out of there in such a hurry I couldn't see the house in the rearview mirror for all the dust I'd kicked up, a rolling red cloud chasing me like a shadow out to the main road. I pulled out and turned right, toward town, and nearly got sideswiped by a propane truck barreling over the rise, blasting its horn. I had to steer onto the shoulder and set the brake and squeeze the wheel with both hands until I got my breath back. I guessed Ash thought it was his daughter showing up that had me acting this way, but the truth was, that hadn't really hit me. All I could hold in my head was the mother, Marlene—her ugly, reptilian eyes, her voice. *I looked just like that myself, about two months gone.*

I leaned across and rolled down the window on the passenger side and sat there gulping air, like my lungs couldn't hold enough. The day was identical to the past twenty or so, hot and still, the asphalt shimmering at the horizon. Across the road, Little David Bates was driving his John Deere combine through the cornfield, down the rows and back again. A grackle watched me from a telephone wire.

I took all this in like I didn't know the landscape like the back of my hand, like I'd never seen it before. Like a blindfold had dropped from my eyes. The blindfold, of course, being Ash. Ten weeks. I counted them off, on my fingers, from that first night I'd taken him out of the rain, to this blazing June morning. Ten weeks, exactly, that I'd seen nothing past his mouth, his arms, the four walls of his room. Little David Bates's corn was as tall and green as I'd ever seen, but dust swirled in the tractor's wake and drifted across the road. How many days since we'd had rain? Since the last time I'd bled? How could I have not noticed something like that? How had I missed the signals? They were all there, plain as the sky over my head: my blooming skin, tender breasts, the unaccustomed rounding of my body, what I'd had the audacity, that very morning, to call "juicy." No appetite in the mornings, drowsing through the afternoons. I'd figured it was love; it was new territory for me, and I didn't know the markers. I'd never been pregnant, either.

I had only to imagine walking into the tiny Mooney pharmacy and asking Dixie Cooley, the blabbermouthed, hawkeyed clerk, for a home pregnancy test, to know I had to take this business out of town. So I drove to the Wal-Mart on the bypass, and made my way to the feminine-hygiene aisle. I'd always breezed by the home pregnancy kits without a glance; married to Mitchell, I'd had about as much use for one as I would a Sherman tank. Who knew there would be so many brands, styles, methods? The directions seemed mysterious, confusing, each kit different from the one before in ways that seemed minor but deliberate. I ended up getting four different kinds, stuffing them into my cart under a twelve-pack of paper towels, on sale for $3.99. If the cashier thought there was anything peculiar about my purchases she didn't let on; her fingers with their inch-long purple nails, each adorned with a tiny rhinestone, never missed a beat as she skimmed my items over the scanner and into a plastic bag. Sixty-three dollars and some change. It seemed like a small price to pay for the revelation of my future.

I drove to my rent house, which I'd barely seen the inside of for the past couple of months, threw all the windows open, and arranged the contents of my shopping bag in a row on the tabletop. On my way out of Wal-Mart, I'd stopped at McDonald's and bought an extra-large Coke, guzzling it all the way home, and now I went into the bathroom and peed copiously into the empty cup. Then I opened one of the kits at random, and stuck the plastic test strip into the cup.

Results in fifteen minutes, the box said. A plus sign meant yes; minus meant no.

I went out onto the front porch. Along the rail, roses were blooming, brash blowsy things with a fragrance that threatened to clobber you, to knock you over and suffocate you. I looked at my watch; fourteen and a half minutes to go. I stepped off the porch, wandered around back. My garden, or what was to have been my garden before Ash got hold of me, languished, barren and mud-baked in the summer sun. In spite of the heat I got a chill, thinking of how my life had been altered, maybe irreversibly, because of Ash, in ways that had nothing to do with tomato plants. My watch said four minutes had passed. I decided four minutes was close enough to fifteen, and let myself, by way of the back door, into the kitchen.

The strip immersed in the cup showed a bright pink +.

Every detail sprang into relief, etching itself in my memory: the heat in the kitchen, the breeze rattling the screen door, the dizzying scent of roses, the sunflower clock ticking softly over the stove. The plastic wand, saying, +, saying, *Yes*. Saying, *Ha!* Saying, *Nothing is what it was, or will ever be the same again.*

I ripped open the three remaining kits and stuck the various test wands into the McDonald's cup. The second hand on my watch marched forward. One of the three strips came up positive in forty-five seconds. The last two took another minute or so.

World without end, amen.

Oddly, my thoughts weren't of Ash, but of my late husband, Mitchell; Mitchell, who for fourteen years treated sex like a penance, and then made me believe, convinced me without a word, that it was my fault I never conceived. It must be the woman's fault, mustn't it, since it's the woman's body that bears, or fails to bear, the fruit? I felt like screaming as I dumped the test kits with their damning evidence into a trash bag and my hormone-rich urine down the toilet. I'd assured

Ash, the morning after our first night together, that I wouldn't—*couldn't*—get pregnant! What was I supposed to tell him now? That I'd taken the word of a foolish dead man, a man whose shame about his body and its urges made me absorb that shame, until I'd suppressed even the possibility of my own fertility? I knew my getting pregnant now, just weeks, maybe days, after taking up with Ash, was no miracle. It was only my body accepting from the universe what had been hovering there, waiting to touch down, all along. Ash was just the angel, the cosmic delivery system, the celestial UPS guy.

This, too, seemed less a display of God's bounty and wonder than some ironic act of retribution. I'd known about Ash's daughter; I knew there was grief there, and regret. But love? The desire to nurture, to guide and protect? A tremor went through me at the thought of my mama's voice, asking me what business I had getting pregnant by a man whose record on fatherhood was dubitable, at best. Or maybe it was Aunt Dove's voice I heard; Mama would have gone straight to her knees, wailing and praying for my lost soul. But the admonishment was the same.

I couldn't just sit there; the news felt so enormous, I thought it must be obvious, ballooning as my waistline soon would be. I decided to drive over and visit Aunt Dove. It was three o'clock; she'd be finished in the garden, napping in front of *Judge Judy* and pretending not to be. I wouldn't tell her anything, I promised myself, closing up the house again, locking the door. I just needed some tribal perspective.

∞

Aunt Dove wasn't napping, though she was in front of the TV; there was a cassette in the VCR, and on the screen an energetic hickory-smoked man with a head like a peeled egg guided a group of people through an intricate series of kicks and jabs. Dove, in her customary captioned T-shirt ("Love and Danger," this one read, "The Party Never Ends") and polyester slacks, moved with the crowd.

"Kee-yah!" they yelled, executing a side kick. Through the storm door I watched as Dove cried, "Kee-yah!" kicking over the arrangement of plastic bluebonnets in the middle of her coffee table and sending them flying.

I rapped at the glass, once, then louder. Dove looked over her shoulder and waved me inside, never missing a beat. The videotaped class moved like mutant kung fu cheerleaders in response to the black man's urgings, while on the sound track a gospel choir sang what sounded like, "Allah rump hey, allah rump hey." I sat down on the arm of the sofa, but just then everything went to watery slow motion and, after a series of ballet stretches and Eastern poses that made me drowsy just watching, the black man bowed to Dove and Dove bowed back, then switched off the VCR.

"Whew," she said, dabbing at the beads of perspiration around her hairline with a wad of Kleenex. "I been doin' this tape ever day for a week and already I feel ten years younger. Do I look ten years younger to you?"

"Every time I see you." I smiled. The week before she'd turned seventy-one.

"I hope you all're in the mood for Kentucky Wonders," Dove said, leading me into the kitchen, where she drew us each a glass of luke-warm tap water. "I guess I picked Kentucky Wonders this morning for two solid hours. Reckon that young man of yours might be ready for a few Kentucky Wonders?"

I knew as well as she did that the beans were Ash's favorites, that she'd planted them specially for him. "I reckon."

Out of nowhere Dove reached out and slipped a hand under my hair, laying her cool, smooth palm against my cheek. "What's the matter, honey? You look peaked."

Just as suddenly she withdrew her hand. She jerked up straight, like someone had stuck a rifle butt in her back.

"Holy Hercules," she declared. "You're pregnant."

❧

"You can't tell anybody!" I said. "Nobody knows. Ash doesn't know. *I* didn't even know, till an hour ago!"

"But it's happy news, honey, ain't it?" She offered me another glass of tap water, which I gratefully accepted. "After all those years with Mitchell . . ."

"If Mitchell walked into this room right now, I'd drive a stake through his cold dead heart," I said, which might have made a lesser woman blanch but only caused Dove to nod avidly, like she could feature it. "And I'd laugh while I was doing it! He made me think it was *my* fault, Dove. That because I was the woman, I must be the one who was defective. And I *bought* it! That's the wacky part—I bought it. I told Ash—" I paused, dabbed a washrag into my water glass, and applied it to my temples "—I told Ash, when we started— Well, when we started, that I couldn't have a baby! Of course he never questioned me, why wouldn't he just assume I had some medical proof, that I'd seen a doctor, had the tests . . . How am I supposed to tell him that this is because my dead husband must have worn his drawers too tight and strangled all his sperm?"

"You could put it just that way, I guess," Dove said with a smile. She smoothed the hair off my face again, and the feel of her hand on my forehead made me feel six again, that there was nothing in the world she couldn't make better. "Ash is a good boy, Lucy Bird. He'll do right by you, don't you worry."

"Do right? What's that supposed to mean? For goodness sake, I'm not worried about whether or not he'll *marry* me."

"You better be," Dove said, "once your mama and the boys find out." My two big brothers had made what could best be described as an uneasy peace with the notion of Ash and me, but I doubted they'd look far for an excuse to draw and quarter him.

"I'm thirty-three years old!"

"And still our sweet baby girl." She put her hand over mine; the skin was pleated and brown and looked as frail as tissue paper. It was, like so many things, an illusion, a trick of the light.

"Mama will murder me," I said, running my thumb over the back of Dove's wrist. "'Lucy's Continuing Descent into Hell,' narrated by Patsy Hatch. Special guest appearance by Jesus."

Dove squeezed my hand. "I wouldn't be frettin' too much about your mama. I have a feelin' she's gonna be more glad-hearted about this than you think. Babies have that way with people. Anyway, she likes Ash, don't she?"

"Of course she likes Ash. She's got two X chromosomes, doesn't she?" I gasped. "I can't believe I forgot to tell you! This all started when Ash's ex-wife showed up at the house this morning, with his fourteen-year-old daughter. Just dumped her out and got in the car and drove off for some job in Chicago!"

Dove clucked her tongue against the roof of her mouth. "Poor Ash. I do hope he's fond of kids." She reached across the table and poked me in the shoulder. "What was the wife like?"

"A witch. She took one look at me and knew . . ." But the word still felt too new, too big, to say out loud.

"I did, too, honey, but that don't make me no witch. If I was you, I'd be studyin' on how to break the news to Ash. 'Cause any minute now he's gonna do like the rest of us. Take a look at you and *know*."

"I don't get it," I said, getting up to help Dove fill a brown paper grocery sack with beans. "How can you tell? It's way too soon for it to show."

"Hmph. Not your tummy, maybe. But it shows." She folded over the top of the paper sack and handed it to me. "That's two pounds, there. Kentucky Wonders. You fix 'em up tonight the way he likes, with the butter and the Dijon mustard." "Dear John mustard," she called it. "Cook up them beans, and give Ash a big ol' kiss and tell him he's gonna be a daddy."

"He's already a daddy. I think he's still in shock over the first one."

"Go on now," Dove said, turning me by the shoulders and giving me a little push toward the door. "Go on home and fix them beans like I'm tellin' you, Lucy. He's gonna be so tickled, you won't know what you was worried about. You'll see."

4

Denny

By the time Lucy got back, the pine trees that ringed the front yard were already throwing shadows across the porch, and the sky was that very intense shade it gets in the last minutes of afternoon, like it's been saving up all its blue for one last stand against the evening. I'd seen that in Dallas, too; it's not only a country thing. You just have to be paying attention.

When Lucy finally pulled her big green Buick up next to my dad's truck out front, I was still sitting at the kitchen table, right where I'd been when she left. Dad had spent most of the time—after he'd called Chicago and left messages at Kent's apartment and Kent's office and the main branch of PaineWebber for Marlene Farrell to please, *please* call and tell him what the hell he was supposed to *think* about all this— fussing about the sleeping arrangements. It wasn't how it sounds, not exactly. It's just that the house wasn't what you'd call finished. Living room, kitchen, one bedroom, and one bathroom, that's all that had been properly fitted out, with walls and windows and fixtures and such. The rest of the place was pretty much a mess, and from the tour I'd gotten looked like it might have been dreamed up by three or four different people with different ideas and possibly different ends in mind. Like, the only way to get to what would be the two back bedrooms was straight through the kitchen; and in the whole twenty-two-hundred square feet of space—I knew that's how much it was because Dad told me—there was exactly one tub and one toilet.

Now, going on five o'clock, Dad was still pacing in and out, worrying about where to put me. You'd think, being a carpenter and all, he'd come up with a plan in fairly short order, but his brain seemed cross-wired and he was having trouble getting anything accomplished; he'd opened another Budweiser and was wandering around fiddling with a tape measure and flipping through blueprints and muttering under his breath. It wasn't his fault, but he was making me feel terrible, like some gigantic package had arrived unannounced and now it was up to him to find a place to stow it, whether he wanted it or not.

The minute Lucy walked into the kitchen carrying a grocery sack, I saw that something was different. She was relaxed, smiling. She looked, I guess the word is, serene.

"Hi there," she said, like she and I were big buddies from way back, like she came home every evening to find me stacking empty Coke cans on her kitchen table. "How've you and Ash been getting along?"

"Okay, I guess." I'd been listening to Pearl Jam on my Walkman, but now I slipped the headphones off to hug my neck. "He's all worked up about where I'm going to sleep tonight."

Lucy laughed, setting the brown paper bag on the sink. "I guess this is not the time to remind him he's been meaning to finish those back bedrooms."

"No, ma'am, I guess not." She opened the bag and peeked inside, then went rummaging in the cupboards till she came up with a shiny silver stockpot, which she set in the sink and started filling from the tap.

"Anyway, I don't see what the big deal is. He has a couple of sleeping bags. You can sleep on the living room couch for a few nights, can't you?"

"Yes, ma'am." My brain juggled this around a few times. Did she mean that in a few nights I might have a real bedroom to sleep in, or that in a few nights I'd be gone, shipped off to Chicago and Ma? Anyway, hadn't she noticed that the living room couch was about ten feet from their bedroom door? If she thought I planned to lie there all night listening to their goings-on, she'd better think again. I'd sleep on the porch first. I'd sleep *under* the porch.

"I wish you wouldn't call me 'ma'am,'" she said. "It makes me feel about a hundred years old."

"My mom makes me."

"I know. My mama did that, too." She was being so nice, I knew she was up to something.

She smiled back over her shoulder at me. "Listen, Denny, I need to ask you a favor."

What did I tell you? I'm psychic when it comes to grown-ups. I should have my own 800 number. "What?" I said.

"That conversation you heard earlier," she said, turning toward me, her voice pitched just below the sound of the water filling the pan. "On the porch, between your mama and me?" I nodded to show I was following her. "Some things were said. One thing, in particular." I couldn't help it, I let my eyes drop to her middle, and she looked down, too, and pulled at the hem of her T-shirt. "Well. Ash—your father—doesn't know. Not yet. I only just found out recently, myself." Yeah, about three hours ago, I thought but didn't say. Come to think of it, I guess Ma's the real psychic in the family. "I mean to tell him, of course, just as soon as the time is right. But, with everything he has to deal with right now . . ." I stared at the tabletop. I'm not stupid; I knew that "everything" meant yours truly. "Anyway, I'd like to ask you to keep it to yourself for now. Our secret, okay? Just between you and me. I hope you understand."

But I didn't; I couldn't think how two grown people had managed to get themselves into such a predicament, much less one of them hiding it from the other, like a baby was some kind of contraband, something you kept in a closet, locked and loaded. This was the 1990s, after all; you'd think even in Mooney, Texas, they'd have heard of condoms.

I didn't get a chance to answer her, though, because just then Dad came clomping out of one of the unfinished bedrooms, lifting the curtain of plastic that served as a wall between it and the kitchen, and without missing a beat Lucy spun neatly around and turned off the faucet and lifted the pot onto the stove.

"Hey," he said, "I thought I heard you come in." He kissed the top of her head, and she turned her chin and tilted her face up to his and he kissed her again, real lightly, on the mouth and then raised his head to look at her.

I don't know how to describe what I saw. There was something in his face, and hers, too, that made it feel like something was pulling loose in me. I was almost fifteen, and I thought I'd seen it all, what passes for love. I'd seen the goofy kids in my school, going steady, and the older ones, all over each other in the parking lot of the Sonic drive-in, across from the high school; I'd seen TV, of course, and I'd seen movies, the ones where it's made up, and some, like the ones Kent kept hidden on the top shelf of Ma's closet in our condo, where it isn't. And I'd seen Ma and Kent, drinking Gallo wine and talking goo-goo talk and giggling in the dark. But this, I knew without anybody telling me, was different. I don't know how I understood that, but I did, just like I knew, in some weird way, that I was meant to see it. It didn't exactly feel, at the time, like a privilege. I felt like I should apologize to them just for sitting there, breathing in and out, three feet outside their little solar system. I didn't see how they could look at each other that way and still be in the world.

"Where've you been all afternoon?" Dad said, leaning over her shoulder to peek in the stockpot. I was surprised he could talk without fairy dust coming out of his mouth, but he looked like an ordinary man now, in his ordinary kitchen, in his ordinary life.

Lucy, I have to hand it to her, was steady as a judge. "Dove needed me to run by and help her with a couple things," she said. "Look, Ash, what Dove sent you. Two pounds of Kentucky Wonders. I thought I'd fix them up with that sauce you like, the butter and Dijon mustard."

"I don't think there's any butter."

"No butter?" No Dijon mustard, either; just a quarter-inch of yellow French's, dried at the bottom of the jar. Lucy stood for a minute looking past him at all those empty shelves in that big shiny Cadillac of a refrigerator. "I guess I should have picked up some burgers," she said.

"I've got a better idea," Dad said. "Let's go into town for supper. We'll take a tour afterward, show Denny the sights. All the landmarks in her old man's hometown." He laughed, a little louder than he should have, and Lucy reached gently past him and shut the refrigerator door, turning her face away so she wouldn't have to see him that way, the man she loved, scared of his own blood, trying too hard.

❧

Downtown Mooney was pretty much what you'd expect: not total nuclear wasteland, but close enough. A town square, historic old court-house, pharmacy, hardware store, beauty shop, bank. Three video-rental places. A Dairy Queen, where we didn't eat, and a café, where we did. After dinner—meat loaf and pecan pie—we walked around the square and Dad and Lucy talked about the town, about who lived in which house and for how long and what had changed since the bypass was built in '87. There were twelve Baptist churches, they said, one for every hundred citizens, not counting one congregation of upstart Methodists. Off the town square were a machine shop, a florist where Lucy said she worked part-time, a tae kwon do studio, a laundromat.

If anything at all had changed here in forty years, you couldn't tell; the place seemed to sag with defeat, like the back room at Goodwill, where everything chipped and faded and marked down ends up. I was embarrassed, and I think Dad was, too; the longer we walked, the quieter he got, until by the time we'd circled back to the café, he wasn't saying anything at all. It wasn't his fault he was born here, but I couldn't imagine what had ever made him come back. It seemed like you must have had to give up on life in some major way to accept this as the best you deserved.

We stopped across the square from the café, in front of what used to be the five-and-dime. A tumbled-down Christmas scene sat in the dark display window, strung with cobwebs. Santa had lost most of his stuffing, and Rudolph's nose was washed-out pink and hanging by a thread. We seemed to be having the same thought, the three of us, a kind of shared gloominess that didn't have anything to do with the season. I knew if I had to spend three months here I would go out of my mind.

Lucy slipped her arm around Dad's waist and tucked her fingers into his back pocket—not lewd, or playful, even, just familiar. "Tomorrow's Wednesday," she said, matter-of-fact. "Round-Up night. Wednesdays and Saturdays, Ash's band plays at the Round-Up. We'll take her out there with us tomorrow night, Ash. Let her see you shine."

He turned his chin an inch and just for a second lay his cheek against her hair, and even though his eyes were closed I saw what was in his face then: something like thanks, only not so small or pale.

Somewhere off the square, a car backfired. Across the street, one by one, the lights winked out in the Dairy Queen. Venus burned like a welder's flame in the night sky. We piled into the pickup and drove home.

❦

Tucked inside my sleeping bag, I made a big show of loading a tape into my Walkman, slipping my headphones over my ears. "You listen to that thing all night?" Lucy asked, passing through the living room with an armload of towels. I said I did. I said it was on an endless loop, that once the tape reached the end it reversed itself and played again. I said I couldn't sleep without music. I said I had plenty of batteries.

As soon as the lights went out, I took off the headphones.

The silence was huge and so total it seemed fake. In Dallas I was used to a lot of night noise: sirens, neighbors, the current of the freeway, always running through your dreams. Here, you could hear the trees sighing in the yard, the dogs snuffling and breathing under the porch, the steady tick-tick of the ceiling fans. After a few minutes I heard Dad and Lucy talking quietly behind their closed door. Their voices were like the freeway current, white and smooth, and although I didn't mean to, I gave in to the flow of voices; for the first time in my life, I let myself wonder how it would feel to have someone look at you with diamonds in his eyes.

Somewhere, Eddie Vedder was making his way toward me, on horseback through the woods, something sparkling and precious in a knapsack, his heart in his hand. We rode all night, nothing but our voices and the wild, wheeling stars, and when I opened my eyes, it was morning.

＊

Over the breakfast table, I watched it dawning on Dad and Lucy that they had no idea, either of them, what to do with an almost-fifteen-year-old girl for a single day, much less a whole summer, even though Lucy, presumably, had been a fifteen-year-old girl herself once upon a time. She stood at the kitchen counter wearing an old striped robe, spooning coffee grounds into a paper filter and trying not to turn green. It was none of my business, but I wondered how easy it could be to keep your pregnancy a secret when it looked like any minute you might puke into the kitchen sink.

Not that Dad noticed; he sat with his elbows on the table, his chin unshaved and his eyes bleary, looking at me like I was holding a gun to his head and demanding all his money. I didn't *ask* for this, I wanted to say; if anything, *I* don't want to be here even more than *you* don't want me to be. If ever a funnel cloud was to swoop down and wipe Cade County, Texas, off the map, that would have been a good morning for it. It would have been doing three people, at least, a great big favor.

They couldn't leave me alone in the house all day, they'd decided, although why they never really said. Maybe they were afraid I'd snoop, or rob them blind, which was pretty laughable; they didn't even have a TV. Or run away, though that might actually have solved a lot of problems for us all. Dad was, according to him, building cabinets for some old lady's fancy house in town and couldn't very well have me hanging around all day; and Lucy had to go to her job at the florist's shop, where someone named Peggy the Great and Powerful would look unkindly on a shiftless teenager hanging around.

After a few minutes, Dad pushed back from the table—the coffee was made now, and there was a box of strawberry Pop-Tarts on the table that no one had touched—and went into the hall and picked up the phone. Except for the hum of the refrigerator, it was so quiet you could hear him punching the numbers. Lucy shifted her eyes to me; I could tell we were both holding our breath. "Pick up the phone, pick up the phone," Dad mumbled. Then, "Marlene, you insane bitch!" he shouted, and slammed the receiver into its cradle so hard the bell made a little yelp of protest.

Nothing happened for five or ten seconds. Lucy stared at me; her cheeks were blazing. Never in my life, not even the worst days at school, had I wished so bad to die, right then, on the spot.

"Ash!" Lucy called.

He came stomping back up the hall in his heavy work boots and stood in the doorway, his eyes as black as I'd ever seen them. It occurred to me that I might get my wish; he looked like he could kill me, or her, or himself. The baby he didn't even know he was having. Any or all of us.

"I won't have this," Lucy said, and in spite of how awful I felt, I looked at her in pure admiration for facing down that big black anger; I pictured myself telling it later, with my last breath, as the police stood over our fallen bodies. "None of this is Denny's fault. You can't punish her for what her mother did."

A weird thing happened then. His whole face changed; the anger seemed to melt right out of his features, until he just looked sort of blank and stunned, like he'd woken up from a dream he couldn't remember. He looked at Lucy, then at me, and in a way it was like he was seeing me, Denise Farrell, his daughter, for the first time. Not that he looked happy about it, exactly. But he recognized me. That much I knew.

"I don't know how to do this," he said in a low voice. I guess it was his idea of an apology.

"Then you better figure it out," Lucy said, and I glanced up at her quick, thinking maybe this was her telling him he'd better get ready to do it a second time, but she just poured out a cup of coffee and handed it to him. You should need a license to have kids; I absolutely believe that. "Denny can come into town with me," she said. I stood up and gathered up my Walkman and asked to please be excused.

❦

I went out and sat on the porch steps for a while and listened to Nine Inch Nails. After I'd been sitting there a few minutes the two dogs — Mutt and Jeff, was how I thought of them — came slinking out from under the steps and started sniffing at my shoes. I stretched out my hand for them to smell and they took turns doing that, the big dog, then the little one, and apparently I passed some kind of test because all of a sudden they started to leap and spin in big joyful circles in the front yard, nipping at each other's hind end and stirring up a cloud of dust two feet high. I couldn't help it, I started laughing at the sight of them, so full of early-morning cheer. It was the best thing to happen to my self-esteem recently, that was for sure.

The screen door opened and slammed. I didn't turn around; I knew it was him. Ma had raised me to be courteous to my elders at all times, but I was pretty sure it didn't count when one of them had just called her an insane bitch on her answering machine.

He sat down beside me on the top step and wrapped an arm around his knees and took a gulp of coffee. The dogs came bounding over and offered him their ears to be scratched, then cart-wheeled off again.

"What're you listening to?" he asked after a minute, even though technically I shouldn't have been able to hear him, with the head-phones and all. They were the open-ear kind, though. Ma didn't want me totally deaf before I was twenty. I tilted the Walkman so he could see the cassette. He nodded, which didn't mean anything other than that, presumably, he could read. I'd seen the CDs stacked around the stereo in his living room: Emmylou Harris, Steve Earle, Hank Williams, Patsy Cline. I liked that stuff, too, though I wasn't about to say so.

"Denny, listen," he began, and it took every bone in my body to keep me seated there beside him and not running off screaming down the driveway. "Everything I've done since you got here has been wrong." He paused like he was giving me a chance to disagree. When I didn't, he went on. "I just want you to know, none of this has anything to do with you."

I was so completely confounded by this that I turned and stared at him: his handsome jaw, his dark eyes, nearer to me right then than he'd been in half my lifetime. "What I mean is—well, I guess you know how things were between your mother and me. I'm sure you've heard the stories."

"All my life," I admitted, and that made him smile.

"But you know, don't you, that there are two sides to those stories." I nodded slowly. He looked into his coffee cup, like the words he wanted might be found in the dregs at the bottom. "Anyway," he said, "I don't mean to speak badly about your mama." Though he had pretty definitely meant to five minutes before, I guessed I didn't have to remind him. "What I'm trying to say is that I would like to ask if you can forget all that. If you could just give me a chance to start again. Just to know you." His eyes met mine with what looked like real difficulty, and though I tried, I couldn't hold them. Even with him so close I could smell his coffee and the soap on his skin, he didn't seem quite real to me; I wasn't quite ready for him to be real.

The moment passed; he let it go, more gracefully than I would have expected. "So, will you come with Lucy and me to the Round-Up tonight?" he asked, unwinding his legs and getting to his feet. Like I had a choice; like anything existed under his roof resembling free will. "It's not Nine Inch Nails, but you might like it."

I bit my tongue so hard I tasted blood; but I heard my voice say, "Sure."

5

Denny

Dad rode off in the truck for his cabinetmaking job, and half an hour later I was sitting up beside Lucy in the front seat of her big Buick, heading toward town. She drove with one hand loose on the wheel and an elbow poking out the open window, her hair whipping around her head in a dark-red swirl and her teeth gritted at the horizon. I'd heard her in the bathroom after Dad left, the toilet flushing and flushing. I watched her profile when I thought she couldn't tell, and tried to imagine telling Ash Farrell you were having his baby. No wonder she looked so grim. Ignorant as I was of the details, I was pretty sure this wasn't planned parenthood.

At Faye's Flowers, Lucy introduced me to her boss, Peggy, who followed me around like Katie Couric, firing nosy questions about Dad's ex-wife and kid, that is, me, nonstop. The shop was small and crowded, or maybe it just seemed that way because Peggy weighed around three hundred pounds and you could hear her breath, wet and wheezy, from any given spot in the room. She was, it turned out, allergic to pollen, which seemed to me like taking a job in accounting when you were allergic to numbers. When I said that, though, she just stared at me with her little red eyes like I'd hurt her soul, and I excused myself and told Lucy I was going to sit in the square.

I walked over to the Sav-Mor drugstore and flipped through the magazines for a while, but when I saw a couple of ladies sneaking peeks at me and whispering behind the pharmacist's counter, I paid three dollars out of the twenty Ma'd given me for the *Rolling Stone* I'd been reading and carried it to a bench outside the courthouse. A man was riding a lawn tractor back and forth in perfectly even strips on the courthouse lawn, over and over, like if he could just do it one more time he'd get it perfect, and across the street people came and went from the Dairy Queen and the café. Some boys drove around the square two or three times in a new Dodge pickup and seemed to be checking me out, but the last time around the driver slowed and rolled down a window and asked, "Hey, girl, you seen Tim Spivey around anywhere?" "I'm not *from* here," I replied, my voice unexpectedly hard and stuck-up-sounding, and one boy looked at the other and said, "Excuse *me!*" and they sped off in a trail of laughter and scorched rubber. I kept my nose in my magazine, after that.

Around noontime I was surprised to see Lucy coming up the sidewalk, swinging a plastic grocery sack. "How's it going?" she asked, sitting down on the bench beside me. She snapped open the bag to produce a couple of peanut butter and jelly sandwiches wrapped in Saran wrap, and handed one to me. "You dazed with excitement here yet? Bowled over by the whirlwind pace of downtown Mooney?" I smiled and bit gratefully into my sandwich. I couldn't believe she'd packed me a lunch. I couldn't believe, after all that had happened that morning before we left the house, she'd even been *thinking* of lunch. But she unwrapped her own sandwich like things were completely normal, like she and I weren't strangers connected by circumstance but ordinary people who did this kind of thing—picnic on a park bench—every day.

She raised a hand to wave to the man tootling by on the mower. "That's Duddy Compton," she said. "He's got OCD. Obsessive-compulsive?" I nodded, my mouth full. Welch's grape jelly; I hadn't had it since I was eight years old. "His wife had him in treatment for twelve years. Now they just let him mow the courthouse lawn. It's cheaper, and it doesn't hurt anybody."

"Nobody except the grass," I said, and giggled. The sandwich was making me sort of giddy, if you want the truth. I had no idea why that should be.

"Nah," Lucy said, grinning. "They just raise the blade."

The hands on the old-fashioned clock in front of the Cade County Bank and Trust lurched into the straight-up twelve o'clock position, and it was like somebody opened the floodgates; all of a sudden the square was full of people, swarming out of the courthouse and the bank, circling for the handful of parking spaces in front of the café. Two dozen people must have stopped to talk to Lucy, including a few in cars or trucks who just pulled right over to the curb when they saw her sitting there. She introduced me to every single one of them. "Ira, I'd like you to meet Ash's daughter, Denny. She's visiting from Dallas awhile." Then they'd go on their way, and she'd tell me some tidbit about them, or say something funny and smart under her breath. I thought it would make you nuts to come from a place like this, where everyone's business was everyone else's—like a safety net, kind of, only made of barbed wire.

A beige Lincoln Town Car, newer by ten years than most of the vehicles in sight, pulled up, and the driver's window went down. Inside was a little bitty white-haired woman who looked like she must be sitting on a booster chair to see over the dashboard. Her hands gripped the wheel at exactly two and nine o'clock.

"Hello, Lucy Bird," she said. "Did you cook up them beans last night, like I told you?"

"Not last night, no. There wasn't—" Lucy cut her eyes at me. "Aunt Dove, this is Ash's daughter, Denny. The young lady I was telling you about."

"Why, hello, honey," she said to me, extending one wrinkled old hand out the window in our general direction. Not knowing what to do, I laid down my *Rolling Stone* and got up and went over and shook it. She had a grip, I'll say that. Her eyes were blue and sharp as laser beams, and her red-and-white T-shirt said, "Cade County for Ann Richards." "I'm glad to know you," she said. "I hope you'll like it here."

"Thanks," I said, taking back my hand. I didn't know what else to say; I couldn't very well tell her I thought her hometown was like something straight out of *Night of the Living Dead.*

"We're taking Denny to the Round-Up tonight to hear Ash sing," Lucy said, getting up and brushing crumbs off her lap. "Want to come?"

"Law, honey, last time you all dragged me out there, some old cowboy started followin' me around all night saying I was his long-lost sweetheart. I didn't get home till one o'clock in the morning." She grinned, her teeth square and strong-looking. "Okay, you talked me into it. Pick me up at seven," she said, and rolled up the window and edged away from the curb and off around the square.

No sooner was she out of sight than a familiar white Chevy truck came chugging up the street. It had started to pull into a just-emptied slot in front of the bank when, all of a sudden, it swerved over and bumped to a halt in front of our bench.

"Ladies," Dad said, pretending to tip an imaginary hat, and without a second's hesitation Lucy ran over to the curb and leaned in the driver's window and started kissing him, in front of God and most of Mooney—hard, with both their mouths open and plenty of tongue. All over the square people stopped what they were doing and watched; Duddy Compton even turned off his mower. Nobody looked especially scandalized; it seemed more regular than that, like the daily episode of a local soap opera. Do you know how hard it is to watch two people making out in front of you in broad daylight? Do you know how it feels when one of them is your *father*? Just when I thought they might be about to start selling tickets, Lucy came up for air and said she needed to get back to work. Dad said he'd give her a ride, and she stepped right up on the running board and hooked her arm around his neck and he eased away from the curb and swung the truck gently around the corner toward the flower shop, with Lucy squealing and laughing, hanging on.

I didn't care if I had to rob a bank to do it; I had to figure out a way out of there.

∾

It took them forever to get ready to go out that night. We ate Dairy Queen hamburgers at the kitchen table, then they disappeared behind their bedroom door. The stereo was on in the living room, the CD player shuffling Willie Nelson and Bonnie Raitt and Asleep at the Wheel, but even over the music I could hear them in there, talking and laughing, the water running almost the whole time in the bathroom. The phone rang, but I don't guess they heard it and I didn't feel right answering it, so I listened to Lucy's aunt Dove leave a message on the machine about picking her up at Kit's house instead of her own. I wondered if Ma would ever call here again. I wondered if she'd gotten Dad's so-called message from that morning.

After what seemed like nine or ten hours, Dad came out of the bedroom and shut the door behind him. His hair was damp and combed back and his face had that pink, fresh-hewn look from a razor, and he wore a crisp white shirt tucked into black Levi's and a pair of well-shined black Tony Lamas. He smiled at me in a sheepish way that seemed half an apology for looking so good and the other half for trying. I didn't see what he had to be embarrassed about; I thought he looked about as smooth as anything I'd ever seen on CMT, although maybe he realized it was a little more than a beer joint in rural East Texas deserved.

He switched off the stereo, then walked over and took his guitar case out of the corner. "Did I hear the phone?" he asked, sitting down in the recliner across from me. He set the case at his feet. My fingers started to itch at the sight of it.

"Uh-huh. Lucy's aunt Dove called. She said to pick her up someplace called Kit's."

"That's Lucy's big brother, one of 'em. You'll meet the other one tonight." He leaned over to unlatch the guitar case. "Maybe we need to get you a scorecard," he said. "So you can learn all the players."

"I don't think I'm gonna be here that long," I said. It didn't quite come out the way I intended. He glanced up at me for half a second, but whatever was in his eyes, I couldn't read it.

"Right," he said, and lifted the guitar out of its case.

I sucked in my breath. It was a black Gibson acoustic with a mahogany neck and a chain of lacy flowers engraved on the pick guard, and its polished surface gleamed like a racehorse as Dad laid it across his knee. He plucked at the strings gently at first, twisting a key now and then to bring it into tune, though the G string still sounded a little off to me. Then, without fanfare, he started to play: something soft and medium tricky, not showing off so much as he seemed to be taking a warm-up lap. His mouth was set in a straight line; he watched his fingers like they belonged to some other man whose secrets he wanted to steal. Then, as suddenly as he'd started, he quit. He raised his head. He seemed surprised to see me there.

"Was that a song?" I asked. "Or just, you know—messing around?"

"I'm not sure yet," he said. "Right now I guess it's somewhere in between."

The bedroom door opened and Lucy came out, reaching behind her to snap off the light. Dad and I stared. She had on a short-sleeved pink dress, low on the shoulders, that ended an inch or two above her knees, and on her feet were a pair of T-strap pumps, the kind that went out of style fifty years ago and then just recently got fashionable again. Her hair was loose and tumbling over her shoulders with a few pieces held off her face by glittery pins, and she held an old-fashioned pocketbook in both hands in front of her. "Ready," she said.

Without once taking his eyes off her, Dad set the guitar in its case and got to his feet. He looked addled, like those boys in the movie where the creature from their science project turns out to be a supermodel. It's funny, but the times Dad and Lucy weren't even touching were the ones when you felt it the strongest, like a force field pulsed, blue and crackling, between them.

"Pinch me, I'm dreaming," Dad said, stepping over the guitar case. Lucy's cheeks were the same color as her dress. "On second thought, don't wake me up." He put one hand on her waist and drew her to him and just held her there for a second, loosely, against his hip, as she touched her nose to the base of his throat.

Dread seeped into me, turning my body cold all over. The whole time I'd been in Mooney, I'd been wearing the same baggy cords, the same sweatshirt with the straggling hem. My hair was brushed today, but still. No one in a dance hall or anywhere else was going to believe I was Ash Farrell's daughter; no one would think he and I even shared a species.

"Denny?" Lucy said. I ducked my eyes, studying the toes of my sneakers. I wondered if it was too late to get out of this, to claim I had a stomachache. Only the pull of that black guitar, of the music to come, was stronger.

"Wait a second," Lucy said, and broke out of Dad's embrace and came over to me. I watched her reach up and twist loose one of the pins from her hair. Without pausing a beat, she swept a lock of hair off my face and tucked it into the rhinestone clip and fastened the clasp. "There," she said, smiling, and I felt my cheeks go hot with pleasure. It was a little bit like putting gold paint on a chicken shack, I thought; but down inside me something started to shine, as tiny and determined as those rhinestones.

"Come on, glamour girls," Dad said, reaching for his guitar. "You're gonna make me late."

❧

I was trying to be cool, walking into the Round-Up behind Dad and Lucy and her aunt Dove, but the truth was, my heart was racing. I never knew a place like this existed outside my imagination. The Round-Up was a real old-time Texas dance hall: long wooden bar, stage at the far end, a concrete dance floor about as wide as a football field. Picnic tables with long benches were arranged in rows toward the back of the room, and already these were filling up with all kinds of folks, old men and little kids, girls all dressed up, couples in jeans and boots, huddled in groups and laughing over bottles of beer. Off to one side people jostled around pool tables under the liquid sheen of a dozen neon beer signs, and you could see straight out past them into a beer garden. A blue haze of cigarette smoke hovered in the rafters, pushed this way and that by the lazy whir of ceiling fans, and the sound system blasted "San Antonio Rose." I felt like I'd died and gone to heaven, like for the first time in my life I'd come awake, really awake, inside my skin.

We moved through the room, Dad with his guitar case in the lead, Lucy behind, talking to Dove, me bringing up the rear. Every second or third person stopped to greet us, to clap Dad on the back, to give Lucy a kiss, to be introduced to me. Girls ducked out of the shadows to peck Dad on the cheek and ran off again, giggling. Men made Lucy promise to dance.

We claimed space near the front of one of the long tables, squeezing in next to a good-looking man in a button-down shirt and a big blond-haired woman in jeans and a fringed Western top who, it turned out, were Lucy's brother Bailey, and sister-in-law Geneva. Geneva acted real excited to meet me, and squeezed past Aunt Dove to sit next to me and ask me a bunch of questions, gulping Miller Lite and shouting over the music. Not like Peggy in the flower shop had done, like she was sniffing out items for *Inside Edition*, but like she really was interested in me.

"Don't mind her," Lucy said to me over Geneva's shoulder. "She's bubble-headed when it comes to Ash. She thinks he hung the moon."

"Well, pardon *me*." Geneva leaned across her husband and said, "You ought to be more grateful to me, Lucy Hatch. If it wasn't for me thinking Ash hung the moon, you wouldn't be in the spot you're in right now." Just then there was a lull in the music as the PA cut off and the musicians onstage started testing their instruments, and Lucy burst out laughing, so hard her brother had to pound her between the shoulder blades and get up and get her a Coke. I guess Geneva didn't know how right she was.

I started to get nervous, watching Dad up there on the platform at the front of the big hall, adjusting his microphone, plugging in his guitar. I don't know why; *he* certainly looked right at home, talking to a bunch of girls who'd gathered at the foot of the stage, laughing at something the drummer was saying. But it scared me to death suddenly that he was going to stink, that everybody would be swooning over his playing and singing, and I'd be the only person in the room who could tell what an amateur, a crank, he really was. I thought I was so worldly, almost fifteen and city-bred. *You know, Denise,* Ma was always saying to me, *for someone with such a poor view of herself, you sure do think highly of your own opinion.* She was right, I guess, even though I couldn't appreciate it at the time.

There wasn't any kind of fanfare, like I expected; the crowd went right on chatting and smoking. The only thing that happened was that a couple of spotlights came up onstage, and the musicians talked among themselves for a few seconds, then Dad nodded to the guitar player, who hit a couple of chugging chords, the bass and drums fell in, and Dad swung his black Gibson acoustic around and faced the microphone and opened his mouth.

Right away I knew I'd been worried for nothing. The song was an old-time one, but what jumped out at you wasn't the tune but Dad's voice. It reminded me of the old Scotch whiskey Kent used to keep a bottle of at our condo, that he said had been aging for years in the dark till it turned this rich, buttery gold. There were other colors in there, too, metal colors, mostly, copper and silver. Some blue. A dark, bruised-looking purple. It was like if you looked hard enough, you could *see* the colors, floating above the dance floor in the smoky air.

As soon as the music started, half the people in the room had tossed back the last gulp of their beers and surged in pairs onto the dance floor, and I sat and watched, half dizzy, as they moved around the huge space like some expert drill team, each couple its own little unit but part of the larger whole. Some of them kept right on talking and laughing, even drinking, like their heads didn't have a clue what their feet were doing. Some, the serious dancers—a handful of younger couples, but mostly the older ones—kept their mouths shut and their eyes forward, their attention tuned like radar to the smooth, tricky-looking workings of their feet.

Even the folks at our table got swept into it; Geneva and Bailey jumped up with a whoop the minute the music started, and Aunt Dove accepted the first offer that came her way from an old man in a beat-up straw hat, and they were all scooting around out there now like their lives depended on it. Lucy must have turned down a dozen offers to dance during the first song alone. I glanced over at her and she looked at me and then back toward the stage, dreamy and a little sad, watching Dad up there singing and grinning into the white lights like she could hardly believe he was real. I knew how she felt; he was only fifty feet or so, a dance floor's width, away from us, but it seemed a whole lot farther.

The song ended and another one began, an old Hank Williams tune, and the mob on the dance floor never broke stride but just kept going, tirelessly, round and round. Bailey walked Geneva over and handed her off and dragged Lucy up off her bench and soon they, too, were gone, melting into the crowd. "Whew!" Geneva hollered and grabbed up her Miller Lite, then just sat there looking like she was having the time of her life. I couldn't imagine why she had a crush on my dad; I thought Bailey was the cutest thing I'd seen east of Dallas, with his long legs and that mustache of his and his shiny white teeth. For somebody's husband, that is, and an older man.

The next song was slow and romantic-sounding and had lots of references in it to summer air and auburn hair, to a place love calls home. The dancer couples slid by in slow clinches, their soles shoosh-shooshing on the concrete floor. Bailey had spun off with Geneva again after depositing Lucy back beside me. I looked over at her, the light on her hair, and it hit me for the first time that Dad was singing about her. That he had *written* this song, about her. It went into me like an arrow. That you could do this: just get up in front of people and sing your songs, put them out there to stand on their own, little offerings to the world.

The band played for an hour, a mix of ballads and fast-paced country songs, and I kept my ears peeled for the unfamiliar tunes, the ones I soon learned to recognize as Dad's own. I looked around me at the lively crowd. Why, I wondered, weren't they paying more attention? He seemed too big for the room. He acted so at ease up there, moving to the music, grinning as folks he knew coasted past on the dance floor, like his whole life centered on this. But I couldn't help but picture brighter lights, cheering voices, his face framed by a TV screen. I didn't see how what he had here could be enough.

I excused myself to nobody in particular and wound my way around the edges of the dance floor to the ladies' room. The door swung shut behind me, muffling the music, only the bass beating through. A couple of girls were in there, putting on lipstick in front of one of the green-flaked mirrors. I peed and flushed, then washed my hands at the far sink. The girls had complicated hairdos and eye makeup, and in their fancy cowgirl shirts and Rocky Mountain jeans, they were as bony as boys. I recognized them from earlier; the blond with the spiral perm had ambushed Dad on his way to the stage, shoving her hips against him, getting her mouth up close to his as they talked. I'd noticed how he'd used his guitar case as a shield, keeping a distance, although maybe he'd just done that for Lucy's sake.

A middle-aged lady in a denim dress came out of a stall. She stepped up to the sink next to mine as I was grabbing a handful of paper towels.

"Well, hi there!" she said. My face in the mirror must have been a blank, because she laughed. "You don't remember me, do you? I'm Judy Moss. I met you this morning on the courthouse square." I nodded, politely I hoped, and dried my hands. "Ash's girl, right?"

"Yes, ma'am."

At the end of the row of sinks, the blond swung her head my way. Her eyes were yellow and heavy-lidded, like a cat's. She looked at her friend, who shook her head and tapped a Salem Light out of a pack.

Beside me Mrs. Moss flapped her wet hands over the sink. "You must be so proud of him!" she exclaimed to me. "We're all proud of Ash. We expect big things from him."

"Yes, ma'am," I said. She was drying her hands, fluffing her hair in the mirror as the blond went on staring at me like I was in a cage at the zoo. If there was any way I could have kept Mrs. Moss there, I would have. But there'd been a break in the music; now it started up again, and she gasped and exclaimed, "This is Sonny's favorite song!" and scooted for the door.

"Excuse me," I said, turning to leave, but the blond waved her hand at me and I froze.

"Hold on, hold on." She turned and set her skinny hip against the edge of the sink and held out a hand for her friend's cigarettes. Her eyes did their slow tour again, starting with the spangled clip in my hair and ending with my Converse high-tops. The shoes, in particular, seemed to enchant her. She stared at them for a long, long time. "Don't you think it's funny, Vonda, that Ash never mentioned he had a little girl?"

The friend—Vonda, presumably—smiled. "I guess y'all never got around to that."

"No, somehow we never did," the blond said, lighting her cigarette. She tossed the burning match into the sink and let it sizzle, leaving a tiny scorched trail in the basin.

"Maybe he thought it would cramp his style," Vonda said, arching an eyebrow at her reflection in the mirror, and starting to add another layer of lipstick.

The blond drew on her cigarette, holding the smoke deep in her lungs as she eyed me. "How old are you, sweetheart?"

It almost made me laugh, her calling me that. She wasn't that much older than me. "I'll be fifteen. In July."

The two girls' eyes met in the mirror, and they started to snort and wheeze, choking on the smoke from their cigarettes. I had no idea what was so funny, though I assumed it had something to do with my appearance, because that's what I always thought, ever since the kids on the school bus in fourth grade had nicknamed me Squatty. Everybody in Mooney knew my handsome, talented father; I figured these girls were snickering at how far the apple had fallen from the tree. But it seemed the only time I could open my mouth was when I was better off keeping my opinion to myself.

"Your father is royalty around here, you know that?" the blond said now, leaning toward the mirror to lift a flake of tobacco off her teeth with one red fingernail. "The bastard prince."

I cleared my throat. "I really need to—"

"Tell me something. Is he still seeing that Lucy person—the little

widow?" I didn't know what she was talking about, the widow part,
but I nodded anyway. "I heard she's moved into his place. So, I mean,
they're living together? It's serious?" *She's pregnant,* I wanted to shout,
how serious would you call that? But I just shrugged.

The rest room door opened and a woman dragging a little boy by
the hand came in, smiling as she steered him through the room and into
one of the stalls. "Now, do it like you do at home, Jamie," she urged. "I
have to go," I said, and turned toward the door.

"Hey! Give your daddy a message for me, will you?" the blond
said, and like the fool I was, I stopped and looked back at her. She
sucked in a lungful of smoke and then exhaled toward the ceiling in
two thin streams, following them with her eyes. "Tell him Misty said if
he decides he wants to come back over to the wild side to give me a
call." She smiled, a tight, shiny smile. "On second thought, he doesn't
have to call. Tell him just to come right on over. I'm sure he remembers
the way."

I'll say this for myself: I didn't tell her to get screwed, but I didn't
promise to deliver her message, either.

The band was taking a break, the room was darker and smokier
than ever, and the dance floor was still packed as the jukebox cranked
up, Vince Gill doing "Liza Jane," all that guitar stuff sounding like
gymnastics, handsprings and back flips. I slipped into my spot on the
bench next to Geneva, who turned and smiled and patted my arm, like
she knew what I'd just been through in the ladies' room.

I felt sick, watching Dad make his way around the dance floor to
our table. Every time a female, six or sixty, approached him, a lump of
misery swelled up in my throat. Bailey offered to get me a Coke, and I
said yes, thank you. He brought it back just as Dad walked up, shaking
hands all around the table, kissing Geneva's cheek, leaning over to give
Aunt Dove a squeeze. Lucy stood up and turned to face him and he put
one knee up on the bench and got her by the waist, and we all watched
as he pulled her hips against his and they smiled into each other's eyes.
It was there, all right, the current between them, although it felt tar-
nished to me now, with no telling whose fingerprints all over it. I had to
remind myself I didn't know him at all; I didn't know what he was

capable of. I wondered if Lucy knew about this Misty. I wondered if she cared.

Somebody handed Dad a beer, and he and Bailey started talking about circular saws. They kept getting interrupted, though, since every five seconds someone walked up with something to say to Dad. The bastard prince. Bailey finally got up to dance with Aunt Dove to a Conway Twitty song, and Dad slung his leg over the bench and sat down facing me.

"Well, Miss Farrell," he said, taking a swig of beer. "How we doing?"

"Okay." I rolled my Coke bottle between my palms.

"How do you like the music? I guess it's not much like what you're used to."

"I like it," I said. "I like it a lot."

His eyebrows went up. I guess he was surprised I'd been listening, or maybe that it was practically the only enthusiasm I'd shown about anything since I'd gotten there the day before.

"Did your mama ever tell you I used to write songs to you?" I shook my head, but the rest of me felt paralyzed, I wanted to hear this so bad. "You had colic when you were a baby, and your mama couldn't ever get you to settle down. All day long she'd walk and walk you, rub your tummy, all that stuff Dr. Spock said to do, but nothing helped. By the time I came home from work in the evenings she'd just be worn out. I mean, hell, who wouldn't be? She'd just hand you over and start to cry.

"Not that I knew what to do any better than she did. But one night she went on to bed, and I just sat you up in your little baby seat on the kitchen table and got out my guitar and started playing. At first you just went right on yelling, like you'd been doing for days. But after a while you started to quiet down a little, and before too long you were just sitting there in your chair and, I swear, you were *listening*. Your face got all still and thoughtful, and you just watched me, with those big eyes of yours. You were so *serious*, like you were paying attention. It got so every evening I'd come home and take you from Marlene and put you in your little chair, and she'd go to bed and you and I would sit around the supper table and I'd make up songs, and you'd listen. So, you see, in a way, you were my first audience." He looked up at me then, for the first time since he'd started talking, and smiled. "I bet you never heard that story before, did you?"

"No, sir." I tucked my hands into my lap so he wouldn't see them shaking. "Could you . . . I mean, what were the songs?" I wanted those songs. In a way, I thought, I had earned them.

"Oh, nothing that ever amounted to much," he said, but just then the Conway Twitty song faded and a Clint Black tune started up and Dad looked over his shoulder and said, "Uh-oh, where's Lucy? They're playing our song." And he set his empty bottle on the table and swung around and swept her up and onto the dance floor. Just like that, gone again.

❧

During the band's second set, I listened extra hard to the songs I knew were originals, knowing that one of them, any of them, might have been something Dad had made up one night around the kitchen table when I was just a crabby baby, back when he and Ma and I were still together. *And happy*, I liked to think, though I suppose that was wishful thinking on my part, since they were living apart a year later, and divorced just after my second birthday. Maybe I thought I'd hear some phrase or chord and be hurtled back in time, strapped into my carrier and listening with every bit of my baby concentration to the music that must have spun itself, those nights, in a web around me, filling my head with stuff I still carried, all this time later.

It didn't happen, though; there was a song about an old car, a song about a dying soldier, lots of songs about girls and heartbreak, but I didn't recognize any of it. For the finale Dad played Van Morrison's "Brown-Eyed Girl" and dedicated it to Lucy.

We were quiet in the Buick, Dad at the wheel, Lucy in the crook of his arm, heading home. The radio was off, the windows down; the only sound was the hum of asphalt under our wheels and Aunt Dove snoring in the backseat, her head propped against the window. We drove to her house, and Dad got out and woke her up and walked her to her front step and waited till she was inside. Lucy settled her head against his shoulder as he started the car again. "You okay back there?" he said to me over the seat back. I said I was. The night flew by in an unbroken streak, the smell of the woods so brisk and green in my nostrils it made me want to cry for all I wanted and thought I would never have.

Dad unloaded his guitar and we filed inside. I felt deflated, like all the shimmer had worn off the evening. I watched him move around the living room, and thought of that Misty girl until my insides were twisted. Lucy put on water for tea, but I said I was tired and climbed into my sleeping bag and put on my headphones and said good night.

Dad went out onto the porch. "Hey, Lucy," he called a minute later, through the screen door. "Come on out here and look at this moon."

She forgot about the kettle, I guess. In a couple of minutes, it started to whistle, and finally to scream; I could hear it even over my Walkman. It went on and on, until I couldn't stand it anymore and squirmed out of my sleeping bag.

The kitchen was empty. I turned off the stove and walked through the house to the front door. The moon was as bright as a coin, the yard washed in silver. They were right up against the side of the truck; I could see him bent over her, her arms around him, and her legs. I could see the way he moved hungrily against her, and the way she moved back, like she couldn't get him close enough. I wasn't completely ignorant; I'd seen those movies, as I've said. I knew I wasn't supposed to watch. Yet there it was again, that idea I couldn't shake. That, even though I didn't understand it, I was meant to see.

I heard her voice, *ah ah ah*, then a little cry, then quiet.

I got back into my sleeping bag, my heart pounding, sick and scared and thrilled with all the things I might or might not ever learn. They were out there a long time. I fell asleep, woke again when I heard them come in, tiptoeing through the living room, shutting the bedroom door behind them. Slept again, finally, and dreamed of music, lost and found.

6

Lucy

Where was the moment, the crack in the surface of our daily lives that would let me hand over to Ash the news I was carrying, something that would surely make everything else that had happened to us look weak and washed-out by comparison? I had never been any good with secrets; I was always blurting out people's private business to the first available ear. But this one was too important not to be allowed its proper due. In the front yard that Wednesday night after the Round-Up, I almost told him; with my back against the truck's wheel well and all Ash's weight and appetite on me, I felt the words rise up in my throat and had to bite my tongue not to shout them out. The moment passed, though; sex has a way of doing that, of overloading the circuits and then shorting out the board, wiping it blank. I forgot, for a few minutes, what I needed to tell him. I forgot that anything could be bigger than this. By the time I got my equilibrium back, we were coiled around each other in bed, and Ash was asleep. I lay awake a long time, listening to him breathe, my fingers resting lightly on the plane of my abdomen, my secret still couched there, safe, beneath the surface.

Morning was no better. Thursdays were always the worst days for Ash. Something about the stage of the Round-Up the night before made the transition back to the rest of his life seem intolerable; how could he be singing his songs for two hundred people one night and building cabinets for contrary old women the morning after? He glared silently into his coffee as the sun shone in the kitchen window. Denny, in the living room, was still asleep. I'd already thrown up twice that morning; I didn't think I could hide it much longer.

"Marlene called," I said, rinsing the coffeepot under the tap.

Ash's head swung slowly around. His eyes were frightful, hooded and hung-over-looking, though I knew he'd only had a couple of beers the night before. For some reason I was never scared of him when I saw him like that, even though I stayed alert to the capacity of his temper. Instead it roused something protective and tender in me. I prided myself, secretly, on guiding him out of his dark and dangerous self, back to the other side, the place where he shined.

"She did? When?"

"Last night. The message is on the machine."

He got up, still in his sock feet, and went into the hall and pressed the playback key on the answering machine. I didn't have to listen; I'd already heard it, could have written the script ahead of time. She was sorry Ash was being inconvenienced, sorrier still he'd felt the need to resort to childish phone games and name-calling, but she didn't see how that changed anything. That the bottom line was, Ash had gotten away without participating in five minutes of his daughter's life for the past eight years, and it was time he made up for that, took some responsibility. That she hoped they could sit down and talk about this sometime as rational adults, although based on his latest phone call this was doubtful, and anyway she was going to be in a training seminar for ten hours a day every day for a week, so he'd just have to wing it, the way she'd done every single day for the past twelve years. That she'd call again, in a couple of weeks, when maybe things had settled down for everyone. Remind Denise to change her shirt every now and then. Tell her to be a good girl. Kent says hi. Click, beep, end of message.

Ash came back into the kitchen, looking miserable. He seemed to be unsure that this *was* his kitchen; he gazed around it, at the appliances and the tableware and me, standing at the sink, like he wasn't sure he'd seen any of it before, like he might have woken up in the wrong house by mistake.

"Am I an awful person, Lucy?" he asked, rubbing his eyes with the back of his hand. "Is there some huge terrible thing I've done that I don't understand?"

Denny stood at the door, blinking in the morning sun. She even slept in those shapeless corduroys. It made me sad, like she didn't think she deserved regular clothes, or pajamas. I saw my rhinestone barrette still pinned to her sleep-matted hair.

"Did Ma call?"

"She left a message," I said, when it became apparent Ash wasn't going to answer her, engrossed as he was in his own big philosophical question. "She's real busy right now, Denny. You think you can stand to stay here a little bit longer, at least? Until your mama and daddy can get things straightened out?"

Denny looked at me, then at Ash, who was staring out the window at some point on the horizon only he could see, like if he only focused hard enough he might get it to burst into flames. If he'd touched her once, even incidentally, since she'd gotten here, I hadn't seen it.

"Okay," she said finally, with the tone of someone who hopes for nothing because it's what she's always known. It broke my heart, and made me want to stab Ash through the jugular. Denny sat down at the table and unwrapped a Pop-Tart and started to nibble on it. Ash turned and left the room, banging his shoulder against the door frame on the way out. In a few minutes we heard his boots on the hardwood, the front door open and slam, the truck roar to life and lurch away.

And so my secret was mine, for another day. I went back to the bathroom and threw up.

∞

Denny was silent, riding beside me into town. I'd already called Peggy and told her I'd be late. It was a hot, windless morning; you had to get up over fifty to get any kind of breeze going. The radio was on, Dolly

Parton warbling "I Will Always Love You," which didn't do much to tamp down the bile that kept rising in my throat.

I glanced over at Denny, gazing straight ahead through the windshield. At first you might have dismissed her as your typical disaffected teenager, but I knew better; I knew that look, so stubbornly neutral, a thin disguise for despair.

The song was more than I could take. I started singing, as loud as I could, drowning out Dolly and her chorus of violins and backup singers, even though the only musical talent I own is the ability to recognize that I don't have any. But I kept singing anyway, as loud as I could, straight through two choruses and the big finale, and by the time the song ended, Denny was laughing. Her whole face was transformed; I saw the possibility there, for some kind of connection. That was my problem; I was always seeing possibilities where no one else could see them.

"What a crock," I said, reaching over to turn down the radio. "If Ash ever leaves me, I hope he's alone and pathetic for the rest of his life."

"He won't," Denny said. "Leave you." I glanced over at her. "How could he leave you?" she asked, and then blushed, as the secret we held between us raised its little polliwog head and howled.

"Well, he might take a hike if he ever heard me sing."

Denny grinned. "I wouldn't blame him." I'd never seen her teeth before. They were exactly like Ash's, the top two just barely overlapping. So maybe she was not just Marlene's alien love child after all.

"Can I ask you something?" she said. "How did you and him . . . How did you and my dad, um, you know. Get together?"

"Well, I grew up here, about a hundred years ago, and your dad and I went to the same school, even though we didn't know each other then, he was three years ahead of me. Anyway, I moved off after high school and got a job in Texarkana. I met a man there, and he asked me to marry him." She nodded, didn't look particularly surprised. "We moved to the country, a place about an hour from here. And for fourteen years I was a farmer's wife."

"Okay." She was waiting to find out why I wasn't a farmer's wife anymore, or maybe if I still was.

"My husband died, last winter. In a terrible accident." My mind flashed to Mitchell high up on the seat of the mower, looking back to see why the blade was stuck, turning and then tumbling . . . I touched the base of my throat, cleared it. "I couldn't keep up our farm by myself, and my family wanted me to come home, so I moved back to Mooney and found myself a little house, and the job with Peggy at the flower shop. And just a couple of weeks after I got back, I met your daddy. On a Wednesday night, as a matter of fact, at the Round-Up. And . . ." I waved my hand airily to suggest the rest.

"You never had kids?" she asked, her eyes on a passing billboard. "You and the farmer."

"We never did." I spared her my supposed-infertility story; I thought even a fourteen-year-old would have been sharper than I'd been in that department.

She took a breath and twisted her body on the seat to face me. "Before my dad met you," she said, "I guess he must have had— You know. Girlfriends."

"Well, sure he did. Sure. In fact, he had a girlfriend when I met him. She wasn't too happy about me."

I laughed, but stopped when I saw Denny's face, and said to myself, *Misty Potter*. It had been a long time since I'd given more than a passing thought to Ash's former fling, but I recalled it all now: Misty inserting herself like a wedge between Ash and me, refusing to budge, having Ash arrested and thrown in jail rather than give him up. Misty Potter, the Blond Avenger, not so many years older than Ash's own daughter. Denny knew; I don't know how, but she knew.

"Listen, Denny," I said. "You can't be mad at your father for stuff that doesn't have anything to do with you. Stuff you don't understand." I didn't think I had to spell out what stuff.

"Aren't you?" she asked. "Mad at him about it?"

"Not so much, anymore."

"I think it's horrible," she declared, with more intensity than I'd known she could muster. "I think it's *repulsive*."

"But you weren't there," I said. "Neither was I. We don't know what was in his head." This sounded feeble, even to me.

"Nothing was in his head. His *head* didn't have anything to do with it."

"You can't judge him, Denny," I insisted. "They were consenting adults—well, almost adults. Nobody got killed. Nobody went to prison." I smiled, but her expression was stony. "You want to know what Ash told me? That it was like an anthropology experiment to him."

Denny screwed up her face in disbelief. "Yeah, that sounds like him," she said, and in spite of myself, I started to laugh. It was so true. It was what my brother Bailey would have called a juicy rationalization.

"You want to know the truth?" I said then, swinging the Buick off the highway and onto the main road into town. "I don't care about it, any of it. It's over."

"Anyway, you and him are—" Her mouth crimped like she was tasting a lemon. "In love."

"Well, yeah. Yeah, we are." And I made up my mind to end it with that. "So, did you enjoy yourself last night?" I hated not to take advantage of this channel that had opened up between us. But she'd turned back to the window.

"I guess."

"It mattered a lot to Ash that you liked it. That you'd think he was good."

Right away I wished I hadn't said it. Not because it wasn't true; it was, I knew in my gut. But she would ask, rightly so, how I knew, if he'd said so. And I would have to say, *No, not exactly*, and things would be worse than before. She didn't ask, though. She just swiveled her head and watched me for a minute, like she was sizing up the depth of my bullshit.

"He's good," she said finally. "Really good."

"Yeah?" I wanted her to keeping going; I thought I was getting somewhere.

"Like, maybe he could even be famous. On the radio. On *TV.*"

We pulled up behind the flower shop and I nosed the Buick into my customary spot under a linden tree. The sun beat down like the fires of hell; even in the shade, the car would be a hundred degrees by the end of the day. I opened the door and swung my feet out onto the pavement.

"Well, I think you should tell him that," I said. Denny looked at me, her eyes wide. "Seriously. I think he would really like to hear it from you."

She made a big production out of gathering up her Walkman and tapes, a beat-up copy of *Rolling Stone*. As she pushed open the passenger door, her face was flat and colorless again.

"I doubt it," she said, and got out and slammed the door and trudged off toward the courthouse square.

❦

Around eleven o'clock, the phone rang in the back of the shop. Peggy answered in the office, then stuck her head out the door and said I had a call.

It was Ash's partner, Isaac King. "Mornin', Lucy," he said. "Sorry to be botherin' you at the shop. I just wondered, you have any idea where Ash might be?"

"Why, he's supposed to be at Mrs. Crouch's," I said. "Where are *you*, Isaac?"

"Well, that's just it. I'm *at* Miz Crouch's, see. And we ain't heard or seen a thing of Ash this mornin'."

I just stood there, the phone a dead weight in my hand. "I don't know what to say," I said finally. "He left the house around a quarter to nine. I thought he was meeting you at the job."

"I did, too. Leastways that's how he acted yesterday. 'See you in the morning, Isaac,' he said to me at quittin' time. He didn't say nothin' about no errand he had to run, nothin' like that. I been pagin' and pagin' him, but no answer. And here I am, and Miz Crouch, well she's about to have a conniption, see, her kitchen is all tore up and there's dishes everywhere and no place to put anything—"

"Isaac, listen. Tell Mrs. Crouch— Tell her Ash drove down to Marshall to get something. Some parts. I don't know what parts, make something up. You stay close to the phone, okay? I'll call you as soon as I find him."

I pressed the bar to disconnect the call, then dialed Ash's pager and hung up. While I waited, I watched the traffic on the street in front of the shop: the sheriff, Bill Dudley, in his patrol car, and Seth and Sean Butler in their new Ram truck with the grill that looked like a cattle catcher. In five whole minutes, those were the only ones who drove by. In the front window, Peggy was building a display around Crystal Sheppard's forthcoming wedding to Bobby Pilger, with a froth of white netting and baby's breath and sugared Styrofoam doves centered around a glossy enlargement of Crystal and Bobby's engagement por-trait, the two of them looking like new-hatched chicks, like the fuzz was still wet behind their ears. I willed my heart to beat regularly, my brain to stay still. Ash didn't call. I don't know how, but I knew he wouldn't.

It occurred to me, right then, just to back out of it. To let Ash run around unaccounted for on his mysterious business, no questions asked. To let Mrs. Crouch fire his sorry ass. To let him lose this job; to let him lose his whole damned home-repair business. To drive myself back to his cobbled-together excuse for a house and load up my stuff and get away from Ash Farrell and his gloomy daughter and never set eyes on him again or utter his name. To raise up my baby without ever, once, letting Ash know.

But I didn't see why he deserved to get off that easy.

I told Peggy I needed to take an early lunch. "Sure, you came in late anyway," she cracked from the window, where, in her lime green muumuu, she'd wedged herself against the plate glass for the whole of Front Street to behold. She'd gotten stuck in there once, when I was on a delivery run; usually, after that, she made me do the displays while she coached. "In fact, why not take two hours while you're at it?"

"Thanks," I said, and grabbed my keys and walked out the door.

I fired up the Buick, without a clue. I circled the courthouse, but Ash's truck wasn't in front of the café or the bank or the True Value. I did see Denny on her bench, and slowed as I passed by. "Have you seen your daddy around?" I asked, but she just shook her head and stuck her chin back in her *Rolling Stone*. I drove past the machine shop, then out through town past the lumberyard, the only other places I could think he might have stopped to do some business. Then I swung the car onto the highway and headed back to the house.

Had something happened the night before between Ash and Misty Potter, I wondered, something that had stirred Denny's suspicion? Was it possible it was starting up again—or that, in spite of all the evidence to the contrary, it had never ended? I found myself bracing for the sight of Misty's sporty silver Mitsubishi parked alongside Ash's truck out front; but the yard was empty, the house closed up tight. The dogs ran in excited, baffled loops around the car, then trotted along behind me as I reversed and turned back up the road to the highway. I drove over to my rent house, even though there was no reason Ash would go there and he didn't have a key. My roses bloomed along the porch rail with their usual intemperance, but there wasn't a soul around.

I knew that, even though her name made her sound like a lap dancer, Misty worked as a legal secretary thirty miles south, in Jefferson, that she had an apartment there. Well, all right, Ash, I said to myself. If this is how you want to play it.

I stopped for gas at the Texaco, then went inside to get a 7-Up to settle my stomach. Ira Deacon took my credit card and ran it through the machine. "You and Ash must have forgot to synchronize your watches this morning," he said, handing over my card.

I stopped signing the charge slip and looked up at him. "What do you mean?"

"He was just in here. Not five minutes ago."

"Ash? Was here?"

"Uh-huh. Filled up the truck and bought him a root beer and a fried pie. Apple, if I'm not mistaken. Was it apple, Lonnie, or cherry?" Lonnie, stocking the beer cooler, confirmed it: apple. "He bought a lotto ticket, too, now that I think of it. Jackpot's up to six million, you know."

"Did he say where he was going?" I asked, picking up my soda, backing toward the door.

"Sure. Imogene Crouch's. Same job he's been working on for two weeks. Said he sure will be glad to get that one behind him. Said—" But I was out the door already, leaving it swinging behind me.

I got to Mrs. Crouch's at the same time Ash did; we pulled in nose to nose at the curb in front of her big fake-Tudor house across from the

First Baptist Church. I cut the engine and just sat there, staring at Ash through our two windshields. He looked to be sizing up the situation, but I wasn't about to make the first move.

Finally he got out of the truck and slammed the door. He came ambling over to me like the king of cool, taking a swig of his A&W, biting off a chunk of fried pie. Apple.

He squatted on the curb, next to my window. He hadn't shaved that morning, and his jaw and upper lip were dark with stubble. He scraped his hair back from his forehand with one hand. I'm ashamed to say how all this made him look to me, how it hit me someplace I didn't really need to be hit, not right then.

"What are you doing here, Lucy?"

"Isaac called me at the shop. He said you hadn't showed up this morning, and he couldn't raise you on your pager. He said Mrs. Crouch was having a conniption."

Ash turned his head slowly and surveyed the house, like Mrs. Crouch might appear on the lawn at any moment, frothing at the mouth. "And your role in this is what?"

"My role in this is detective, apparently. Or watchdog, or whatever kind of bitch you want to call me. My Lord, Ash. Isaac asked me to try to find you! I checked a couple places, then Ira Deacon at the Texaco happened to tell me you were on your way here. It's obviously not the big deal it got made it out to be."

"Obviously." He was still staring at Mrs. Crouch's front door, which in fact opened presently. Isaac stepped out onto the porch—portico, Mrs. Crouch called it, even though strictly speaking it wasn't—and waved. Ash raised a hand in response and held it there, aloft but inert, like he didn't have the wherewithal to move it.

"Why are you acting this way?" I asked. "Isaac works for you. You work for Mrs. Crouch. If you had some personal business, some reason you knew you'd be late, why didn't you just let one of them know about it? I'd just as soon not have gotten in the middle of it, frankly. I didn't sign on for this."

"Yeah?" He lowered his hand and swiveled his face back toward me. "What *did* you sign on for? If you don't mind me asking."

"Good question." Orange spots danced in front of my eyes; I thought I might be bursting a blood vessel. "I must've seen your name on a bathroom wall. 'For a good time, call Ash Farrell.'"

"You trying to tell me you haven't had a good time?" He smiled as I turned the key and started my engine. "I seem to recall you were having a pretty good time along about midnight last night, outside under that shiny old moon." He stood up and stretched his legs. The front door of the house opened again, and old Mrs. Crouch came out, along with her collection of little yapping dogs. Before she'd even started our way, I could see her mouth moving.

Ash leaned over and put his elbows on my windowsill. His face was inches from mine, and I couldn't decide if I'd rather kiss him or pull away from the curb and watch him topple headfirst into the street. "Do you tell me all your business, Lucy?" he said. "Do I know everything about you there is to know?"

"What are you talking about?" Something flip-flopped inside me, but try as I might, I couldn't read his eyes.

He tucked in his elbows and straightened up. "Turn, turn, turn," he said cryptically, as Mrs. Crouch descended across her lawn toward us, the dogs barking and leaping like a bunch of crazed wind-up toys. Ash started humming the old sixties song under his breath.

"What?" Up till then he'd only pissed me off, but now he was starting to scare me.

"'A time for every purpose under heaven.' Go back to work, Lucy. This won't be a pretty sight."

I nudged the car away from the curb, watching in my rearview mirror as the old lady swept down on Ash with her fists raised like Mike Tyson. Ash had his arms crossed in front of his chest, a classic coward's stance. My money was on Mrs. Crouch.

7

Lucy

 I didn't know how to fight with Ash. We were still new in love, and hadn't had any practice. Anyway, I wasn't exactly sure we *were* fighting. I collected Denny from her bench in the square at the end of the day, not knowing what in the world I'd gotten into.

I'd never been much of a cook, wasn't inspired to be, but that evening I stopped at the Food King and bought steaks and potatoes and butter and Dijon mustard. Tonight, I swore, no matter what, I would fix up Aunt Dove's beans. A time for every purpose under heaven. Denny had picked up a Stephen King paperback at the checkout stand, thumbed through it, and asked if she could have it. By the time we got home, she was on chapter two.

I invited her to come into the kitchen with me, that even if she wanted to read her book at the table, I'd appreciate the company. I asked if she minded the radio, and she said she didn't. I stood at the sink gazing out the window at the woods gathering dark and the sky a brushstroke of blue beyond, scrubbing the potatoes and listening as George Jones sang and Denny quietly turned pages and thinking I had everything I needed, right then. There were times I was more comforted by Ash in the abstract than by the presence of him. I wanted to think about making love with him in the front yard under a three-quarter moon. I wanted to think about living happily ever after. I didn't want to think about what might actually happen an hour from now, when he got home.

He drove up not long after, pausing to stomp the dust off his boots on the mat, singing "Why Baby Why?" as he came up the hall and into the kitchen. We'd been listening to the same radio station, apparently. He kissed me behind the ear. He smelled like sweat and varnish and the outdoors and something else, that dark note I could always detect but never identify. "What's this? *Supper?*" he gasped, clutching at his chest. I made a face at him and he turned around and looked at Denny. She was trying to ignore him, but I could tell it was a struggle; every time he was around I could feel something in her yearning toward him, a sensation I well understood.

He glanced over her shoulder, then reached down and turned back the cover of her book and scanned the title. "*Ooooh,*" he whispered, fluttering his fingers in what I guessed was supposed to be a spooky way. Denny rolled her eyes, but she couldn't hold back a grin. It gave me a pang, her gratitude for the littlest scrap of his attention. And yet I couldn't say I didn't know how it felt, that craving. Ash's greatest gift, even more than his music, was that the minute he aimed his sights at you, you were the brightest thing in the galaxy. For as long as it lasted. I didn't blame Misty Potter for hanging around, acting loopy. It would be tough to let go of, once you'd had it.

He opened the refrigerator and took out a Bud. "Do you need me for anything?" he asked, moving back to the doorway, twisting open his beer.

"Not at this precise moment," I said, meeting his eyes with mine full of intent, then ducking my chin when he started to smile.

"Call me when supper's ready," he said, and in a minute the front door opened and closed, and presently the sound of his guitar came floating in through the screen. I turned off the radio so I could hear him. *Walk through this world with me,* he sang, *go where I go . . .*

That was Ash. He could never just say "I'm sorry" like other people. Everything came with a score.

⚭

Supper was congenial. The food was decent if not dazzling, and Ash regaled us with the story of Mrs. Crouch coming after him on her front lawn with her dukes up. The way he told it, he'd stopped to run an errand, and was only a little late. He seemed to be making a point.

After we finished eating, Denny asked to be excused and took her book out onto the porch. Ash tipped his chair back on its hind legs and opened the refrigerator and got out a fresh beer, then sat and watched me as I cleared the dishes from the table and ran the sink full of soapy water.

"That's enough, Lucy," he said. "Come here a minute." He set the four legs of his chair square on the floor, and because I was a besotted fool, I let him pull me into his lap. He pressed his mouth against my hair, and I leaned into him and closed my eyes and said a prayer, the kind God laughs at and files away with the requests for football victories and good weather and stock-market tips: *Never change. Stay forever.*

"You've been holding out on me," he said.

I raised my head. "What?"

"You told me you didn't know how to cook."

"I told you I'm not a *born* cook. I know how, I just don't care for it much."

He smiled. "Anyway, thanks for the beans. You know just how I like them."

"My pleasure."

And there it was, the opening into which my shiny little announcement might fall. It sat there, beckoning, while my throat closed around the words like a yoke, squeezing the life out. It felt like we'd woken up one morning a pair of happy ships on the same sea, but that a wind had blown up from out of nowhere and we were drifting in opposite directions. *Where are you going, Ash?* I thought, feeling his eyes on me, feeling his heart beat. *Where are you now?*

"Is Denny okay?" he asked then, surprising me; it was not where I'd thought the conversation was headed.

"I think so," I said. "She seems sad, though. I wish you'd . . ."

"What?"

"I don't know. Do something. With her, for her. I know she thinks she doesn't want to be here, but she's so hungry for something, Ash. She's only fourteen," I reminded him. "You're her father."

"A gig I never enlisted for," he said, so bitterly that I drew back quickly to look at his face. "I was twenty years old when Marlene got pregnant," he said, "and Catholic, to boot. I thought I was a big man. Doing the right thing." He took a swallow of beer. "Boy, was I wrong about that."

I pushed myself off his lap and turned around and swept an armload of plates into the dishwater. The sickness I felt went so deep it made my bones hurt, like the marrow was dark and malignant.

"I guess you think that's a pretty shitty attitude," he said, setting his bottle on the table.

"I guess I don't think it helps Denny very much," I said. "Denny, the human being. Brought into the world by a couple of people who care more about their own interests than hers." I dropped the skillet into the water with a rocking splash and turned to him. "You cannot hold that girl accountable for what you did! Or what you wished you didn't do. You want to be a man? Then face it, Ash. She's here, now. Yours."

He got up and stood staring at the backs of his hands on the rail of the chair. I watched his shoulders work underneath his T-shirt, a nerve jump in his cheek. "This is the last thing I need to be hearing right now," he said, "thank you all the same."

"Ash," I said as he walked toward the door. "Ash!" The front door banged.

I finished cleaning up the kitchen, putting the pots away. Beyond the window, the remnants of sunset lingered in the trunks of the pines.

I wiped my hands on a dish towel and went out onto the porch. Ash's truck was still in the yard. Denny sat on the step wearing her headphones, scratching my little dog Steve Cropper's ears.

I sat down beside her and the puppy shifted his focus to me; his tail flogged my calves, and he drooled rapturously as I wriggled my fingers under his chin. "What a slut," I said, and Denny made a small sound, though whether it was laughter or something else, I couldn't tell. In the near-darkness I could feel the heat coming off her face.

"Who would ever think to name a dog Steve Cropper?" she asked.

"Same person who already had a dog named Booker T.," I answered. "Not too subtle, was it?" She let the headphones slip around her neck. "Where is Booker, anyway?" Denny jerked her head in a vague way in the direction of the empty road. "Is that where your daddy went?"

"Uh-huh."

"Well, he's liable to miss dessert. You want pie? Dove made it. Lemon cream."

She shook her head. It was a perfectly lovely summer evening, warm and almost breezeless. Stars poked through the dark velvet scrim overhead. Mosquitoes swarmed. How, I wondered, had everything changed so fast? Venus was in the exact same position it had been two nights before, but everything was different. For the first time since I'd met Ash, I felt like I needed a map of the sky.

Denny and I sat there until the moon began to rise, and then we got up and said our heavyhearted good nights, and went to bed.

❦

My back was to the door, my eyes on the clock—not quite midnight— so I heard but didn't see Ash come in, heard him sit down in the rocking chair to pull off his boots, heard the soft rustling of his clothes coming off, falling to the floor. He slid under the sheet. His skin smelled like nighttime, like secrets.

"I know you're awake." He rolled toward me and laid his hand lightly on my hip. "Aren't you talking to me?"

"I can't talk to you, Ash. No one can talk to you. The minute you hear something you don't like, you just start walking."

The ceiling fan ticked. Under the porch Steve Cropper whined softly, dreaming his doggy dreams. My heart beat in my chest like a stone. "Will you listen to me, then, at least?" Ash asked. "Will you do that?" I didn't say yes, but I didn't say no, either.

"All I meant earlier," he said, "was that I wish Marlene and I had been more careful. After about the first three weeks, we had no business even being together, much less thinking we could settle down and raise a baby. And all of us got punished for it, you see? Denny most of all."

I turned to face him, twisting myself up in the sheet. The moon made a stripe of light across his face, his silver-and-black hair. It seemed like God must be taunting me, putting all I wanted at arm's reach and yet as far from me as the source of that light.

He put a hand in my hair, working it in deep, his callused fingertips pressing against my temples, my scalp. He ran his thumb across my cheekbone, over my lips. I felt like a snake being hypnotized. I forgot that sixty seconds earlier he'd been wanting me to talk, and that now he seemed bent on keeping me quiet. I let myself be charmed.

❧

Ash was up early the next morning; I came half awake hearing him get into the shower, then again as he came in and bent over me and kissed my neck. I smelled bar soap, coffee, toothpaste, that heady morning brew. "Don't get up," he whispered. "I'll see you tonight." And he walked down the hall carrying his boots and let himself out the front door. I heard the truck start up, then pull out. Sleep was such a blessed haven; I closed my eyes and drifted.

When I woke again it was past eight, and I had to scramble to get washed and dressed and into the car to make it to work on time. Denny rode beside me without a peep, blinking her sleep-swollen eyes. This weekend, I swore to myself, everything would change. We would decide what to do about Denny. I would tell Ash everything. If we could just get through till tomorrow night: Saturday night, Round-Up night. I let Denny off in the square without ten words exchanged between us, feeling like I'd just dropped off a hitchhiker, some pale, sullen stray. It wasn't completely Ash's fault, I knew, that he hadn't fallen head over heels in love with his daughter on sight. I had to tamp down the urge to drive past Mrs. Crouch's, to see if Ash's truck was out front. I steered into my parking spot behind the flower shop, opened the car door, and leaned against the trunk of the linden tree for a few minutes, until the churning in my head and stomach passed. I pulled myself upright, hung on.

❧

At noon I walked up to the square to share another brown-bag lunch with Denny. We ate our peanut butter and jelly without speaking, for the most part; it was getting hard to act cheerful when you could feel the weight of the place, the circumstances, dragging her down. I'd grown up without a father, too, but there had been compensations: two brothers, a dear devoted aunt, a mama who, though she'd hit a rough patch and tended to quote Jesus like he was her next-door neighbor, was at least present, had never dumped me on a stranger's doorstep and flown off two thousand miles to become a stockbroker. Ash was fond of describing Marlene as a gypsy when she was young, unbridled and free. Well, she was reined in now, and the product of their wild oats was right in the middle of my life, with an unhappiness as big as Texas.

We were finishing up our sandwiches when Ash's truck came puttering into the square and over to the curb.

"Hey there," he said through the open window. "I'm new in town. Y'all know where I can find some loose women?"

I glanced at Denny, who stared at the ground, fighting a smile. When Ash talked silly like that, it was like him blowing on embers; you could practically see her start to glow.

"You ought to try a place called the Round-Up," I said. "There's this hunk named Ash Farrell who plays music there. He's got more women than you can shake a stick at."

"Nah." Ash squinted through the windshield. "I heard Ash Farrell settled down."

"I guess that depends on your definition of 'settled.'"

"I guess it does." He never knew what to do when you didn't accept his little witticisms, when the embers failed to catch and burn. "Hey, guess what?" he said. "Mrs. Crouch is having a card party. Her whole house is full of little old ladies with pink hair, drinking tea and playing pinochle, so I got the afternoon off. I have to run up to Texarkana to the music store, pick up some strings and stuff for tomorrow night. You want to come?" He was, by some act of divine intervention, speaking to Denny.

Her whole face lit up, like a switch had been thrown behind her eyes. It made me ache inside. I'd seen it happen, over and over, could recite a litany of the kinds of craziness and heartache that could ensue; I felt sometimes like a walking, breathing casualty myself. But I nodded at Denny, made myself smile. *Take it*, I thought. *Take it, while you can.*

She scrambled around the truck and climbed in, abandoning her Walkman and Stephen King book on the bench beside me. "Could you take my stuff home?" she called across Ash through the window, and I said I would.

He revved the engine a couple of times. I was afraid to look at him. I was afraid he'd be watching me for some sign of appreciation, like I was supposed to fall to my knees and sing "hallelujah" to him for this. But all he did was tell Denny to fasten her seat belt, and said they'd pick up something for supper, and then he put the truck in gear and they drove off.

Hallelujah, I sang, gathering Denny's belongings and walking slowly back to the shop. And threw the rest to God.

8

Denny

His truck was a mess. It looked like he lived in there, literally; the floor was heaped with empty Coke cans and cassettes and junk-food wrappers, and there were clothes and tools and maps and blueprints stuffed behind the seat so high they were starting to spill over the headrests. He was fond of Mrs. Baird's fried pies, apparently. A plastic Jesus was stuck to the dashboard, His face painted in a miniature grimace, like He couldn't believe that this, of all places, was where the Son of God should end up.

I nearly couldn't get my seat belt fastened, the fabric was so cracked and stiff. "How old is this thing?" I asked as we drove by the machine shop, and a crew of black men in work clothes raised their hands as we passed.

"This truck? Older than you," Dad said. "Not quite as old as me." An air freshener shaped like a pine tree swung from the rearview mirror, along with a beaded rosary. I reached up and touched the little ivory cross, and Dad smiled. "That's more superstition than anything else," he said, like he was apologizing.

"I thought you were Catholic," I said. "Or you used to be, but you lost it."

He laughed at that. "I lost it, all right. Your mama wiped the Catholic right out of me." I hoped we weren't going to get into another discussion about Ma. Every time the topic came up I felt weird inside, like I should be defending her, even though I didn't want to. Try as I might, I could not feature my parents together. I'd seen their wedding picture once, both of them with their hair long and dark, their arms around each other's waist, their eyes shining. I didn't know those people, though. Neither one of them seemed to exist anymore, or to have any connection to me.

He turned north on Highway 59. It took a while for the old truck to get up to speed, and it shimmied a little right around fifty-five and then flattened out again as it settled in at sixty. The day was hot, and pine trees blurred by our open windows, a haze of fragrant green. I looked over at him behind the wheel and my heart opened up. I didn't mean for it to, it just happened. All of a sudden I was glad, glad, glad to be there. I wished we could keep driving forever.

The truck was ancient and decrepit, but it had a good tape deck. Once we got up to cruising speed, Dad started fumbling around under the dash and came up with a cassette he managed to get into the slot.

"You ever hear of Butch Hancock?" he asked. "Songwriter out of Austin, by way of Lubbock?" I said I hadn't. "Well, listen up. You're about to get an education."

It was a woman's voice that came out of the speakers, though, an old-time prairie voice, sweetness and hunger stirred together:

> *If you were a bluebird, you'd be a sad one*
> *I'd give you a true word, but you already had one*
> *If you were a bluebird*
> *You'd be crying, you'd be flying home.*

I sat up straight in my seat, listening hard. It was a strange song, with its references to raindrops and hotels and highways, strange but beautiful, too, and I wanted to digest the words and make sense of them, to etch the music into my bones.

The tune played out, and Dad looked over at me. "If I ever wrote a song that good, I'd quit," he said. "Just say, 'Yup, that's it. I can stop now.'"

"No, you wouldn't." It seemed to surprise us both, coming out of my mouth.

"Yeah, you're right. I wouldn't." He laughed, and all of a sudden I felt like laughing, too. But I didn't. I remembered the doll whose string broke on my seventh birthday, followed by eight years of silence. It was important to be grateful for whatever gifts were given.

❧

After three days in Mooney, I wish I could say Texarkana was an improvement. It was bigger, that was one thing; it had Target, Taco Bell, some passing acquaintance to the twentieth century. You could buy a car here, a computer, Chinese food. Otherwise, don't make me laugh.

We drove through the downtown area, past office buildings and shopping complexes, and turned in, finally, at a strip center that had seen better days. There were a wig shop, a liquor store, a couple of boarded-over storefronts. In short, it looked pretty much like down-town Mooney. Dad pulled in in front of a peeling sign that said FOUR STATES MUSIC. "Here we are," he said, and we got out and went through the plate-glass door.

If I close my eyes now, I can remember the way that place smelled. I never knew what it was, exactly: wood and resin, leather, metal, all the things guitars are made of. And something else, something that was separate but still part of the blend, something I couldn't name. What it would be like, I guessed, if tears had a scent. The place had such a big, sad soul; I fell into it like I'd gone down the rabbit's hole.

Dad shook hands with the man behind the counter, a skinny dude with long gray hair and a Fender T-shirt so old it had holes under the arms. "Twigs, this is my daughter, Denny. Denny, this is Twigs. He owns this place. Plays a decent six-string, too."

I shook the hand the man held out. His fingers were long and gnarled and had those telltale calluses that Dad's, and every guitar player's, have. He smiled at me like he'd known me forever.

"Pleased to meet you, Denny," he said. He was the first person Dad ever introduced me to as his daughter, and the first person who hadn't looked at me like some botched DNA experiment when he heard we were related.

They started talking about strings, and I wandered through the shop, down the rows of guitars hanging from the walls like the carcasses of prized animals. I wanted to touch them so much my hands shook, but I was afraid. Things seemed to be going so well. I didn't trust myself not to mess them up.

At the back of the room was a boy sitting on a metal folding chair, his face hidden by a piece of white-streaked hair, bent over an old Martin D-45. His fingers danced over the frets like little demons, possessed. The music was beautiful and scary and, as always, I started trying to figure out how to soak it in before it stopped, like there might not be enough in the world to hold me, like if I didn't heap my plate right up to the ceiling, the buffet might run out. I thought of my dad playing to me at the kitchen table when I was a baby, and wondered if my whole life I hadn't been trying to get back to that feeling.

The boy looked up and saw me watching. "Hey," he said. He didn't seem all that surprised by the look on my face; he acted like trying to suck music into your soul was a perfectly understandable reaction. He was about my age, maybe a year or two older.

"Hey," I answered back. The guitar was the color of maple syrup, with an abalone inlay, barely a fingerprint on its glossy surface. It looked like what God created between the sixth and seventh days, the final and most perfect thing. "That was nice," I said.

"Thanks," said the boy. "Do you play?"

I shrugged. We were both kids, with a certain level of cool to maintain.

"You with Ash?" the boy said, motioning with his chin to the front of the store where Dad leaned with his hip against the counter, talking to Twigs.

"I'm his daughter." It felt so peculiar to say that, like a confession I'd been working up to my whole life.

"Ash is all right," the boy said. "Pretty good guitar player."

"Pretty good," I agreed.

"Twigs thinks Ash is gonna be a big star," the kid said then. "Gonna go to Nashville, get on the Opry, take home all the prizes. Get him a big house and a Cadillac and a bunch of shiny suits. Be the Cowboy Man."

"The Cowboy Man?" I didn't know what to make of that.

"Denny?" Dad called from up front, and I told the boy I had to go. "Give us a call when y'all get to Nashville," he said. "Me and Twigs'll come up, drink margaritas, hang out by the pool. Maybe Ash'll need a couple of pickers for his band." He grinned and ducked his head and in a couple of seconds his fingers were flying again.

"What was that about margaritas by the pool?" Dad said as we were climbing back into the truck. "Was that boy making a date with you? Because I'm telling you right now, no. You're too young."

I looked over and saw that he was smiling. He was teasing me, of course. No one would imagine me having a romance. No one would imagine there was anything special about me. Well, someday they'd all be sorry. They'd be so surprised they'd drive their stupid Cadillacs straight into their stupid swimming pools. I couldn't wait.

"It's only two o'clock," Dad said. "What do you say? You want to run by the mall?"

"The *mall*?" You should have heard my voice, like he'd asked me to go to Egypt.

"Sure. Hell, we're red-blooded Americans, aren't we? Isn't it our patriotic duty to keep the economy going?"

❧

It was a pretty sorry mall: not like North Park or the Galleria in Dallas, with the shops full of things made for magazine-ad people, jewels and clothes and fancy electronic gadgets for their houses. This one was more ordinary, with a Gap and a Foot Locker and a Sears and a food court. Still, I was kind of thrilled, walking into the place with Dad, looking around at the neon and glass. I felt, well, red-blooded. American. I imagined myself back in Dallas, curled on my bed, talking to my classmate Sandy Keene on the phone. "I went shopping," I would say. "With my father." And she would be quiet for a second, out of awe and appreciation. Sandy's parents were divorced, too.

We got Cokes at a snack bar and then wandered around for a while, looking in store windows. "What do you think of that?" Dad would ask, pointing, and I'd label it boring, or okay, or the kiss of death, and we'd move on.

The minute I let my guard slip and admitted I liked something, he pounced. It was a pair of pants in the Gap window, and I really did think they were cute. On the five-foot-ten-inch, hundred-pound model in the display, they were cute. "Try them on," Dad said. "Come on, I'm buying."

There was a minute there, shimmying into those pants in the dressing room, where it crossed my mind that my father was ashamed of me. That he and Lucy had ganged up behind their bedroom door and plotted this whole thing, that she told him not to bring me home without something clean and decent to wear. It pissed me off a little, to tell you the truth. As a rule Dad's clothes were just as crummy as mine, but there was something about him that made you not even notice that what he was wearing was faded or wrinkled or threadbare half the time. What good, I wondered, had my father's genes done me? Why, oh why, had I gotten his stupid front teeth, and not his cheekbones?

Then something happened; I looked at myself in the mirror, and something inside the glass seemed to shift. I looked different. Not five-ten, not a hundred pounds. Not supermodel material, not even close. But nice. The pants, for no reason I could name, suited me. I decided in a flush of feeling to get them. To let my father pay.

He looked so glad when I came out of the dressing room and said, "Okay," like I'd been admitted to Harvard. "Let's get some shirts, too," he said, and stood by while I picked out an armload of T-shirts, green and yellow and lavender, Easter egg colors. I guess I was being, in my own way, girlie.

It went to my head. We walked into the one high-end department store in the whole mall, and I made a beeline for the cosmetics. "What do you want?" Dad asked as I stared into one of the glass cases. "Get something."

"I'm not allowed to wear makeup," I said. "Ma won't let me."

Immediately he started laughing, and I did, too. Ma wasn't around, obviously.

"Maybe a lipstick," I said.

I made my way straight to the Chanel counter. The women behind the cases looked cool and forbidding with their black cloaks and shellacked features, but I didn't care. I was drunk with power, of being a girl out shopping with her father, two dedicated consumers. I started spinning the lipstick carousel. I wanted something pink and expensive.

"Hi," one of the clerks said, walking up with a little smile. "Can I help y'all?" She looked like she was from France, but her voice was pure East Texas.

"Yes, you can," Dad said. "This young lady would like a lipstick."

The woman—girl, she was, really, college age—glanced at me and couldn't think what to say. Then she looked at Dad, and her face rearranged itself again.

"How about a makeover?" she said to me, though her eyes were on Dad. "It's a lot of fun and it doesn't cost anything."

"A makeover?" I repeated. You'd have thought she'd said, How about a Mercedes convertible? It seemed too grown-up, out of my reach. Dad smiled, raised his hands as if to say it was up to me. I dropped my Gap bag on the floor and clambered up onto the tall black stool, and the girl came around the counter with her little brushes and kits. A badge on her cloak said her name was Cyndi.

"Are you a performer or something?" she said, draping me with a black cape. She was looking at me but talking to Dad. " 'Cause you look real familiar."

"Oh, yeah," he said, grinning at me over her shoulder. "I'm a singer, maybe you've seen me on TV. And this young lady is my—" We all waited; Cyndi held her brushes aloft. "My publicist." I barked out a laugh. I couldn't help it; there was no way I was going to be part of his little scam. "Okay," he said, leaning his elbows on the counter. "She's my daughter."

"Really?" Cyndi said, coming at me with a sponge and a bottle of foundation. "Do you have a video? Because I swear I've seen you somewhere before." Notice how the business about the daughter got skimmed right off the top, like the rind on an old hunk of cheese. It was amazing how she managed to work on my face, a very intimate part of my anatomy, for fifteen minutes without paying one second of attention to me. "Wow," she went on, "your wife must really appreciate you doing this." Schlepping me around the mall, she meant, though of course that wasn't what she was getting at at all. She may have had on two pounds of makeup, but she was as transparent as glass.

"There is no wife," Dad said. He looked at his hands. "Denny's mother and I are divorced."

"*Really,*" said Cyndi with such fake sympathy I expected violins to start playing in the background.

"He has a girlfriend, though," I volunteered. "They're madly in love. They live together." *She's having his baby,* I just about blurted out. *They have sex in the front yard at midnight.* "She's really, really pretty," I said, "a lot prettier than this," and I swept my arm around to indicate the posters of models with their creamy skin and perfect features. "And nice. She's so *nice.*" I didn't care if he thought I was cramping his style. He'd thank me, in the long run.

"Oh?" Cyndi asked, looking over her shoulder at Dad to confirm or deny all this. He raised his shoulders in a shrug.

"It's true," he said. "Guilty as charged." It didn't really spoil the party, though. Two minutes after she started on my face, the other Chanel girls started coming over, drawn like flies to honey by the sound of Dad's voice, his laughter, his arms all ropy and brown among the gleaming bottles and tubes. By the end of my makeover, I looked like I was thirty years old, and Dad had a handful of business cards. He paid for my lipstick—fifteen dollars, and he didn't bat an eye—and we walked back out into the mall.

He stopped in front of Smoothie Heaven and studied the embossed cards in his hand: Cyndi, Janice, Mary Anne, the phone numbers over those little interlocking *C*s. "I don't guess I'll be needing a makeover," he said, and tossed them in a trash can. It was a good thing. If he'd put those cards in his pocket, I'd already sworn I was walking home.

We bought hot pretzels and sat down on the edge of a fountain to eat them. The fountain was tiled and full of coins, pennies mostly, a few nickels and dimes, the odd quarter. I guessed you were supposed to make a wish, but it seemed senseless to me. Like you could bribe God by throwing money at Him. Like He could be had for a puny twenty-five cents.

"You like Lucy, don't you?" Dad asked after a minute. He wasn't looking at me but at the pretzel in his hand, half chewed, the paper grease-stained and crumpled.

"Sure," I said. "That stuff I said back there, to the makeover girl? I wasn't making it up, if that's what you mean." He just kept staring at his pretzel like it was some kind of charm, that if he only gazed long and hard enough, all its mysteries would be revealed. "You *are* madly in love," I said. "Aren't you?"

He raised his head then and smiled at some point I followed with my eyes but couldn't see. "Madly," he said. He sounded sad, though, and tired. The skin around his eyes was creased. I guessed it was hard work, being madly in love. When would you sleep, eat, think about music?

"We need to get her something," he said, standing up and throwing half a perfectly good pretzel in the trash. "A present. Any ideas?"

I scanned the row of stores around the fountain. We were, I kid you not, directly across from a Motherhood Maternity, its window full of headless mannequins with watermelon bellies under their smocks and jumpers, and the sight of this made me panicky, reminding me of things I didn't want to think of, would rather not have known. I needed my father to be madly in love with Lucy Hatch. I thought if he lost that, I would lose him, too, him and his big multicolored voice and his black guitar, all those songs, like a well full of dark, sweet water I'd just barely tasted.

I suggested perfume.

We went back to the department store and sniffed dozens of bottles, but nothing seemed right. My Sin was dismissed as too racy, White

Shoulders as too prim, Tommy Girl as too young, Tabu as too old. "This is what Ma wears," I said, holding up a bottle of Poison, which cracked him up. Beautiful, he said, was in Lucy's case redundant—he actually used that word—as was Happy, although I didn't see how you could have too much of either, even bottled. "What about Obsession?" I asked, only half joking, but he shook his head and picked up another bottle and held it to his nose.

"Here," he said. "Smell." I did. It was soft, clean, classic. I turned it over and looked at the label. Eternity.

Yes, I said. It was perfect.

❦

He decided he wanted it gift-wrapped. While we were waiting, he wandered into the men's department, and I tagged along, admiring my unfamiliar, newly sculpted face in the surfaces of things. At the end of my makeover, Cyndi had given me a little card that showed me how to re-create my new look at home. The products she'd used, all told, came to three hundred sixty-seven dollars and fifty cents.

He stopped in front of a rack of shirts. The one hanging in front was long-sleeved, a dusky olive green—silk, I was pretty sure. Dad lifted the hanger off the rack and held the shirt up to the light. The color shifted, going green to gold and back again. It reminded me of the Arabian nights, of tents and camels and dancing girls.

"What do you think?"

"About what?"

"This," he said. "This shirt."

"It's nice," I admitted. "For who, though?"

"Who do you think? For me."

I started laughing. It wasn't very polite, I know; his face got completely still. "Sorry," I said, "But where do you have to wear a shirt like that?" I pictured him building cabinets in a green silk shirt, checking the oil in the truck, eating chicken strips at the Dairy Queen.

"I was thinking tomorrow night," he said, a little defensively. "At the Round-Up."

This sent me into hysterics. A whole afternoon in his company had gotten me overheated, I guess. As I've said, I never know when to hold my tongue.

"Why don't you just rent a tux?" I said. "Maybe we can find Lucy an evening gown." He just stood there, the shirt hanging limply from its hanger. I took a breath, checked the laughter. "Okay, but seriously. Why would you wear a silk shirt to the Round-Up?"

All sorts of stuff went through his face. His mouth opened, like he was going to say something, then closed. The whole world, it seemed, was made up of people with things they weren't telling anybody.

"Oh, my God!" It was one of Ma's favorite phrases, but till that day I don't think I'd ever used it before in my life. "This is about her, isn't it?"

"Who?"

"That girl. Misty."

Dad looked stunned. The arm holding the shirt dropped to his side. "Jesus Christ," he said. "How did you find out about Misty?"

"You mean it's *true*?" I was practically shouting, right in the middle of men's wear. Behind the cash register, two clerks exchanged a glance. Go ahead, call Security, I felt like saying; arrest this man. The thought of her sticky red lips and her scrawny body made me want to retch. I turned around and started marching off the floor.

"Denise!" he said sharply, but I kept walking. He was bigger than me, though, and faster. He grabbed my arm, and I felt the ball of his thumb go into the soft skin of my triceps as he pulled me around. He was looking at me hard and strange, like he was trying to read my mind.

"I'm not seeing Misty," he said. "Not since I met Lucy. Why did you think I was?" He was still holding my arm, tight. Of all the ways I'd imagined my father touching me—hugging me, squeezing my hand, brushing my hair—this one was not on the list. I stared at his T-shirt, inches from my eyes. "Denny," he said again, quietly. "Who were you talking to?"

"Her."

"Her? You mean *Misty*?" He laid his head back and stared at the ceiling. "For Christ's sake," he said. "I ought to get a restraining order." He let go of my arm. "Do you want to tell me about it?" I shook my head no. I thought if I repeated what she'd said to me, the words would come out of my mouth like little black toads.

"Denny, listen," he said, "I want to tell you something. It's real important, but you can't tell anybody, you understand? It's a secret."

All the air had gone out of the day, all the light and shimmer. I felt like my shoulders were bowed with other people's secrets; I didn't think I could take the weight of another one. If I'd had more backbone, I'd have yelled, "No!" would have demanded he drive me straight to the bus station and buy me a ticket for Dallas, or Chicago. But I didn't. I was fourteen years old and, for some reason, everybody wanted to tell me everything.

"You know Twigs?" Dad said. "The guy who runs the guitar store?" I nodded. "Last fall he helped me make a tape of some of my songs. I've been sending the tape around to different people, record companies and management folks, mostly, in Nashville. Well, I met a man from one of those companies in Austin a couple months ago, and he's coming to the Round-Up tomorrow night, to hear me play."

"Oh, my God!" There it was again; twice in one day.

Dad smiled at the shirt dangling from his hand. I started bouncing up and down on my toes. I was galloping from one end of the emotional racetrack to the other so fast, I'm surprised I didn't leave skid marks.

"But why? Why is it a secret? You ought to be telling the whole world!" I was so excited. Nashville, the big house, the swimming pool, the Cadillac; I could practically reach out my hand and touch them.

"Not yet," he said. "Not until . . . Well. I mean, it could turn out to be nothing, after all. I don't want everybody getting all worked up over it, and then the guy goes home and nothing happens. Does that make sense?"

It did. It was a perfect reason for not telling Geneva, or Aunt Dove, or his drummer, even, any number of people who were attached to the music by a shoestring. But Lucy was his girlfriend, his partner. Didn't she deserve to share his nervousness and, maybe, his disappointment as much as his happiness? How was it possible to be madly in love with someone and at the same time shut them out of your dreams?

I thought then of the boy in the guitar shop, and something sank inside me. I pictured it all clearly: Dad in his shiny suit, in a crowd of music people, sipping a margarita by the pool. There he was at the middle of it, all right, but nobody else I knew was in the picture. Not me, not Lucy, not Twigs, nobody. Martina McBride, maybe, Faith Hill, and who could relax with them around? He would shed East Texas and everything attached to it.

The funny thing was, I understood. He couldn't not do it; keeping your light under a bushel, Ma called it when she was admonishing me. It was a sin against God, and even if you thought sometimes you didn't believe in Him, did you really want to get sent to hell to find out? That first night at the Round-Up, when I'd thought its walls weren't enough to hold him, I hadn't know how close the truth was, that it was breathing its big damp breath right outside the door.

"So, this record-company man," I said. "He's not going to like you if you don't have a fancy shirt?"

"Well, I don't think it's a requirement. But I want to make a good impression."

"You will," I said.

I brushed my fingertips against the collar of the silk shirt. Someday, I believed, I would think back on this day as the closest I'd ever come to my father. It was what he did. He beckoned you, and then, when you were blinded by the dazzle, he slipped away. Lucy knew it, too. Misty didn't, which only proved how stupid she was; she was like a rat who just keeps pressing the lever, again and again, even when the reward is gone. But Lucy knew. I felt sorry for her, thinking about it. I was only his daughter; I would grow up, fly away, tell stories about it someday. Lucy was in love with him, though. No wonder her secret made her feel tangled up inside. She must have known, somehow, that she was going to have to settle for part of him, a little chunk of brightness in her hand. Maybe it would make her rage and scream and beat her fists against the sky, or maybe it would be a comfort to her. I didn't know.

He paid for the shirt, and we picked up our package at the gift-wrap counter and got out of there.

9

Lucy

 Saturday morning, Aunt Dove called to invite Denny and me over for lunch and to work in her garden. Denny wasn't thrilled about the idea, I could tell, although her mood had lifted considerably since she and Ash had gotten back from Texarkana. Neither one of them wanted to talk much about the trip, but when she walked in carrying an armload of new clothes, a lipstick, even perfume for me, I didn't press it.

When we got to Dove's, though, Denny fell straight under the spell of the garden, the Far Eastern statuary, the prayer flags flapping down the rows of peppers and beans and tomatoes. Before long she was right in the middle of things, pulling weeds and plucking bugs like she'd been born a country girl.

"You had that talk with Ash yet?" Dove asked. Denny was outside gathering tomatoes for salad, and Dove and I were in her kitchen cutting up a chicken. The flip side of morning sickness, for me, was that by midday I felt hollow and ravenous; I believe I could've swallowed that chicken raw and whole.

"I haven't had a chance. Things have been so topsy-turvy since Denny came. We almost never have a minute to ourselves, and then when we do . . ."

Dove gave me a look. "Uh-huh. Can't put the brakes on the old love train, you mean. How you figure you all got into this spot in the first place?"

I flushed, remembering what had happened the night before, how Ash and I had come awake as if from the same dream, forgetting Denny in her sleeping bag on the other side of the door, forgetting there was anybody else in the world . . . At breakfast Denny wouldn't look at either one of us, and after she'd gone off to brush her teeth, when I mentioned to Ash that I wished he'd think about finishing out one of the back bedrooms so we could get our privacy back, he'd snapped.

"I'll put it right at the head of the list," he'd said, pushing back from the table and taking one last gulp of his coffee. "Finish Mrs. Crouch's kitchen. Rehearse my band. Play my gig at the Round-Up. Establish world peace. Oh, yeah, fix up a room for Denny. Ash Farrell, Superman."

He set down his empty mug, the stoneware ringing against the countertop. "I have to go. I'm heading straight to band practice from Mrs. Crouch's, and from there to the Round-Up. You and Denny can manage to get yourselves there on your own tonight, can't you? I'll see you later."

"Nobody's asking you to be Superman, Ash," I'd said. But by then he was gone.

"I can't explain it, Dove. Ash just seems different, these past few days. Sometimes he's high as a kite, and sometimes you want to duck for cover." She looked at me sharply, and I shook my head. "Oh, he's temperamental sometimes, sure, but mostly he seems so, so *detached*. Like at the same time he's sitting right there at the breakfast table, he's a million miles away." I lay down my knife and passed the cutting board to her. "It's like he's got a secret."

"Ha! That'd be something, wouldn't it?"

She took the chicken from me and started rolling pieces in flour and dropping them into a skillet full of hot Crisco. I sat down at the table and watched my aunt move deftly around the kitchen, from sink to stove to countertop, her actions as exact and economical as a ninja's. When I was little I thought Dove had all the secrets to the universe, but now I wondered if the biggest one was that she knew how to fry a chicken.

"You know," she said, after the fryer was immersed and sizzling, "you got to do it pretty soon. It's not just that Ash needs to know, though he does. But you need to be gettin' to the doctor, start takin' care of yourself. For your own sake, Lucy Bird, and the baby's." I nodded, shamefaced; I knew. But Dr. Crawford, Mooney's white-haired old obstetrician, had delivered me and my brothers, and my sister-in-law Geneva was his head nurse. I couldn't exactly pop in for a prenatal visit and maintain my anonymity.

Dove stopped and studied me a minute, her face solemn. "How you figure Geneva's gonna take this?" she asked. It's a wonder she never practiced mind reading as a day job.

"I don't know. She and I never talked about it, why neither one of us has kids. I sort of thought maybe she and Bailey decided against it. They're so crazy about each other, I thought they'd decided just the two of them was enough."

"Oh, no, honey. She started goin' to Dallas six, eight years back, for them fertility treatments. The kind where you lay up on a table and they stick a needle in you and forest your eggs."

"Harvest, Dove. They harvest your eggs. My goodness, she *told* you this?"

"Oh, sure, the whole family knows. Your mama, of course, thinks it's a big sin—men doing the work of the Lord."

I nodded; I could just imagine. "Why do you suppose nobody ever told me?"

"Well, you was gone, honey, all those years. And ever since you been back, let's face it, you been a little preoccupied." She grinned at me and I smiled back. "Don't you be worryin' about Geneva," Dove said, lifting the chicken pieces with tongs and turning them in the sputtering grease. "So long as you've got what you want, I expect she'll put aside her own wants and be happy for you."

"But I don't *know* what I want," I said. "I just can't get a handle on it, Dove. I've had five days, almost, to get used to the idea, and no matter how hard I try, I just can't fathom the idea of an actual baby. It doesn't seem real, somehow."

"That's 'cause you ain't told Ash," she said. "I reckon once he knows, it'll get real fast enough."

The back door opened and Denny came in carrying a bucket of tomatoes, her face pink from sun and effort. "I've never seen tomatoes like these in my life," she said, setting the bucket on the tabletop. "They look like they belong in the *Guinness Book of Records*."

"You stay here with us awhile, Miss Denny," Dove said. "We'll show you things you'll never see in the big city."

"I don't know," Denny said doubtfully. "Maybe." She peered into the skillet. "We had fried chicken *last* night," she said.

"No, ma'am," I replied. "We had KFC last night. This is honest-to-God home-fried chicken. You need to learn the difference if you mean to be part of this family."

I watched this register, my last remark. I half expected Denny to stick her nose in the air, to wander out of the room and plop herself down irritably in front of the TV. But she surprised me, not for the first time in the past five days. She smiled. And pulled up a chair at the table.

∞

Denny made a big production of getting ready for the Round-Up that night, putting on her new pants and a yellow shirt, pinning my rhinestone barrettes in her hair. I sat her down at the kitchen table and dabbed a little blush on her cheeks and swiped a mascara wand over her lashes, and then let her finish it off with a slick of her new lipstick. As she rode beside me in the Buick through the early evening, humming under her breath to the radio, I believed I could feel her straining toward something up ahead in a way that reminded me, more than I would have thought possible, of her father.

The Round-Up was packed, and Ash was nowhere to be found as we slid into our usual spot alongside Bailey and Geneva, both of whom looked like they'd been drinking for a couple of hours already. "Have you seen Ash?" I shouted to Geneva, but I couldn't make out her answer over the blare of the jukebox and the corresponding crowd noise. Bailey got up and went to the bar and brought us back Cokes, which I accepted gratefully. I hadn't realized how worn-out I was; but for the caffeine and the noise level, I didn't think I could hold my eyes open.

The band came on at eight o'clock, Ash smiling at the rush of welcome from the crowd, strapping on his guitar. He was wearing a shirt I'd never seen before, of an iridescent hue that shimmered under the lights. "One. Two. One two three four," he counted, off mike, and the band swung into "Guitar Town" as the crowd jostled and surged as one body onto the dance floor and then, like magic, paired off into individual grooves. The next thing I knew, Bailey was up off our bench and pulling Denny up by the hand, and I watched as they began a plodding course around the perimeter of the dance floor, Denny's eyes never leaving her feet, Bailey steering her like she was an unruly sailboat on a high sea. My heart surged unexpectedly with affection for both of them, and I snuck a glance at Geneva, but her eyes were trained on the stage in their usual wistful gaze.

Ash came over during the break between sets, but although he kissed me and spread greetings all around, he disappeared as quickly as he'd come, and a few minutes later I saw him talking at the bar with a man in an expensive Western-cut jacket and jeans. By the time the second set began, all I could think was that, in an hour or so, I'd be able to go home and sleep. It suddenly struck me as silly, my sitting through every single one of Ash's performances, week in and week out. There was a greeting card Peggy sold in the shop that had a verse on it about finding spaces in your togetherness and letting the spaces be filled with love. How were we supposed to find those spaces, Ash and I, when I sat glued to this bench week in and week out, my cheery little face trained on his every note and move? What was I trying to prove? Even your favorite song can make you a little sick if it plays in your head twenty-four hours a day.

Then Ash stepped up to sing a song he'd written about us, "A Place

Love Calls Home," and I felt guilty and low. There were plenty of women in that room who would have given a limb to have Ash writing songs about them, to stand up and declare himself so nakedly in front of two hundred people. What was wrong with me, that I didn't appreciate all I had?

I let Bailey coax me up off the bench and onto the dance floor. He and Denny had been practicing most of the evening, and he'd returned her to the table all pink and pleased-looking. "How did you manage that?" I asked him as we merged into the sea of dancers.

"I just told her that if she was gonna keep coming out here with us every week for the rest of the summer, she was gonna have to learn to two-step. Listen, how about if Gen and I take her home with us tonight? Give you and Ash the night to yourselves?"

"Really? You'd do that?"

"I told her we'd take her to IHOP. She can't wait."

It took a long time after the show for the hall to clear out. Finally, Dub came around and started pulling benches out from under people and taking their beer bottles. Denny went off with Geneva and Bailey so eagerly, I can't say it didn't hurt my feelings a little. While Ash packed up his guitar, I went over to the bar and asked Dub's wife, Jackie, for a cup of water. The man I'd seen Ash talking to earlier, the one in the fancy jacket and jeans straight off the rack, was standing at the end of the bar holding a Coors Light. He looked at me and nodded. I smiled and glanced away. By the time Jackie handed me my water, the man was at my side.

"Let me guess—Lucy, right?" Early thirties, potbellied, with one of those two-inch-long ponytails I'd seen on men in magazines but never within a fifty-mile radius of Mooney. There was a fancy cologne scent to him and something else, a sheen of otherness, of opportunity and privilege, of some place dangerous and far away.

"Have we met?"

"Oh, no. I recognized you from the song. 'A Place Love Calls Home'? Your hair," he explained, and laughed as I reached up to touch it with self-conscious surprise. "That, and I saw you and Ash together earlier. It wasn't that long a leap."

"Are you a friend of Ash's?"

The man smiled, settling his hip against the bar. "I hope to be. I hope to be a good, good friend of Ash's." He transferred his beer bottle to his left hand and extended his right. "Tony Amate," he said. "Arcadia Nashville."

Just then Ash came sliding up and pumped Tony Amate's hand. "Hey, man, thanks for waiting," he said. He swept his damp hair off his forehead; his silky new shirt was soaked through and sticking to him.

He leaned over and kissed me lightly, then snaked his arms around my hips. "I see you've met my muse."

"I have. And it's no wonder, I must say." Tony Amate smiled his oily smile at me. I felt like somebody's prize pig, like somebody had stuck me on a platform and hung a ribbon on me. "Listen, man, have you got a couple of minutes?"

"Sure," Ash said, disengaging his hold on me. "I might be a while here, Lucy," he said against my ear. "Why don't you run on home? We'll talk later." I shot him a look that said, *You're damn right, later,* and watched it hit the surface of his dark eyes and bounce right back. He turned to Tony Amate, who was babbling about seeing me again sometime soon, and they walked off in the direction of the empty stage.

❧

The parking lot was almost empty: employees' cars scattered near the perimeter, Ash's truck, my Buick sitting way out by the road in never-never land, a white Ford Taurus with a Hertz sticker that must have belonged to Mr. Arcadia Nashville. Misty Potter's silver Mitsubishi Eclipse gleamed under a halogen lamp on a pole. No one was inside, though. On a hunch I swung back around and approached Ash's truck. There was Misty, slouched against the hood with one of her sleazy friends, laughing and smoking cigarettes. They got quiet as I walked up, and without a glance or a word shoved themselves off the bumper and ground their butts under their heels and sashayed off across the parking lot. The Eclipse's engine roared, and the car peeled out of the lot in a spray of gravel.

I climbed behind the wheel of the Buick, but couldn't make myself start it up. I wasn't sleepy anymore; if anything, I felt too alert, like someone spinning a radio dial in the middle of the night, whizzing straight past the polka music and the antacid ads and the call-in evangelists, miles of white noise and static, in search of the one voice that would tell me what I needed to hear.

At last, here they came, Ash and the stranger, Tony Amate, lingering for a minute or two near the front door, finally shaking hands and turning their separate ways. Tony Amate got into the Taurus and started it up and pulled out onto the highway, south, toward town.

Ash unlocked his truck and set his guitar case inside. I hit my headlights, and watched as he turned in my direction, a hand raised to shield his eyes. He squinted into the glare for a second or two, then closed the truck door and came walking across the parking lot toward me.

He crouched beside my open window, his dark jeans pulling taut across the front of his thighs.

"Hey, this is really cool and all," he said, "but I'm afraid I have to pass. I'm a one-woman man now. My days of sex in the parking lot are over." *Thank you, Ash,* I thought. *Thank you for reminding me of the sex you've had in the parking lot.* I wondered what kind of gymnastics were necessary in a Mitsubishi sports coupe. "What are you doing out here, Lucy?" he said. "You should be home asleep by now." I shook my head, but I couldn't seem to get rid of the static. "Where's Denny?"

"Spending the night with Bailey and Geneva. I told her we'd pick her up in the morning." I forced my eyes off the steering wheel and looked at him. "Arcadia Nashville is a record company," I said, just in case he thought I didn't know.

"Yeah."

"So, that guy, Tony Amate, just happened to be in the neighborhood? He works for a record company in Nashville, but he took a wrong turn and wound up in a dance hall five hundred miles away?"

"No," Ash said, "it wasn't a wrong turn." I let a silence open up and stretch out, since it wasn't mine to fill. "Last fall," he said finally, "my buddy Twigs and I made a tape of four of my songs. I've been sending them around for a few months now."

"Around."

"To record labels, music publishers. I hadn't had much interest till now."

"But Tony Amate is interested?"

"Remember in the spring, right after I met you, when I went to Austin?"

"Of course I remember." It had stormed for four days straight, and Ash had driven back to me in a raging flood.

"There was this big music festival, and I got booked into one of the showcases. Tony heard me there, just a short set in a club, me and my guitar. We've talked a few times since." I thought of Ash's disappearance earlier in the week, his silence at the breakfast table. "He wanted to see the whole show, hear the songs with the band. If he liked what he heard, well . . ."

"Well?"

"He can't say anything for sure, not yet," Ash said. "But he claims he likes my stuff a lot." I nodded at what I was hearing, but I felt numb. "I should have said something, I guess. I just didn't want the whole town getting worked up over it and then have it not amount to anything, you know?"

"I'm not the whole town, Ash," I said, but he acted like he didn't hear me.

"I've worked my whole life for this," he went on. "Right now, tonight, is as close as I've ever been. I just didn't— If it doesn't happen, it's gonna be hard enough to live with myself. I didn't want to have to carry everybody else's disappointment, too."

I didn't know what to say. I felt like I was out there somewhere suspended in space, one of those bodiless radio voices, scanning the airwaves like a phantom. I wasn't sure Ash and I were on the same wavelength anymore. I wasn't even sure he was listening.

The Round-Up's sign blinked twice and then went dark, and Dub and Jackie came out, locked up, and drove away. Ash stood up, shook the kinks out of his legs. "I wish you'd say something," he said, but when I opened my mouth, I tasted tears in the back of my throat. I didn't cry in front of Ash; except for making love, I never had. I'd always believed that as long as I could say that, I'd be able to find my own way home, but now I wasn't sure.

"Scoot over," he said, opening the car door, and I moved over into the passenger seat and let him behind the wheel.

We sat in silence, listening to the occasional car pass by on the highway. He was two feet from me; I could hear his breathing, smell his skin, and still it felt like we were caged in our own little glass boxes, separated by the things we wanted, spoken and unspoken, possible or not, ours alone.

"What is it you want, Ash?" I said. "Do you want to be famous? See yourself on TV, make a million dollars, have people screaming everywhere you go?"

I watched him give the question some thought. "I don't know if I can explain it, Lucy. I guess I just want a chance to be heard."

But you have that, I thought, *right here.* The whole northeast corner of Texas was in his pocket: a hall full of happy, dancing people twice a week, and Ash in the spotlight at the center of it all. Nashville, on the other hand, would be nothing but commotion. How could you ever expect to make yourself heard over all that racket?

He started the car, and we rolled slowly across the parking lot and pulled in next to his truck. "Come on," he said, pushing open the door, leaving the motor running. "I'll follow you home."

❧

As Ash unlocked the front door and set his guitar case inside, I crossed the porch and sat down in the swing. The chains squeaked as I curled my legs underneath me. "I'm going in," he said, but I didn't answer him. The screen door opened and closed, and lights started coming on inside, and I heard water running in the kitchen.

He came out again a few minutes later with his hands wrapped around a blue-striped mug. "I made tea," he asked. "You want some?"

"No, thank you." It was a warm, muggy night; scraps of cloud trailed like ghost fingers across the moon, and moths swirled in the pale orange glow of the porch light.

"You gonna stay out here all night?" He propped his hip against the porch rail and sipped his tea.

"I hadn't really thought about it."

"You know, it's our first night in nearly a week without Denny around."

"I know." And we were quiet awhile.

He tipped the dregs of his tea over the porch rail. "Can I get you anything?" he said. "A cushion, anything?"

"No, Ash," I said. "I don't need a thing from you."

"Yeah, well, don't bother sugarcoating it." He reached to open the screen door. "Good night, Lucy."

"Sweet dreams, Ash."

Inside, one at a time, the lights went out. Through the window screen I heard water running in the bathroom, and finally the bedroom went dark as well. There was nothing but a wall of logs between us, but it felt like that wall that runs right down the middle of China; it felt like I'd never known a soul who lived on the other side.

⋙⋘

I woke with daylight coming through the white curtains, in Ash's bed, as naked as the day I was born. The clock beside the bed said half-past ten, and though a breeze stirred the curtains, the room was hot and bright. The house smelled of coffee, and there was a wet towel over the knob of the bathroom door. Even unconscious, it seemed, my body, like a compass to true north, kept coming back to Ash.

I sat up, pushing back my hair, tamping down the morning's first surge of bile, and wondering, not for the first time, how I had landed here, what had propelled me here, and what held me. Then I heard the noise: a high-pitched keening sound, like an animal in pain. Or a power tool. An electric saw.

I looked out the window. Ash's truck was backed up to the side of the house, the bed piled high with lumber, and his workbench was set up in the yard. After a few minutes the saw stopped, and I heard hammering. Construction sounds. He was making a room for Denny.

Denny

 Part of me was dying to hang around the Round-Up and see what happened with the record-company man, but to tell you the truth, it scared me a little bit, too. When I said good night to Lucy, she acted like she didn't really hear me, and she looked kind of sick, the way she did in the mornings. I'd seen the guy hanging around the bar all night in his fancy coat and his little ponytail, sticking out like a sore thumb. I wondered if Lucy knew about him yet, what she would say when she found out. I was sort of sorry I was going to miss it.

But the chance to go with Bailey and Geneva was too good to pass up. They loaded me into Bailey's big old pickup, and we drove all the way to Marshall and had breakfast at IHOP at one o'clock in the morning along with all the truck drivers and stoner college kids. Other than Lucy's aunt Dove's fried chicken, it was the best meal I'd had since I got to East Texas. It was such a relief to be eating with real people for a change. No offense, but most of the time Lucy and Dad had other things on their minds than food. Bailey kept telling jokes and flirting with the waitress, and Geneva and I laughed the whole time, wolfing down our pancakes. They even let me drink a cup of coffee, and Bailey paid and left a big tip. I started sort of pretending they were my parents instead of just another set of grown-ups I'd gotten handed off to when things got inconvenient, and on the way home I fell asleep in the back of the truck.

I woke up partway when we got to their house, and Geneva led me inside and into a guest room done up in lots of flowery prints. I was so happy to be sleeping in an actual bed, I almost cried. They had little soaps and embroidered towels in the bathroom, and Geneva gave me one of her nightshirts to sleep in, which was way too big for me, but smelled like Ivory Snow and was as cool and soft as a breath against my skin. I slid under the comforter and just looked around the room for a while, not wanting to turn off the bedside lamp. It was so pretty and snug. But I'd be lying if I said I didn't fall asleep thinking about Nashville.

In the morning Bailey and Geneva made me get up and go to church with them. I'd barely set foot in a church in my life, other than once in a while on Christmas Eve or Easter, but it wasn't as bad as I'd expected. You never heard such a bunch of singers in your life. At my elbow Bailey belted the hymns with plenty of energy but no regard for the tune, while Geneva sang in a quavery soprano and I hummed along under my breath.

Afterward we drove back to their house and ate cold chicken and potato salad for lunch—I was starting to feel like I might start laying eggs any minute, these people were so crazy about chicken—then Geneva wondered out loud if she ought to give Lucy a call. "She said she has to work Crystal Sheppard's wedding this afternoon," she said. "Maybe she'd like us to run you home." It made me feel kind of bad. Things were so normal at hers and Bailey's house; I'd been secretly hoping they might decide to keep me another two and a half months.

When we got to Dad's, Lucy was just coming out of the house, in a yellow dress with her hair hanging down her back. It was hard to believe she was the hired help—she looked pretty enough to be in the wedding herself—but there were rings under her eyes, and her skin looked like someone had pulled it too tight across her bones. I always thought pregnant women were supposed to be soft and round, but since I'd gotten there, in a matter of days, Lucy seemed thinner and more delicate than before.

She directed us around the side of the house, and there was Dad's truck full of lumber and tools, and he was measuring and cutting plywood on a bench set up in the yard.

"Hey," he said, "what do you think?" His T-shirt was ringed with sweat, and he had wood chips all over his clothes and in his hair. Last night at the Round-Up was like another lifetime, a million miles away.

"What?" I answered. It hadn't taken long for me to learn to be wary of his offerings, the way they so often came with strings dangling in all directions.

"What do you mean, what? I'm fixing up your room. You've gotta help me out a little bit, though," he said. "Unless I can convince Geneva to pitch in."

"Anything for you, Ash," she said lazily, taking a seat on the open tailgate of his truck. Bailey had told me Geneva's idea of manual labor was leaving a list of instructions for the maid.

"We can't stay anyway," Bailey began, "we've got a wedding—"

Right then, Lucy's Buick started up, and we all watched her back up and make a loop in the front yard and drive off down the road, leaving the dogs trailing behind in the dust. Dad stared after her like he was concentrating hard on the sound of her engine so he could commit it to memory, maybe describe it later.

"Everything okay, bud?" Bailey asked. His voice was offhand, but you couldn't help but hear the steel in it.

"Sure," Dad said. He held the tape measure against a sheet of plywood, and bent his head over it.

"Well, I've been meaning to ask you something, since it's sort of come up."

"Yeah? What's that?"

"When are you planning to stop shacking up with my sister and make things official between y'all?"

"Bailey Hatch!" Geneva jumped off the tailgate and faked a swing at Bailey, who laughed and ducked but kept his eyes pinned on Dad.

Dad straightened up from the workbench and looked square at Lucy's brother. Both of them were smiling, but their eyes were flinty. If they'd been dogs, they'd have been pissing all over the place.

"First of all," Dad said, "I'm insulted you would call this a shack." He made a broad sweep with his arm, and they all laughed. "As you can see, improvements are in progress. Second of all, your sister has been a widow for, oh, about four and a half months now."

"Three of which she's been living with you," Bailey replied. He had a point, I thought.

"Technically speaking," Dad said, "Lucy still has her own place." I was surprised by this; it was the first I'd heard of it.

"Which she hasn't spent one single night in since she took up with you," Bailey said. I had to hand it to him, he was cool as a cop, laying out the facts.

"Has Lucy said anything? Is she unhappy, do you think?" Dad glanced from Bailey and Geneva and back again, like he was daring them to disagree.

"Sweetie," Geneva said, "if she was any happier, she'd be floating around on little angel wings." She seemed kind of nervous when she said it, though; I couldn't help but think Geneva had noticed the stains under Lucy's eyes.

And I had to bite my tongue, swallowing back the one big thing I knew that could change it all. I wondered how Dad would feel about making things official once he knew there was a baby on the way. Or maybe he did know, and that's what Lucy driving off in such a rush was about. For the first time, in a slow, cold roll, it occurred to me that maybe Lucy wasn't planning on having a baby after all. I'd had sex ed in school; I knew not only where babies came from but that plenty of people who conceived them never gave birth to them. There were lots and lots of ways.

"Bailey, I swear," Geneva said then, stepping over to put her arm through his, "you're starting to sound more like your mama every day."

"Well, I can't help it," Bailey said. "I guess I just think everybody ought to be as settled and happy as I am with you. Even old Ash here." He smiled, letting Dad know he was off the hook, for now.

"To be as settled and happy as you, I'd have to be married to Geneva," Dad pointed out, and he and she grinned at each other.

"Speaking of making things official," Geneva said, "if we don't get a move on, babe, Crystal and Bobby will have gotten married without us."

Dad watched their pickup as it disappeared down the road toward the highway. He went on watching the road even after they were gone.

"Okay, okay," I said as soon as their engine had faded away, "what happened?" Dad dragged his eyes back to me like he'd been sleepwalking. "Last night!" I said. "At the Round-Up! The record-company man!" Did he honestly think I wouldn't remember?

"Well, you know, Denny, it's like I said. It might or might not happen. It's too soon, really, to say." His voice sounded scoured dry, like he was discussing some boring event from the evening news and not the biggest thing ever to happen in his life.

"But he must have given you some idea! I mean, did he say he liked your product? Did he say he'd get back to you?" My mom was in business; I knew the kind of talk these people used.

Dad smiled, so small the corners of his mouth barely moved. "He liked the product, okay? Yeah. He said he'd get back to me."

"So, did Lucy find out? Is that why you and her are fighting?"

He'd picked up the saw, but when I said that, he laid it down again. "We're not fighting," he said. "Who said we were fighting?"

We turned our heads toward the sound of another engine making its way up the road. It sounded like it was having some trouble; it sounded, in fact, like it was on its last legs. In a few seconds, an old pickup—so old it made Dad's Chevy look like this year's model—came belching and wheezing into the yard, and Dad drew an arm across his forehead to wipe away the sweat and wood dust and stepped out from behind the workbench. "Here's Isaac," he said, lifting a hand to wave, and the truck pulled up alongside Dad's and shimmied to a halt.

The man at the wheel beamed, showing a gap between his front teeth. As he swung down from the cab, I saw that he was short but well built, his arms with that same corded-wood look Dad's had, from working with his muscles all day.

Sitting up in the passenger seat was a young woman so beautiful I couldn't keep from gawking; her skin looked like coffee stirred with cream, and she had the most amazing hair I'd ever seen, a gold-brown cloud that radiated a foot from her scalp, like cotton candy spun out of bronze. She was pregnant, gigantic, even though the bed of the truck was already crawling with kids who went spilling out into the yard the second the truck stopped rolling, swarming over my father and theirs and everything in sight. Two little girls, their hair pulled tight in pigtails, wrestled for Dad's attention, and he scooped up one in each arm and held them on his hips while a boy, bigger than the rest, checked out the power tools, and a couple of littler ones scrambled into the bed of Dad's truck and started climbing the stacks of lumber like it was McDonald's Playland.

"Isaac, this is my daughter, Denny," Dad said, setting the little girls on their feet. "Denny, this is Isaac King. And this ravishing creature," he said, going around the far side of the truck and opening the door, "is Rose. Rose, my daughter, Denny."

"How do you do," I said, hanging back as she eased down from the cab and smiled at me. She looked like someone out of the past and not of this place, like an ancient tribal queen. But here she was, in deep East Texas, one hand in the small of her back and the other on the huge, tight swell of her belly under a cotton housedress, watching her children tumble out of control and acting like she owned the world anyway.

Dad lay a hand on her stomach. "How's the reverend?" he asked, and Rose laughed and patted his hand and said the reverend was fine. "I appreciate you loaning me your husband for the afternoon," Dad said. "Seeing as it's Sunday and all."

"Ha! You're doin' me a favor," Rose said, reaching out to grab one of the smaller boys by the collar as he was about to do a swan dive over the side of the truck. "Like I don't got enough trouble underfoot with these young ones." She and Isaac smiled at each other, and I decided there must be something in the water up here that made all these ordinary-seeming people so goofy in love.

Dad turned to Isaac. "Did you bring your guitar?"

"Ssh!" Isaac pretended to whisper, but Rose smacked him on the arm anyway.

"What're you talkin' about, guitar?" she said. "You said you was buildin' a room for your girl!"

"Which I am doing, as you can see," Dad said, gesturing at the lumber and the tools. "But we're gonna have to take a break sometime." He smiled at her and she returned the smile with a look that let him know she wasn't falling for his smooth talk and his crinkly eyes. I realized I might have just met the first woman in Cade County, Texas, who was unmoved by my father's charm, who let him know without a word that he wasn't selling a single thing she wanted to buy.

"Never mind," Dad said, "we'll get by." Rose leaned over and pecked Isaac on the mouth, and started gathering her kids and herding them back into their truck. "Sure I can't persuade y'all to stay awhile?" Dad asked, plucking one of the tiny girls off his leg and handing her into the bed of the pickup. "Lucy's working a wedding in town this afternoon. She'll be sorry when she hears she missed you."

"We got to run by my mama's and help out a bit over there," Rose said. "Ever since she had that business with her heart she has trouble doin' what she used to, and still she wants a big old dinner ever Sunday. We'll be back for Isaac 'round suppertime. We'll say hello to Lucy then."

She spent some time positioning herself behind the wheel, getting the seat belt arranged over her belly. "You boys have fun," she said. "But not too much fun. Remember, it's Sunday. Good to meet you," she said to me, and cranked the old truck's motor and put it in reverse. "You kids sit down back there!" she hollered, and they all dropped in place like little soldiers as she turned the truck in a wide circle in the side yard and swung it out onto the road.

⚬⚬

I don't know what Dad thought he needed me for. Fixing up my room, it looked like, was nothing more than a poor excuse for getting together with his best friend and telling tales and drinking beer. The minute

Rose drove off, Dad went inside and came back out with one of those little six-pack coolers and started handing out the Buds. Isaac had a moment's hesitation, it being the Lord's day and all, but only a moment's. Within half an hour they'd finished the six-pack and started on another.

I sat on the tailgate of the pickup and just listened to them, mostly, soaking up their stories and high spirits. Every now and then a board would get cut, or Dad would recall that I was present and give me some kind of half-assed order, like hand him the hammer, or another beer. It was the promise of the music that kept me sticking around; that and just being in their company, studying on their friendship. At first glance you'd have to wonder what in the world they had in common, but you could tell by how easy they were with each other that the connection was old and true. I tried to guess what they might have talked about without a fourteen-year-old girl around.

After about an hour they decided they'd done enough work, and I followed them to the front porch, thinking to myself that if they continued at this pace, I'd still be sleeping on the couch when I was twenty. I didn't care, though, because Dad went inside and came out carrying more beers, and a Coke for me, and his guitar. I sat down in the creaky swing and tried to make myself invisible as he and Isaac cracked themselves another cold one. I thought maybe they'd forget I was there and I might accidentally hear something real.

Dad went first, with a song about a sailor in a storm saying goodbye to his sweetheart as the ship goes down. Then Isaac took a turn, singing about a man walking in a graveyard searching for his true love, who might or might not have been dead, it wasn't really clear. He accompanied himself on Dad's Gibson; his style, though not showy, was sure, and he had a deep, strong voice. What I loved more than anything was watching Dad watch Isaac sing; he looked like he was in church, like he'd never heard anything so holy.

They started passing the guitar back and forth, and together they sang a whole slew of old blues tunes, Robert Johnson, Leadbelly, Mance Lipscomb, some of it sad and serious, some of it joyful, with Isaac stomping his boots against the porch steps for percussion. I wanted to be part of it so much my throat hurt, but I think Dad would've flown off to the moon before he'd have suspected such a thing.

They were doing some old Ray Charles song when Lucy's Buick came rolling into the yard. As she swung her legs out of the car, Dad made a chopping motion with his hand and they stopped on a dime and he started belting out, in his best Elvis imitation, "One night with you is what I'm praying for . . ."

Lucy came sauntering up, watching him with a little twist to her mouth. She looked about a million times better than she had earlier; her face was full of color, and in one hand she carried what must have been the bride's bouquet, a bunch of roses and baby's breath held together by a cluster of gaudy-colored ribbons. She put her hand on Isaac's shoulder and he covered it with his, and we all watched Dad, who was singing his heart out, hamming it up for all he was worth. As he strummed the final chord, he looked up and pretended, not very convincingly, to have just noticed Lucy standing there.

"You are so full of shit, Ash Farrell," she said. "You see?" she said to Isaac. "You see what I have to put up with?"

"Would you mind watching your language, please?" Dad said. "There are minors present." I waved at Lucy from the porch swing as Dad took a swallow of beer. "So, how was the wedding?"

"One for the record books, I would think." She settled herself against the porch rail. "The groomsmen were so hungover from the bachelor party they could barely hold their heads up. The flower girl threw up Hawaiian Punch all over her dress, *before* the ceremony. The bride's father broke down during the toast—just sobbed his heart out, like it was a funeral instead of a wedding. Oh, and the band! You want to guess, Ash, what Bobby and Crystal's first dance was? 'Brick House.'" Dad laughed out loud, like it was a perfect choice.

"The flowers were nice, though." Lucy seemed thoughtful as she studied the bouquet in her hand. "I guess Denny might as well have this," she said, leaning forward and tossing it to me; it landed with a gentle *poof* in my lap. "I don't expect I'll be needing it."

Dad opened his mouth and closed it again, two or three times, like a fish in a tank. "Shut up, Ash," Lucy said good-naturedly, and went up the steps and through the screen door, letting it bang shut behind her.

"Shit," Dad said. So much for watching your language with minors present. Slowly he set the guitar in its case and fastened the clasps. "How long have you and Rose been married, Isaac?"

"Nine years, May," Isaac said. He looked like he was about to bust to keep from laughing as Dad said again, "Shit," and picked up the guitar case and went inside after Lucy.

Isaac pushed himself up off the step and brushed his hands on the front of his work pants.

"I don't know why he thinks he can fight it," he said. "I been tellin' him and tellin' him. Those two is *destined*." And he smiled his big, gap-toothed smile at me, like destiny was a bunch of flowers done up in colored streamers. Something to be thankful for.

11

Lucy

 There's something about weddings that makes people sit back and ruminate on their own love lives. For Bailey and Geneva, they were fond reminders of how lucky the two of them were to have each other. Aunt Dove claimed to feel vindicated in her belief that she'd done the right thing by staying single. My mama loved an excuse to get all weepy over the tragedy of her own marriage, and for days afterward we'd get to relive the infamous Day Your Daddy, Raymond Hatch, Left Us. When I was married to Mitchell, I used to sit in the hard-back pew and stare at the hopeful, upturned faces of the intended and wish with all my heart that I had what they had: true love, a fresh start. So, now that I'd been granted what I'd wished for, why was I so hesitant? Watching Crystal Sheppard exchange vows with Bobby Pilger, their voices young and earnest, all I felt were cold chills, although the air-conditioning in the church had quit an hour before and everyone around me was fanning themselves and sweating.

I'd be lying if I said I hadn't thought of marrying Ash. I'd had the daydreams most women do, of a frothy white dress and bridesmaids lined up like a row of after-dinner mints, banks of flowers and a triple-decker cake that looks like a snow queen's castle. It was easier than I cared to admit to picture Ash standing at the altar in a dark suit coat, his face grave and handsome, his hands folded, a white rosebud in his buttonhole. Oh, I could picture the wedding just fine. But I'd *been* married; one thing I knew, if nothing else, was that the wedding has precious little to do with the marriage. You can have the biggest send-off in the world, champagne and confetti and cheering crowds, but none of that makes a bit of difference if the boat won't float.

Bobby and Crystal's reception was at the Indian Mound Country Club, an unassuming little place with a nine-hole golf course and a postage-stamp pool, and a banquet room that Peggy and I had festooned in the bride's chosen colors, mauve and teal. The band was tuning up in the corner, a bunch of college boys from Little Rock in white tuxes and shaggy eighties-style haircuts. Guests started trickling in, someone tapped a keg—it's a myth that East Texas Baptists don't drink, which is why they almost never have their wedding receptions in the church hall—and before long the wedding party arrived and the revelry got underway.

I was standing back by the groom's cake, watching the musicians, when Geneva walked up with a plastic cup of beer in her hand. She motioned to me, and I scanned the room for Peggy and then slipped off with my sister-in-law to the hushed beige refuge of the ladies' room. My stomach had settled down, and I'd been sneaking shrimp puffs and cheese crackers for half an hour and was feeling fine.

"How did you and Denny get along last night?" I asked, parking myself on a padded ottoman and watching Geneva shake her cigarettes out of her purse. She claimed she was a social smoker, but her definition of "social" included any activity involving another human being, even those on radio and TV.

"Oh, fine, she's a good girl. Bailey managed to get her wrapped around his finger—big surprise, huh?" I laughed. "We took her to church with us this morning."

"Gosh, maybe we ought to send her over to your place for keeps."

Geneva fumbled her lighter out of her bag. "The real question is, how did you and *Ash* get along? House to yourselves and all that?" She arched her eyebrows at me in the mirror.

"Ha! I sat out on the porch swing all night." Well, most of the night; there was the little matter of lost time, whatever had caused me to wake up bare-naked in his bed at ten-thirty that morning without an inkling as to how I'd gotten there.

Geneva stared at me. "You're kidding, right?" I shook my head, but I didn't feel like going into the story of the guy from Nashville with her. "Honey, don't *tell* me these things! You know I'm Ash's biggest fan. I'm counting on you to live my fantasy." She lit her cigarette and took a hit, exhaling in a cloud that made me cough and fan the air in front of my face

"Speaking of Ash," she said, settling back on the chaise, "you shouldn't have run off in such a hurry this morning when we brought Denny by. Your brother just about called him out, right in his own front yard."

"Called Ash out? About what?"

"About when he intends to make an honest woman out of you."

"Oh, my—" I put a hand to my mouth, but a scrap of a laugh escaped anyway. "Well, what did he say?"

"Bailey just asked him, flat out, when he intended to stop shacking up with you and make it legal. Ash reminded him you'd only just lost your husband, but Bailey's no slouch in the math department, as you know. He reminded Ash that you'd been living with him three out of the four and a half months since Mitchell died."

"Is that true?" I said, almost to myself. It sounded scandalous, like something one of the Gabor sisters would do.

"Ash wanted to know if there was any cause to suspect you were unhappy with things the way they are. I said no, I'd never seen you happier, in fact, and Bailey backed off and turned loose of his leg, and that was that."

Geneva looked at me bold-faced, tapping her cigarette against an ashtray. "So, what about you?"

"What about me?"

"Don't tell me you haven't thought about it."

"I don't know, Gen. I mean, it's true—my husband just died."

"Oh, bull," she said. "Do it, Lucy. Do it quick. Before somebody else tries to ride him off into the sunset." She was right, I guessed, though the likeliest candidate right then was probably Tony Amate. Tony Amate held the keys to a kingdom I would never even enter.

The ladies' room door swung open, and one of the bridesmaids stuck her head in. "Any single girls in here? We're about to throw the bouquet."

"*Oh*, no!" I exclaimed.

But Geneva was bigger than me and twice as determined. She steered me into a gaggle of tipsy, fragrant girls, who whispered and smiled knowingly at me as I slipped into the pack. I clenched my arms tight to my sides while Geneva waved gaily from the sidelines, like a soccer mom.

The new Mrs. Bobby Pilger came tripping over, her feet tangling in the train of her satin gown, a cup of beer sloshing in one hand and her bouquet in the other. I knew that bouquet; I'd personally wired the stems of roses and baby's breath, tied the cascades of ribbon. It had never occurred to me that I might be meeting up with it again under more intimate circumstances.

"Ready?" Crystal cried, and the girls and the watching crowd all hollered their approval. The drummer hit a flashy roll and Crystal turned her back to us, swigged her beer, then raised her pitching arm and let fly.

A big, orgasmic "Ah!" went up as the little knot of unattached women parted like the Red Sea and there I stood, solid as a fence post, all alone in the clearing. The bouquet hit me square in the forehead, bounced off, and went skittering across the floor. The whole room cheered.

"See there," Melba Campos said, retrieving the bouquet and pressing it into my hand. "There's no getting out of it now. You're a marked woman."

The band launched into "Forever and Ever, Amen," and I stood surrounded by laughing, milling, three-quarters'-drunk people, clutching the bouquet to my abdomen like a shield and thinking to myself, *You don't know the half of it.*

☙

I didn't see it then for what it was, another window opening, then closing. The perfect window, really. When I got home, I tossed the bouquet to Denny with a wisecrack about not having any use for it, but when Ash followed me into the house, his expression was so hangdog I couldn't stand it, and sent him back outside while I stirred up a pot of chili for supper.

The men worked steady for another couple of hours, and then Rose drove up in their old truck with all those babies bouncing around in the back like jumping beans, and we sat on the porch as the day waned and the kids ran shrieking after june bugs in the yard and the long evening stretched out full of violet promise. Sitting in the half dark with Rose in the crook of Isaac's arm and his hand like a bulwark on her belly, it seemed things would never be more right. I saw Ash studying them, too, his face sad and tender, and I wondered if he craved their contentment. If it was something he might have chosen for us if he'd thought it was possible.

In bed that night, I watched his face as he lay on top of the sheet, gazing at the blades of the ceiling fan as the light through the window glass spilled across his torso and his face; he looked like an antique statue, something carved over months and years by the world's most painstaking hand. I rolled over and lay my hand on his chest and was surprised, as I always was, by the warmth of his skin, the steady thump of the heart beneath. There were times, even after three months, when I had to remind myself that he wasn't chiseled stone.

"Isaac and Rose seem so happy, don't they?" I asked, and held my breath at what felt like a leap of bravado.

"They are," Ash replied. "I envy them, in a way."

I propped myself on my elbows and looked at his face. "You do? Why?"

"Because things are so simple for them. Love, work, babies. A little music and a little good food."

"Are you saying you wish your life was like that?"

"Of course not," Ash said. "I only wish it was all I wanted."

He reached up a hand and gathered my hair at the base of my neck. He seemed to be looking for something in my face, and without meaning to, without even realizing I was doing it, I reached in and snapped the window shut again, before he could see inside. I didn't have to ask Ash what he wanted. What I wondered, listening to his breathing deepen and slow, was whether there was a place in it the right size and shape for me.

❦

In the morning I felt terrible, guilty and sick. I was only sleeping a few hours a night anymore; I'd wake from some unremembered dream and then lie for hours next to Ash, counting his breaths and the trip-hammer of my own heart. The next day the pain seemed lodged against my breastbone like the point of a knife. There was, I knew, a thin, thin line between omission and a flat-out lie.

I'd lobbied for Denny to be allowed to stay at the house while we went to work, that we couldn't have her sitting on a bench in the court-house square for the rest of the summer. Ash had given in, but grudgingly, and was determined to find some way to make her "account" for her days.

"She's a kid, Ash, this isn't boot camp," I reminded him, handing him his coffee, and he said sourly, "Yeah, but." I understood that he believed she should be spending her time constructively, but I couldn't see that telling her to keep her hands off the stereo or his power tools was much help to anybody.

"Why would I want to touch your stupid Skilsaw, anyway?" Denny said, biting into a Pop-Tart. "Except it's probably the only way I'll ever get a place to sleep around here."

"You'll get a place to sleep when I'm finished with Mrs. Crouch's cabinets," Ash said. "Have you got something to read?" She held up the Stephen King novel, which she was two-thirds of the way through.

He got up and left the room, and came back with a dog-eared copy of *Horseman, Pass By*. "Here," he said, tossing the book on the table in front of Denny. "I want you to read the first fifty pages of this. I expect a report tonight at supper."

"Fifty pages!" Denny squealed. "This is worse than *school*!" Ash just shrugged and sipped his coffee, looking a little smug, I thought. "And I can't listen to the stereo, *ever*?"

"We'll see how you do with the book report first."

"What about my Walkman?"

Ash pushed back from the table and set his coffee cup in the sink. "You just get those pages read. Then we'll talk about the rest." He went out, and in a minute we heard water running in the bathroom.

"I think he hates me," Denny said, gazing bleakly at *Horseman, Pass By*.

"He's just trying to act fatherly," I said. "It's not like he's had a lot of practice lately."

She looked sharply at me. Ash had put on his boots and was coming back up the hall.

"Lucy!" she whispered. "When are you going to—"

I reached over and snatched the remaining Pop-Tart out of her hand, stuffed it into the garbage disposal, and flipped the switch. Denny stared at me with her mouth dropped open, then shoved her chair back from the table and grabbed her Walkman and ran out of the room. She nearly collided with Ash in the doorway; he flattened himself against the jamb as she careened through. The disposal continued to grind away, even though the Pop-Tart was history, antimatter, by now.

"What happened?" Ash mouthed at me over the disposal's roar. I shrugged. "Denise!" Ash yelled, but the front door banged. I turned off the switch and the disposal churned its way into eventual silence.

"Leave her alone, Ash," I said. "You'll only make it worse."

"Goddamn it," he said, "I wasn't cut out for this."

I kept my palms on the countertop and my eyes on the window, even when he came over and lay a hand on my hip, and finally he sighed and gave me a kiss on the jaw and said he'd see me that evening. I stood there until I heard his truck start up and pull out.

What I'd said to Aunt Dove a couple of days earlier was true; I hadn't yet seemed able to connect the fact of pregnancy with an actual baby. Even last evening, watching Rose and Isaac, what I envied was the sweetness of expectancy, the way it drew and held them together, not the squalling, messy, human result.

I left Denny a peanut butter and jelly sandwich on a plate in the refrigerator, and a note on the kitchen table, tucked in between Stephen King and *Horseman, Pass By*. "Be patient with us," I wrote, "We're doing the best we can." I signed it "Love, Lucy." But I didn't see her again before I got into my car and left for work.

∞

Around lunchtime, Peggy handed me a dozen roses and a slip of paper with a scrawled address. It was a slow day in the shop, not a single Monday-morning floral apology for a lovers' quarrel or a single week-end death, although Florence Bingham at the Golden Years retirement home had fallen from her wheelchair at the Saturday night ukulele concert and broken her hip.

The address was vague, just a number in the ninety-nine hundreds, off the state highway. "You don't know where this is?" I asked Peggy, who was busy filling out an order sheet and didn't look at me. "I mean, is it a residence, a business, what?"

"All I know," Peggy said, "is they want you there by noon. Now get a move on." It never crossed my mind I was being set up, that even Peggy Thaney with her enlarged, overburdened heart could be a fool for love.

The ninety-nine hundred block of Highway 133 began two miles north of town, with County Line Liquor. I slowed the van and eased it onto the shoulder, scanning for numbers, but the buildings were few and far between: an auto-body shop, a couple of abandoned shacks with caved-in porches and no glass in the windows.

I was looking for a spot to turn around when I came upon the Piney View Motor Court. Sure enough, the numbers etched onto the glass of the office matched the ones on Peggy's note. I was about to pull up to the first cabin with the hand-lettered "Vacancy" sign in the window when I saw Ash's pickup, all the way in back, in front of number ten.

I drove slowly across the parking lot, trying not to laugh out loud. I'd been so preoccupied, I'd never stopped to consider the last order we'd had for pink roses, my favorite flower: the morning after the night Ash and I met, the bouquet left like an act of contrition on the seat of my borrowed truck.

Maybe this wasn't what it seemed, I thought, pulling in next to Ash's truck, taking care with the roses even though, apparently, they'd already found their recipient. Maybe this was one of those interventions like they do with drug addicts or cult members, where your family and friends gather and force you to admit your powerlessness over your circumstances. I could see their faces now: Dove, Geneva, Bailey, Ash. *Admit it, Lucy; there's something you haven't been telling us.* It was, in some weird way, almost a comfort to imagine this.

I knocked on the door. "It's open," said a muffled voice, and I turned the knob and let myself into the cottage.

The room was so dark, it took a moment to get my bearings. In spite of the fact that the Piney View was a notorious assignation spot, I'd never been there; the boys I dated in high school had gone for parked cars, not motels, and then I'd moved away and married Mitchell.

Then a pool of yellow light fanned out from a lamp, and in the middle of that pool was Ash, on top of a nubby brown spread, his arms crossed on the pillow beneath his head, wearing nothing but an old familiar smile.

"Faye's Flowers," I said, crossing to the far side of the bed and laying the bouquet on his chest. "Special delivery."

He caught one of my hands in his, and I sat down on the mattress beside him. He lifted the bouquet and studied it for a moment, then drew out a single rose and placed the remaining bunch on the bedside table. He put the rose between his teeth. I started to laugh. Ash, his teeth clenched tight on the prickly stem, didn't blink. I was still laughing when he pulled me down beside him and started to unbutton my blouse.

"Wait a minute," I gasped, as the rose got flattened in a fragrant crush of petals between us. "I think there's been a mistake here. I'm just the flower deliverer. Are you sure you weren't hoping for Misty Potter?"

"I'm not, and have never been, *hoping* for Misty Potter. And I sure as hell never bought her roses." He lifted my skirt and snaked his hands underneath, pulling my hips against his. I might have been a little apprehensive about this single-minded ardor if I hadn't been so instantly aflame. Biology, chemistry, destiny, God; I don't care what you call it. No matter what was going on between Ash and me, the one thing I never doubted was that we would always find each other this way.

"Honestly, Ash," I said, as with a flick of his wrist my underpants went sailing into some shadowy corner. "The Piney View Motor Court? I mean, it's not like we never . . . I mean, just last night . . ."

"I remember last night," he said. "I remember it fine." My blouse was gone; *pop* went my bra hook, and the new fullness of my unbound breasts spilled into his hands.

He lifted his chin to look at me, the whole length of me, so hastily undressed and so plainly aroused, and grinned his satisfaction, and if I'd been in any other temper or position I'd have smacked him, but he had something I needed just then.

"You know what bothered me about last night, though?" he said. "You were so damned quiet. Your face was up against my shoulder, and I could feel all this, this wildness inside you, but the whole time you barely even breathed. And at the end, there was this tiny little *squeak*.

"I miss the noise, Luce," Ash murmured, his body settling over mine. "I want to hear you yell. I want you to raise the roof off this place. Okay? Can you do that for me?"

Well. He'd paid for the room, after all, and the roses. I didn't want to seem ungrateful.

∾

"Does Peggy know about this?" I asked, my face pressed sleepily against Ash's shoulder. "I got the idea she was in on it, somehow."

He laughed. "You mean you think I called up and disguised my voice and ordered a dozen pink roses delivered to room ten of the Piney View specifically by Miss Lucy Hatch? Sure, Peggy knows."

I raised my head and looked at him. "Peggy knows I'm screwing you in a thirty-dollar motel room on my lunch hour?"

"First of all," he said, "the room was thirty-six dollars, plus tax. Second of all, it's been way over an hour. And I wish you wouldn't call it 'screwing,' Lucy. It cheapens the beauty and sanctity of our relationship."

I smiled at the bowed curve of his lower lip, that tiny check-shaped scar underneath. I'd never asked him how he got it. A punch from some jealous husband, a plate hurled by a jilted lover. Or maybe just a fall from some childhood bicycle. Ash was never as great a legend in his own mind as he was, much of the time, in mine.

"There's a place for beauty and sanctity," I reminded him. "But a thirty-dollar motel room is a place for screwing."

"Thirty-*six* dollars," he repeated, smiling, but he was staring at the ceiling, and in a few seconds, his mouth started to move. I sat up under the sheet and watched him, but he was oblivious to me, and soon I heard him humming under his breath. *Hm, hm, hm,* he'd go, then mutter a couple of words, then *hm, hm, hm* again.

"Ash Farrell!" I exclaimed. He held up his right hand, palm out, to hush me. "Are you writing a *song*?"

He rolled over and yanked open the drawer to the bedside table. Finding it empty, he tumbled out of bed and started foraging around the room until he managed to lay his hands on a Gideon Bible, and without a breath of compunction opened it and ripped out the flyleaf.

"That seals it," I said, "you're going to hell for sure," as he came over and sat back down on the mattress, his eyes doing another quick scan of the room. He looked back over his shoulder at me.

"Have you got a pen?"

I did, unfortunately. I had a little pack I carried with me when I made deliveries, with change and the portable credit card machine, and the pen I handed clients to sign the charge slips. Even so, I considered lying about it. *No,* I should have said. *Forget it. Come here, and let's get every one of our thirty-six dollars' worth.* He read my mind, though, and I sighed and got him the pen. It would never be said that Lucy Hatch stood between man and art.

I climbed out of bed and collected my clothes, but Ash stayed curled over the torn flyleaf, scrawling and mumbling. I went into the bathroom and turned on the taps in the tub until the cold, rusty trickle became pink and lukewarm, and then I stepped into the shower and let it wash the beauty and sanctity of my afternoon with Ash down the drain. When I came out, dressed and twisting my damp hair into a ponytail, Ash was still writing.

"I have to get back to work," I said, leaning over to kiss him on top of the head. There was no indication that he heard me. "Ash?" I said.

He raised his head. He looked like he was in some sort of ecstatic trance, like he'd just seen straight into the burning face of God. All of a sudden, any jealousy I'd felt for his romantic past, for that silly tramp Misty Potter, his young wife, Marlene, the others I could only imagine, seemed frivolous. *This* was the real contest; how in the hell were you supposed to compete with God?

I picked up the eleven unmangled roses from the bedside table, and my change bag. "That'll be twenty-seven fifty for the flowers," I said. "No charge for the delivery."

Ash reached reflexively for his wallet and handed me a twenty and a ten. I counted out two ones and two quarters and laid them on the table. He'd sat back down and was bent over scribbling again, his head cocked slightly, like a voice only he could hear was dictating in his ear. I peeked over his shoulder, but it looked like hieroglyphics to me, like it was in some lost language I was never meant to know.

"Thank you for your patronage," I said, my hand on the doorknob. "Have a nice day."

Ash smiled distractedly, and gave me a little wave. I left him there, still writing. I hoped I wouldn't have to explain to Peggy how he'd stiffed me on the tip.

12

Denny

He was trying to drive me insane. It was the only reason I could think of for why he treated me the way he did: one day all beery and friendly, him and Isaac working together on fixing up my room, letting me sit and listen in on their jam session; then the next morning a maniac again, telling me hands off the stereo and his stupid tools, assigning me chapters in some prehistoric cowboy book I'd never heard of, like I'd landed in remedial reading in summer school. I should have just stayed in Dallas and taken my chances. I should have sat down in the middle of the driveway and refused to get in the car with Ma. Nothing could be worse than this. Except, maybe, one thing; now, all of a sudden, Lucy was in on it, too. When she snatched that Pop-Tart out of my hand, I just about died. I know she was just trying to keep me from asking about stuff that was none of my business, but still, I felt like she'd all of a sudden switched sides and lined herself up with the devil.

I ran out the door with Dad hollering my name, but he didn't keep it up or come after me, which only proved my point, that he cared more about exerting his brand-new parental supremacy than he did about the actual welfare of me, his daughter. I kept on going, across the road and into the woods, the dogs at my heels.

When I was sure no one was following me, I sat down on a stump and listened. I was still close enough to the house to hear what was going on, and sure enough, not two minutes after I left, Dad's truck started up and drove away, and about ten minutes later, Lucy's Buick did the same. It was the first time I'd been alone since I'd landed in Mooney, almost a whole week before. I got little chill bumps just thinking about it. I could do whatever I wanted. I had no money, no car; to tell the truth, I didn't know how to drive. But I was on my own.

It was nice there, in the woods. I slipped off my headphones and put my Walkman in the pocket of my sweatshirt. High over my head the trees made a canopy of sweet-smelling green, and the ground under my feet was soft with crushed pine needles, and after a while I could pick out the sounds of three or four different birds. The dogs had gotten on the scent of something and started running in circles, then all of a sudden dashed deeper into the woods. I decided to go after them.

I lost sight of them pretty quick, but I could hear them moving around in the underbrush, and I kept going until I came out in a little clearing. I poked around and found the remains of an old building: crumbling steps, a couple of blackened cornerstones, the charred-out hulk of a potbellied stove. Everything else, it looked like, the woods had reclaimed.

Just beyond the ruined foundation, I discovered an old graveyard. It wasn't much more, really, than a patch of ground, set off by a border of broad, flat stones, but the space inside had been cleared, and the markers, though they looked ancient, were upright and mostly legible. I walked slowly among the stones and read the names and the dates out loud. Eustice Washington had died in 1927, at the age of a hundred and two. Alvin Getty, born 1912, had only lived four days. The most recent stone was 1943, two whole generations ago. There was no question it was a place for spirits, but I felt welcome there. They probably didn't get that many visitors; I figured they were glad to see me.

I sat down on the stone border and looked around. It was a pretty place, with a slash of blue sky overhead and the clean scent of pine all around, and I listened to the dogs and the birds and the wind in the trees until I realized that my heart had stopped pounding and I didn't feel like I needed to cry anymore.

Part of my brain, the sensible part, was telling me to go back to the empty house and throw my stuff into my duffel bag and just get the hell out of there. But I was less than a month from my fifteenth birthday; my heart, most of the time, felt too small for all the things it was trying to hold. The fact was, I was a little bit in love with East Texas, and with my father and Lucy, too. As confused and sad as I felt right then, this had in some ways been one of the best weeks of my life. I had been in a honky-tonk, a guitar store, a garden full of Buddhist trinkets, a Baptist church, an old country cemetery. I'd gotten my first lipstick—Chanel, to boot—and learned to two-step. I'd eaten more fried chicken in a week than I had the whole rest of my life. My father had turned out to be a better musician than I could have hoped for. And there was more music, I knew, where that came from; somewhere were the songs he'd written for me as a colicky baby. Wasn't that proof, no matter how shabby, that he'd loved me once? How could I leave until I had that in my hand?

The dogs came crashing back through the woods and into the clearing, looking depressed. Actually, just Booker looked depressed; Steve Cropper wasn't smart enough, I don't think, to realize they'd been after anything, he'd only been along for the ride. It would be wonderful, I thought, to be that dumb, not to know or care what it was you were chasing after. I rubbed their ears and they licked my hands, and I got up off my rock and said good-bye to the old ghosts and walked back out of the woods.

The house looked strange to me, knowing that I had more or less free reign. It occurred to me that my father telling me what to do and not to do while they were gone was nothing but a lot of bluff. Unless he'd had the place wired for surveillance—and I didn't think he was *that* paranoid—there was no way he'd be able to know what I was up to. You could tell he hadn't figured out yet the basic rule of parenting, that the minute you tell a kid not to do something, she will right away make that thing her number-one project.

I got nervous, stepping through the front door, letting it latch quietly behind me. "Hello?" I called down the hallway, just to hear the sound of my voice, any voice. If somebody had answered me, I'd have had a heart attack. But it was all coolness and silence inside, nothing but the hum of the air conditioner and the appliances in the kitchen.

I went into the bedroom and snooped around a little, but there wasn't much to see—no dirty books in the night table, no sex toys. No birth control, obviously. I guess they were too pure for all that, or maybe they were just better at hiding the stuff than I was at finding it. There was an old picture I'd never seen before of Ma and me as a baby, tucked way down in a drawer full of socks, and one of a big, sunburned man in overalls and a feed cap under a pile of Lucy's T-shirts. Even the contents of the bathroom cabinet were boring: Tylenol, dental floss, Milk of Magnesia.

I was hungry—after having my breakfast jerked out of my hand and stuffed down the garbage disposal—so I went into the kitchen to look for something to eat. I saw the note on the table, in between my Stephen King novel and the horse book, but I didn't pick it up, not right away. I opened the fridge and found a peanut butter and jelly sandwich on a little plate, Lucy's idea of a peace offering, I guessed. It crossed my mind just to leave it there, to let her find it untouched when she came home that evening, to let her know I wasn't that easily bought. My stomach won out, though. I ate the sandwich in about four bites, standing over the kitchen sink. Then I opened the cabinet and got out the Pop-Tart box, and gobbled two, for good measure. It seemed like I was always hungry, that nothing was enough to fill me up.

I leaned over the table and looked at the note, although I didn't actually touch it. "Be patient with us. We're doing the best we can." I hated to tell her, but that's exactly what I was afraid of.

I wandered into the living room, wondering if there was any way I could get away with playing his CDs without him knowing it. Cases were scattered around the stereo, and the ones in the rack weren't in any kind of order, but I still couldn't help but think he had some way of checking: a system, a sixth sense. Maybe he dusted for fingerprints. I was feeling cocky, but not that cocky.

That's when my eye landed on the guitar case in the corner.

In a lot of ways, I was young for my years. I'd never had a date, much less kissed a boy; I barely even thought along those lines, except in the most soft-focus ways. But the way I felt about guitars was the way I was sure it must be to fall in love. I ached for the engraved fret board, the metal strings under my fingers, the tension of trying to fit my hands around a C-sharp chord. If I'd been a different kind of girl — maybe just a prettier one, or sillier, like a lot of kids my age — I'd have been sneaking in boys through my bedroom window. I, Denise Farrell, daughter of Ash by blood if not by design, was crazy for guitars. And now he'd gone off and left me alone with one.

I didn't see how I was doing anything wrong, at least not anything he could hold me accountable for. He hadn't actually *mentioned* the guitar on the hands-off list. It just never dawned on him that I would have the urge to touch it, much less a clue what to do with it. It wasn't the only way my father sold me short, but it sure was the most considerable.

I set the case on the floor, flipped back the latches, and raised the lid. The Gibson sat in its form-fitted nest, its glossy black body catching the light. For a little while, I just sat and looked at it. I wasn't working up courage so much as the proper respect. It seems to me that what a musician needs more than anything is respect for the instrument, that if you approach it like you would a stray animal, with just the right balance of attraction and fear, only then will it reward you.

I held my breath as I lifted the guitar out of its case and laid it across my knee, letting my fingers move for a minute or two soundlessly, without pressure, over the strings. I had a little no-name practice guitar of my own back in Dallas, but compared to this, it didn't even rate. If Dad had walked in the door right then, he'd have had to wrestle me to get the thing out of my hands. This was the sensation I most identified, then and always, as happiness.

My father's songs were in there, I realized. But so were mine.

I didn't do much, that afternoon. Some simple scales, a quick run-through of "Wildwood Flower." A bridge of a Pearl Jam song I liked that I'd been working up to for a while. And then, from memory, the dozen or so bars of the song I'd first heard Dad play on this guitar, here in this room as we were waiting for Lucy to get dressed for the Round-Up, just a few nights before. The notes seemed fixed in the instrument, like my father had planted them there for me to find. I played till I felt my blood get warm, till I felt my heart sit square in my chest again. I sat for a few more minutes with the instrument on my knee: honoring it, giving thanks. Then I took the polishing cloth out of the case and wiped my fingerprints away, and set it with as much tenderness as it had ever known back in its hard-shell bed, and stood it upright in the corner again, its secrets hidden but reachable, and everything right with the world.

I went into the kitchen and sat down at the table with the Pop-Tarts and opened *Horseman, Pass By*. More than anything, what music makes possible is forgiveness.

❦

It was not quite three o'clock when Dad came home. I was still at the kitchen table, having finished my required reading and the rest of the Pop-Tarts and gone back to Stephen King, when I heard him pull into the yard and come across the porch and into the house. He didn't call out or announce himself in any way; maybe he'd forgotten about me, or figured I was still gone. I heard his boots cross the living room floor and then go back out again, and even though I kept my eyes on my book for a couple of minutes, the suspense was killing me.

I got up and crept to the door and looked out through the screen. He was sitting on the top step, the guitar across his knee.

I went cold all over, thinking that somehow he'd found me out. But I knew him well enough by then to know he'd have come straight into the kitchen with all his guns drawn: Shoot first, ask questions later. I could see his mouth move from time to time, and his hands hesitate on the frets as he tried one chord, then another. I set my book on the hall table and pushed open the door.

"What are you doing home?" I said. Much as I believed I hated the quarrelsome aspect of our relationship, I can't say that I didn't do my part, sometimes, to fan the fire.

He smiled, though. The monster from the breakfast table was gone. When my father smiled at you, I'm not kidding, it was like New Year's and the Fourth of July all rolled into one; you never saw such fireworks, and they'd be there long afterward, even after you closed your eyes.

"I'm the boss," he said. "I get to come home when I want."

"You don't get paid for it, though," I pointed out, but instead of getting mad, he laughed. I watched his hands for a while, listening to him humming quietly. "You're writing a song," I said, "aren't you?"

"Mm." He played another bar or two, then looked up again. "Want to hear it?" I tried to be cool and not nod my head off, and sat down.

The song was okay—not the best I'd ever heard, but hardly the worst. "It's not finished," he said about halfway through, which was pretty obvious. It was about people having sex in a motel room, from what I could tell, though he'd dressed it up some in prettier pictures. "Thirty-Dollar Room" was the name of it, I figured from the refrain. This couple in the song kept meeting, all through their courtship and their marriage and finally their old age, in the same thirty-dollar room, to keep the romance in the relationship alive. "Side by side they lay/and watched the world fall away." Nice, if not very imaginative, though I guess if we were all waiting for an original idea, there'd be no country-western music.

He set the guitar aside and reached into his pocket and unfolded a piece of paper, smoothing it flat on his knee.

"What's that?" I leaned closer to look. There was scribbling all over the page, in what looked like Chinese; printed at the top were the words, "Courtesy of the Gideons," and machine-stamped above that were the words, "Property of Piney View Motor Court. Do Not Remove!"

"This? My song," he said. "Oh, the paper, you mean? Well, it was the closest thing to hand. I guess I owe the Gideons a songwriting credit."

"You were at the Piney View?"

His head snapped up. "How do you know about the Piney View?"

People were never giving me any credit for anything, like I didn't have eyes or ears like older people. We drove right past the Piney View on the way to the Round-Up, coming and going, four times all told in the past week. I didn't know anything at all about the Piney View, to be honest, except that I'd seen quite plainly with my two callow eyes that it was a motel, and that there was no reason I could think of for my father to have been in a motel lately. No reason, except one.

"You're dis*gu*sting!" I yelled, jumping to my feet, causing him to rear back from me like I might be about to punch him. "You have the most beautiful, wonderful"—I paused, remembering the Pop-Tart incident, but promptly forgave it as something he'd provoked—"the most wonderful girlfriend in the whole world, and you have to go off to a nasty old motel, to, to . . ." It wasn't that I couldn't think of the right word. I knew the word, all right, and several more like it, but I knew I'd never live to tell about it if I used one. "To be with some, some horrible, disgusting, horrible girl who's probably planning to rob you, or give you some disease—"

He'd started laughing, which only made me madder.

"Don't expect me to cover for you," I said in what I hoped was a no-nonsense voice. "I'm telling Lucy, whether you like it or not."

"Denny, for goodness sake," he said. "Would you settle down and let me explain it to you?"

"I don't want an explanation!" I said. "I know what you did to my mother! I know you'll never change."

I gasped, hearing that come out of my mouth. I hadn't even known I was thinking it, much less that it sat so near the tip of my dangerously unloosed tongue.

"Sit down," he said, his eyes so black they seemed to be all pupil. There was no question from the tone of his voice that I had a choice in the matter. I sat, but I scrunched myself up as tight as I could against the porch post, and crossed my arms over my chest for good measure.

"Denny, look. A lot of bad stuff happened between your mama and me, I won't try to say otherwise. We were two unhappy people who didn't know how to help ourselves, so I guess the only thing we could do was take it out on each other. And on you, too, even though we never meant to." He glanced at me, then away again. "I don't know all the things your mama's told you about me, and I'm pretty sure I don't want to know. But you have to believe me when I tell you that I was true to her, every minute of every day we were married to each other. She always wanted to believe I wasn't, but I was." He smiled, a little. "I was still Catholic then. I was too scared of going to hell to fool around."

"You don't think about hell anymore?"

"Oh, I think about hell, every day. If nothing else, it's a good song-writing subject."

"So, then, what about the Piney View?"

"Lucy and I were at the Piney View this afternoon," he said. "Together."

"You and *Lucy* were in the motel room?" I couldn't have been more surprised if he'd said the queen of England. "But you . . . But you . . ." I waved my hand to take in the porch, the house, the general direction of the bedroom. This was one more time honesty, I knew, would not serve me. There was plenty going on in that house, and outside it, too. Even my Walkman turned up to ten could only drown out so much.

"I didn't know this would be so hard to explain," he said, and I was happy to see he'd gotten red in the face. "It was just a— A treat, for Lucy, from me. She's been a little blue lately. I thought she could use some cheering up." I looked closer at him; it occurred to me, not for the first time, that he knew more than he was letting on. "She seems kind of preoccupied the last few days, don't you think?"

"Well, I don't really know her that well," I said. "Maybe she's just tired."

"You know, if I didn't know any better . . . This is just the way your mother acted when she was first pregnant with you."

My stomach dropped, landing somewhere around my knees. I felt like some bottomless vessel that people just kept pouring stuff into, stuff I had no business knowing; I just never could make myself say, "No more."

"What do you mean, know better?" I said.

"Lucy can't have babies. She told me so when we—well, when we first got together."

"She did?" My brain was busy taking all the little colored pieces it had been given and rearranging them this way and that, trying to make them fit the puzzle, but so far all I had were corners and edges; there were still big chunks missing out of the middle. "You mean a doctor told her this?"

"Mm-hm. Well, sure, I guess so. She was married for fourteen years. She must've seen a doctor about it sometime. Anyway, Lucy wouldn't keep something like that from me," he said. "And I think I'd be able to tell."

Well, what signs would you be looking for? I wanted to ask. *Sickness, tiredness, absentmindedness?* The things that made my father shine at the things he did best were also the ones that could be the most irritating, tied as they were to his almost total lack of ability to see beyond the end of his own handsome nose.

"Maybe she's scared," I said, going out farther on that particular limb than I had any business being.

"Scared? Of what?"

"That you'd be mad."

He laughed. "That's crazy! If it was possible, and Lucy could get pregnant, you mean? Why would I be mad?"

I wasn't going to answer that; I made him think about it. My father hadn't wanted a child fifteen years ago, and he wasn't convinced he wanted her now. The ease with which I accepted this should have galled me, but it was, as I've said, a chapter in a book I'd been hearing all my life. Why else would I have been so greedy for his kindness and his company? I knew how flimsy it was, how suddenly it could end, no explanation necessary: *Sorry it didn't work out, here's your ticket, have a nice life, good-bye.*

"Look," I said finally, "it's probably nothing. She'll be fine in a day or two." A line, I realized, had been drawn in the sand and somehow, without meaning to, I had stepped across, out of the Farrell camp, and onto Lucy's side.

"I hope so," he said. "You know, don't you, that we're going out to Isaac's this weekend, for Juneteenth?" I shook my head, never certain until I was actually strapped into the seat belt that these invitations included me. I knew about Juneteenth, from Texas history in the seventh grade; I knew it was the anniversary of when Lincoln freed the slaves, or when the word finally made its way to Texas, at least. In Dallas there were neighborhood parades every year, and blues concerts. "They do this out at their place every year. There's barbecue, the real deal, a pig in a pit, and everybody brings their instruments and sits around the yard and sings until the next morning, just about."

I wondered if we would be the only white people. I knew I shouldn't care, but I did; I wasn't sure I could stand all those eyes watching me, saying to themselves, *Now here's a shoddy specimen; you call this a white girl?*

"There are kids there?"

"Oh, sure, all the way from babies to teenagers. You never saw such food in your life, and I guarantee you've never heard such music. I've been going for eight years now, ever since I first met Isaac. This is Lucy's first time, though," he said. "And yours," he had the grace to add, letting me know I was included. I said I couldn't wait.

"You know," he said, "we never did hear back from your mama in Chicago, did we?" I shook my head no. It was surprising, really, how little I'd thought about her this past week. It seemed like the minute she'd driven away all this other stuff had started that had sucked me in like a whirlpool.

"Do you miss her?" he asked. It's no wonder I'm psychic; when they loaded that particular character trait, I got it from both barrels. I didn't know if the true answer was the best one, but I decided to take a chance.

"No, sir."

"We won't keep bothering her, then," he said, and stood up. "Are you hungry? Maybe we ought to start supper, have it ready when Lucy gets home."

I followed him into the kitchen, where he opened the pantry and started foraging. He held up a jar of spaghetti sauce, and I nodded. For the next few minutes, I watched him move around the kitchen, putting a pot of water on to boil, dumping the sauce into another pan, adding in some brown-and-green-flecked things from little shaker bottles.

"I didn't know you could cook," I said as the aroma of sauce began to fill the room.

"I'm not sure you can call this cooking, strictly speaking." He put the tip of one finger into the heating water, then pulled it quickly out again. "But you have to remember, I've been a bachelor for thirteen years, almost. I'd have starved to death a long time ago if I didn't know how to stick some Ragú in a pan."

"Unless maybe your girlfriends did it for you." I don't know why I couldn't stop picking that particular scab.

He stirred the sauce with a big metal spoon. "Well," he said, "it's been a long time since I've known anybody who cared much about whether I was getting enough to eat." In another tone of voice it might have been a brag, but I could tell he didn't mean it that way; in fact, he sounded a little sorry for himself. "Your mama was a wonderful cook, I recall. She used to make this fantastic lasagna. Six layers—it took her all day, rolling out the pasta, blending the cheeses, making the sauce."

"Typical," I said, but he was tripping on his own now, right up Memory Lane.

"And some kind of chocolate cake, for my birthday, with cherry filling, and frosting about a mile high . . ." He opened a jar and took out a fistful of pasta and dropped it into the boiling water, but his eyes were miles away.

"You really remember that?" I asked, and his gaze lifted from the place it had traveled and landed again on me.

"Sure I remember it," he said, like he was wondering why I'd ask.

"Ma always claimed you forgot all about us when you left. She said you wiped her and me and those years right out of your mind."

I hadn't meant to hit a sore point dead-on, but I could see I had. He adjusted the flame under the spaghetti as the water came back to a boil.

"Let me tell you a story, okay?" he said. "Right after Marlene and I got married, we moved into a little bitty two-room house on the south side of downtown Dallas, a place called Opportunity Park. Lord, we were poor, and your mama hated the place, coming as she had from a well-to-do family. But we were lucky, too, nothing bad ever happened to us there, at least not because of the neighborhood.

"The house was a wreck, something breaking or leaking practically every day, and your mama thought I ought to be able to take care of it, but I was so busy working, just trying to afford rent and food and stuff, there was never time to keep the place from falling apart. It was clean, though—your mama was a stickler for that—and you had a little crib in the corner of the bedroom that we bought at Goodwill and painted yellow, and she stenciled a little row of ducks along the headboard." He wasn't looking at me as he spoke but into the sauce, which he stirred as slowly and thoughtfully as he seemed to be choosing his words.

"The day you were born, I was at a job in the northwest part of town. We were putting up drywall when the word came over the radio that a storm was coming, marching right on down from the Panhandle, bringing tornadoes and buckets of rain. We were battening down the hatches and just about to beat it out of there when the call came on my boss's two-way that Marlene had gone to the hospital.

"I jumped in my truck—not the one I have now, believe it or not, this one was even older and cruddier—and started speeding across town, and the sky was getting darker and darker, and the wind was howling, and finally it started to rain. It was so bad, pretty soon my windshield wipers weren't doing any good at all, and even though everybody else was giving up, pulling off the road, I kept going. It took me an hour to drive eight miles—most of the roads were flooded, and I couldn't see to go any faster than that. We found out the next day that there had been seven tornadoes, all over Dallas County, and there I was, a hell-bent fool, right in the middle of them.

"I got to the hospital and parked and ran inside, soaked to the skin—I'd had my head out the window the last couple of miles, just to steer—and somebody took me up to the maternity floor with about two minutes to spare. Well, there was your mama, all strapped down to this table and her belly under the sheet so big I thought that instead of a baby coming out, somebody must've put two or three more *in* there, but— My Lord, what a sight! Even though she was sweating and yelling and cussing me every step of the way, I don't think I ever saw her look so wonderful. She was in her element, even though she'd kill me for saying it, and for telling you about it now.

"And all of a sudden, there you were—red and squalling, looking like you'd landed someplace you hadn't asked to be and were plenty mad about it. They cleaned you up and wrapped you in a blanket, and the nurse handed you to me, and I carried you over and let your mama see you. I remember pulling back the blanket with one finger and all of a sudden you opened your eyes. They weren't like regular baby eyes, all blank and blue; you looked like you had all the secrets to the universe. I was just twenty-one, and I'd never given much thought to the subject of reincarnation, but I had no doubt the first time I saw you that you'd been here before." He smiled and checked the clock. "And to think," he said, "I almost missed it."

He turned off the burner under the spaghetti and tipped the pan into a strainer in the sink, and a cloud of steam rose, obscuring his face. "So next time your mama tries to tell you I don't remember," he said, "you come ask me. I have plenty more stories where that one came from."

My heart was racing. I felt like I'd just come awake from some tangled dream to find my real life was a more blessed thing than I'd known. "Why did you leave?" I blurted out, so fast the question got past my lips before my tongue knew it was there.

He turned around, the steam from the spaghetti slowly settling. "Oh, Denny," he said. "I can't— Please don't ask me that." He reached to turn off the flame under the sauce. "I'm afraid I don't agree with your mama on that one," he said. "There are some things I believe it's better for you not to hear."

I watched as he upended the strainer over a platter, the noodles slithering out in a rubbery mass, then added the sauce. "You think we ought to wait for Lucy?" he asked, but when I answered, "No!" a little louder than I'd intended, he nodded and said, "You're right. We'll save her some. Let's eat."

It was not even five o'clock in the evening, but the light in the room had changed, the way in summer, dusk can stretch out for hours and hours. It was warm in the kitchen, peaceable. I decided to be grateful for the slightest favors, to accept grace where I found it. We closed our eyes and said our separate thanks, and we had our supper.

13

Denny

On Saturday afternoon, while Dad had band practice, I went with Lucy to Aunt Dove's. It was weird how much I enjoyed being in her garden, with a pair of shears in one hand and a metal bucket in the other, wandering up and down the rows while the little statues stood guard and those colored flags flapped in the breeze.

One of the most surprising things to me about East Texas was how at home the outdoors made me feel, something I'd never known I cared for. At supper just the night before I'd gone so far as to mention my place in the woods, the burned-out building, the old cemetery. I spent hours there every day, sometimes just sitting on the slab listening to the birds and the bugs, sometimes moving among the graves, picking up junk and weeds, polishing the names and dates with the tail of my shirt, keeping my ears open for whatever might start whispering from between the trees.

Dad had looked at me with sudden interest. "Oh, you found Little Hope."

"What?"

"That old ruin used to be Little Hope chapel. There was a fire back in the fifties, and they couldn't afford to rebuild. Some of the families still come out and tend the graveyard, though, a couple of times a year. Our road is named for it, didn't you know?" He picked up his iced-tea glass, smiled. "Heavy-duty stuff in the air over there."

"Spirits," I said, and Dad nodded.

Lucy shuddered and got up from the table. "You all hush," she said, reaching to collect our empty plates. "You're giving me the creeps."

"Oh, no, Miss Lucy," Dad said, watching her set the dishes in the sink. "Only friendly ghosts here on Little Hope." And he'd glanced over and winked lazily at me. He knew, like I did, we were surrounded by sweet old souls.

I gathered the beans and mint Dove wanted, but when I tried to let myself in through the back door, it was latched. I knocked but no one answered, and when I peeked through the window, the kitchen was empty.

I walked around to the front and went in, listening for voices. I heard them, finally, in one of the bedrooms. "All I know is, I have to get rid of it," Lucy said. "As soon as I possibly can."

I stopped dead, sucking in my breath. Dove said something I couldn't make out, then Lucy said, "I just don't know where I'm going to come up with the money. I can't very well ask Ash for it," to which Dove replied, "I don't see why not. If it wasn't for him, you wouldn't be stuck with the thing in the first place. Anyway, honey, you know I'll always float you a loan." "Oh, I couldn't," Lucy said, "not for something like this. And where would I even start to look?" "Geneva will know," Dove said matter-of-factly. "You need to ask Geneva."

So, my suspicions were right; not only was Lucy planning to get rid of her baby, but Aunt Dove was involved—offering to loan her money, to make arrangements, all behind Dad's back! I'd thought my loyalties lay with Lucy on this, but all of a sudden I felt myself swinging back toward the Farrell camp. Dad might have wanted a baby about as much as he wanted a fatal disease, but he at least deserved to be told. And it was my little sister or brother we were talking about, maybe the only chance I'd ever get. I was all for women's choice, but it seemed to me we ought to have a say about it, too.

They came out of the bedroom, Dove carrying a sewing basket and Lucy an armload of fabric, and even though I knew my face was burning, they didn't act at all caught out to see me. "Did you get that lemon balm I wanted, honey?" Dove asked, and I said I had, and followed them into the sunny kitchen, biting down, one more time, on my tongue.

∞

I intended to speak to Lucy the first chance I had, but the moment never came. Dove decided she wanted to come along to the Round-Up, and so we took her with us when we headed home that evening to clean up and change. Lucy was quiet but cheerful, and I thought she must be acting so calm all of a sudden because she'd set her plan in motion. I knew it was her life, her body. I couldn't have said why I cared, except that she had trusted me with her secret; it seemed I had some stake in the outcome. The baby inside her—fetus, if you want to get technical about it—was half Farrell, just like me. I thought if I didn't speak up on its behalf, it would never have a voice. Dad and Lucy were as lovey-dovey as ever, sliding around the dance floor during the break in their usual eye-locked trance with his hand on her butt, but I had a knot in my throat as big as a golf ball.

Geneva noticed how quiet I was, and when the lights came up and people started to filter out, she leaned across the table and asked if I wanted to help drive Dove home and then go with them to IHOP. I didn't, not really, but I also knew I didn't want to be under my father's roof that night, not with Lucy being such a hypocrite, smiling like a snake while the wool got pulled farther and farther over Dad's eyes, so I said all right. Lucy reminded me that we were going out to Isaac's the next day for Juneteenth; she said they'd stop by and pick me up the next morning before Bailey and Geneva left for church.

I wasn't hungry, but Bailey ordered me peach pancakes anyway, and I managed to cheer up some when the food came. Geneva kept trying to draw me into conversation, and Bailey to joke me out of my silence, but I've never been too good at putting a smiley face on things, and after a while they just left me alone, although don't think I didn't see the little looks they kept shooting at each other across the table when they thought I wasn't paying attention.

We were halfway back to their house, speeding through the woods in the dark, when Geneva said, out of the blue, "You know, Denny, sometimes it's hard to talk to the people closest to you. Sometimes it's easier to ask for help from somebody who might not know you so well. Who can listen without being judgmental." And suddenly, plain as day, I could hear Aunt Dove's voice saying, "Geneva would know; you need to ask Geneva."

I unbuckled my seat belt and leaned forward between the front seats.

"That doctor you work for," I said to Geneva. "He's a ladies' doctor, right?"

"Dr. Crawford?" Geneva said. "He's an obstetrician and a gynecologist. Those are ladies' things. Why?"

"If somebody wanted to get an abortion," I said, "could they go to Dr. Crawford? Or would they have to go someplace else—like another town?"

Bailey's eyes swung around and found Geneva's in the dashboard light. "Jesus Christ," he said.

"Pull over, Bailey," Geneva ordered. "Right now."

He steered the truck onto the shoulder and brought it to a stop, letting the engine idle. They looked at each other again, then turned to face me in the backseat, where I'd sunk into the corner. My heart was tripping so fast I thought it would burst. All I knew was that I had betrayed Lucy, and that losing her goodwill was the one thing I didn't think I could stand.

"Denny," Geneva said in what I guessed must be her professional voice, "tell us the truth now. Are you in trouble?"

"*Me?*"

I nearly laughed, at the craziness of it and then the beautiful logic. How could they know that the most intimate contact I'd ever had with any male was dancing at the Round-Up, that at the ripe old age of almost-fifteen I hadn't even had my first period? It was funny, when you thought about it—except that all I felt was relief, that I still held Lucy's secret, cupped safe in my hand.

"Oh, no!" I said. "No, it isn't *me*! It's a—a friend. Someone back in Dallas. She, she thinks she might be pregnant and she doesn't know what to do."

"There are clinics," Geneva said, "in Dallas. Some very good counselors, too."

"Yes, but . . ." My brain often didn't work at the same speed as my mouth. It was a big problem. "Yes, but she can't do it there. She's afraid of someone finding out."

"Someone like her parents?" Geneva asked. "How old is your friend, Denny? Is she your age?"

"No!" I said. "She's older. A *lot* older."

She and Bailey traded another look. I saw him shake his head, just barely, side to side. They thought I was lying, which frankly didn't concern me nearly as much as them getting at the truth.

"Well," Geneva said, "Dr. Crawford couldn't help, anyway. We don't perform abortions at the clinic. The nearest place around here is Shreveport."

"How much does it cost?" I asked. "My friend doesn't know if she can come up with the money." The phrase "Quit while you're ahead" never entered my mind. I thought I was on a roll.

"It's a couple hundred dollars," Geneva said. "But really, Denny, your friend can't be involving you this way. She needs to talk to a professional. I'd be glad to set it up for her, if you like. If you'll give me her name and number, I'd be glad to have someone give her a call."

"That's okay," I said, faking a big yawn. "This is all she needs to know right now, I think. I'll tell her what you said. It's been really helpful."

I leaned my head against the headrest and closed my eyes. There was no sound in the cab but the faint whistle of Bailey's breath through his teeth. Finally he put the truck in gear, and we eased back onto the highway and rode in silence the rest of the way home.

Geneva came into the guest room just as I'd slid between the sheets in one of her borrowed nightshirts. She sat down on the edge of the mattress and put her hand in my hair, her fingertips brushing the clasp of one of Lucy's shiny barrettes.

"I know we're not your blood kin," she said. "But we'll do whatever we can for you. You just have to tell us the truth."

I could only nod. I wasn't faking now, I could barely hold my eyes open. Her hand in my hair reminded me of Ma, although Ma hadn't touched me that way in a long time.

"Okay," Geneva whispered, and I thought, just before she turned the lamp out, that I felt her lips brush against my forehead. But I may have already been dreaming.

∽

Lucy and Dad were late picking me up the next morning. Geneva and Bailey had already locked up the house to go to church and were standing beside the truck, wondering whether just to leave me there on the front porch, when the old green Buick came chugging around the corner with Dad at the wheel and pulled up to the curb. "Hop in," he called to me, tooting the horn and waving at Bailey and Geneva as they backed the pickup out of the driveway and drove off.

I climbed in back and slammed the door. Lucy grinned at me from the passenger seat, her arm stretched along the back of the seat, as Dad put the car in gear. "You look nice," she said.

I glanced down self-consciously. Geneva had loaned me a top she claimed to have outgrown twenty years ago, a white peasant-style blouse trimmed in red and yellow embroidered flowers, and I'd washed my hair in their shower with jasmine shampoo.

"Thanks," I said. "So do you." Her hair was down, and she was wearing a pink-and-white-striped sundress, and her shoulders and bare arms were light gold and sprinkled with freckles.

"All I know is," Dad said, "I've got my work cut out for me, keeping an eye on the two of you all day long."

"Oh, we can take care of ourselves," Lucy said breezily, "can't we, Denny?"

I did what I always did; I agreed with her.

The rest of the way there, Dad entertained us, I guess you'd call it, with a speech on Emancipation Day. My father loved Texas history and could talk about it for hours, whether you encouraged him or not, and he actually knew more about Juneteenth than I would have expected. The original edict, he said, was issued by President Lincoln on the first day of January 1863, but it wasn't until June 19, 1865, that General Granger arrived in Galveston to let the slaves in Texas know they were free. Nobody knew for sure, Dad said, how it was that it stayed such a well-protected secret for two and a half years after the rest of the country knew, though it was obviously to the wealthy slave owners' advantage to keep the news to themselves, but it seemed to me like one more insult—that those people deserved some kind of reward for the years when, by law, they were free but no one got around to telling them. But how did you pay back something like that? Time is the one thing you can never get back when it's gone.

I wish I could say that the history lesson boosted my confidence, but by the time we got to Isaac's, I was a mess of nerves. I had never been so conscious of the color of my skin, getting out of the car with Dad and Lucy, wading into a crowd of dark faces. My whole life I'd gone to school with kids of every color; probably a third of my eighth-grade class was black. But I had never interacted much with those kids, never really felt welcomed or understood. I'd never thought about that before, but I did now. I wasn't completely convinced no one would call me out and ask me to account for the actions of my ancestors in 1863.

Isaac came over and helped Dad lift a big cooler out of the trunk, and gave me a squeeze on the shoulder and Lucy a hug. People were arriving by the carload, swarming around the yard and porch of the small frame house, carrying armloads of food and babies, while kids of every size ran screaming through the grass like wild Indians. Over at the edge of the clearing, I could see the pit in the ground, could smell the cooking meat, and my mouth started to water. Then I saw the guitars on the porch piled up like Christmas presents, and I forgot about food.

Rose came out of the house carrying a covered dish. "Did you ever?" she asked, sweeping her chin to indicate the size of the crowd. "Every year I say I'm not doin' this again, and every year I get roped into it, somehow." She smiled at Isaac, who was snatching up one of their little boys as he darted by.

"Well, we're glad you did," Lucy said. "Can I give you a hand?" She reached for the dish Rose cradled against her belly, which Rose gave over gratefully.

"Law," Rose said, "I believe I may up and have this baby even before the party gets goin' good." She and Lucy walked off together toward a long table spread with a checked cloth and covered with platters and bowls.

I trailed after them for a while, looking over the food, smelling the mingling aromas. "Try this," Rose said, handing me a buttermilk biscuit so flaky it practically fell apart in my hand. She laughed at my expression as it dissolved in my mouth. "Here, have another."

Dad and Isaac were the ones to start up the music. They sat down on the porch on a couple of folding chairs, Dad taking his guitar out of its case, Isaac producing a beat-up blond Yamaha, and before too long they were honking and wailing away on "Got My Mojo Working." They hadn't done two verses before some other men joined them, one with a string bass, one on mouth harp, and the third with nothing to add but his loud, deep voice, shouting out the lines of the chorus in a call and response that got the people in the yard to stop what they were doing—setting out food, chasing after kids—and hollering out, too.

It lasted about ten minutes, and by the time it was over, there were a dozen men up there with guitars and other instruments, all sweating and laughing, clapping each other on the back. Dad looked, if you'll pardon the expression, like a pig in shit. The man on Isaac King's front porch that afternoon seemed to have nothing to do with the one I knew from the stage at the Round-Up, wooing the drunks and the dancers with his silky voice and his clever lines. It seemed like all he wanted was what he had right then, to be one of those happy, blended voices, raised in celebration.

More and more players joined in—accordion, banjo, even bongo drums—and I sneaked closer to the porch as the afternoon went on, until I felt brave enough to sit on the grass right down front, at the feet of a couple of old ladies in their Sunday best with paper plates balanced on their laps, sipping sweet tea and nodding their heads to the music. Lucy came over and handed me a plate heaped with barbecue and beans and mashed potatoes, which she made me take even when I said I wasn't hungry. "Honestly," she said, looking down at me, "sometimes I see so much of him in you, it scares the bejesus out of me." And she went back and took her place in a circle of shade trees with some of the other ladies.

One of the old women sitting nearby leaned out of her lawn chair and flapped her hand at me. "Why, you'd be Ash Farrell's little girl. I seen you before but I didn't make the connection."

"Yes, ma'am." I was white like he was but not good-looking like he was, was what I guessed she meant.

"Goodness, I remember your daddy from when he wasn't yay high," the lady said, holding her hand about a foot off the ground. "His mama and I used to work down to the feed mill together, right after his daddy run off. I guess she musta had that little boy underfoot more than she knowed what to do with, or maybe he just reminded her too much of her old man. Oh, that Frank, handsome as Rock Hudson and worthless as the day is long!

"Anyway, she come a little undone, I guess you'd say, and that's when they took her down to Rusk, and the county put the baby to stay with that family, who was they, Ona?" The other woman was either deaf or ignoring her. "He was a right pistol, your daddy, always into somethin' or other. We was all surprised he stuck around here long enough to finish school, though a course his mama was back by then, not that he ever set foot in her house again. Then, when he come back for good after he took off to Dallas, why, you coulda knocked this whole town over with a feather. That's where you come in, I reckon. He's done real good for hisself, though, ain't he? Got him a house and steady work, and singin' down at Dub Crookshank's place, and a real nice girl, too, Patsy Hatch's youngest, that lost her husband." She eased off one shoe to massage a swollen heel.

I took a swallow from the plastic cup of iced tea in my hand. "His mama," I said. "Whatever happened to her?"

The lady glanced up from her poor puffed-up foot to look at her companion, who shrugged, as if to say, You opened this can of worms, you dish it up. "Why, she's still 'round, last I heard," the first lady said, stuffing her foot back into the shoe like a sausage into a casing. "Livin' out at her peoples' old fishing camp, over toward White Pine. Used to come into town ever so often, take some money outta the bank, drive around with her nose in the air, like she's too good for the rest of us." She studied me for a second or two. "You mean your daddy never took you to meet your grandma?"

"I thought she was dead." But I realized as I said it that he had never once talked about his childhood to me, and that I had never asked.

"Aw, she's alive enough, last time we seen her. Mean as a bear and crazy as a loon. If your daddy's been keepin' you outta her hair, I guess he got his reasons."

The musicians launched into an old hymn, "Touch the Hem of His Garment," like the lazy pace might cool things down a little, and I was just about to get up and look for Lucy and some more iced tea, when a new face came out the front door and took his place among the players, nodding all around, settling a fiddle on his shoulder. He was taller and younger than anybody else up there, but the thing that stood out most was the way he was dressed—like someone not just older, but from an older time, in a necktie and high-waisted pants and suspenders. He touched the bow to the fiddle, and with a nod from Isaac fell in and started to play.

All around the yard, conversations died, fans stopped flapping, little kids quit running wild and stood still to listen to what came out of the fiddle, like poured honey, like it had all the sweetness in the world down inside it. For a minute I forgot the heat, the crowd, even the boy holding the fiddle; it was almost like I couldn't see the player for the gleam of the music, the way it bobbed and weaved in and around the other instruments and the voices, shining its light on them. I hadn't developed that quality yet myself, of knowing when to hold back, but I knew it was what separated the best musicians from the ordinary ones. *Amen*, the grandmas next to me shouted out when his solo ended, but the boy just blended back into the group as simply as he'd come forward, and after one last token verse and chorus, the song ended.

Nobody seemed to want to follow that performance, and the musicians decided to take a break. I'd lost sight of the fiddler, so I got up and tagged after Dad for a while, admiring the easy way he moved through the crowd. I thought if there was anything of value I could take from my father that summer, it would be to learn to copy that ease, the way he always managed to adjust himself to his circumstances. I knew I had a long way to go.

At the food table he glanced back and caught me following him, and for half a second his face took on its old cloudiness and I thought I was in trouble, but just as quickly it softened again.

"You having a good time?" he asked as I squeezed in line next to him and he picked up a paper plate.

I nodded, watching him fork meat onto his plate. I was dying to ask him about my grandmother, but this didn't seem like the place. "When does the music start up again?"

"Oh, after everybody's had a chance to get the feeling back in their fingers, I guess. You know, Denny," he said, "there are plenty of kids here your age. Wouldn't you like to meet a few, maybe make some friends?"

A hot wave of dread washed over me. It had nothing to do with the fact that I was one of three white folks out of a hundred. It was that, white or black or any color of the rainbow, I was the same girl I'd always been, shy and tubby, plain as a paper bag. How could I explain this to my father, who wore his confidence the way he wore his looks, like he knew it would always pave his way? I was shocked by the tang of hate I felt for him, sour and brassy on my tongue.

"Hey, Curtis!" Dad called to a man I recognized as one of the musicians, a couple of places ahead of us in line. "Your girls here today?"

"Oh, sure, they're around someplace," Curtis said, helping himself to three or four squares of cornbread. "That Rhonda, I can't make her stay still for nothin'." He saw me and smiled. "Why, hello," he said.

"Curtis, this is my daughter, Denny. I was hoping she might meet some of the other kids. You think you could introduce her to your two?"

Curtis handed over his plate to a woman in jeans and a tube top, saying, "Hold that for me a minute, will you, sweet pea?" and motioned with his chin that I should come with him. I couldn't even look at Dad, I was so mad. I shot a beseeching glance at Lucy as we passed, but she was talking to somebody and didn't see me.

There were four girls sitting in a row on the tailgate of someone's new truck, two of whom Curtis introduced as his daughters, Rhonda and Angel. The younger one, Angel, was a little bit like me, ordinary and kind of baby-fat, but I knew at first glance that her big sister was another story, her long legs in cutoff shorts, hair in a smooth, shoulder-length flip. With one slow blink of her green-shadowed eyes, she sized me up and got ready to file me under "Not Worth the Trouble."

I don't know what they'd been doing when Curtis and I interrupted, but as he went back to the food they studied me and each other with cagey, sideways looks.

"So," Rhonda said, examining her fingernails, "you're Ash's girl." *Seeing as you're white as Crisco,* I heard between the lines, though I wasn't that impressed with her powers of deduction. "Where you come from after all this time? We never seen you before."

"Him and my mom got divorced when I was two," I said. "I lived with her in Dallas. Till now," I added, I didn't know why.

"That your new mama?" Rhonda asked, and we all looked across the yard at Lucy, who stood in the circle of Dad's arm wearing an expression that made me want to shout out in warning, the way you do in horror movies when you know the heroine is about to make a fatal mistake.

"I guess so," I said. "I mean, I guess they're thinking about it."

"Better think quick," she said. "Baby on the way, Rose says. And if there's anybody knows about babies, it's Rose."

I was trying to think up a retort for this when a new voice said, "Excuse me. Denise?"

I looked up, and up. He seemed to be all limbs, legs and arms and long, thin fingers, the same fingers I'd seen working the frets of his fiddle like it was a thing he knew better than his very own name.

"How do you do," he said with a nod. "I'm Erasmus King."

He was the same color as chocolate milk, with the whitest teeth I'd ever seen. Under his close-shorn hair his ears stuck out a little. I slid

off the tailgate, onto my feet. Maybe it was a combination of that nod
and his last name, but something about him seemed to demand a royal
response, and I guess I must have bowed a little, because he laughed.
All my life I'd wondered what the word "mellifluous" meant, and now
I knew.

Rhonda hooted. "What're you talkin' about, Erasmus! Nobody here
but plain old Raz."

He ignored her. "I saw you down front," he said to me. "You looked
like you were in church."

There was so much going through my head at once I could barely
process it. He was a foot taller than me, easy, though maybe not so
much older, a year or two. The sleeves of his button-down shirt were
neatly rolled to the joints of his elbows, and on his feet he wore polished wing-tip shoes. It was summertime in Texas and way too hot for
such a getup, but Erasmus King looked as cool as jazz.

"Your dad sent me over to say hello," he went on. "I've known him
just about forever. I guess I started sitting in with him and my uncle
when I was six or seven, over at my grandfolks' place in Rodessa."

"Your uncle?"

"Isaac," he said. "His brother J.D.'s my dad. My folks split up way
back. I live in Dallas with my mom."

I could feel my jaw hanging like a trapdoor. "I— Mine, too. I mean,
I do, too."

"Yeah?" He seemed interested, if not amazed, by this coincidence,
but then I, even in my borrowed peasant shirt and fresh-washed hair,
probably didn't make the first impression on Erasmus King that he had
on me. "Where do you go to school?" he asked.

"I'll be a freshman at Patterson in the fall." I'd forgotten completely
that, not five minutes before, I'd been hinting to Curtis's girls that I
meant to stay in Mooney. "What about you?"

"I'm on scholarship at Beaux-Arts," he said. "Junior year."

"Oh." My heart had leapt up and was beating its wings against my
collarbone, making it hard to breathe. Beaux-Arts was where the gifted
and talented kids went, the ones who went on to study at Julliard and
Princeton and the Rhode Island School of Design. *I know you,* I wanted

to say; *I'm one, too.* But I couldn't do it, it wasn't the place and I didn't have the words. It made me nervous, the way he was looking at me, and I glanced around at the other girls, saw the younger ones poking each other with their elbows, Queen Rhonda staring at me with her eyes so hot I'm surprised my hair didn't catch fire.

"You want a Coke?" He reached into a cooler in the back of the truck and handed me one, the old-fashioned green glass bottle beaded with condensation, full of ice slivers.

"They really call you Raz?"

He smiled. "I tried taking back my given name when I got to school in Dallas, but here at home, I can't seem to shake it."

"I'm Denny, by the way," I said, "not Denise."

"Well, it's good to know you, by any name," he said, and held out his hand, and we shook. His palm was damp, from the Coke, but otherwise he looked as fresh as talcum.

The guitars and squeeze boxes and mouth organs were being taken up again. At the first chord from Dad's guitar, the G string as always just a little flat, Erasmus said he had to get going. He rolled his Coke bottle across his forehead—the only sign I saw that he felt the weather like the rest of us—and said he'd see us later.

Rhonda pushed herself off the tailgate and stood staring down at me, in cork-heeled sandals and a blouse tied in a knot at her rib cage. Someday she would make some man—maybe more than one man— wish he'd never been born.

"Hey, girl."

I thought about Erasmus King, and straightened my spine. "My name is Denny."

"Denny. You better think about where you're fixin' to step."

"What are you talking about?"

"Watch those feet, is all I'm saying." She turned to her sister and their friends. "This party's a big bore. Who feels like dancing?"

The girls jumped up and headed toward the house, tugging down their shorts in back, plucking at their hair.

Rhonda stopped and looked back at me. "You coming, or you need a printed invitation?"

I didn't stop to think twice but ran, along with the others, to the grassy clearing in front of the porch as the musicians swung into "Baby Scratch My Back" and the sky above us scrolled from blue to purple to deep, satiny black, wheeling with stars, more stars than surely a human eye had ever seen, while down below on earth we whirled and raised our arms to heaven, one body with separate, beating hearts, on Emancipation Day.

⚮

The party really might have gone on till morning, like Dad said, except that just before midnight, Rose's water broke. Right in the middle of "Crawlin' Kingsnake," somebody started shouting, and one instrument at a time the music died off, everybody looking around and murmuring in confusion, and then here came Rose, with her mama on one side and another lady on the other, waddling slow and stiff-legged up through the yard, toward the house. "I hope y'all ain't quittin' on my account," she said as Isaac jumped down from the porch and started to help her up the steps. But right then her eyes got wide and her whole face pulled tight, like someone had turned a screw behind it, and they went on in the house and things started breaking up. I was sorry; I'd been having a fine time, dancing with Curtis's girls and sneaking glances at Erasmus King and hoping it would last all night.

"Why do we have to leave?" I asked when Lucy came around to collect me. Dad was still up on the porch with the rest of the musicians, though they were starting to pack up the guitars and fold up the chairs. "I'm not one bit tired."

"Rose is getting ready to have a baby. Don't you think she's entitled to a little peace and quiet?"

"They're going to the hospital, though, aren't they?"

Lucy laughed. "Not everybody goes to the hospital to have a baby."

"You mean she's having it *here*? At *home*?"

But it made sense, when I thought about it; once you'd done it six times, it was probably like falling off a log, and that seemed to me even more reason to let the party go on, that Rose might just as soon be surrounded by people laughing and playing music. How I felt about it didn't seem to count, though. Lucy headed off to gather up our things, and I hung around the porch, hoping Dad wouldn't notice and feeling foolish till I managed to catch Erasmus's eye and then trying to act like that wasn't what I'd had in mind the whole time.

He came down the porch steps, his fiddle under his arm. "I've seen a lot of parties get busted up for a lot of reasons, but this one beats them all," he said. "I was watching you dancing with Rhonda and those."

My backbone prickled. "So?"

"Nothing. You looked like you were having a good time, that's all."

"Yeah, well, white people need fun, too," I said. I didn't plan it to come out the way it did, and we both started laughing at how it sounded, like something you'd see on a bumper sticker.

He shifted his fiddle to the other arm. "How long are you here for?"

"I guess just long enough to load up the car."

"No, I meant this summer. Are you staying awhile or going back to Dallas?"

"I'm supposed to be here till the end of August," I said. "My mom won't take my dad's phone calls, though. So I guess it's sort of up in the air."

"Well, I'm here all summer," he said. "Maybe I'll see you around."

Leave it to Dad to pick that exact moment to come lumbering across the yard carrying his guitar case, grinning like a fool and stinking of beer. He clapped Erasmus on the back of the neck with his free hand.

"Look at this kid," he said happily, to no one in particular. "The first time I saw him he didn't even come up to my knee. And now—"

"And now you don't even come up to *my* knee," Erasmus said, slipping Dad's embrace, smiling in embarrassment.

"Where'd you learn to play like that?" Dad asked. "You were pretty good when you were just a squirt, but . . . Hey, maybe I'll take you with me to Nashville! How'd you like that? Didja hear I'm going to Nashville?"

"I didn't know it was for sure," Erasmus said, cutting his eyes at me.

"It isn't," I said. "He's drunk. Dad, you're drunk."

He put his arm around me. "So what if I am? What a day! What a fine, fine day! Thank you, Mr. Abraham Lincoln!"

"We better go," I said to Erasmus. Before we get any whiter, I thought to myself; before we start taking the credit not just for Mr. Lincoln but for Martin Luther King Jr. and Nelson Mandela, maybe even Jesus and the apostles.

I managed to turn Dad around and point him toward the driveway. It was like piloting a stubborn little boat, one that wanted to go with the tide of fancy and not where it ought to for its own good. I looked back over my shoulder at Erasmus as we bobbed and weaved, saw him watching us with a regretful look on his face. I was pretty sure I knew what he was thinking.

But then, right before I turned away, I saw his mouth move.

It said, "See you."

14

Lucy

 I knew Ash had been drinking all day, but it wasn't till I saw Denny steering him toward the car and heard him singing "I'm Happy Working for the Lord" at the top of his lungs that I realized just how much beer he'd really had. He stowed his guitar and the empty cooler in the trunk and got into the passenger seat as I slid behind the wheel and Denny climbed in back and cranked the window down. There was a heat coming off her like a fever.

But Ash, in a haze of Bud Light and goodwill, didn't seem to notice.

"Hey," he said, twisting halfway in the seat to look at Denny as I navigated the winding driveway out to the main road, "you sure were cutting the old rug out there tonight."

"'Cutting the rug'?" she said. "You make it sound like a bunch of old farts."

"That's me," Ash replied cheerfully. "An old fart." In the backseat Denny gave an indecipherable snort. "How did you and Curtis's girls get along?"

"Okay."

"What'd you think of Raz? Kid's something else, isn't he? Smart as a whip, plays like an angel. Even if he does dress like he raided his granddaddy's closet."

"Yeah, he was nice." Her voice was practically inaudible, and there was a wistful note in it I didn't think most men, even sober, would have heard.

So I was surprised when Ash said, "What?" He slung his arm over the seat back. "Tell me what's on your mind, baby girl. Talk to me."

"How come you never told me about my grandmother?"

I took my eyes off the road long enough to glance at him, but his face was inscrutable, like it was hewn of wood.

"Nothing to tell," he said.

"That's not what I heard," Denny said. "I heard she's living over in White—"

"Denise," Ash cut in, "I don't think you understand me. There is nothing to say on that particular subject, all right? Not now, not ever."

"But I don't—"

"Denny," I said, and she gave a little bark of disgust and threw herself against the seat back in a dramatic fashion, and we followed the slashing white line on the highway without speaking, the rest of the way home.

As we pulled into the yard, the dogs came scooting out from under the porch and ran a couple of circuits around the car. Ash opened the trunk and set the cooler in the dirt. Denny got out, moving light on her feet. I could still smell her shampoo as she passed me, that and something else, something I didn't recognize and couldn't put a name to. She didn't call out good night or anything else as she let herself in the front door, letting the screen bang shut behind her.

I went into the bedroom and unzipped my sundress and slipped into my robe. Ash came in a minute or so later and shut the door.

"You sleepy?"

"Not really. A little."

"Well, what do you say? You want to break out the José Cuervo and the Hank Williams records and have us our own little party? Or how about we head down to the creek—Flat Creek, down behind Dub's place? Like we used to last spring? Spread out our blanket on that big old rock and see what happens?"

I laughed and shook my head. But I felt a pang at the mention of Flat Creek. I'd gotten it into my head, through a combination of tricky math and superstition, that that blanket at Flat Creek was the reason I was in the mess I was in now, weaving myself deeper in a skein of lies every minute of every day.

"So what about it?" Ash said to my reflection in the bureau mirror. "You up for a little Hank and José?"

I studied his face as it floated over my shoulder, the familiar planes and contours reversed, everything the opposite of what I'd known. My memories of our night at Flat Creek were crystal clear: the scratchy wool blanket and the cool flat rock beneath, Ash's body in the moon-light and the sensation of opening to him, opening and being filled with a shower of silver stars. Well. I'd had a little whiskey, I admit. But I was convinced the stars had been real, as real as the rock and the moonlight, and so, too, was the end result.

He stepped up behind me and put his hands on my shoulders. "I was thinking tonight, Luce, what things could be like in a couple years, if this Nashville deal comes through. We can get the hell out of Dodge. Sell the house, pack us a couple of knapsacks, and take off. See the whole country from the back of a tour bus, maybe. Just you and me. Wouldn't that be something?"

"Sell the house? *This* house?"

"Well, yeah. What do we need to be tied down here for? I mean, sure, maybe later, when we're old and feeble and need a place to sit on the porch and watch the sunset. But, hell, we're young, both of us. Why not just grab what we can, while we've got the chance?"

"*If,*" I reminded him. "*If* we get the chance." But the words felt lodged against my windpipe like bits of gravel.

Ash's hands dropped to his sides. "You don't think it's gonna hap-pen, do you?" he said. "You think it's all a big joke. Tony Amate and Arcadia records and all of it."

"No, Ash, I don't think it's a joke. It'll happen. I know it." In fact, I hadn't known till I heard in my own voice how surely I believed it.

"You don't want it to, though."

"I just— I guess I think it's not that simple."

"Well, why isn't it? Why isn't it simple?"

"Have you thought about Denny? What about her?"

"Denny's here for the summer, Lucy. Only till I can get her god-damned wing nut of a mother to take her back to Dallas."

I'd started to twist the sash of my robe, rolling the ends into plaits and then letting them unfurl. "I guess I was hoping different."

"Different, how? You mean you want her to *stay*? Permanent?" I didn't answer him, just kept twisting and twisting the sash. "Jesus, do you hear what you're saying? We'd be full-time parents!"

"I know."

"Well, hell! I thought we agreed when we first took up together that neither one of us wanted that."

"I never said that! I never said I didn't want it! I just said I—that I didn't think it was possible."

"Because you can't get pregnant, you mean."

I shrugged, watching Ash's face as the fog of alcohol burned off and something clean and sharp below the surface began to show through.

"You did say that, did you not?" he said. "At your kitchen table, the morning after the first night we spent together, didn't you look me straight in the eye and tell me you couldn't have a baby?" I nodded. "So, it seems pretty black-and-white to me. Either you can get preg-nant or you can't. Lucy?" He pronounced my name like he was trying to cleave it with his teeth.

"Well, I can," I said. "I mean—I did. I am."

He sat down on the bed, then stood up again.

"You are shitting me," he said.

I almost laughed then at the way things kept turning back to bite me, the way my Harlequin-romance expectations went on dying hard. Weren't expectant fathers supposed to fall on their knees when they heard the news, weren't they supposed to guide you to a chair and insist you put your feet up, bring you flowers and magazines and pickles and ice cream, rub your back, nuzzle their faces against your belly in awe at the miracle of procreation? You'd think I'd have managed to tamp down those expectations, to have realized by now that Ash was not a man I could put in a mold. Still, in my own dumb way, I'd hoped for better than "You're shitting me."

He looked sober now, in every sense of the word. "But you— You said—"

"Stop telling me what I said! I know what I said!"

"So, you lied?"

"No!" I raised my palm. "As God is my witness. I thought it was true."

"You said you were infertile! At some point, a doctor told you this, right?"

"Not exactly."

"Jesus! What does that mean, 'not exactly'?"

"It means— Well, Mitchell just made me believe it, somehow."

"Your *husband* Mitchell?"

"He never *said* so, not the words! It was just, just something he made me *feel*. That all the time we were married and I never got pregnant, it was my fault."

Ash turned toward the mirror and slid his hands through his hair. "Jesus H. Christ on the cross," he said. He caught my reflected gaze and held it. "How long have you known about this?"

"Not too long."

"An hour? A day? Because anything else is too long."

"A couple of weeks. Since Denny came. I found out that day."

He turned to face me. Who was this, I wondered, someone whose features I'd memorized with my eyes and my fingertips, someone I thought I knew better than I'd ever known a living soul? There was no trace of my sweet Ash in this face, no sign of the man who'd laid me down on a wool blanket under a sky of silver stars, the moon on his shoulders and the whole wide world in his eyes.

"Quit looking at me that way!" I said. "You act like I'm some, some kind of criminal. It was a mistake!" Terrible word; wrong word. "No, I—I didn't *mean* for it to happen. I didn't *know*!"

Ash swept his keys off the bureau; they landed with a heavy-metal clank in the palm of his hand.

"Let me tell you something, Lucy," he said. "I made a mistake, too, once. It's lying right on the other side of this door, right now, just as real as can be. Do you understand that? Do you know what it means?"

The tread of his boots heading out of the room and down the hall was heavy, deliberate, giving me an opportunity, I knew, to run after him, to plead with him not to go, at the very least not to drive after he'd been drinking. I didn't do it, though. My heart felt like a plank.

I listened to the sound of his engine grinding, struggling to turn over. After a minute or two, the front door banged and his footsteps came back up the hall. I guessed he didn't care if he woke up Denny, or maybe he figured she was awake already, listening to every ugly thing that passed between us, including but not limited to the word "mistake."

He loomed in the doorway, his anger making him seem larger, drunker than before. "Where are your keys?"

"Excuse me?"

"My goddamned truck won't start. I need your keys."

Was he kidding me? Let him go out and total my car, and kill himself in the process? If there was any justice, I'd get to do it with my own two hands. But then, who would I sue for child support? I saw my life unfolding before me: the welfare office, the courthouse, *The Jerry Springer Show*. No, if somebody had to leave, it might as well be me.

At the back of the bedroom closet was an empty box I'd used to carry my clothes and belongings, one load at a time, from my rent house to Ash's over the course of the first weeks we were together. I pulled it out and set it on the bed, then opened a bureau drawer. How to decide what, in a single trip, to carry? When time was of the essence and I didn't know if, much less when, I'd be back? I had to nudge Ash out of my way in order to navigate between the bureau and the bed. "Could you step aside, please? You're slowing me down."

"Now hang on just a minute," Ash said as I scooped up an armload of underthings and dropped them into the box. "How did *I* get to be the bad guy here? What did I do?"

"Let's see." I turned to him, hands on my hips. "You called me a liar, for starters. Then you tried to run off. The only reason you're standing here right now is because your truck won't start." He glanced down, guilty as charged. "You act like this is all something I did on purpose, Ash, to mess up your big plan. But what about *my* plan? You know what? I don't think you care. I think you want to ride around the countryside with a bunch of girls screaming and tossing their panties at you, and I don't think there's a place for me. Not for me, or Denny, and sure as hell not for a baby."

"Are you done?"

"No, I'm not! How dare you suggest I'd do this to, to catch you, or trap you, or ruin your life! How dare you act like I haven't thought about the consequences! I loved you, and I gave myself to you, and this is what came of it! You can call it a mistake, or you can call it a miracle. Do you want to know why it was so hard for me to tell you? Because for two whole weeks I've been scared to death you'd look me in the eye and say, 'You're shitting me.'"

He watched in silence from the doorway as I tossed in a set of electric rollers, two pairs of jeans I wouldn't be able to button in a month. I found the photo I kept tucked away of my late husband, Mitchell, and I slipped that in, too.

I picked up my box and brushed past Ash, leaving a scattered trail of socks and hair clips behind me. I had my purse, my keys. I was still in my robe, but I didn't figure it was likely I'd see anybody I knew on the highway in the middle of the night, and I didn't feel like pausing to get dressed, didn't want to take a chance on breaking my momentum.

Denny sat up on the couch as I made my way in the dark through the living room. "What's going on?"

"Nothing," Ash said. "Go back to sleep."

He followed me as far as the front steps while I shoved the box into the trunk of the Buick, but when I looked back at him over my shoulder, he reconsidered what he'd been about to say and just stood there with his mouth hanging open.

I whistled for Steve Cropper, who jumped into the backseat with his tongue lolling, delirious as always to be going for a ride. Just as I was shutting the door, Booker jumped in, too, and ran across to the passenger-side window and stuck his head out, barking with anticipation.

"Hey!" Ash yelled, but I was starting up the engine and acted like I couldn't hear him. My feet were bare, dusty from the yard, the pedal cool and solid under my sole as I pressed it down. I wrestled the car into Drive, and didn't look back.

The rent house was stifling after being closed up for so long, and I went around throwing open windows and turning on fans, feeling a welcome rush of coolness come off the grove out back, the heavy scent of roses drifting in from the front porch. The kitchen clock said ten after one. I wasn't one bit sleepy, but in a perverse way I could only blame on hormones, I was hungry.

I sat on my front porch step in my robe and dirty feet, eating cold kidney beans out of a can, feeling mosquitoes feasting on my bare limbs, and listening to the dogs rustling around under the house. Two new rules, I swore to myself, from this day forward: absolute truth and decent nutrition. In the morning I would make a list, go to the grocery store, call Dr. Crawford's office and set up an appointment.

Meanwhile, the beans tasted wonderful, thick and soupy. I sat in my little pocket of heat and dark, slapping at my arms and legs and scanning the skies for the North Star, the one my aunt Dove had taught my brothers and me to locate and wish on every night before bed. Inside the house the phone rang—eight times, ten—then stopped. I got to my feet, stretched, wished on the brightest star I could find; it might not have been the right one, but it was the only one I could find. Then I went inside and made up the bed and lay down and waited for morning.

15

Denny

 I had a pretty good idea what happened that night. I was wide awake anyway, thinking about the picnic and the dancing, and the way the sound of Erasmus King's fiddle had spilled out over the yard all sweet and gold, like something you'd serve over pancakes right off the stove. I heard their voices behind the bedroom door, rising and falling and then rising again, and even though I could just make out a few words, I figured it could only mean one thing.

Why she chose then, that night, to tell him, I didn't know. Maybe she thought the beer and the party would've softened him up, or maybe the fact of Rose and Isaac's new baby brought it up. She must have thought it would come out differently than it did, though, and not ending up with everybody clomping up and down the hallway in the dark, slamming doors and firing up their engines like the Daytona 500. Dad stayed outside, on the porch, a long time after she left. I guess I drifted off, finally; I halfway heard him crossing the floor, the bedroom door latching behind him, and then what seemed like minutes later the sky leaking all watery and yellow through the curtains over my head.

I got up and pulled on my clothes and went into the kitchen, where the red light on the Mr. Coffee was on, the pot half empty. I found Dad in the yard, the hood of the truck up and his hands black to the wrists with grease. I let the front door slam behind me, and he jerked his head up and glared at me. I was pretty sure I knew a hangover when I saw one.

"What are you doing? Where's Lucy?" I asked, tearing the wrapper off a Pop-Tart.

"Christ, don't shout," he said, even though I hadn't. "Piece of shit Chevy," he muttered, peering into the mess under the hood. "There's more crust in here than a loaf of Wonder bread." He picked up a blue-striped mug off the running board and took a swig.

"Look, I heard y'all last night," I said. "It's no use acting like nothing happened."

"Goddamn it, I know I have jumper cables around here someplace. Look at these terminals, would you? It looks like they came off the goddamned *Titanic*."

"Dad?"

I'd been about to say how jumper cables weren't much good if all you had was one vehicle, but when he raised his head again, slow and stiff, and looked at me, I thought he looked as glum as it is possible for a human being to look, his face creased and unshaved, his eyes blood-shot. "Can you cut me a little slack, please?" he said. "Last night was bad, and today isn't starting out any better. My woman ran off, she took my dog, my truck won't start . . ."

I had to work to keep my face straight. "Sounds like a country-western song to me."

"And one more thing—my daughter's a smart-ass."

"Where'd Lucy go?"

"That would be hard to say for sure." He swirled his coffee, drained it, stared into the empty mug. "She didn't slow down long enough to leave a forwarding address."

"I guess she must've really been mad."

"I'll tell you what she is. You're gonna hear it anyhow, so I might as well tell you. She's pregnant."

"You're just now figuring that out?" I finished my Pop-Tart in four quick bites and crumpled the wrapper in my hand.

"What are you talking about?"

"You're the one who claimed you'd know by looking at her. Ma did, and that was just from seeing her the one time."

He stood there opening and closing his mouth, like a fish.

"You mean you knew about this? You and your mother both?"

"Uh-huh. I'm pretty sure Aunt Dove does, too. And Rose, and Curtis's girls at the picnic . . . It looks like you're just about the end of the line."

He gave up trying to make sense of things and sat down on the running board, his neck drooping and his head sagging between his knees. He looked whipped, but I wasn't so sure. It would've been just like him to be running tunes through his head, rhyming up "baby" and "maybe."

Just then I heard the sound of an engine turning off the highway onto Little Hope Road. "Who's that?" I asked as a heavy-duty truck with a flatbed and a winch came into view, lumbering through the dust and the potholes.

"I called Isaac's brother J.D. for a jump. Raz answered the phone. Seems everybody's still over at Isaac's, passed out, so he said he'd come."

"You mean that's Erasmus King?"

Without waiting for an answer, I turned and ran for the house. I splashed my face with water, stuck a toothbrush in my mouth just long enough to substitute the taste of Colgate for Pop-Tart, ran a brush through my hair, and pinned it back from my face with the sparkly barrettes Lucy had given me. My shirt was pretty grungy, but at least it was clean, and it was all I could manage on such short notice. At the last second I picked up my Whisper Pink lipstick and slicked it over my mouth.

The whole thing took less than two minutes, so by the time I made it back to the front yard, Erasmus was still lining up his dad's truck nose to nose with the pickup. After some more maneuvering, he opened the door and swung down, wearing a pair of dark blue coveralls that said DARNELL in stitched red letters over the breast pocket. They were too short for him at the wrists and the ankles and sagged like a parachute everywhere else. He grinned when he saw me and I grinned back at the sight he made.

"Boy, you saved my life," Dad said. "Seeing you drive up is about the only thing that's gone my way since yesterday."

"Oh, yeah, why's that?"

"Don't get him going," I warned Erasmus. "He'll start telling you his sad story and he'll never stop."

"You looked pretty happy last night," Erasmus said, opening the back of the truck and taking out a set of jumper cables.

Dad shook his head gloomily. "Did you ever feel like there was a real turning point in your life? I mean, a moment you could look back at and say, 'There—that's where it all went to hell?'"

"He's a kid, Dad. I told you," I said to Erasmus, who was standing there holding the cables and looking nervous.

"Come on, let's get this crap heap running," Dad said. "I've got stuff to do, and I can't do it without wheels."

Together they clamped the jumper cables to the battery terminals, and Erasmus got into the tow truck and cranked it up. The big engine roared, and Dad turned the pickup's key and after two or three clicks the motor coughed and sputtered, and a big cloud of blue-black smoke came shooting out of the tailpipe. They gave each other the thumbs-up through the windshields, and Dad sat there revving the motor for a couple of minutes while Erasmus got out and unhooked the cables and stowed them back in the wrecker.

Dad gestured at me and I walked over to the pickup, fanning the exhaust from my face. "I'm going to Wal-Mart to stick a new battery in this thing," he said. "Then I'm—well, I don't know what I'm gonna do. I've got my pager. You call me if Lucy shows up, or if she calls. If you hear anything. *Anything*, you understand me?" I nodded my head, even though I think we were both pretty sure what the chances of that happening were.

Erasmus was standing next to the tow truck, and Dad motioned him over, too. "Tell your daddy I'll write him a check for the jump tomorrow, okay? Meanwhile, this'll cover your trouble." He slipped a ten-dollar bill out of his billfold and passed it through the window.

Erasmus shook his head. "I can't take that, man. My dad'd kill me."

"Take it and shut up about it. Consider it your reward for being the only person who survived yesterday sober." Erasmus smiled and folded the money in his palm. Dad sat looking at him for a second or two as the pickup chugged. "How old are you, Raz?"

"Sixteen."

"Let me give you a piece of advice, okay? Steer clear of women. I've been mixed up with them since I was younger than you, and nothing good has ever come of it. Not one thing."

"Thanks a lot," I said, but he was gunning the motor again. "You kids behave," he yelled out the window as he wrenched the transmission into first and roared off up the road, trailing a cloud of sooty smoke behind him.

Erasmus and I stood side by side in the yard, watching him go. It was a hot, bright late June morning, the sky as smooth and blue as a platter. Cicadas hummed in the pine trees, and dust floated over the surface of the road in a red haze.

"What was that about?" Erasmus asked finally, when things were quiet again.

I gave him the short version, pieced together from what I knew and what I was only guessing at. He listened with his head cocked, like he was trying to hear the words between the words, to puzzle out the meaning hidden there.

"You have to kind of feel sorry for him, you know?" I finished. "I mean, he thinks he's so, so cool about everything, but really, he's clueless."

"Yeah, well, that's grown-ups for you," Erasmus said. He slid the zipper of the coverall down a couple of inches, showing a dark green T-shirt underneath. "I've got a new little cousin. A boy. They named him Reverend, can you believe that? Reverend King. Hasn't anybody around here ever heard of birth control?" I smiled and shrugged, but I wasn't sure how to feel about the topic of babies just then. "Would you mind if I wash up before I take off?" He displayed his greasy palms.

I led him into the house and showed him the bathroom, where Dad kept a big bar of Lava in a dish by the sink. After a minute or so, Erasmus came out of the bathroom with the coveralls folded over his arm. His T-shirt looked brand-new, his jeans pressed. On his feet were a pair of basketball shoes that looked like scaled-down space stations.

"I can't believe this place," he said, his eyes scanning the living room. I looked around, too, trying to see it like a stranger would. The furniture didn't match and was a little worse for wear, but the room was homey and, mostly, tidy, if you ignored the stacks of CDs scattered across the rug like parade confetti. "The first time I came here I was about ten, I guess," Erasmus explained. "I remember Ash said it was a work in progress, but in all that time, nothing's changed. He's still got sheets of plastic instead of walls and the same ugly couch. The stereo's new, I guess. Hey, Harman Kardon speakers."

"He's still just got one bedroom and one bathroom, too." I gestured to my rumpled sleeping bag. "Guess who's been sleeping on the couch for three weeks. Do you want a Coke?"

I popped the tabs on two cans and poured the Coke into glasses, and added ice from the Fridgidaire's built-in dispenser. "It's kind of funny, isn't it?" Erasmus said as he took a glass from me. "That the best room in the house is the kitchen? I didn't think Ash was all that interested in cooking."

"The bedroom's nice, too," I said, then chomped down on my lip when I realized how that sounded. Erasmus was looking out the window, though, and didn't seem to hear me.

"It's pretty here," he said. "Peaceful. You can hear yourself think."

"How long did you live around here? Till your parents split up, you said."

"Yeah, when I was four. I've been back to visit every summer, though." He took a sip of Coke. "It's the weirdest place. Like a little piece of the world that got shut off from the rest. You know what I mean?" He looked at me over his shoulder. He seemed to be weighing whether or not to say what was on his mind or keep it to himself.

"What?" I said. I wanted to hear it.

"The sheriff stopped a couple guys on their way out to Uncle Isaac's place last night. They had a load of fireworks under a tarp in back, and a jug of kerosene."

"No way."

He nodded. "Maybe you've seen them in town. Skinheads, with tattoos all over?"

"Seth and Sean Butler," I said. They liked to cruise the courthouse square in a shiny Dodge pickup with a chrome skull for a hood ornament, blaring heavy-metal music out of the tape deck. I'd seen their shaved heads and homemade tattoos and figured them for small-town play actors, knocking over mailboxes and causing a ruckus.

"They hang out with an older guy by the name of Tim Spivey. Spivey was down in Huntsville for six years, for possession and theft. While he was in, he hooked up with the AB."

"The AB?"

"Aryan Brotherhood. White supremacists? The guys who like to tie black people to the bumpers of their pickup trucks for entertainment."

"You mean—the Butler brothers are tied in with this AB? *Here?* In Mooney?"

"They just about made it to Uncle Isaac's picnic. They'd been mouthing off in town, though. The sheriff heard about it and laid out for them. Caught them about half a mile from the house."

Erasmus tipped back his head and drained his Coke in several long swallows. My own mouth felt parched, like it was full of road dust.

"But it's okay now, right?" I said. "The sheriff took them to jail?"

"Driving around in a pickup full of fireworks isn't against the law. Not even for skinheads with Klan symbols carved on their arms." He turned to set his glass on the drain board.

"But I— It doesn't make any sense. How could something like that happen here?"

Erasmus studied me in the square of light that fell across the floor from the window.

"Did you ever hear the story about those little girls in Alabama who got blown up by a bomb in church? A long time ago, in the sixties?" I said I hadn't. "Well, one of the men who did it was from around here. Everybody knew he did it. He used to brag about it around town. He claimed the law couldn't touch him. And you know what? They couldn't. Because folks around here protected him. Like he was a *hero*." I swallowed, trying to scare up some spit, but there wasn't anything I could say that would be the right thing. "You think because your dad and my uncle are big buddies that this is some kind of, of fairyland. But it isn't."

"I guess you better get out of here, then." I finished my Coke and put the glass in the sink. "We shouldn't even be talking to each other, right? I mean, what's the point? You probably shouldn't even be in this kitchen." I was really mad, but I couldn't have said why, exactly.

I stood at the sink with my shoulders squared off as Erasmus walked out of the kitchen and down the hall, shutting the front door softly behind him. After a minute, I went out, too. He was standing on the porch staring out over the roof of the tow truck toward the trees.

"I better get the truck home," he said without turning around. "Sure as I'm standing here, my dad's getting paged to pull somebody out of a ditch. Look, I wasn't— I didn't mean it to sound like I was blaming you for, for how things are. It's just that, well, I get to go back to Dallas in a couple months, but my dad, my granny and granddaddy, Uncle Isaac, they've lived here their whole lives, and they won't budge. I get scared for them. Sometimes I don't think they see how it really is."

"Wait a minute," I said. "I want to show you something."

Without a bit of compunction I got Dad's guitar from its spot in the living room and carried it onto the porch. I flipped the latches and lifted it out of the case and sat down on the top step and set it across my knee, taking a second to bring the flat G string into tune. Erasmus stood leaning against the porch post, his arms folded across his chest, his face a cool blank. I closed my eyes a second, held my breath, and then I jumped in.

I sang the song Dad first played me in the truck on our way to Texarkana: "If you were a bluebird, you'd be a sad one . . ."

Afterward, I set the guitar back in its case and closed the lid. I couldn't quite name the expression on Erasmus's face, other than that he kind of looked like he'd gotten the wind knocked out of him. And then all of a sudden he smiled, puckering his chin, stretching his cheeks, winding up in crinkles at the corners of his eyes.

"Man," he said. "Oh, man, oh, man, oh, man. Why didn't you say something? Why didn't you come up on the porch yesterday at Isaac's?"

I shrugged. I felt like my face was burning up.

"I don't know. I haven't . . . I mean, nobody really knows." How could I tell him it was a piece of me I'd held on to for my own, something no one could touch so long as they didn't know it was there? How could I say it was meant as an offering, proof that we were more the same than different, where it counted, under the skin?

"Not even your dad?"

"Nope. Just you."

"Did he write that?"

"No. I learned it from him, though."

He considered this for a second. "I wish I had my fiddle," he said.

"Me, too."

"Maybe I could bring it over sometime."

I nodded. "That would be good." If you looked hard you'd have thought he was blushing, just like me.

I walked him into the yard, watched as he climbed up into the high cab and rolled the driver's-side window down, then swung the truck backwards and headed down the road, tapping the horn a couple of times on his way out. I stood there watching the dust settle, till I could hear the bugs again, the breeze ruffling the tops of the trees, thinking how the world could change in a heartbeat, while you were doing something else, while you weren't even paying attention.

I went back inside, replaced Dad's guitar case in the corner, washed the drinking glasses and dried them and put them away, then I walked down the road to Little Hope. It was so hot the stones seemed to shimmer under a bone-white sky, and the only sound was from a hive of wasps off somewhere in the trees. I found a shady spot and stretched out and replayed the morning in my head, every sweet note of that song, Erasmus's ear-to-ear smile.

Next thing I heard was Dad's pickup clattering past on the dirt road. I scrambled to my knees, shook the grass burrs out of my hair, and ran back toward the house as fast as I could go. He was getting down from the truck as I came into the yard, and I knew from the slouch in his shoulders that he hadn't found Lucy or, if he had, he hadn't made much headway.

"Isaac and Rose have a new baby." He tried to smile, but I could see it was taking everything he had. "A little boy named Reverend."

"Erasmus said the sheriff caught some white boys heading out to Isaac's last night," I said. "With fireworks and kerosene."

"Those goddamned Butlers," Dad said. "Hanging out with ex-cons, acting like their great-great-granddaddies down on the plantation. I've butted heads with them a couple times myself. Somebody needs to clean their clocks."

"Did you find Lucy?"

"Well, yes and no. She was at work, but she wouldn't see me. Peggy wouldn't even let me in the door." He shook his head and went on up the steps and into the house.

I waited a minute, then followed him inside. His hands were braced on the rim of the kitchen sink and his face pointed at the window, but I knew he wasn't taking in the view.

"Dad?"

"Hmm."

"Did you eat?"

"What?"

"I could make you something. A peanut butter sandwich, maybe."

He looked over his shoulder at me then, his eyes glancing off mine, red-rimmed and wet, and it dawned on me that whatever had happened the night before was bigger than I'd thought, that maybe he'd finally found himself up against something he couldn't weasel or charm his way out of.

He took down a glass from the cupboard and ran it full from the tap and drank it straight down. "Maybe later, baby girl," he said, setting the glass in the sink, and brushed past me and out of the kitchen without meeting my eyes. In a few seconds I heard the bedroom door close.

I thought about going after him, picking up his guitar; I thought about sharing my secret. But no matter how hard I tried to talk myself into it, all day long, I couldn't bring myself to knock on that door.

Lucy

"One more time. Explain it to me."

Peggy wrested a huge wreath of white carnations out of the cooler and passed it to me, and I hauled it over and parked it next to the door, along with several others similar in style and heft. I'd arrived at work that morning to learn that our postman, Harvey Peel, who'd been admitted to the hospital the Friday before with chest pains, had had a massive coronary and passed away Sunday night. Harvey had been carrying the mail in Mooney for thirty-seven years, and it seemed that every single customer of the U.S. Postal Service wanted to honor his passing with a floral tribute.

"You told Ash you're having a baby and then loaded up your stuff and moved out of his house?" Peggy asked. "Before the two of you even had a chance to talk it over?"

"That's pretty much it," I admitted. Peggy made a clucking sound with her tongue against the roof of her mouth. "Look, I don't know what everybody's so worked up about," I said. "I'm not saying it's permanent. I just need a little time to think about what happens next."

"What happens next," she answered, "is that you've got yourself a baby. A baby and no husband."

"I don't get it," I said. "All this business about making an 'honest woman' out of me—it makes my skin crawl! I mean, I don't need a man to, to bestow that on me, do I? I don't need a man to have a baby with, either! Well, to *have* a baby, sure, but to raise it up—"

"Lucy," Peggy broke in, handing me two big sprays of chrysanthemums, "I believe you're missing the point."

"Which is what?"

"Which is not whether you need a man to raise a baby, which, if you'll pardon my two cents, based on my own personal experience, you most certainly do. The point is, whether you have no kids or ten of them, you and Ash are meant to be together. Did you ever think that maybe this is just God's way of cementing the deal?"

I bit my lip as the phone rang, keeping to myself my opinion of God as master mortarman, while Peggy popped in back to answer it. She leaned into the doorway a second later and motioned that it was for me. "Not Ash," I said, half question, half warning, but she shook her head and mouthed, "Bailey."

"Wow, Lucy, you sure do know how to kick-start a sleepy old Monday," my brother said as I stuck the phone between my chin and shoulder.

I wondered if I'd ever get used to knowing that in this town no business was ever truly your own. "How'd you hear?"

"The sun's been up, what, three whole hours now? There can't be a soul between here and Texarkana who hasn't heard."

"I hope you didn't call me up to lecture me. Peggy's pretty well got that covered," I said loudly, knowing she was eavesdropping from the front room.

"Seems like it's a little late for that anyway," he said, and I laughed and admitted it probably was, at that. "Naw, I'm just checking to see if you need anything." I thought of telling him that what I needed was a man whose first response to the news that we were having a baby wasn't "You're shitting me," but I let it pass. "I wanted to make sure you aren't stuck, that you've got a place to stay."

"I'm at the rent house, for the time being," I said. "Everything's okay."

"Aren't you about to broil alive out there? Geneva and I have an old window unit in the garage, from before we put in the central air. I wish you'd let me —"

"I'm fine, Bailey. Honest."

"You know, Lucy . . ."

"What?"

"Did you stop to think maybe you need to, well, give Ash a chance to deal with this in his own way? Seems to me that if you just hit him upside the head with it and then jump in the car and take off, it isn't really fair to think he's gonna handle it like a champ."

"Did *you* stop to think that maybe I cleared out to give Ash a chance to deal with it his way? He's got plenty to think about, and so do I."

Bailey cleared his throat. "You aren't— Shit, how do I say this. You do mean to keep the baby?"

"Of course I do! What made you think I wouldn't?" But he didn't answer me. "I've never for a second meant not to. It's a . . ." What? A marvel? A blessing? I wasn't sure, to be honest, if I believed in those things. Then I heard Peggy's voice: *cementing the deal.* "It's fate," I said. God as master mortarman. "I've been trying to call Geneva at the clinic. I've left two messages, but she hasn't called back."

"Well, it's Monday. You know how that is. Whup, there goes my pager. Listen, give me a call if there's anything I can do, you hear?" He hung up.

I delivered two vanloads of flowers to the Rest Haven funeral home, then tried dialing Geneva again. The clinic operator put me on hold for three or four minutes, at the mercy of an orchestra medley of Beatles tunes, before the line clicked and my sister-in-law said hello in a clipped, breathless voice.

"Hi," I said, "it's me." No response. "Remember me? Lucy Hatch? The scarlet woman?"

"I remember," she said. "What's up?"

"Well—nothing. I mean, everything. I was hoping to talk to you."

"What for?"

"Lord, Geneva, since when do I need to pass a quiz to have a conversation with you?" She was silent. "What's going on? Did you and Bailey have a fight?"

"Look, I really don't . . . I can't get into it right now, okay? The other nurse is on vacation and I'm like a one-armed paper hanger."

"Can you have lunch? I was planning on stopping for a sandwich over at Dove's."

"Maybe. I don't know." She sighed into the mouthpiece. "I'll try, okay? I'm not promising, but I'll try." And, like Bailey had a few minutes earlier, she left me standing with a receiver dangling in my hand.

"Don't look now," Peggy announced as I walked back into the showroom. She jerked her thumb in the direction of the display window, through which Ash's pickup could be seen pulling up to the curb.

"Oh, no!" I said. "Not here, not now!" But Peggy was already headed toward the front door, throwing it open so forcefully the sleigh bells tied to the knob on a silver ribbon sounded like a burglar alarm. She stood blocking the entrance, three hundred pounds in a turquoise muumuu trembling from head to toe with righteous indignation.

"What do you think you're doing here?" she said as Ash circled the truck and stepped up onto the sidewalk. I ducked behind the greeting card rack, where I had a clear view but couldn't be seen.

"Unless you're deaf, dumb, and blind, then you know damn well what I'm doing here," he said, "so I'll thank you to step aside and let me do it."

"You move your hind end off my property, Ash Farrell, or I'll call Sheriff Dudley to do it for you."

Through the window I could see Ash plain as day, the skin stretched tight across his cheekbones, the whites of his eyes shot through with red. He looked like he'd slept in his clothes. He stared at Peggy like she was the latest in a string of petty annoyances, like she might be the final and most irksome straw. He opened his mouth to speak but she cut him off.

"Now, you listen here," she said. "I know you prob'ly don't believe it, but I'm on your side. Not that I'm letting you off the hook, hear, but I think you got a bum deal. Y'all two have got yourselves in a spot, sure enough, and in my mind, nobody's interests are being served by y'all acting this way, 'less maybe it's the gossips over at the DQ. Lucy's a hothead, you'd be the last one surprised to hear that. I don't think what she's doing is right. But she doesn't want to see you right now, and I got to respect her wishes.

"Now you run along like a good boy, all right?" Peggy's voice had softened both in volume and tone, and her multiple chins had stopped quaking. "Go home, sober up, get yourself some sleep. You give Lucy some time. She'll come around, I guarantee."

Ash dragged the toe of his boot along a crack on the sidewalk. "I've done some things I'm not proud of, and that's the truth," he said. Hearing him almost made me smile. It was his morning-after act, pure and simple, full of rueful pronouncements, leading into the turning-over-a-new-leaf stage, wrapping up with a grand finale full of happily-ever-after.

"Tell her something for me, will you?" he said to Peggy. "Tell her—tell her I'll be back tomorrow. Tomorrow, and the next day, and the next day. Will you do that? Will you pass that on for me, please?"

"'Course I will," Peggy said gently. "Now you get on home and get some rest. Just set back. Everything's gonna be fine, you wait and see."

We watched, Peggy from the doorway and I from my spot behind the greeting cards, as Ash climbed back into the truck and cranked the key. We stood there until the blue cloud from his tailpipe had settled over the street, and then Peggy came back inside and let the door sigh shut behind her. The sleigh bells gave one last, paltry jingle, like they'd used up all their energy on Ash's appearance.

"I know," I said as she leveled her gaze at me and held it. "Don't you say a word. I know."

✖

At twelve o'clock I walked the six blocks from the shop to Aunt Dove's. I let myself in the kitchen door and found her mixing up a bowl of tuna salad.

"Sorry I didn't call ahead. You having company?"

"Just you," she said. "I had a feelin' you'd turn up."

We smiled at each other. "I guess that means it's all over town."

"Over and back by now," she agreed, turning to set the bowl on the table. She was wearing her white hair cropped short, as well as a T-shirt from Dwight Yoakam's 1994 tour, which I was reasonably sure had bypassed Mooney.

"You know, it's funny," she said.

"What is?"

"I always thought Bailey was gonna be the wild one. When he gone off after school to rodeo, I figgered, Well, here we go. Gonna get himself mixed up with some tramp, get her pregnant, break his neck, wind up a bum."

"He just about did break his neck," I reminded her, sinking into a chair and slipping off my shoes. It had actually been a hip and his collarbone, but it kept him off the circuit long enough to come home to Mooney and fall in love with Geneva and turn into a regular solid citizen: a churchgoer, a business owner, a faithful husband. At least I was pretty sure he was a faithful husband; my conversation with Geneva earlier had me a little worried.

"'Course your brother Kit always was square as a block, never had to worry about him none, and there you were, tucked away down on the farm, married to Mitchell. Who'd of b'lieved when you came back to town you'd wind up the main dish at Burton's café?"

"Thanks for the vote of confidence."

"I never thought I'd hear myself say this," she went on, setting out a loaf of store-bought bread, "but I do believe you are your daddy, Raymond Hatch, all over again. The minute things got dicey, he'd hit the ground running."

There was a brand-new bag of Fritos on the table, and I ripped into it. "You know, it's real interesting to me how it seems like everybody in town has already taken sides. I'm starting to wonder if Ash isn't driving around with a campaign sign and a bullhorn." Dove didn't reply. "Maybe I had a reason to take off like I did," I said. "Maybe things happened that nobody knows about but Ash and me."

"Be that as it may," she said, pulling out a chair across from me, "sometimes you've got to face up to the tough stuff, Lucy Bird. Did you ever think for five minutes of just settin' still and lookin' things in the eye?"

I pushed my hands through my hair and stared at the ceiling. "I need to think, Dove. In Ash's house I can't hear myself think."

"Aw, bull hockey," she said. "In my day we never did have no time to think about stuff the way folks does nowadays. We was too busy doin' what needed doin', tryin' to keep our heads above water. Things needed sayin', we said 'em and went on about our business. And you know what? I don't know that we was any worse off for it. This is your mama's fault, I reckon, puttin' dreamy-eyed notions in your head back when you was a youngster."

"First my daddy, now Mama," I said. "Can't you decide who's fault it is I'm such a mess, or are you just hanging it on anybody you can find?"

"Sometimes I wish I'd just smacked Patsy upside the head one time when she got to actin' loopy over your daddy, Raymond Hatch. Maybe it woulda got her outta her nightgown and got her to put down the hootch long enough to see what kinda pitcher it made for you kids."

"It's something to live up to, all right," I said. "Did you think maybe all I'm doing is trying to hold up the family image?"

Dove helped herself to the Fritos and began to chew one thoughtfully. "Nah, you ain't like your mama, not really. Not crazy. Just mule-headed."

"Gosh, I wonder where I got that." I held up a teaspoon, and smiled when she caught a glimpse of herself reflected in its silver bowl.

"I am, at that," she said, picking up her iced tea. "Old, too."

"Don't make me laugh."

"Naw, I mean it. I had a lot on my mind, these past coupla weeks."

"Like what?" Was she sick? Or worse? I tried to keep my voice casual, but my heart was thumping.

"You listen to me a minute. I never had no kids of my own, and that was fine by me, I never wanted nobody but you and the boys, no way. But this child . . ." She nodded toward my belly, and I caught myself smoothing the tail of my shirt over the nonexistent bulge. "Aw, I know Kit's got his brood, and I'm fond of 'em, even if they do act like wild animals half the time. But this one's gonna be something else, Lucy Bird. The day you come here with that glint in your eye, I knowed it, and I know it still. I feel like it got made under a special star."

She leaned forward, spreading her hands, hard and brown, on the tabletop. "Don't you see? This ain't no time to be runnin' around the countryside actin' like a coupla silly teenagers. You and Ash got to start pulling together. You got to be *ready*."

I leaned back in my chair and watched a butterfly light upon the kitchen window, a shock of orange against the blue beyond, like a trick of the light, then gone.

"Suppose we can't?" I asked, swallowing a lump in my throat.

"Cain't what?"

"Pull together."

"What makes you say that? Not some little two-bit fight."

"It wasn't a fight, not exactly. It's— I don't think Ash wants to be a father, Dove. It's not on his—his agenda, I guess you'd call it."

"Did he say that?"

"Not in those words. But he was painting this picture of how he wants it to be, after Denny goes back to Dallas. This thing with his music could really take off. I don't think being a family man is part of the plan."

"Well, if I know you, you just dropped it on him like a bomb and then shoved on out the door."

"So?"

"So, maybe if you'd of given him two heartbeats to mull it over he'd of had another comeback." I shook my head doubtfully. "Think about it, Lucy Bird. You let fly a piece of news that's gonna change the man's life and then 'spect him to do a one-eighty as soon as it lands. Maybe he needs a couple days to paint the barn another color, huh?"

I laughed. "What's that supposed to mean?" I said, when through the window over the sink I saw Geneva coming up the walk. She tapped her knuckles against the door and came inside.

"Hope you've got enough for one more," she said, turning to wash her hands at the sink. Her nurse's scrubs were printed with little pink cherubs, but her spine looked as stiff as a drainpipe. Dove had been busy making up tuna sandwiches while we talked, and she divvied them up onto plates as Geneva poured herself a glass of tea and eased into a chair.

Nobody said anything for a few minutes. Dove and I looked at each other across the table as Geneva pulled the crust off her sandwich.

"My transfer came through," she said finally, and looked from Dove to me and back again. I didn't know what she was talking about. "I put in for a position at Golden Years. It's not my background, geriatrics, but, hey, it's so hard to find nurses right now, they were glad to see me."

"But you've been with Dr. Crawford, what, twelve years?" I said.

"Thirteen," she confirmed. "Time for a change, don't you think?"

"I thought you loved your job."

"I did, at first. I just never—" She rolled the crust into a ball between her thumb and forefinger. "You know, when I started working in an obstetrician's office, I always figured I'd be the one on the examining table someday. But now— Well, I can't keep going in and seeing all those pregnant women, all day every day, and act like it isn't eating me up inside. It's too hard." She looked at me, her eyes full of tears. "Congratulations, by the way."

"Geneva." I reached out my hand but she snatched hers away.

"Don't," she said. "Don't *comfort* me, okay? I already feel like a shrew. You're my sister-in-law and I'm supposed to be happy for you. So I'm happy, okay, goddamn it! *Happy.*"

Dove pushed her chair back and stood up. "Maybe you girls need a few minutes to yourself," she said. I tried to make eye contact, to beg her not to leave me, but she picked up the plate with her half-eaten sandwich and carried it out of the room, and a few seconds later the sound track of *The Bold and the Beautiful* poured in from the living room.

"You want to start?" I said to Geneva. "It sounds like you've got a load on your mind."

She shook her head; tears splashed onto the flowered tablecloth. "I'm a horrible person."

"Why's that?"

"Because I don't want to be talking to you. I don't even want to *look* at you." The anger in her voice brought me up short and kept me silent.

"I mean, here you are, knocked up like a bowling pin, and I just want to scream. Why is everything so, so slapdash for you? You don't even want it!"

"Wait a minute—who told you that? Bailey said the same thing! Where is this story coming from?"

She picked up her tea glass, studied it, set it down again. "Last Saturday night," she said, "we took Denny to IHOP. On the way home, she started asking questions. About how to get an abortion—where to go, how much it cost. She said she was asking for a friend. They all say that, of course, but she— Well, I just couldn't believe it was her. But this morning, when I heard about you, I called her up. And she admitted it, that she'd overheard you and Dove talking. About needing to get rid of it, not knowing where to go."

I was speechless, running the news back and forth in my mind. I had no doubt Denny had heard *something*. But what could Dove and I have been discussing that she misconstrued so wildly, and why?

"Geneva," I said, "I don't know what Denny's talking about. I promise you, I mean to go through with this. I never for one second thought of anything else." She dabbed at her eyes with a wadded-up paper napkin. "Is that what you're so upset about? You thought I didn't want to keep the baby?"

"You remember that day a couple months ago when I took a few days' sick time?" she asked. I thought back, said I did. "Well, I had a miscarriage."

"Oh, Gen. Oh, God."

"My sixth one. Six times I've been pregnant, and six times I've lost it."

If you'd asked me the night before or first thing that very morning who my best friend was, I'd have said my sister-in-law. I realized now there were things about her I'd never known, dark places she had never let me see.

"I don't know what to say," I told her. "I'm so sorry. I didn't know this, any of it."

"I've had every test in the world, every kind of treatment. Nobody knows what the matter is. I can get pregnant, all right, but for some reason I can't carry one to term." I heard her breath whistle past her teeth. "I made it all the way to fifteen weeks once, about five years ago. That was the worst one. Don't look so shocked. We didn't tell anybody, only Dove. So, you see? Here you are . . ." She laughed, but the sound was like someone skating down the blade of a knife. "Bailey doesn't want to try anymore. This last one was the hardest, for him. He says he doesn't think he can do it again.

"Look, Lucy, I'm just trying to tell you that it's— I *want* you to be happy, I want to be happy *for* you, but it's just so hard, and I don't know how to fix it. I'm afraid I might not be able to be around you very much for a while. I mean, I want to say everything's gonna be like it was before, but right now I can't see how." She wiped her eyes and looked at me. "I know, I'm a bitch. Bailey will kill me when he hears what I said to you."

"You just told the truth." But I felt an ache inside, the small, safe place that had always been my relationship with Geneva gone dull and dark, like a burned-out star.

She tossed down her napkin and stood up. "I've got to get back. I told Dr. C. I'd only be gone half an hour. With Rita on vacation, the place is falling apart at the seams."

I stood up, too. I wanted to hug her, or be hugged by her, but that everyday act of consolation felt as far away as China.

"When does your new job start?" I asked.

"Two weeks from today."

"I have an exam with Dr. C. next Monday." I'd made the appointment first thing that morning.

"I heard."

"You don't have to be there if you don't want to."

She glanced toward the window, then back to me. "I guess you've probably had about as much advice as you can stand today," she said. "But don't let Ash off easy, Lucy. You make him do right by you."

"Famous last words." I smiled.

"They might be, if Bailey gets a hold of him."

"Poor Bailey. He still hasn't gotten over me kissing Tommy Rupp in the back of his Firebird when I was sixteen."

"No, he hasn't, and don't you forget it. I have to go."

"I know."

"I love you."

"I know that, too." But before I could return the sentiment, she was out the door and gone.

I sat down again heavily and stared at the tabletop. A few minutes later the TV went off and Dove came back into the kitchen. She carried her empty plate across the room to the sink.

"Something wrong with my tuna salad?" she asked, nodding at my untouched sandwich and the one Geneva had only pulled apart with her fingers.

"I'm not so hungry."

"Well, I ain't havin' no grandniece or -nephew born cravin' nothin' but salt and grease, so if you wanna get out of here and get on back to work, you better put somethin' in your stomach besides Fritos."

"I can't believe it," I said. "I can't believe you knew all this and you never *told* me."

"Weren't mine to tell." She dried her hands on a dish towel and folded it over the edge of the drain board, then turned to me. "Look here—remember when you walked in here a coupla weeks ago with your news? How would you of felt if I'd gone against your wishes and spread it all over town?"

"I might not be in the fix I'm in now." But it wasn't a joke, and we both knew it.

"You know what your problem is?"

"No, but I bet there's somebody in the bloodline you can blame it on."

"You 'spect everbody to drop everthing and be runnin' around wavin' their arms and yellin', 'Hallelujah.' But a baby ain't a trifle, Lucy Bird, some shiny thing you show off to all your friends and then tuck up out of the way on a shelf. It takes time for folks to make the shift sometimes, clear out a little space in here." She tapped her thumb against her chest, nailing Dwight Yoakam right between the eyes.

"I know that."

"You think? I ain't so sure."

"So, what am I supposed to do?"

Dove leaned across the table and snatched the Fritos just as I was sneaking my hand toward the bag.

"You know, for once I think I'm gonna keep my mouth shut and let you figger it out for yourself."

⚯

After work I took my new-made list and stopped by the Food King. I got orange juice, cheese, bananas, broccoli, things I hadn't tasted in so long they looked exotic to me, piled in multicolored abundance in my cart.

"Eating for two," the checker, Marcel Compton, observed as she rang up my purchases.

"But shopping for one," I pointed out, and she clamped her big old lipsticked mouth shut and counted out my change.

Back home, I opened up the house and turned on the fans, and ate cold deli chicken and potato salad off a Chinet plate, sitting on the front step. Afterward, I sat and watched the dusk creep up, the long, slow fall into night I loved so much, and thought about fate, and luck, and second chances. About how I, Lucy Breward, the farmer's wife, just when it seemed the game was fixed, had gotten called up to spin the wheel again; about my brother and sister-in-law, how they'd have walked through fire for the chance I'd been so casually given, and the man who, maybe not so casually after all, had given it to me. I wanted to reach some kind of peace with that, but I never did, not exactly. I threw sticks for the dogs, and counted stars, and listened to the sound of my heart beating in my chest, pumping my blood with impunity, all the places it needed to go.

17

Denny

 The next morning Dad was a brand-new man. I woke up early hearing his pickup pull out, but by the time I was dressed and chewing on a Pop-Tart at the kitchen table he was back, driving the truck around the side of the house. I got up and looked out the window and saw him drop the tailgate, then carry the Skilsaw and his toolbox out of the shed. I washed my hands and grabbed a Coke out of the refrigerator and went out to join him.

"Hey, look who's up!" he said, helping himself to a long swig of my Coke straight from the can. He'd showered and shaved, and his eyes that had looked so awful the day before were bright and clear. A little *too* bright, if you asked me.

"What are you so cheerful about?" I asked. For somebody whose whole life was coming apart, who hadn't come out of his bedroom the past sixteen hours, he was acting way too chipper.

"It's a great day to be alive, Denise," he said. Now I was really worried. "What have you got on tap this morning? Maybe you could hang around and give me a hand." I noticed that the truck bed was full of lumber.

"With what? How come you aren't working?"

"Oh, we finished up at Mrs. Crouch's last Friday. I've got a kitchen remodeling coming up for Mrs. Wells Mackey, but that's not till next week. Meantime, maybe you and I can take care of some stuff around here that needs doing."

"Like what?"

"Like your room, for starters. And a room for the baby." I couldn't believe the way he said it, so offhand, like it was what he'd been picturing all along: a comfy little family home.

I looked at him close and hard. "Have you talked to Lucy?"

"I thought I'd give her a little space to breathe the next few days."

"She doesn't know about this, then?"

"It'll be a surprise."

"Dad?"

"What?"

"Are you on drugs?" Really, I couldn't think what else it could be, but he laughed like I'd said the funniest thing in the world.

"Get on over here," he said. "Let's see if we can make a carpenter out of you."

It was fun, working side by side with him that morning, listening to him whistle and mutter and cuss. I wasn't much help, but he seemed to like having me there, to have somebody to try out his stories and dumb jokes on, to fetch him Cokes and drywall screws. So I was kind of disappointed when the phone rang mid-morning, but Dad waved at me to answer it. I was thinking so hard about Lucy, about the idea of us all living under that roof like a regular family, that I had to stop and catch my breath a second when I heard Erasmus's voice.

"What are you doing?" he wanted to know, and I said he wouldn't believe it if I told him, which I did.

"He's like another person," I said. "Like aliens stole his brain during the night and left this, this normal happy person inside his body."

"Well, I was wondering if I could come over later on," Erasmus said. "Bring my fiddle."

"Oh." My own brain was acting funny; I'd laid up half the night thinking about playing music with Erasmus, but now, at the sound of his actual voice, I'd forgotten all about it.

"I can't get that song out of my head," he said. " 'If you were a train stop, the conductor would sing low . . . ' "

"I know."

"You haven't told him, have you?"

"Not yet."

"Well, maybe you should think about doing it while he's having a good day." But I couldn't picture it, couldn't imagine taking the chance on ruining Dad's new frame of mind, no matter how weird it was or where it had come from. "Anyway, what about it? Can I come? I've got to help my dad out at the shop today, but what about this evening, after supper?"

"I—I have to ask."

"Go do it, then. Put the phone down. I'll hold on," he said, before I could even say I'd think about it.

"Who was that?" Dad wanted to know when I made my way back outside. He was playing it cool, keeping his eyes fixed on the board he was measuring, but I could tell he hoped I'd say Lucy. I felt bad having to tell him the truth.

"Erasmus?" he repeated, and laid down the tape measure and looked up. "Erasmus King?" I started to say something smart about how many people named Erasmus did he know, but something about the look in his eyes stopped me. "What did he want?"

I picked up a sketch Dad had made with a pencil on the back of a hardware store receipt and pretended to study it. "He's just— Well, he's waiting for me to ask you something."

"What would that be?"

"He was wondering if he could maybe come over later."

"Over here? What for?" I shrugged. I knew I should tell the truth, but I couldn't find words to fit. "Do you mean he wants to call here?" Dad asked slowly. "On you?"

"No! I mean, I guess so. I mean—he just wants to visit awhile, is all! He said he'd bring his fiddle." There. It was out; halfway, anyway.

To this day I wish I had a picture of the look that moved over my father's face. Part of it sent a chill down my spine, and part of it made me want to laugh out loud, seeing how I had a sway over him I never knew before.

"Well," Dad said. "Well," and for half a second, I swear to God, his eyes watered up, the way they had in the kitchen the day before when I'd offered to make him a peanut butter sandwich. "Well, fine," he said finally, looking down at his hands. "We'll have us a jam on the porch."

"I could ask him for supper," I said, real fast, before he could change his mind. "You could cook hamburgers on the grill."

"Sure," Dad said. "We'll run to the Food King after a while and get what we need."

And just like that, I crossed over into another kingdom, and was standing there looking at my father from the other side.

⚮

He managed to frame out two doors and two windows before he decided he'd had enough construction for one day, and we climbed in the pickup and headed into town. We made a quick pass through the Food King, grabbing up hamburger meat and buns and all the fixings, then Dad pointed the truck toward the middle of town. There was some kind of big to-do at the Baptist church, the parking lot full to overflowing, and Dad steered over to the curb in front of Mrs. Crouch's house, the old lady whose kitchen cabinets he said he'd finished last week. I thought maybe he had some leftover business with her, but he cut the engine and just sat there, his wrists draped over the steering wheel and his eyes fixed on the church across the street.

"What's going on?" I knew Baptists liked to worship more than normal people, but this was an awful big crowd for the middle of a Tuesday afternoon.

"Harvey Peel died," Dad said without taking his eyes off the church. "The mailman."

"Well, are you going in, or not?" I said. It was hot out, and I was thinking we shouldn't have bought hamburger meat if we were planning on stopping off on the way home for a funeral, but Dad just shook his head. When it was obvious we weren't going anywhere anytime soon, I opened the door and got out and sat down under the shade of a pecan tree in Mrs. Crouch's front yard. I'd heard she had a fearsome temper and a bunch of nasty little dogs, but I wasn't about to fry in the front seat of a decrepit old pickup, no matter what kind of mystery mission Dad was on.

Then the front door of the big brick church opened, letting out a wedge of organ music and cool air, and a small figure in a blue dress slipped out, and all of sudden it all came clear. I stood up in the grass and watched as Lucy lifted her hair off the back of her neck, squinting into the sun. It only took her about five seconds to locate the pickup; it was almost like she knew beforehand it would be there. She didn't look happy, exactly, but she didn't seem mad like I would have thought, either. She stood without moving for a minute, then stepped out from under the church's covered entryway and started toward us across the parking lot. She stopped in the middle of the street, her arms folded over her chest like she was hugging herself. Her dress was the color of the sky in a Bible picture, and her hair was loose down her back, and if the ache that came up in me from seeing her there was a sign, I could only guess how my father felt.

"How's the service?" he asked, his hands still on the wheel.

"Over," she said. "If you came to pay your respects, you're a little behind schedule."

"Poor Harv," Dad said. "I knew the man my whole life, but I never really *knew* him, you know what I mean?"

"Too late now," she said. "What are you doing here? I thought you finished up with Mrs. Crouch last week."

"I did. Denny and I've been working around the house today. Finishing out those extra rooms."

She nodded. "Well, that should up your resale value."

If he knew what she was talking about, he let it pass. "We came into town for some groceries. We're having company for supper." He turned and nodded at me, and Lucy raised her eyebrows expectantly. "My daughter has a gentleman caller."

"Erasmus King," I said. "It isn't any big deal, though."

"Is that so," Lucy said. I wished all of a sudden that she would be there to help get ready, braiding my hair for me, singing in her terrible off-key voice to the radio, maybe baking up something for dessert.

"Feel like joining us?" Dad asked. "There's enough food for an army."

"Sorry. I've got plans."

For the first time since she'd come out the door of the church, Dad took his eyes off her and turned his face toward the windshield. He seemed to be studying something in the road with terrific concentration.

"How long do you think you can keep this up, Luce?"

"Six more months, at least," she said without missing a beat.

"You've got to talk to me sometime."

"Sometime. But not today."

"When, then? You think six months is a long time, but it isn't. It'll be gone before you know it."

"Right. You try tossing your guts every morning and swelling up like the Goodyear blimp and see how fast *you* think it goes by."

"You don't look a thing like the Goodyear blimp," he said. "You look great. Blue must be your color."

"Truer words were never spoken." She smiled a funny little smile and smoothed down her dress in the front. "Anyway, give it time."

"See, that's what I'm trying to say. We haven't *got* that, Lucy—time. I mean, one minute we're in front of the Baptist church and the next thing you know, he's graduating high school."

"Who is?"

He nodded in a nervous way toward the waist of her blue dress. "That one, there."

For a long time Lucy stared at Dad, her hand going to her still-flat stomach like she was urging whoever was inside not to worry about a thing.

"You know something funny?" she said. "I can't help remembering how you were when I met you, you and that old silver tongue of yours. That wasn't all that long ago, either. What do you suppose happened?"

"My whole life came discombobulated, that's what happened."

Across the street at First Baptist, the heavy wooden doors swung open and a bunch of men in dark suits wheeled a trolley with a big bronze coffin toward the hearse sitting at the entryway, and Lucy said she had to go. "Damn it, Lucy!" Dad said. But she was already walking away, tossing her hair. "When are you gonna start listening to me?"

"Just as soon as you start saying something I want to hear." She paused for a second, turned back. "Y'all have fun tonight," she said, her eyes aimed at me. "I want to hear all about it."

"When?" Dad called out the window. People were pouring out of the church in their dark clothes like ants across the parking lot, heading to their cars, and in a few seconds Lucy was lost in the swarm. "When?" he said again, but softer this time. Like it was just dawning on him that not only couldn't she hear him, she wasn't even trying.

∽

I left Dad in the kitchen fussing with the supper fixings and went to take a shower, but when I came out again, in my Gap pants and a clean T-shirt, brushing out my damp hair, he took one look at me and his face sagged.

"What?" I said, feeling my mood drop like a ton of bricks.

"Well, you— Not that you don't look just fine. But don't you want to think about maybe fixing yourself up a little bit? It's not every night we have company for supper."

"Fix myself up, how?" I was thinking if he wanted a storybook princess, it was a little late to be getting in his vote.

"Well, I don't know," he said. "Whatever it is you girls do. To your face, or your hair, or whatever."

I threw my hairbrush at the table, where it rebounded off the fruit bowl and went skidding across the floor.

"I don't *know* what girls do," I said. "Nobody ever showed me! Lucy could have, but she isn't here, because you ran her off! You fucked up. You *always* fuck up. You're a moron."

I thought I'd feel better, but I didn't. I stepped over to the counter and picked up a knife he'd been using to slice tomatoes; it was still dripping juice and seeds, and don't think I didn't picture plunging it into the side of his neck, his and then my own. Erasmus would show up and find Dad and me in the middle of the kitchen floor in a pool of our blood, his running right into mine so you couldn't tell where one left off and the other began. On second thought, probably our blood was different colors, mine some wishy-washy, second-rate kind.

"Watch your mouth, Denise Farrell," he said. "Remember who you're talking to."

"It's true, though, isn't it?" I said. "Tell me what you'd call it. You fucked up."

He looked out the window a minute, taking long, deep breaths, then turned and set his hip against the countertop and crossed his arms over his chest. I could smell sawdust on him, a trace of the soap he must have used that morning. No matter how crazy it was, I couldn't help hoping this was the moment he'd finally take me in his arms and admit he'd always loved me, that I was the daughter he'd yearned for every day we were apart. I guess he'd never seen any TV movies-of-the-week, though, because all he did was say, "Please put that knife down, before you hurt somebody."

I felt full of rage inside, lit with it. I felt like if I opened my mouth, diamonds and pearls would rain out on the ground and the whole world would fall in wonderment at my feet. And still my father would be standing with his arms crossed, calling me by my given name, telling me to put the knife down, not to say "fuck."

I set the knife in the sink, gently, like it was a delicate surgical instrument, and stomped past him and down the hall to the bathroom. The mirror was still covered with steam from the shower, and I made a ball of my fist and rubbed a clear spot in the middle. There I was, Miss Potato Face. Unless a plastic surgeon happened to show up at the front door in the next few minutes, I was stuck.

A plastic tortoiseshell headband Lucy had left behind sat on the edge of the sink, and I picked it up and shoved it through my hair. It actually looked worse that way, straight back off my face and hanging limp behind my shoulders, my forehead shining like a dinner plate. I took the cap off my Chanel lipstick and swiveled it up out of the tube. I didn't even care if I was getting it on straight. I hated my father with a fullness that felt almost holy, hated him for being handsome and not having the good grace to pass it on to me; hating him for noticing that, for caring. Hated him for chasing Lucy off when I needed her most. Lucy would have found some way to make the best of this. Lucy, like Erasmus, saw something else when she looked at me, something more than mouse-brown hair and stubby legs. To them, unlike Dad, I was more than the sum of my parts.

Then all of a sudden there he was, his face floating in the mirror glass over my shoulder.

"Denny," he said, watching me paint my mouth with coat after coat of Whisper Pink, until it looked like I'd inhaled an entire cone of cotton candy. "Come on, now. Cut it out."

"Better?" I asked, turning around to give him a full-face view. "Am I gorgeous enough for you now?"

He reached out and took the lipstick out of my hand and replaced the cap. "Look, you were right, okay? I fucked up. First Lucy, now you. Every time I've opened my mouth the past couple days, it seems like I've stuck my foot right in it."

I felt tears pressing at the base of my throat, working their way up. "Lucy should be here," I said. "Right now. Tonight!"

"She isn't, though," he said. "She's taking a—a sabbatical."

"What's that?"

"A break. Time off."

"That's crazy!" I said. "She's having a baby!"

"We all are. Lucy and me, and you, too. Did you think of that?"

I tore a square of toilet paper off the roll and started rubbing the mess off my mouth. "Don't go trying to hang your stupid accidents on me."

"Well, now, I'm not so sure anymore it *was* an accident."

"What are you talking about?" I said, even though I didn't really think I wanted to know.

"Don't you believe in providence? Destiny?"

I stared at his face in the glass. "Uh-oh," I said. Now he was getting flaky on me. Or religious; I wasn't sure which was worse.

"Look, I'm trying, okay?" he said. "I've got a long way to go, but I'm trying."

He started to walk off, but stopped when I said, "Dad?"

"What's that?"

"Lucy's coming back, isn't she? This—this sabbatical. It'll be over in a couple days and she'll be back. Right?"

He met my eyes in the mirror and held them, and I remember wondering if he would lie to me, if he'd say what he knew I wanted to hear instead of what he really, in his heart, believed as true. He looked at me so hard I wasn't sure where his pupils ended and the irises began, until his eyes seemed like pure pools, reflecting everything that floated beneath their glassy dark surface. Then, right at the moment I might have seen all the way clear to the bottom, he turned away, and I listened to him go back up the hall to the kitchen, without telling me anything at all.

❧

Dad went outside to fire up the grill, and we managed not to say too much to each other till Erasmus drove up, with his fiddle in its case and an icebox cake in a beat-up tin pan. "My granny made me bring this," he said, holding out the cake like it was an apology. "There's more food at Uncle Isaac's than all of us could eat in a week." He was dressed like he'd been for the picnic, high-water pants, long sleeves, suspenders, and I couldn't help thinking he looked like he belonged in an old photograph, the edges blurred and sepia-toned.

I took the cake, which was sweating under a film of Saran wrap, pretending I didn't feel my father's eyes on the both of us. "We'll have to get over to Isaac's in a day or so, check out that baby, won't we, Denny?" Dad slipped a platter of hamburger patties out of the refrigerator and made a spot for the cake.

The two of them went out to the yard, fussing with the charcoal and all that stuff men like to do, but I didn't particularly care for being left in the kitchen and so I wandered out there and stood and listened to them talking. It made me mad, a little, that Erasmus was acting like he'd come to see Dad and not me, but then I reminded myself that he'd known Dad a lot longer, that they had more in common, at least on the surface of things, than he and I did. They were talking about music, no surprise there. Erasmus was going on about somebody named Stuff Smith, and Dad was telling him how he ought to take advantage of everything he could learn at Beaux-Arts, jazz and bluegrass and classical. "So, we're gonna jam a little bit later on, am I right?" Dad asked. Erasmus shot me a look behind Dad's back but I shook my head, and he just said, "Yes, sir, I'd like that."

Dad straightened up from fussing with the fire. "What's this 'sir' business all of a sudden?" he said, smiling. "Not on my daughter's account, I hope." I had to pretend like I was busy with the platter of hamburger patties, like I didn't feel my face going ten shades of red.

They talked all through supper, about records they liked, and Dallas, and people both of them knew. I could hardly get a word in edgewise, but I liked listening to them, the easy way their voices slid in and out around each other's, the way Dad treated Erasmus like an equal and not some dopey kid. He was making an effort, I knew, on my behalf; and it's true, it was better because of him, I had to give him that. Like I was the kind of girl who had gentleman callers every day. Like what had passed between us in the kitchen earlier had happened to some other father and daughter.

I got up to clear the table, and Dad and Erasmus went into the living room. I could hear them talking in there, then the stereo started up, the new Ralph Stanley CD Dad had gotten by mail order a couple of days before. I stopped still for a minute with my wrists in the dishwater and listened, letting that old mountain music pour through me from my scalp to my toes. Someday, I thought, I would make music like that, so pure it was like a field of snow where no creature had ever set foot, not even anything tiny, like a fox or a bird. Someday I would be a hundred years old, and people all over the world would come to hear me play my perfect, untouchable music.

I waited till I heard them go out onto the front porch, until I heard guitar and fiddle come out of their cases and the sound of fingers being touched to strings. They started out with something loose and bluesy, getting a feel for each other's style, for where things were headed. Dad took the lead, and Erasmus followed, and they spent a few minutes letting their instruments loop around each other in a lazy way, like they had all evening to get where they were going.

I slipped out the screen door and over to the porch swing. The sun had started to go down behind the trees, and the air was heavy with heat and red dust and the sound of crickets; and just for a minute it seemed like it might be all right to think about spending your life in Mooney, Texas, where time seemed to wait outside the circle of pine trees like it had other places to be and better things to do, where if you never saw anything brighter than the evening star, just beginning to burn white against the dark blue sky, it would be all right. I knew better than to trust that feeling, I knew we were under some kind of spell, because of the music, but I liked it anyway.

They did a handful of tunes, moving from blues to country to something that sounded like jazz, and sitting there in the swing with the night coming on I halfway managed to forget my place in all of this. I was in a reverie, I guess you could say, thinking about Lucy and the baby and Dad going to Nashville, so that when he said my name, I jumped about a foot straight up in the air.

"What?" I came back to reality with such a thump, I thought I'd fall out of the swing.

"You're about a million miles away over there."

"Yes, sir."

"I just asked if you had any requests. Anything in particular you feel like hearing?"

"Actually," Erasmus said, before I could speak up, "I've got one."

"Well, let's hear it."

"How about the bluebird song?"

It was almost completely dark now; all I could make out was a white shirt, the fiddle a shadow in the crook of an arm. I knew he thought he was helping me out, but I still felt like I could wring his skinny neck.

You could hear the surprise in Dad's voice. "You mean Butch Hancock's bluebird song? I didn't know you knew it."

"Denny played it for me."

"Have you been messing around in my tapes, Denise Farrell?" Dad said. "I'll thank you to ask before you go taking stuff out of the truck without permission."

"Okay." I pushed out of the swing and stood up. "May I please borrow your guitar?"

In a way, I wished the porch light had been on. I'd like to have seen the look on his face, instead of just having to guess it from the tone of his voice when he said, "Say again?"

"You said I should ask permission. I need to use your guitar, please."

He handed it over without a word. I can't even begin to guess what he was thinking when I took a seat on the step below him and spent a few seconds tweaking the G string into tune. I pulled in a breath and glanced around, but Erasmus's face, Dad's face, everything was hidden in the moonless night. Just as well, I thought, to do this like it was just me, alone. Like I'd done it a hundred times before.

The darkness was like a glove, something warm and snug-fitting that held me in its palm. I let the first few notes of the song spool out of me on their own, and before too long I was caught up in it, the way the words and the melody twined themselves together to make something with bones and a soul and a beating heart. I was just coming into the second verse when Erasmus fell in behind me with his fiddle and I remembered I wasn't alone, after all; I let a little piece of the load go to him, and let him steer us along. Oh, it was worth it, everything I thought it would be, my voice and that fiddle and Butch Hancock's lines as fine as anything Shakespeare ever thought up: "If you were a hotel, I'd lean on your doorbell/I'd call you my home."

Afterward, the silence felt so big, I thought it would choke me. Even the bugs were quiet, like they'd been listening and were trying to decide what to think. Then, all at once, they took up their buzz-saw whine, everything back to the way it was before.

Dad got to his feet and opened the screen door, and the porch light came on. It was a puny sixty-watt bulb, and under it his face, and everything else, was the color of a melted-down Creamsicle.

I stood up and held out the guitar, but he didn't reach for it, didn't do a thing but stand there looking at my face in the orange light. I felt the way I did on Christmas morning, watching Ma unwrap whatever it was I'd bought for her that year, wondering with a churning in my stomach if the gift would mean as much to her as it had to me, if the spirit in which it was offered would carry half the weight of the gift itself.

"I only borrowed the tape one time," I said. "Just to learn the song. I put it back the next *day*. It's right where it's always been, right there on the floor mat."

"Never mind that." I was sort of wishing he'd blow up at me, to be honest, anything but his face a pale blank and my guts twisting like a bucket of worms. "Raz? You knew about this?"

Erasmus stood slapping his bow against his thigh over and over in a nervous rhythm. "Only since yesterday."

Dad nodded his chin, one time, like he'd come to some hard decision. Then he did something he'd never done before, not once anywhere except in my dreams. He reached up his hand and slid it underneath my hair, against the back of my neck, so that the base of my skull was resting in the bowl of his palm. The heat of his skin was like a live wire connecting us, his blood and mine, as sure as anything I'd ever known.

He gave my neck a squeeze and then took his hand away. "What other tapes did you borrow?"

"Only a couple. Emmylou Harris, and Kitty Wells. But I put them right back! You never even knew they were gone!" I was still holding the guitar in front of me like a venomous snake, but he ignored me and sat back down on the step.

"Miss Kitty and Miss Emmylou," he said. "The last of the honky-tonk angels. Well, go on, then. Let's hear you earn yourself a place."

I looked to Erasmus for help, but he just stood there, all goofy- and glad-looking.

"Can we have the light off, at least?" I said. "I don't think I can do it with the light."

From his perch on the step, Dad started to laugh.

"You better get used to it, baby girl," he said. "I've got a feeling the light's about to start shining on you all the time."

18

Lucy

 I'd come in on my day off to help with Harvey's funeral, so that evening, after we'd transferred the flowers from the church to the cemetery, then, afterward, carried most of the bouquets and potted plants to the hospital and to Golden Years, Peggy sent me home and told me not to come in till Thursday. I started to protest about needing the paycheck, but Peggy insisted I needed some time to myself even more, that she'd break Faye's Flowers's sixty-year-long standing policy and give me a paid comp day.

The unexpected time off caught me unawares. I got up late, thinking I'd clean house, but that chore took little more than an hour, so I took flour and Crisco down from the pantry and a couple of pints of Dove's berries out of the freezer and baked a pie. That made the house too hot for human habitation, so I called the dogs and we took a long, meandering walk, and when I got back, my brother Bailey's truck was parked in my yard.

He came stepping out the front door onto the porch, a bottle of Coca-Cola in his hand.

"What, you just wander off and leave your house standing wide open, in the middle of a Wednesday afternoon?"

I took the Coke from him and drank, savoring the chilly burn on the back of my throat. "Be serious. Who's going to drive all the way out here just to go through my crummy little house? Anyway, it's too hot to close the place up. Don't ask me what possessed me to turn on the oven. You want some pie? It's Dove's dewberries."

We went into the kitchen and he stood at my elbow while I cut us each a slice of pie, and we carried our plates back onto the front step and settled there, side by side.

"You've got something on your mind," he guessed, forking up a bite of crust and berries.

"Oh, I was just thinking that the last time I made a pie was the first time Ash ever came out to this place," I said. "I didn't even know what he was selling, then."

"Ended up being kind of expensive, didn't it?" Bailey asked. "What he was selling."

"You think so? It doesn't seem like it to me." I glanced at my brother, but he was studying the uneaten bite of pie on his fork. When, I wondered, was the last time I had really looked at Bailey? Had those grooves been etched around his mouth all along, had his eyes always had that droop at the corners? I'd spent so much time over the past couple of days brooding about Geneva, I hadn't given much thought to what it had been like for Bailey, whether he'd let himself grieve for those lost babies, their names and their faces, who they might have been, or if he'd learned in time to steel himself for loss, to look at it as nothing any more but a procession of failed biology experiments.

"So, I hear Geneva gave you a piece of her mind," he said.

"Well, it was pretty much all news to me."

"Things have been rough for her."

"For you, too, I bet."

He let his eyes glance off mine, then back to his plate. "If it was up to me, we would've quit a long time ago. But she— She just can't let it go. That's been the hardest thing. Seeing her so hell-bent, and nothing I can do to change her mind."

"But aren't there other ways? You could adopt."

He sighed. "See, that's the thing, right there. It seems like it's gotten to be about something other than a baby, you know? I mean, about having a child to raise up. Somehow she sees it as all about *her*. About not being good enough, deserving enough. I think that's why she came down so hard on you. Like you took her prize."

"But it's not a contest. I don't deserve this any more than she does."

Bailey smiled sadly. "Well, I can't talk sense to her. Nobody can."

"She isn't even speaking to me at the moment."

"So I heard. She told me she acted like a bitch."

"No, she didn't. She just said some hard things. She was honest."

"Well, she can't cut you out of her life. Not forever."

"No, but maybe she just needs to come to grips with things her own way." I sat back against the porch rail, remembering Aunt Dove in her kitchen two days before, and smiled in spite of myself.

"What?" Bailey asked around a mouthful of pie.

"Oh, I was just thinking of something Dove said. About giving Ash a chance to sort out how he feels about being a father. She said, 'Maybe he needs a couple days to paint the barn another color.'"

Bailey laughed. "That's gonna be some paint job."

"You think Ash is an incurable reprobate and not fit to raise a child? Is that what you're saying?"

"I don't know, Lucy. I guess Ash is probably as well equipped for the job as the next guy." He was fiddling with his fork, mixing juice and crust. "Won't know till you let him have his say, though, will you?"

I spun and looked at him, and his ears turned red. "Bailey Hatch!" I stood up and set my plate on the rail. "He put you up to this, didn't he? Ash sent you here, to plead his case! I can't believe he'd do something so, so underhanded!"

"But I—"

"Wait a minute. Ash *would* do something that underhanded, but I can't believe you'd go along with it!"

"Well, he dropped by the job site this morning. I probably wouldn't have believed it either, before. But he really seemed—I don't know, Lucy—contrite. Sincere."

"Notice what you just said," I pointed out. "He *seemed* sincere. Ash Farrell, master of illusion." I didn't know why I was being so hard on Ash, except on principle. The whole thing—my moving out of Ash's house, this token resistance—suddenly showed itself as an exercise in futility. I might just as well have been petitioning for the sun to come up in the west.

I tipped my half-eaten pie into the dirt, where the dogs scrabbled over it like beggars, then put my hands over my face and started to cry. Bailey got up and put his arms around me and I sobbed into the front of his Oxford-cloth shirt. It felt wonderful, therapeutic, like something forbidden by my religion.

"I'm sorry," I said finally, pulling my face out of his shirtfront to wipe my eyes. "My hormones are all over the place, I guess."

"Well, since you're riled up anyway, can I keep going?" Bailey said. He ran a finger under his collar, like it was binding him. "He wants to know if he can come out and see you. Just to talk to you, is all. Now, don't start up the waterworks again. Just think about it a minute, okay? Let's carry these plates inside and then you can answer me."

It was funny, in a way. From the first day of our courtship, Ash had charged straight in, steering me where he wanted me to go; even the first few nights I'd spent apart from him, laid low after a trip to finish up the last business of my husband's life, Ash hadn't harbored two seconds' doubt that I'd be back, that our feelings for each other were matched both in depth and steadfastness. It was only now, months later and so much water under the bridge, that he'd finally found the nerve to ask the thing he never once had in the beginning: permission. It was encouraging, I thought; a sign on the road to enlightenment.

Bailey and I took our plates inside and set them in the sink. "I really wish you'd think about letting me bring out that AC for you, Lucy," he said as we went back onto the porch. "It doesn't seem right, you being out here in this heat, in your condition."

"Well, my condition's not all that comfortable to begin with." I slid my arm through his, and we stood together on the step, enjoying a lick of breeze from the trees across the road, a moment's respite. "I'll think about it, okay? I'll let you know."

"I have to run," he said. "We've got a crew out at that new subdivision west of town, and a rookie with a backhoe dug up an electrical line." He leaned forward and gave me a peck on the corner of my mouth, a rare demonstration of affection, or solidarity.

I smiled at my brother as he climbed up into his truck and closed the door and the driver's-side window went whirring down. "So, what should I tell Ash? That you're thinking about it?"

"Oh, I'll be home tomorrow around three," I said. "Tell him he can come on out then, if he hasn't got anything better to do."

Bailey drove off, laughing, like I'd just told the funniest joke in the world.

∞

Peggy had asked me to stop by the café on my way in the next morning and pick up a dozen doughnuts. It was past nine and the breakfast crowd had thinned out, though the usual suspects—old men, mostly, who had nothing to do but drink coffee and gossip all day—were still curled like fossils over their china cups. Carol, the waitress, waved at me from behind the register.

"Hey, there! We were just talking about you."

"Why doesn't that surprise me?"

"Actually, we were talking about Ash," she said. "About last night at the Round-Up. This place has been buzzing all morning."

"What happened last night at the Round-Up?"

"Oh, it was something, to hear folks tell! One big pity party." I shook my head to show I wasn't following her. "Nothing but heartbreak songs. Every blue old thing Ash could dredge out of the songbook, and not a single lively tune you could step out to, either. A bunch of people complained to Dub, but he just threw up his hands and said Ash is an artist and there wasn't nothing to do about it but let him air his misery in public."

"Was this a joke?"

"Oh, no, honey. He was pouring his heart out, absolutely for real. Two full sets. Dub said he never sold so many whiskey shots in one night in twenty-five years."

"Most of them to Ash, probably."

"One or two, maybe. But he knew what he was doing, Lucy. They say there wasn't a dry eye in the house." Carol looked at me meaningfully, as laughter swelled up like a bright bubble in my chest, aching to escape. He knew what he was doing, all right, just like he knew I'd hear all about it in town the next morning. Part of me was annoyed with Ash for being such an exhibitionist, but another, bigger part of me was truly sorry I'd missed it.

The bell over the door jangled, and Saul Toomey, one of the regulars, stepped in, doffing his feed cap. "Hey there, Lucy," he said with a toothy smirk. "You been in to work yet this morning?"

"Peggy asked me to stop off for her doughnuts first," I said, as Carol brought out a white box and laid it on the counter. I studied Saul's face, feeling a tiny tickle at the base of my spine. "Why?"

"Looks like your boss been decoratin' again," he said. I told Carol to put the doughnuts on Peggy's tab and jumped into the Buick and sped around the corner and down two blocks to the corner of Front and Second Streets.

I couldn't see the window, obscured as it was by the little knot of people on the sidewalk out front. I drove around back and parked, then went in through the rear door. "Morning!" Peggy sang out as I rushed in, laying her box of doughnuts on the counter, and kept going straight on out the front.

The group on the sidewalk split in two to make way for me. "Yes, ma'am, Peggy's outdone herself this time," Constance Struthers, the county clerk, said as I took in the display: a gigantic swag of fake ivy and little white lovebirds festooning two blown-up photographs—my high school yearbook senior picture, my hair parted down the middle, my smile as big and guiltless as a two-year-old's, alongside a grainy black-and-white print of Ash onstage at the Round-Up, his eyes closed, his mouth open in some note suspended forever, soundlessly, in space. At the top, pink paper letters six inches high spelled out the day's burning question: "A Match Made in Heaven?" Suspended at odd intervals were red and white construction-paper hearts, left over from last year's Valentine's window, offering up the alternatives: "Yes,"

"No," "Yes," "No." And, finally, at the foot of the scene, a bald plastic baby doll in a toy high chair gripping a pink-and-blue pennant in its fist: "Vote Here!!!"

"Oh, for crying out loud," I said, pushing my way back through the front door. "Peggy!"

She waved, her mouth full of sweet fried dough. On the counter was a shoe box covered in white paper with a slot in the top and a red paper heart with "LUCY + ASH 4EVER?" in black block letters glued to the lid.

"This is too much!" I said. "Peggy, this is just—"

The front door opened and Constance Struthers and Millie Campbell, the courthouse secretary, stuck their heads inside. "Where do we vote?" Millie sang out, and Peggy motioned them over and handed them little slips of paper and pencil stubs from the Indian Mound golf course. They took their time, making out their votes like they were deciding the fate of the universe, then dropped their ballots into the box. "God bless you, dear," Constance said to me, and they went back out the door.

"That's sixteen yes," Peggy said, putting a couple of little tick marks on a pad next to the shoe box, "and two no."

"You've had eighteen votes already?" The shop hadn't even been open half an hour. "Wait a minute—who voted no?"

"I'm not at liberty to say," Peggy replied, and handed me a doughnut as the door opened and three more members of the electorate walked in.

❧

By the time I got ready to leave that afternoon, we'd sold four single and two bunches of roses, two mixed spring bouquets, a schefflera, and an orchid, and the vote stood at 111 to 4. I drove home and splashed some water on my face and brushed my teeth and changed my blouse to something cotton and sleeveless, and turned the fans on high. Ten minutes later, stirring up a pitcher of tea with ice and mint, I heard Ash's truck come clattering up the front road.

Through the screen door I watched him swing down into the yard, watched Booker and Steve Cropper come tearing around the corner of the house and do little jigs of welcome on their hind legs as he stood rubbing their ears. "Hey, guy, hey, guy," he murmured as they butted his knees with their heads and Steve Cropper peed a happy little puddle in the dirt.

Ash came up the steps and rapped the backs of his knuckles against the door frame. He was still in his work clothes: Levi's, faded tan T-shirt, scuffed boots.

"These are pretty sorry guard dogs you have here, lady."

"Yeah, but you ought to hear them play 'Green Onions.'"

"Can I come in? Or are you gonna leave me out here with the rest of the dogs?"

"It's open. There's tea, just made," I said as he came into the kitchen, and I filled him a glass and handed it to him and watched him drain it, then hand it back for a refill.

"I've got pie, too. Dewberry."

He shook his head. "That old trick worked once, but it won't again," he said as we pulled out chairs at the table and sat. His eyes seemed as sad and faded as the oilcloth beneath our hands.

"I told Bailey the last time I made a pie was the first time you were here. He thought I'd gotten the poor side of the bargain," I said.

"He can be one tough son of a bitch, you know it? I wish I could figure out why I like him."

"Well, somehow you two have wound up in the same corner." We sat in silence for a while, listening to the fans hum.

"Your brother said Geneva came down pretty hard on you the other day."

"Did he tell you why?"

"Yeah, the bare-bones version. What a screwed-up world this is, huh? Half the folks having babies they don't want and the other half wanting ones they can't have." He picked up his tea glass, looked into it, set it down again.

"Your public relations skills haven't improved any since Tuesday."

"Give me a break here, will you, Lucy? Didn't you say to me, right at this table, in fact, that it wasn't possible for you to get pregnant?"

"I told you—Mitchell just made me believe that, somehow. That all the time we were married and it never happened, it was my fault. It was stupid, I admit. But don't you remember when we started up together, you and I, how ignorant I was? I'd been married fourteen years, and I didn't know anything!"

"Your mama didn't ever tell you where babies come from?"

"I'm saying that Mitchell and I didn't *talk* about this stuff! As far as he was concerned, sex was what the bulls did to the cows in the barnyard. Like it shamed him, almost, to touch me." I was surprised by the power this memory had over me, the dark cloud it laid over my heart.

"But the thing I keep coming back to over and over is, why didn't you *tell* me? The very first day you found out?"

"I don't know if I can explain it, I don't even think I understand it myself. I just kept waiting, for the right time, so it would be a happy thing. So that we could be happy about it, together. And instead, the longer I waited, the more tangled up it got, first with Denny, then this business about Nashville, the record-company man . . . I don't know how to make it work, Ash. I don't know how the things you want and I want are ever going to come together."

"There's a middle ground," he said. "There always is. You just have to hunt a little harder sometimes to find it."

"I'm scared," I said, setting down my glass, surprised by the sound of my voice in the quiet room. "I'm scared I won't have anything left in my heart for a baby. That I've given it all to you."

He looked at me so hard I had to close my eyes, and when he reached for my hand this time I didn't protest, but leaned with all my might toward the feel of his thumb sliding across my knuckles, calling me home.

"I don't think it works that way," he said. "I think when a baby comes you—you make room, somehow. Alongside the other. Maybe your heart gets bigger. But it doesn't cost you, that much I do know. Not the way you mean."

"Aunt Dove says this baby got made under a special star. She says we have to stop carrying on like this, that we've got to buckle down and figure out how to raise it. But how do we do that, Ash? I don't know if you and I are on the same road anymore. I'm not sure we ever were."

He drained his tea, rattling the cubes in the empty glass. "Remember, when you went to close up Mitchell's farm? You came back talking all tough, about how you couldn't give yourself over to me like you had to him. Like you knew ahead of time that's how things were bound to turn out between us, and that you meant to put the brakes on before it could happen. But there aren't any guarantees, don't you know that by now? It seems like you want all the answers, and we don't even know the questions yet."

"Well, then, maybe that's where we need to start," I said. "With the questions." I watched as he traced the pattern of vines on the oilcloth with his index finger. "There's something else, isn't there?" I said. "Something you haven't said."

"Look, I don't want this getting more complicated than it already is," Ash said. "I think from here on out we lay things out on the table, right away. No more sneaking around, keeping secrets, waiting for the best time to talk."

"So, talk." My heart was doing loops in my chest like a crazy moth.

"The record-company guy? Tony Amate? He called yesterday. They want me to come to Nashville."

I looked through the screen door, at the dogs scuffling and rolling in the dirt, the gaudy heads of the roses along the porch rail. "Permanently?" I asked. "Or just for a—a visit?"

"Just for a few days, next month. He wants to set up some meetings, introduce me to some people. After that . . ." He held up his hands, then placed them flat on the table.

I pushed back my chair and set our glasses in the sink. I heard the scrape of Ash's chair on the linoleum, felt the heat and mass of him as he stepped up behind me, the scent of his skin so familiar and fundamental, I had to close my eyes to keep my equilibrium. He put his hands on my shoulders, lightly, like he was waiting to see if there'd be a shock or a singe, and without even thinking about it I turned my head and lay my cheek against the backs of his fingers, felt their rough warmth through my own thin skin.

"Ash," I said, as he lifted my hair off my neck and pressed his mouth against the spot where his fingers had been. I turned, and he planted his hands against the sink edge on either side of my waist and slanted his hips against mine. What took my breath away was not the smile on his lips but the dead-level look in his dark eyes. "This is how we got into this mess in the first place," I reminded him.

"Is that what you think we've got? A mess?"

"I'm having a baby, and you're going to Nashville. What would you call it?"

"See, that's where you and I are coming at this from two different directions. Why does it all have to be one way or the other? It's like you can't let yourself see things unless they're black or white."

"Okay, then—how do you see it, if it's not black or white?"

"I guess I'd start by looking at the things I want and trying to figure out how I could have a little piece of all of them."

"For instance?"

"Well, for instance—don't you think they allow wives and kids in Nashville?"

"You haven't got a wife."

The smile had reached his eyes by now. "No, and I can feel my prospects shrinking as we speak."

"Is this just another joke to you? Like the time you pretended you meant to pay Dewey Wentzel a hundred dollars to let you out of jail so you could spend the night with me? I should have slammed the door in your face right there! What was I thinking?"

"You know, it never ceases to amaze me, what kind of a knave you take me for. It was five hundred dollars, not a measly hundred. And it was no joke. Ask Dewey, if you don't believe me, since he threatened to book me with contempt. And in case you don't remember, you *did* slam the door in my face. Or at least tried to run me through with a pitchfork."

"Oh, I wish I'd just let Misty Potter have you! I wish you'd driven into the Trinity River and drowned!"

"Well, I just about did," he said mildly. "I wasn't about to let that happen, though. Not knowing what was waiting on me on the other side. Pitchfork or no pitchfork."

"Go away," I said, giving him a halfhearted shove. "I know what you're doing, only this time it won't work."

"It already worked." But he read the look on my face and quickly held his hand up, Indian-scout style, as if to declare his innocence of all charges.

"What about what *I* want, Ash? You talk about what you want, but what about me?"

"So, tell me," he said. "What do you want?"

I tilted my chin and looked into his eyes. They were black as earth, pupils appearing to meld into the irises to form a smooth dark surface in which I saw nothing but my own likeness, reflected back.

I shook my head. It didn't seem enough to say that all I wanted was what I had there and then: the way I'd come, in time, to see myself in Ash's eyes. "All I know is, I feel like I have to be able to say before we can get to what comes next."

I followed him onto the front porch and watched him hoist himself behind the wheel. He whistled once, short and sharp, between his teeth, and Booker scrambled onto the running board and then jumped in a graceful arc into the bed of the pickup.

"You think about what I said while you're working it all out, will you?" Ash said.

"About what?"

"My proposal."

"What proposal?" I asked, but Ash was gunning the engine and didn't hear me. He waved as he steered the truck in a loop and headed back up the road.

"Did I miss something?" I asked Steve Cropper. "Did you hear a proposal?" But the dog's only response was to scratch himself behind the ear, and we watched the truck disappear in a mantle of dust.

19

Denny

 Nothing was the same again, after that first night
Erasmus came for supper. Once in a while I actually
missed it, the good old days when I was invisible.
Now I'd catch Dad watching me sometimes when he
thought I wasn't paying attention, and he'd have this look on his face
like he was trying to crawl inside my head and pick apart what was
going on in there, like everything I was thinking was suddenly beautiful and enchanting, which, trust me, it was not. It pissed me off a little,
to tell you the truth, that the old Denny hadn't been worth two minutes
of his time, and now, because of some random little thing, some fluke of
nature, I'd all of a sudden turned into this object of fascination. It made
me act contrary, made me slam doors and stay in the shower until I
used up all the hot water in the tank and act like sometimes I couldn't
even hear him when he was talking to me.

"He's driving me crazy," I told Erasmus one night on the phone.
"He can't talk about anything but music. All he wants me to do is sing,
sing, sing."

"Are you kidding me?" Erasmus said. "I'd give anything to have my dad treat me that way. He still thinks I'm gonna be a mechanic when I get out of school. He thinks music is like a, a bad habit. Embarrassing, you know? Like, maybe if he doesn't pay attention, I'll just grow out of it."

"It's insulting, though, isn't it?" I said. "I mean, I'm not any different than I was before."

But it wasn't true. The way Dad looked at me *had* changed me, made me see someone other than that flat-footed, stringy-haired girl I'd always seen looking back from the mirror. Oh, the feet and the hair were still there, same as they ever were. But something else was different, something about the way I lifted my shoulders now when he spoke to me, how I held my chin. If I was playacting at first, well, that was all right. Playacting was how you got by on the surface of things while, underfoot, the groundwork was shifting.

※

He spent the rest of the week working on my room and the nursery, stringing electrical wires, laying the flooring. Isaac came over on Friday to help Sheetrock the walls, and Rose and her sister Flora and the kids drove out that evening to pick him up. It was my first time to see the Reverend, who turned out to be not much to look at, I'm sorry to say, his face gray and puckered, his eyes tight shut. Still, I have to say that I understood then how it was to love something at first sight, the promise of all he'd be. I didn't want to hold him, hadn't ever held a baby before, but everybody teased me until I stuck out my arms and let Rose lay the bundle in the yellow blanket across them. He was heavier than you'd think someone only five days old could be, and I wished he'd open his eyes, but he didn't; he just hiccupped once and screwed up his face and slept on, but my heart opened right up and took him in anyway. I knew I had no claim on him, not really, but some part of him seemed to fasten itself to me. All the rest of the day, I could not stop smiling.

I slept in my new room that night for the first time, spreading my sleeping bag out on the floor. Dad had wanted that stuff that looks like wood but isn't, but I'd held out for wall-to-wall carpeting, and it felt soft and springy under the nylon shell of the sleeping bag. After he said good night, I lay on the floor staring at the moonlit square of the uncovered window and tried to count my blessings, to tote them up one by one, but before I could make it past Erasmus's sticking-out ears and the Reverend's raisin face, I was asleep.

⚮

Dad woke me up the next morning leaning over me with a cup of coffee, telling me to get up and get dressed, we were going to Texarkana. "Why?" I asked through a fog of sleep, but he wouldn't tell me, just said to hurry up or I'd miss Christmas.

We drove to a place on the west edge of the city called Deep Discount Furniture, a warehouse stocked to the rafters with unfinished wood and fiberboard pieces, bunk beds and cocktails tables, every size bookcase you can imagine. "No daughter of mine should have to spend half her life sleeping on the floor," Dad said when we walked in, but a little of the spring went out of his step as we lifted tags and looked at prices. There was a set with a canopy bed and dresser and pair of night tables that kept drawing my eye, but I knew from the look on Dad's face that it was out of our range. "How come you don't just build me some furniture?" I asked. "Like you did your bed, and the kitchen table?" He laughed. "Someday, baby girl. When I'm done making my fortune, I'll make sure you've got the prettiest goddamned bed you ever saw." And so we settled on a twin bed with a four-drawer dresser and night table in unpainted pine.

We waited for a couple of husky kids to carry out our assortment of flat boxes and lay them in the bed of the pickup. I thought Dad would be bossing them around, directing things like he always did, but I turned around and found him back on the sidewalk in front of the store, staring at a display in the window: a crib, a changing table, a rocking chair, and a dresser, all painted shades of yellow and green, and a quilt with a row of baby chicks embroidered along the hem folded over the rails of the crib.

He went back inside, leaving me to guard the truck, and came out again carrying one more flat box, which he added to the stack. He battened the whole thing down with a couple of bungee cords, then we drove to Home Depot and he vanished inside, leaving me to guard the truck, and came back out twenty minutes later with two cans of honey finish, which is what I'd said I wanted for my bedroom set, and a single can of the lightest green you've ever seen, the color of hope itself.

"We've got one more stop to make, okay?" he said, as we headed into the middle of Texarkana. I felt a flutter of excitement when we turned in and parked in front of Four States Music, remembering those guitars hanging from the wall like the keys to a kingdom.

Both of us shook hands with Twigs, and Dad hung back at the counter while I wandered off down the rows of Gibsons and Fenders. The boy on the metal chair wasn't around, and the store was as quiet as a church, the rows of hanging instruments gleaming like pirate loot in the soft bands of sun from the windows.

"Pick one," Dad said. He was standing right behind me.

"What?" I thought I must have wax in my ears, that maybe Ma was right and my Walkman was making me hard of hearing.

"You heard me," he said again. "Pick one."

My eyes blurred for a second, staring at the instruments in front of me. The old Martin D-45 I'd heard the boy playing on our last visit was locked in a case at the end of the row, but no sooner had my eyes drifted that way than Dad said, "Not too fancy, now, I'm a working man." He winked at me then, as if to say, *But not for long.*

I trailed down the aisle until I found a Washburn acoustic, with a natural finish and a spruce top. I deserved better, I knew, but I wasn't about to start an argument; and anyway, there was something, right from the start, about the way the Washburn fit into my hands, its heft as I lifted it gently from its rack. It seemed, like Reverend King had the night before, to belong in my arms.

My heart was racing as I sat down on one of the metal chairs. I took a couple of practice runs, then pitched myself headlong into "Rocky Top," and in seconds I'd lost myself, aware of nothing but the blur of my fingers on the frets. They say music is just math, but I've never quite believed it. How does that explain the way the notes curve and thrum against the inner membrane of your ear, how your brain gathers them and sends them to your soul?

Dad and Twigs applauded when I finished. Then, "Sounds to me like the G string's a little off," Dad mused, just to keep my head from getting too big, I guess.

"You must be tone deaf," I shot back. "You always tune yours flat."

"Get the case," he said to Twigs. "We'll take it."

I went out to sit in the truck while he paid for the guitar. He came out carrying it in its soft-side gig bag and tucked it carefully behind the seat. Then he jammed the key into the ignition and just sat there, staring straight ahead through the windshield. I was scared; the look on his face wasn't that different from the one I'd seen all those mornings over breakfast, the one when he'd stormed up the hall and called Ma an insane bitch over the telephone.

"Did I do something wrong?" I said finally—opening myself up to the full scope of my failings, practically handing him a pad and pen.

In the afternoon sun, the creases around his mouth and eyes gave him a mellow look. They say women get wrinkles, men get character, and I had a terrible feeling my father was going to be one of those men who looks even handsomer at sixty than he did at thirty-five.

"You know the other night, when you asked me about my mama?" he said. I sat biting down on my lip, not wanting to make a sound for fear of interrupting his momentum. "I was just a tiny kid, and it's all kind of mixed up in my mind, but it's like there's a, a sound track to what things were like then, you know? I just have these little snapshots of her in my head—standing at the kitchen window, sitting on the edge of her bed—but every time I think of that time, it seems like, she was singing. I don't remember the songs, not clear. But the first time I heard Brenda Lee on the radio, I thought it was my mama. That's how good she was." He looked over at me. "I always thought maybe she passed on a little piece of that to me. But I can't— Jesus, I close my eyes listening to you, and I hear her like it was yesterday."

I didn't know what to say. I thought about my grandmother, who I'd never seen, pictured a young woman in red pedal pushers and her hair up in a scarf swishing her hands slowly, contentedly, in a sink full of sudsy water, in time to the music in her head.

"I want you to understand something," Dad said. "The guitar is not a gift. It's not a bribe or a peace offering or an apology. It doesn't have anything to do with me. You don't owe me a goddamned thing, Denise, and I don't want you feeling beholden to me. But you owe it to yourself, and you owe it to God, to use it the very best you can. Is that clear?"

"Yes, sir."

"Good. Now, let's go home and see if you have any talent for assembling furniture."

∽

I didn't, but it didn't matter, since in his usual manner he took over the proceedings, ripping open boxes and strewing boards and tools everywhere, and after about an hour watching him sweat and cuss, and him hollering at me to bring him his second beer, I got out of there and called Booker and we walked down the road to Little Hope cemetery. Everything looked the way it usually did, all peaceful in the sunshine, nothing moving but the occasional bird overhead and Booker sniffing through the long grass. Dandelions had sprouted around a few of the older stones, and I yanked them up, then pocketed a gum wrapper that had blown in on some stray breeze.

I climbed up on the flagstone fence and surveyed the scene around me. For the first time I thought to question why we're taught not to make a sound in cemeteries, why it is we suppose the dead want quiet. Wouldn't things be quiet enough, lying forever in a box in the ground?

"Listen," I said, as loud as I could without yelling, but the only sign that anyone heard me was Booker pulling his nose out of the dirt.

I only knew one song by Brenda Lee, the one that goes "I'm sorry, so sorry . . ." But I poured my whole self into it, swaying my hips, raising my arms skyward as I belted out the chorus, imagining my grandmother doing the same thing forty years before at the kitchen sink. Was it really possible, I wondered, that she had, without ever knowing me, handed down her gift? How was it that we shared this thing and had never once laid eyes on each other? I finished with a flourish, feeling light-headed, but when I listened for a ghostly response, all I heard was my father's voice from down the road, yelling my name like the house was on fire.

I took off running with Booker on my heels, and found Dad in the kitchen, twisting the cap off another Bud.

"Where'd you get to?" he said, but I could tell he wasn't really mad. He sat down at the table. He looked beat.

"Checking out the cemetery," I said. "Just making sure things were okay." I remembered the gum wrapper in my pocket, took it out, and deposited it in the trash. "Did you want me for something?"

"Your room's done, if you care," he said. "It needs paint. Maybe we can take care of that tomorrow." I started to go look, but he stopped me. "Hang on a minute. You had a call. Lucy was wondering if you'd like to come over for supper."

"What for?"

"Nothing in particular. Just lonesome for some girl talk, she said. You want to clean up a little bit and I'll run you over? She's got tuna salad and key lime pie."

I didn't quite trust him—Lucy, either, for that matter—but I had to admit I was lonesome for her, too. Also, my curiosity was killing me: How was she getting along in her little house, what made it such a sweet escape from my father and me? In a way I hoped things were falling apart around her, and in a way I hoped she was blooming, showing Dad, plainer than words, how she could manage on her own.

She was standing on the porch waiting for us, wearing shorts and a loose-fitting top with little yellow flowers on it, and the first thing I thought, even before I realized how glad I was to see her, was that all of a sudden, in just the few days since she'd run off from Dad's house, it seemed like, she looked pregnant. Not all puffy and swollen, the way some women get, but her boobs and belly were definitely rounding out the front of her clothes, and there was a softness to her face where before had been all angles. She smiled at me, but her eyes slid off over my head to where Dad sat behind the wheel, idling the engine and looking right back at her. If anything, the blue arc of electricity felt stronger than ever, leaping from one of them to the other and back in the heat.

"I've got an errand to run," he said finally. "How about if I pick her up around nine?" Lucy said that would be fine, and he revved the engine a couple of times and drove off.

The house wasn't much, but it was a pretty place, surrounded by pines, and a row of big-headed pink roses—damask, I learned they were called—blooming all along the porch rail. "Are you hungry?" Lucy asked. "Knowing your daddy, he's still stringing you along on Coca-Cola and Pop-Tarts."

"We had Taco Bell, in Texarkana."

I followed her through the screen door and into the kitchen. There was a box fan in the window but it was hot as blazes in there, and Lucy had a fine sheen of sweat over her skin, like honey on a ham.

We took the food she'd fixed from the refrigerator and carried it out back where she'd set up a card table and a couple of folding chairs. I ate eagerly, although Lucy seemed to be just scooting her food around on her plate. The tea was sweet and cold and had little sprigs of mint floating in it. All in all, it seemed to me Lucy was faring for herself with a little more substance and flair than she had at Dad's house, but I didn't want to say so. I guessed she had to do something with her time when she wasn't having sex twenty-four hours a day.

"So, how was your supper with Erasmus?" she asked, after I'd eaten two servings of tuna and a roll and was starting on the pie. It was delicious, cool and tart on my tongue. "I hear you had a little surprise afterward for your daddy."

"Who told you about that?"

She laughed. "Secrets don't stay secret around here for long. You must've figured that out by now." And she ran her hand over the small new curve of her belly. "Poor Ash," she said. "He must feel like everything's gone topsy-turvy on him. So, tell me the truth—are you and Erasmus King an item?"

I scrunched up my face at her like I didn't know the meaning of the word. "We just get together and play music. That's all."

"He's a nice-looking boy."

"I guess." I kept my eyes on the table.

"All right. Another subject." She cut into her pie, lifted the fork to eye level, studied it a second, and then set it back on her plate. "I was hoping you might tell me about your conversation with Geneva. How in the world did you get the idea I was thinking of not having this baby?"

"One morning at Aunt Dove's, I heard you and her talking in one of the bedrooms. You were saying you had to get rid of it, but you didn't know how to go about it, or where you would get the money. You said you couldn't ask Dad, because it was his fault, and Dove said for you to talk to Geneva."

Lucy clamped her hands to her face and reared back in her chair, so hard the front two legs came off the ground. "Oh, Lord!" she cried. "Denny! We were talking about trading in the *car*! I meant it was Ash's fault because he'd gotten me the deal on the Buick in the first place! Geneva's sister's husband owns a used-car lot, up in Atlanta. Oh, my," she said, lifting her hair off her neck and fanning herself with a stack of paper napkins. I was so mortified, I lost my appetite; I actually set my fork down halfway through my pie.

"Oh, honey, don't be embarrassed," she said. "It doesn't even matter, not anymore."

"I just don't understand it," I said. "How things were just fine one minute, and then it got all messed up."

"Seems we were all sitting on secrets, when it would've been better to lay things out like they really were, right from the start. I guess we're all a little bit to blame for that."

"You need to come home," I blurted out, and for a second her whole face lit up with surprise. Then she smiled, but there was something far off in it, a downhearted cast to her eyes.

"I wish it was that easy," she said.

"Why isn't it?" I asked, feeling that crazy flood of fear and release I

felt when I knew I couldn't hold my tongue. "You love him, don't you?"
She nodded. "Then what's so hard about it?" I said. "He doesn't know
what to do without you! He—" *He's making a crib for the baby*, I almost
said, *the softest green you ever saw.*

Lucy shook out her napkin and laid it on the table. "I wish I could
make you understand it," she said. "It doesn't make sense to anyone.
Not to my family, not to Ash, sometimes not even to me. It's just that—
well, six months ago I was a settled-down married woman, living on a
farm. Then my husband died, I moved back here, I met your daddy . . .
I never expected to fall in love, much less have a baby. I guess I feel like
this is my last chance, you know? To make sure my feet are on the
ground, that this really is me, Lucy Hatch, inside this body, before I
turn into somebody's mother, or somebody's wife."

"Do you believe in love at first sight?" I asked as we started gathering up our empty plates. I was thinking about the Reverend, the way
some part of him I didn't even know seemed to belong to me.

"Well, it sure didn't happen with your daddy and me." I was surprised to hear that, and said so. "Oh, he was awful, the night we met!
I'd seen him sing beforehand, of course, and I admit it was quite a
show. But afterward, when Geneva introduced us, he'd had a drink or
two, and he had that Misty Potter hanging all over him, and I thought
he was crass and rude and just completely full of himself. You know the
way he smiles sometimes, with just the one corner of his mouth turned
up? Like he knows something you'd rather he didn't?" She imitated
this, so dead-on that I started laughing.

"So, what changed your mind? I mean, no offense, but your first
impression doesn't sound that different from the way he usually is."

"Well, for starters, he showed up at the flower shop the next morning. He was very smooth, very charming, the exact opposite of the
night before. He pretended he'd had a fight with a girlfriend—Misty, I
thought—and he asked me what my favorite flower was, and when I
told him pink roses, he bought a dozen and walked out. When I left to
go home at the end of the day, the roses were sitting on the front seat of
my truck."

"And you *fell* for that?" I thought it sounded just like him; it was so transparent.

"Oh, that was just the beginning! He offered to help me with my garden, and when he showed up, he'd brought me this fat, squirmy puppy." She nodded toward Steve Cropper, lying in the shade. "He drove out one night and parked in my yard and sat on the tailgate of the truck and serenaded me. A couple of days later a pipe in my kitchen broke, and he fixed it.

"Everybody tried to tell me he was chasing me. I'd never been chased, and just couldn't believe it." She elbowed open the screen door, balancing a stack of plates on her hand, so that I could go through. "So I tried to put a little bit of distance between us, and we had a—a falling out, I guess you'd say. But we made up, sort of, up at Willie B.'s Barbecue. The next night I went back to the Round-Up, and I danced with him for the first time." We set our dirty dishes on the kitchen counter-top. "The whole town, by then, knew what was going on. It would have been very, very tough to fight it."

"Did you, though? Fight it?"

"A few more days," she admitted. "He had to go to Austin, on some music business. We were having a terrible storm, the roads were all flooded, the bridges were washed out, but he made it back, straight through. It took him twelve hours. He was just about dead on his feet when he got here. Just about," she repeated, and smiled to herself, stacking the plates one by one in the sink. "And that was it," she said, sparing me the gory details. "The next day I went home with him, and never left."

"Till now."

Lucy looked up at me, startled seeming, like she'd forgotten she was in her own kitchen and not his.

"I hope you don't think I'm endorsing starting off a relationship the way your daddy and I did," she said. "I hope when your turn comes, you'll be more sensible than we were."

"Don't worry," I said. "I told him already, I'm never falling in love as long as I live." Even as I said it, the sound of Erasmus's fiddle seemed to move through my head, like a spun thread of pure gold.

Lucy laughed. "I don't imagine that when it happens, you'll have much to say about it."

She dried her hands on a dish towel, and we went outside and called Steve Cropper and set off on a rambling walk. Evening was coming on; the road lay in a trough of purple shadow, and the sounds of birds and insects getting ready for night kept us company. We wandered a mile or so, then doubled back, and were within shouting distance of the house when we heard Dad's truck making its way up the road behind us, the engine chugging under the hood.

"Well, do I get her back?" he asked, dangling his arm out the window. I started toward the truck, then ran back and gave Lucy a hug. She held on in a way I knew had nothing to do with my father, that was meant for nobody but me.

"I know I'm not supposed to ask this," he was saying to her as I got into the cab beside him, "but is there anything you need? Anything I can do?" She shook her head. "Well, if you think of anything, call. If you just want—"

"I know. I will."

"Sweet dreams, then."

"You, too. Both of you."

He eased the truck into gear and turned around in the yard and we headed back toward the highway, watching Lucy shrink to nothing in the rearview mirrors.

"So," he said, "how'd it go?"

"Okay. Fine. The pie was terrific." But I knew from the way he was looking at me that that wasn't the answer he was waiting for.

"She'll be back," I said. And he nodded and smiled, and pressed the accelerator to the floor.

❧

He'd been to Wal-Mart and bought me a set of sheets for my bed, yellow with springs of pink rosebuds, a matching pillowcase, a feather pillow, a blanket.

"I wasn't sure what you'd think of all this," he said, standing beside me as I looked at the pile of plastic-wrapped packages. "If you hate it, we'll take it back." I just shook my head; I couldn't say that, of all the things he'd done in the past few days, the fact that he saw me as worthy of pink-flowered sheets just might be the most surprising.

He'd spent the evening painting the crib, and called me into the back bedroom to see. It looked, for all intents and purposes, like the one in the furniture store window, the green as pale and tender as the underside of a new leaf. "It's perfect," I admitted.

"So, what do you think of Jude?" Dad asked. "For the baby."

"Jude, like the song? 'Take a sad song and make it better'?"

He laughed. "Sort of, yeah."

"It's all right for a boy," I said. "But the baby's a girl, I think."

"Is that right."

"Yes, sir. Her name is Sophie."

He just smiled and switched off the light. He continued to stand there, though, outside the room, looking in at the crib, in a square of moonlight. It gave me a chill, seeing it that way, cold-looking and empty, but from Dad's face I knew that wasn't what he pictured at all. It seemed to me that the ability to see what you wanted might be almost the same thing as having it, like if you just concentrated hard enough, whatever it was would take shape before your eyes. If I'd been a different person, or he had been, I'd have touched him then, would have slid my hand in his and pretended to share his vision. We weren't those people, though.

He looked down at me. "Sophie," I said.

"In your dreams," he answered, and we went to put rose-printed sheets on my bed.

20

Lucy

 I felt more at loose ends than ever after I'd seen Denny, watching her and Ash drive off in his rattle-trap truck. I tried to make myself busy around the house, but all weekend I found myself stopping in my tracks, imagining where they were, what they were up to. Ash's band practiced on Saturdays, and of course, it was Round-Up night. I went to bed with a book, but wound up staring at the ceiling at two A.M., wondering if solitude and contemplation were all they were cracked up to be. Sunday morning, I let Dove drag me to Willie B.'s for lunch, then back to her house to watch a movie on HBO. The barbecue gave me heartburn, and the movie, a romantic comedy starring Michelle Pfeiffer and one of the doctors from *ER*, made me so blue, I left before the last half hour. "You know what your problem is, Lucy Bird?" Dove said, not taking her eyes off the screen as I gave her a hug and headed for the door. "You never want to stay still long enough to see how things work out."

By Monday, I was in a state. I gave myself a talking-to, driving around in the van on my morning deliveries: *Whatever happened to both*

feet on the ground, to getting reacquainted with the sound of your own voice? But in fact I'd been watching for him all along, waiting for Ash to be Ash, to sweep me off my feet, daring me to resist. I looked for his truck downtown at lunchtime, but it wasn't there. Any other Monday, I'd have seen him at the bank or the hardware store, have passed him somewhere on our various rounds. But today, he didn't seem to be anywhere.

❧

My appointment with Dr. Crawford was set for three-thirty. I was nervous, even though there was nothing to be worried about; I knew, from a book Dove had gotten me from the library, that my development was right on schedule. Dr. Crawford, in spite of being a small-town doctor in his seventies, had pretty much seen it all in his fifty-year career, and wasn't apt to be shocked by one more unwed mother, even one he'd delivered more than thirty years before.

The scariest thing, I decided, driving over to Dove's beforehand, was that the doctor visit made things authentic, in a way they hadn't quite seemed before. The row of test strips with their little pink plus signs, the morning sickness, the sudden, rapid rounding of my body in the past couple of weeks, all seemed dim and dreamlike compared to the thought of Dr. Crawford smiling at me across his desk and telling me what my estimated date of confinement would be. "Confinement"— what a perfect word for it, like a prison sentence, life without parole. What was wrong with me, that the idea made me jittery inside? I was supposed to sacrifice myself to motherhood willingly, eagerly, and never think twice. What was I so afraid of forfeiting in the process?

"I'll go with you, if you want," Dove said, handing me the usual glass of warm tap water, but I told her it wasn't necessary. The clinic was only four blocks from her house, and I was early. I decided to leave the Buick in her driveway and walk.

For years Dr. Crawford had had his practice in a small clapboard house near downtown, but a few years earlier he'd moved, along with a handful of other doctors, into the flat, rambling building that had once been Mooney's elementary school. The waiting room—the former school cafeteria—was large and bright and filled with women: women with toddlers, women with infants, women with bellies as big as battleships, even a couple of flat-stomached women who kept their eyes fixed guiltily on their magazines. I took a seat and picked up a copy of *Motherhood Today*, but the articles about breast pumps and car seats seemed to dance on the page, refusing to sit still. There was so much to learn, so much I didn't know. A young woman across the aisle from me cradled a swaddled bundle in her arms, gazing into the folds of the blanket with such rapture that I felt a fresh wave of panic. Maybe I was too old to be a mother. Maybe I was just too mean.

By the time the nurse came out to fetch me, I had perspired straight through my blouse. At the sight of my face, she slipped her arm around me. She had dark, creamy skin and a reassuring smell about her, talcum powder and buttered toast. A plastic tag on her chest gave her name as Aurelia. "Hatch," she said, glancing at my chart. "You'd be Miss Geneva's sister-in-law we been hearing so much about."

"I was sort of hoping she'd be here this morning," I said, but the woman just murmured something I couldn't make out and instructed me to step on the scale. I was surprised I'd gained only four pounds; but Aurelia said it was typical to lose a little at first, then start to gain, after the morning sickness stabilized and the appetite returned, as mine had, with a vengeance.

I sat down in a molded plastic chair to let her strap a blood pressure cuff to my arm. Over her shoulder was a bulletin board where notices of various classes and services were posted. "Pain-free Childbirth," said one, a testimony to something called Trance-Birthing. "Banish the fear, worry, and pain before, during, and after," it read. "Call upon your innate birthing instincts." I made a strangled sound in the back of my throat, and Aurelia looked up at me, then at the flyer. "What if I don't *have* any innate birthing instincts?" I said. Aurelia smiled, but I could tell she had no clue what I was talking about.

She led me to a room and left me to change into a thin cotton gown. I sat with my legs dangling over the edge of the examination table, listening to the paper covering crunch underneath me as I fidgeted. The room was so cold my teeth were chattering.

Aurelia came back in carrying a chart and a pad. "Just a coupla questions, before we see the doctor," she said, uncapping a pen. "What was the date of your last period?"

"I have no idea."

"Excuse me?"

"I'm sorry, but it's the truth. All I know is that it was before the third week of March, which is the first time I—the earliest this might have happened. Getting pregnant, I mean." I shrugged. "That's it," I said. "That's all I can tell you. I just don't know."

"Well, dang," she said. "How am I supposed to explain that to Dr. Crawford?"

"Explain what?" the old white-haired doctor asked, entering the room, peering at me over his half glasses. "Lucy Hatch," he said. "Didn't I just deliver you, a couple of weeks ago?"

"A little longer than that, I think."

He took my chart from the nurse and skimmed it. "Age thirty-three. And this is your first pregnancy?"

"Yes, sir."

"Hmm."

"Is that a problem?" In two minutes I'd already flunked two tests, and those were just the ones I knew of.

"Atypical," he said. "Certainly not unheard of. No cause for alarm." He looked at Aurelia. "Estimated date of confinement?"

The nurse shot me a look. "Seems there's some question about that."

"Oh, well, not for long. Scoot up here," he said, and patted the metal stirrups like a kindly grandfather offering a pony ride. I gazed at the ceiling as he probed and prodded, then smoothed the cotton drape over my raised knees. "Twelve weeks," he said matter-of-factly. "That sound about right?"

I sat up. "Are you sure?" I saw myself standing in the kitchen the morning after my first night with Ash, telling him with nonchalance that I couldn't have a baby, while already, at that very moment, our little boy-and-girl gametes were locked in each other's arms, swimming upstream into ever-after land.

"Not a hundred percent," he said. "But I've been doing this awhile.

I guess I'm right my fair share of the time." He smiled and patted my arm. "I'd like to do an ultrasound, though. Since there seems to be some uncertainty. Okay?"

"Something's wrong," I said after the doctor left and Aurelia gave me a cotton cloak to wrap around me in order to walk down the hall to the sonogram room. "There's something he doesn't want to tell me."

"Nothing's wrong." She steered me into the hall. "There's only so much the doctor can tell, just by feel. The picture will let us know, from the size of the fetus and the heartbeat, how far along you are." *Since you've provided no useful information at all,* her sideways glance seemed to say, but she just smiled and pointed. "This way."

The sonogram room was occupied; I had to wait for a few minutes on another plastic chair in the hall. Would I have done things differently twelve weeks before, had I had an inkling of what was to come, of my butt freezing through a sheet on a cold plastic chair, the beginning of this long, uncertain road? If I'd looked a little harder, would I have seen the telltale gleam at the back of Ash's eye? And would I have gone ahead anyway, laying myself wide open to all he had to offer: his heart, his home, the great cresting wave of the future? "Lucy," I heard him say, his voice as real behind my closed eyes as the night we'd met. As if he were not some figment of my imagination or memory, but present. Here.

My eyes flew open and I stood up, clutching the cotton drape around me, watching Ash come up the fluorescent-lit hallway, one foot in front of the other and his eyes never leaving my face. In my memory sometimes the image blurs and the details get confused. Sometimes he's running, sometimes moving so leisurely someone seems to have slowed the film. His shirt may be blue, gray, green. But the look on his face is always the same. I'd expected this, I realized, watching him come, but I don't think I fully understood until that moment just how deep it ran.

"Sorry I'm late," he said. "They didn't want to let me back here without a warrant. What'd I miss?"

"Well, I peed in a cup, and stood on the scale. The nurse said I have perfect blood pressure. Ash, what are you— How did you know to come?"

"Never mind that. You mean they didn't tell you anything else?" It was hard to say if he was relieved or disappointed.

"Dr. Crawford thinks I'm twelve weeks along," I said. "He wants to do an ultrasound, to be sure."

The technician stuck her head around the door frame. "Ready?"

Ash reached for my hand, and I laced my fingers in his, our palms lying flat and clammy against each other's. "Can I come?" he asked, looking at the technician, who looked at me. I nodded so hard I felt like one of those dashboard dogs with the bobbing head.

The technician identified herself as Colleen, and appeared to be about sixteen years old. "This your first?" she asked cheerfully, helping me onto the table.

I was trying to decide how to answer when Ash spoke up. "Together," he said. "I've got a daughter, not quite fifteen." Like he'd done it all by himself.

"Then you probably want a boy this time, right?"

"I don't think it matters what I want. Denny says it's a girl," he told me. "She says her name is Sophie."

"Well, it's too soon to know that today," Colleen said, loosening my gown to smooth some sort of jelly onto the mound of my abdomen. "We can't usually determine gender from an ultrasound until at least twenty weeks, and a lot of doctors prefer to wait till thirty. This one will show us the size of the fetus, though. I understand there's some question about the date of conception?" I blushed and nodded, and was thankful Ash opted for once to keep his mouth shut.

We watched as Colleen tweaked some dials on the machine, then picked up a wand and ran it slowly back and forth over my belly. I glanced at Ash, but his eyes were fixed to the image on the screen, a mix of static and vague watery shapes. "Did you have this with Denny?" I whispered, but he just shook his head and squeezed my hand.

"There," Colleen said, pointing. "See that? That's the heart." The room was quiet. I couldn't take my eyes off the screen. It was nothing but a pulsing dark blur, so small and so stubborn. Nothing ever ends up looking the way you expect it to.

"Look," I said, "it has your black heart," and Ash pinched my arm and we all laughed, which was the only way I knew to keep from crying.

Dr. Crawford came in and bent close to peer at the screen. "Well, congratulations, you two," he said. "You've got a good, strong heartbeat there. We're looking at, oh, let's say December twenty-first for an EOC." He sounded so casual, like he was picking a golf date. It was too soon, I thought. I couldn't possibly be ready by December twenty-first. I knew nothing about breast pumps, or car seats, or Trance-Birthing. I didn't know anything at all.

They sent me off with a big bottle of vitamins and a photo of the ultrasound, the black blob that, before we knew it, would be disrupting our sleep, demanding food and stories, electronic equipment, the keys to the car, would be heading off to college, taking drugs, having sex, getting arrested. I stopped at the front desk to book my next appointment, then walked with Ash to his truck in the parking lot. So much had happened. Where did we start? What could we say?

"Where's your car?" he asked, squinting in the late-day sun. His shirt, I made note, was gray.

"I walked from Dove's."

"Hop in, I'll ride you back over."

He opened the passenger door, and I reached inside to set the ultrasound photo on the dashboard. The light filtered through it from behind, a mess of spots and wavy lines, as indubitable as anything I'd ever seen.

Ash laid his fingers lightly in the small of my back. I could smell him: soap, wood, that one dark note at the bottom that I would never be able to name.

"There he is," he said. "Jude Hatch Farrell."

"Jude? You mean, like the Beatles song?"

"No, I mean Jude, like the patron saint of lost causes."

I turned around, and he drew me into his arms, my face pressed hard and damp against his throat. For fourteen years I'd shared my life with a man but never felt that any part of me belonged to him. Maybe, with Ash, I'd been straining too hard to see the horizon, looking for a question I couldn't even name, when it was enough, after all, to feel that my heart—a cause I'd thought was lost forever—was finally safe, at home.

"Ash?"

"Mmm."

"I want to go home."

He cupped his hand under my chin and lifted it and looked into my eyes, making sure, I guess, that he understood which home I meant. Then he nodded, and helped me up into the truck, and shut the door solidly behind me.

21

Denny

I didn't believe in fairy tales. The way I saw it, life was full of things hiding behind bushes and under rocks, waiting to trip you up—although, come to think of it, maybe that's a fairy tale all by itself. I didn't believe in glass slippers, or kisses that turned frogs into princes. I didn't believe in over the rainbow.

But for about five minutes, one evening that summer, I forgot all that. I'd been sitting at the kitchen table reading one of Dad's old guitar magazines when I heard his pickup come racing and honking into the yard. I dropped my book and ran as quick as I could make it to the front door. Just in time, it turned out, to see him jog around the truck and open the passenger door and scoop Lucy into his arms and carry her, laughing and fussing all the way, up the steps and onto the porch.

"What happened?" I said, pushing open the screen as he set her on her feet. "What's going on?"

"Want to see your little brother's first picture?" Dad said, waving a piece of paper in front of me.

I took it from him and squinted at it, trying to find anything I could recognize in the mess of squiggly dark lines and splotches, but it was no use.

"He means your sister," Lucy said. "Sophie." I looked up at her, and she gave me a big shiny smile and came forward and hugged me hard. You could feel the happiness in her, pulsing under her skin, like a live thing trying to get out. It scared me a little bit, their happiness, how huge and ungainly it seemed, like any minute it would start weaving around out of control until it finally hit something and broke into a thousand pieces.

"It's a girl?" I asked. "How can you tell?" The only thing in the picture I could make out at all was a black spot that looked a little bit like a peanut.

"Wishful thinking, that's how," Dad said, circling Lucy from behind with his arms. "It's a conspiracy, if you ask me. Y'all want me outnumbered."

"You're already outnumbered," I pointed out, which set them both off laughing. "Is it true?" I asked when Lucy stopped for a breath. "This is Sophie?"

"Oh, honey, we don't know yet. Maybe not for a couple more months, even. But the doctor says there's a good strong heartbeat. He says the baby will be here in time for Christmas."

Christmas! It sounded like another lifetime to me, like I was already watching it all from some place far away, a little miniature Dad and Lucy and baby Sophie around a sweet-smelling tree, a perfect picture of comfort and joy.

"In the meantime," Dad said, "I'm trying to convince Miss Lucy here that it's in her own best interest to marry me just as soon as possible."

"Why?" I asked. "Is it in her best interest, I mean."

"Well, hell, what's the matter with you women? What other reason do you need?" He shook the peanut picture in our faces, while Lucy winked at me, as if to say the proof was standing right in front of him, wearing a loose blue blouse and a little cat smile.

"Denny's got a point," she said. "I spent my whole life before I met you living by the book. I've kind of gotten used to being a scarlet woman. I'm not sure I'm so eager to give it up.

"I haven't spent six months on my own since I was nineteen years old," she said. "And what about you? You're going to Nashville! Maybe you ought to think about whether or not you want to be tied down."

He held up his wrists, which were thick and blue-veined but otherwise didn't have a mark on them. "I've been tied down since the first time I laid eyes on you," he said. "Couldn't hardly sleep for the rope burns. See?" I could feel things getting heavy and made a move toward the front door, but without taking his eyes off Lucy's face he said, "Hang on a minute, Denise. I need a witness here.

"I've done a lot of dumb things in my time," he said to her. "Running after the wrong things, while the real ones got away. Well, it took me a while, but maybe I've learned. How to know the real things when I see them. When to quit running and hang on.

"You got away once, but I can't let it happen again. So marry me, or don't marry me, I don't care either way. But stay."

It was so quiet then, nothing but the far-off sound of a truck out on the highway, the wind in the pines. I kept thinking I shouldn't be standing there, this was too small and too private, but there was always that piece of me that, no matter what, couldn't turn away. How many chances would I ever get to look love in the face and hear its true name?

Lucy started to cry. Dad went to put his arms around her, and she gave him a feeble little push, but he just laughed and held on. She looked so small, standing there in the circle of his brown arms, his chin nestled in her tangled red hair. It didn't seem like such a slight body could hold what I knew she held: her love for my father, the baby they'd made.

"Come on inside," he said into her hair. "Let me show you what we've been up to since you left."

I listened to them make their way back the hall and through the kitchen, heard Lucy's little exclamation of surprise when she laid eyes on my new bedroom, their voices finally dropping out of earshot as, I guessed, he showed her the baby's room, four bare walls and that pale green crib. My stomach growled, loud, and I wondered what the odds were that anyone but me was interested in supper. Booker came up the steps and butted me in the shins in a sociable way with his snout, but even though this was my favorite time of day at Little Hope, I didn't feel like walking. In a minute Dad and Lucy crossed back through the living room, and with a soft click, the bedroom door closed.

I tiptoed down the hall and lifted the phone off the shelf and dragged it the whole length of the cord, into the kitchen. Erasmus was home, thank goodness; he answered on the second ring.

"Well, you don't sound very happy about it," he said after I'd related the events of the past few minutes. "Isn't that what you wanted? For Lucy to come back?"

"Yes, but—" I thought about what it was I wanted but couldn't say. For a second, on the porch, I'd felt like we were joined, all four of us, me and Dad and Lucy and the baby, a family. Now, already, they'd forgotten me, slid back into themselves; and I wondered if this was how life would always be for me, always on the edge of things, a ghost girl, outside looking in. "Never mind," I said to Erasmus. "I'm just hungry, I guess."

"Yeah? Me, too. My dad's got a new girlfriend and he's never home for supper anymore. How about I come get you and we go get a DQ Dude or something?"

I was changing into a clean shirt when I heard noises in the kitchen. I poked my head out of my room and saw Dad at the stove in his Levi's and bare feet, putting on the tea kettle. He must have had some sixth sense because without even turning around he said, "Come on in here," and I went and sat down at the table.

"Erasmus is coming over," I said, trying to make my voice casual. "He's taking me to the DQ for supper."

"That's good." I don't think he really heard me. He looked so mellow, padding around the kitchen, taking down the Constant Comment and a pair of mugs, humming "Blue Moon of Kentucky."

"So, you're really getting married?" I asked.

"Well, I'm not sure Miss Lucy is fully persuaded." He reached into the pantry for the plastic honey bear. "You're in favor of a wedding, aren't you?"

I thought of the look on Lucy's face, the way her body seemed to throb with feeling, the way she'd cried into his shirtfront. I thought of her gladness that was like a bumper car, ricocheting off everything in sight, how stubborn and unsteady it seemed.

"I guess so, sure. But this isn't gonna turn out like you and Ma, is it? Like, you're just doing it to give the baby a name, and then in a couple of years you'll take off?" I heard myself say it and I saw the dark gathering in his face, but it felt like it was all happening far away, at some cool remove.

"Do you think I'm proud of how things turned out, Denise? Do you think it gives me pleasure to know how I failed you and your mama, both?" His eyes burned, and I couldn't hold his gaze. "I married your mama for the only reason I knew," he said. "That I loved her so much I didn't want to live without her. And you. Both of you."

"Ma said—"

"I don't give a damn what your mama said! I meant to spend my life with her! I tried the best I could to be what she wanted, even when she didn't *know* what she wanted, even after she knew what she wanted wasn't me. She kept kicking me out, and I kept going back! Sometimes I wonder if that craziness of hers was nothing but an act, just to get me to give up, finally, and leave the two of you alone. You know that story I told you when you first came here, about how I used to sing to you at the kitchen table? She couldn't stand it, that we might have something that belonged to just us two! She didn't want me to love you. She thought it would take away from her love for you. Her great, big, old vulture love."

He turned and set his mug in the sink, the stoneware ringing against the stainless steel. Nothing he'd have done then would have surprised me, not even if he'd sprouted wings and flown through the kitchen window to roost with the owls in the piney woods. But he just grabbed hold of the edge of the counter and stood there, his head bowed, the muscles in his shoulders working like snakes under his skin. I could smell him, the damp, musky smell that was all over the house that summer, the smell of his and Lucy's blended skin.

I knew what had happened. We had belonged to each other, he and I, and my mother had stood up and blocked the way. She had seen what was there, the thing that ran through his blood and into mine, and she had flung up her arms to try to stop it. He was my real, my true parent, not her, and she had known, and had divided us, made up stories, kept him away.

Until now, when it was too late; now that I was growing up, taking shape, with the beginnings of urges no one could explain, gloom and greed and fury. My mother must have been scared to death when she heard the sound that came out of my mouth, the way my hands found their way to a guitar. No wonder she hadn't stuck around for the reunion. No wonder she hadn't called in a month. I was pissed off at both of them, to tell you the truth. Why hadn't he fought for me, yelled and fumed until my mother gave up her hold? And what about me had made me so unnecessary, had failed to keep their interest? They'd managed to fashion their own, separate lives, and I was lost, suspended between the two of them in some foggy nowhere land, not belonging in any kind of real way to either one. She was gone, and even though he was as close as my fingertips, I couldn't reach him.

I listened to him go up the hall, and the rusty screech of the hinges on the front door. I followed him, stepping out onto the porch as he put his hands in his pockets and looked out into the coming dark.

"Anybody tells you they have no regrets in this life, Denise, don't believe them," he said. "Anybody who says he's got nothing he wouldn't do over again is a goddamned liar."

"Yes, sir," I said, though I could only guess what it was, exactly, he was talking about.

He slipped his hand under my hair, against the back of my neck, and held it there. I felt the ridge of skin at the base of his fingers, their thickened tips; I felt every single beat of his regret. One star pulsed overhead in a sky blue as ink. Somewhere, far in the woods, a creature let out its sad, strange cry. He took his hand away and put it back in his pocket as a pair of headlights turned in off the highway.

❦

I still don't know how I talked him into letting me go. All I can think is that he must have weighed letting me take off in the dark with a boy in a twenty-year-old Chevy Impala against having the whole evening to swing naked from the light fixtures with Lucy, and guess what won?

I tried not to think too much about it, sitting across the front seat from Erasmus and letting the night come in through the open windows. If this really was a date, I didn't feel any of the things I was supposed to feel—no cold sweats, no butterflies in my belly. Erasmus sat so easy behind the wheel, his shoulders loose, steering with one wrist like he'd been born to drive. My heart beat a little bit faster looking at him, it's true, but I wasn't thinking about love. Love, as I saw it, was fighting and making up, running away and proposing, swinging naked from the light fixtures. This had nothing to do with that. I felt like we were part of the same circle, Erasmus and I, leaves on the same tree. I thought of a word Lucy told me Dad used to describe when they'd met, the way they'd come to see each other: "countrymen."

It was Monday night, but the Dairy Queen in Mooney was hopping. We stood in line at the counter, ordered our sandwiches and fries. The whole way into town, Erasmus had been telling me some long, complicated story about the tow job his dad had sent him out on that morning, how he'd gotten lost somewhere in the next county and by the time he found the place where he was supposed to be, the guy's neighbor had come along with his new heavy-duty pickup and they'd pulled the car out of the ditch themselves, and he was still telling it even as we found a booth and cleared aside the dregs of somebody else's meal and sat down to eat our supper.

I was about to unwrap my sandwich, laughing at the picture of Erasmus driving back to town in the tow truck trying to think of a way to come up with the cash for the job so he wouldn't have to tell his dad he'd gotten beat to the punch by a farmer with a king cab, when a shadow fell across our table, blocking most of the overhead light. Till then, I realized I'd never seen the Butler boys, either one of them, up close before, and that this one—I didn't know if it was Sean or Seth, they looked just alike to me, even though everybody said they weren't twins—was a lot bigger and uglier than he ever seemed behind the wheel of their Ram truck. His skin was terrible, a mess of angry red pimples, and he stank of beer and gasoline.

"Whatta ya think you're doin'? This's our table."

"Well, you left your trash all over it," I said. "About six kiddie meals, it looked like."

Just like that, the other brother materialized, crowding into the aisle, smelling even worse than the first one.

"I don't think you hear what we're sayin'," the first brother said, but even though I'd spoken, he was looking at Erasmus, not me. "This is *ours*."

He placed his hands on the table, a shoulder's width apart, and flexed his arms. Around our booth, conversations had fallen off; the girl behind the counter stood watching us over the register.

"Let's go, Denny," Erasmus murmured, his eyes fixed on the table, and started gathering up our untouched supper.

"No!" It came out louder than I intended, so that everyone in the place who hadn't been listening now was. I leaned toward Erasmus, circling my food protectively with my arms. "No!" I whispered. "They can't just . . . We can't—"

"Some problem here, folks?" A yellow-haired lady with a chest like a battleship came out from behind the counter with a tag on her red polo shirt that said DORLAS, MANAGER. It looked to me like Dorlas could take both Butler brothers single-handed.

"These got our table," one of the Butlers said. "We want it back, is all."

"It *isn't* theirs!" I said. "They weren't even in the restaurant when we got here! They're just trying to push us around, for no reason."

"Well, now, honey," Dorlas said, "what would they be trying to do a thing like that for?" Her mouth twisted up, a bitter crimp disguised as a smile. Then, just that quick, it was gone. "You two run on," she said to the Butlers. "I done told you, I can't be havin' you all in here ever night, stirrin' things up. I got a business to run."

"Some business," the first Butler said. "Garbage collection, looks like." But they made their way toward the door, taking a swipe at a

stack of red plastic baskets on top of one of the trash bins and sending
it flying in all directions.

Everyone in the place watched as they crossed the parking lot and
got into the Ram. The engine started with a roar, and the driver revved
it a few times and then flipped on the headlights so the high beams
shone straight in through the big plate-glass window. The tires spun
and smoked, and a woman with a little boy sitting right inside the window got up and snatched him out of the booth and rushed out the side
door without even bothering to gather up what was left of their meal.
Finally the truck swung in a wide backward arc and screeched out of
the parking lot, leaving a haze of exhaust and burned rubber.

I pushed away the rest of my sandwich. I wasn't hungry anymore.

"You Ash Farrell's daughter?" Dorlas said to me. "That right?"

"Yes, ma'am."

She cut a glance at Erasmus, then back to me. "Your daddy got any
idea where you're at tonight?"

"Yes, ma'am. He does."

In slow motion, the place started to come back to life: the milk-shake
machine whirring, the murmur of voices. Dorlas nodded one time, like
she wasn't convinced, and went back behind the counter.

Erasmus stood up and slid out of the booth. I started to say that
we'd paid for it, we might as well eat it, but the look on his face cut
right through me, and without a word I got up and followed him out to
the car.

The whole way down the highway to my father's house I kept watch
for headlights behind us, a truck grill with a death's head leaping silver
and grinning into our rearview mirror. But the night was as quiet as the
one before, the woods thick and close, like they were full of secrets.
Half a dozen times I opened my mouth to say something to Erasmus,
and half a dozen times I shut it again. I was in way over my head, and
I knew it; it wouldn't have done either one of us any good to say so.

The house was dark except for the front-porch light and the bulb
over the stove hood, shining through the kitchen window. "I think we
should wake up my father," I said.

"Why, Denny? What is he gonna do?" Erasmus's voice was flat and tired, more like he was sixty instead of sixteen. "I told you. It's just how people are here. It's never gonna change."

"But those boys," I said. "They can't just, just go around picking on people, trying to mix things up. It's—well, it's against the law, or something."

He reached across the seat and grabbed my hand. His own felt sticky and damp, and I thought of his cool, dry palm the evening we met, of the way he'd stood with his shoulders back and his spine so straight, like he was beholden to no one.

"Swear you won't say anything to anyone about this. Not even your dad. *Especially* not your dad."

"But I—"

He pressed my hand, hard enough to hurt. "*Swear.*"

I made my own little deal with God, standing on the step watching Erasmus's taillights disappear like some night creature's red eyes, into the trees. I wouldn't disturb Dad and Lucy; but if they came out to see about me, I would tell the truth about what had happened, not just the Butlers but the Dairy Queen manager, too, all of it. I stood listening to the Impala's engine fade, till the bugs and birds took up their usual chorus. I double-locked the front door and went into the kitchen and opened the refrigerator, but it was no use. My appetite was gone.

22

Lucy

 I woke to the smell of coffee and sounds from the kitchen, and I got up and pulled on Ash's old denim shirt, fastening it as I went up the hall. Ash and Denny sat side by side at the kitchen table, sipping from his blue-striped mugs. Something about the way the sun came through the kitchen window made the bones in Denny's face stand out, in a way I hadn't noticed before.

Ash smiled at me in the doorway. "What are you doing up so early on your day off?"

"I heard you all in here and thought I was missing a party." I sat down next to him and he covered my hand with his free one and ran his thumb over my knuckles. "Ash, is that coffee your daughter is drinking?"

"Will you take me to Wal-Mart today?" she asked me. "I want to get some curtains for my room, and a bedspread. Some paint for the walls."

Ash squeezed my hand. "I told her you'd help her," he said. "I hope that wasn't presumptuous."

"You? Presumptuous?" I said, as Denny got up and set her cup in the sink. She skirted the table and went off down the hall, and in a minute we heard the shower running.

"What's going on?" I asked. "Did something happen last night with Erasmus?"

"Jesus, did you see her face? She looked like she'd rip me down the middle just for asking."

"Well, maybe I can pry it out of her later."

"In the meantime, get over here," Ash said, and drew me onto his lap. The sun shone like melted beeswax through the window and he kissed me voluptuously. "So, how are *you* feeling this morning?"

"About what?" I took his hands and guided them over, then under, the denim shirt I wore.

"Like you don't know what. Like I didn't spend half the night working my powers of persuasion."

"I guess I don't understand the big hurry. Anyway, I kind of like this part. The persuading."

"It's just that I don't see any sense in waiting, is all," he said. "Why not just go ahead and call the judge, see if he can't squeeze us in between fishing tournaments?"

"Now, that's a romantic notion. Oh, you're no fun at all!" I declared as Ash laughed and began to extricate himself from the jumble of our limbs.

"Do you know who I'm working for today, Lucy? Mrs. Wells Mackey, that's who."

Mrs. Wells Mackey—Loretta—was one of those good-looking fifty-year-old women who's never quite gotten over the fact that she's used up her best years on an unappreciative man in a small town. Mrs. Mackey liked to drive her little Audi coupe to Dallas and shop a couple of times a month, then parade around Mooney in outfits most of us would never see outside the pages of the Neiman-Marcus catalog, stirring things up. Her hair was several expensive shades of blond, and for Christmas a few years before her husband had given her a brand-new set of breasts, two sizes bigger than the old ones. She remodeled her house the way the rest of us might order a cone at the Dairy Queen, on a whim. It was rumored that Mrs. Mackey stepped out on her husband from time to time, though none of these stories was ever substantiated; she had to live among us, after all. Still, I can't say I was thrilled to hear about Ash being so handily in her line of fire. She seemed like the kind of woman who'd greet the mailman at the front door in a fire-engine-red silk kimono without a stitch on underneath. Mr. Mackey was in cattle and was away a lot, on business.

"Well, good," I said. "Before you go, let me remind you what a real woman feels like. Just in case you go getting any offers you can't refuse." Ash opened his mouth but I pressed my hand over it. "Hush. This won't take two minutes." I set to work after the buttons on his Levi's; and sure enough, by the time the water stopped drumming in the bathroom, we'd made our steamy, fragrant tangle and separated again, smiling and self-conscious in the morning light.

"I need another shower," he said, standing up to tuck the tail of his shirt back into his jeans.

"Don't you dare. You let Mrs. Wells Mackey know what you've got at home."

He lifted his hands to his face and inhaled. "Mm. You took care of that, I think."

"I'm marking you," I said. "So you don't forget your way home at the end of the day."

"God," he said, circling me with his arms, "will you marry me?"

"I'm thinking about it. I might even have your baby, too. How's that for an offer you can't refuse?"

By the time Ash drove off, Denny was out of the bathroom, and I showered and dressed in shorts and one of my loose-fitting tops, and sandals, and she and I set off for Atlanta, twenty miles north. We drove for several miles with only the sound of the road rushing through the open windows and Willie Nelson's nasal twang coming out of the radio.

"So, how was your evening with Erasmus? Did you guys have a good time in town?"

"Great," she answered. "Time of our lives."

"You know, Denny," I said slowly, "I was wondering how you feel about starting high school in the fall. I mean, are you excited? Do you think it will be fun? Do you miss your friends in Dallas?"

"Oh, sure, I'm thrilled. *All* my friends are just *dying* to see me."

"Well, you're in a jolly mood this morning," I fired back. I couldn't believe how bitchy I sounded, and she didn't indulge me with a come-back. "Let me ask you this. What would you do if you could do any-thing you wanted at the end of the summer?" Out of the corner of my eye, I saw her take her eyes off the passing scenery and look at me. "Really, I was wondering what you thought about staying here."

We merged off the highway onto the six-lane divided bypass; a semi roared by on our left, rocking the Buick's heavy chassis, filling the car with diesel fumes. "You mean, live here?" she asked. "With you? Permanently?"

I kept my eyes straight ahead on the wide silver tail of the eighteen-wheeler up ahead. "Well, nothing's permanent, is it? I mean, we don't know what's going to happen with this record-company guy. He may want Ash to come up there, or . . ." My brain seized up like it did every time I thought of Nashville; I couldn't help picturing Ash and me like the cover of some Dolly Parton/Porter Waggoner album from the six-ties, in form-fitting spangles and shellacked yellow hair, lounging next to a guitar-shaped swimming pool.

"You don't want him to make it," she said, "do you?"

"I want him to have everything he's ever wanted," I said. "And I don't want anything to change."

"But you don't want to leave here?"

"I want it to be possible, somehow, for Ash to do what he does and for this to be the place he comes home to. Me, and you, and the baby." I almost couldn't bear what was in her face. How in the world had it fallen upon me, this urge I felt to hold and keep her? "I can't promise you anything," I said. "I shouldn't even be discussing it with you. It's up to your mama and daddy to decide. I only want you to be thinking about it, okay? If it was up to you, whether you'd go back to Dallas, or stay."

We pulled off the bypass into the huge asphalt parking lot in front of Wal-Mart, already teeming at ten o'clock in the morning, and made our way inside past the branch bank and the optometrist and the life-size plastic Ronald McDonald that always seemed poised to mug somebody.

"Look, you've got to help me figure out what to do about this wedding," I said as Denny commandeered a cart and we headed for the housewares section.

"You mean you decided? I thought you were still making up your mind."

"Well, your daddy does seem to be in an awfully big hurry. It makes me nervous, somehow."

"How come?" She stopped in front of a display of bedspreads and fingered a pastel floral one.

"I guess because things have been so crazy the last few weeks. It seems like it might be nice to give it all a chance to settle down. I guess I don't see a reason to rush."

"But he got you pregnant."

"Oh, good Lord," I said as she picked up a pillow sham printed with daisies. "Listen, Denny, I feel like you deserve to know that your daddy did not get me pregnant." She looked at me in astonishment. "Well, yes, he did. I mean, yes, the baby is his. But it wasn't his fault. We . . . Oh, shit."

"You mean it wasn't an accident?"

"Well, it wasn't planned. But it wasn't prevented, either."

"You *tricked* him?"

"No! I—of course not!" How had I gotten myself into this? "We didn't think it was possible," I said, and murmured a silent little prayer that it would be enough.

"Jeez," she said, "were you guys *dumb*." I couldn't argue with that.

We proceeded to the curtain aisle, our cart still empty. "I just want to say one more thing," I said. "I wouldn't marry your daddy just because I'm pregnant. I mean, that's not the only reason. It isn't even the big one."

"What is?" She held a swatch of white voile up to the light.

I watched her and struggled for a way to say what I felt, some way to distill everything I felt for Ash, the whole broad sweep, into a phrase or two fit for his daughter's ears. *Because I know him on some level that goes beyond the present and the physical, that comes from the sky and the earth and was here before we were and will be here after we're gone. Because I cannot get enough of touching him. Because he found a glory in me. Because I want to see these things go on.* I was still trying to sort it all out in my head when Denny, for the first time all morning, smiled: her real smile, the one with her father's teeth.

"Never mind," she said. "I guess I know. Can I have these?" She waved the voile curtains, on sale for eleven ninety-nine. I nodded yes in grateful silence, and she tossed the package into the cart and we made a slow circle back to the bed linens.

She chose, finally, the daisy-print bedspread, and in the paint department we picked a pale, creamy yellow off a chip and handed it to a high school kid to mix up for us. While we waited, we wandered over to the electronics section and watched a few minutes of *The Young and the Restless* on a bank of television sets. "Maybe somebody will give y'all a TV for a wedding present," Denny said. I laughed and said I hoped not.

We pushed the cart over to the music department, where Alan Jackson and Tim McGraw and the Judds were stacked in rows five high and three deep. "It's weird, isn't it?" Denny said, scanning the aisles. "To think about seeing him here."

"Who?"

"Dad."

I stopped and thought about it. A year from now, would somebody be standing in Wal-Mart listening to Ash's voice come through the overhead speakers and stop to think that the auburn-haired girl in "A Place Love Calls Home" had a name, a face, a ring on her hand, a baby on her hip? It was one thing to have him singing about me in front of our hometown every week at the Round-Up; how would I feel when people in Toledo or Tampa were cueing up the stories of our life for their morning commute or their nightly jog or their happy hour?

We paid for our merchandise, then got back in the Buick and drove straight to Mrs. Wells Mackey's house. She and Mr. Mackey lived on a nice-size spread west of Mooney, in a six-thousand-square-foot ranch house on a couple of hundred acres with a stock tank and a windmill and a detached four-car garage. We drove through a front gate decorated with wagon wheels. Ash's old truck was parked in the circular drive, nose to nose with a blue van that said DEB'S CATERING.

"Wait here," I said to Denny, who had her nose in a copy of *Bride's Magazine* she'd finagled me into buying at the checkout at Wal-Mart. "I'll just be a minute."

I stood on the step wondering whether to ring the bell, when the front door opened and a young woman in black slacks and a white smock came out. "Oh! Hi," she said. "From the flower shop, right? I'm the caterer. You must want Loretta."

"No, I'm here in an unofficial capacity," I said. "I'm looking for Ash Farrell."

"Hold on. Last I looked, they were finishing the crudités and starting on the cheese biscuits." She vanished inside for a minute, and when she returned, Ash was trailing her, a miniature carrot in one hand. "Lucy!" he said. "What a surprise."

"Well, I was going to apologize for interrupting your work, but I don't guess I have to," I said as Deb opened the back of the van and lifted out a big stainless-steel chafing dish. "What are crudités?" I whispered.

"Nothing but a fancy name for cut-up vegetables." Ash held up the tiny carrot, then popped it into his mouth. "Loretta and Wells are having a couple of his clients over this evening, and she decided to lay in a few rations."

"Which explains why you're helping her sample them."

"We've been going over blueprints all morning. I managed to scare up an appetite."

"Well, can you tear yourself away from your teeny-weeny vegetables a minute?" I said. "I want to talk to you."

We crossed the lawn, toward the fence that separated the yard from the stock tank out back. Pecan trees spread their branches over the water, and a scattering of Holsteins grazed on the far bank.

"Mrs. Mackey asked me this morning what cologne I was wearing," he said.

"What did you tell her?"

"That it must have been my fiancée's. Her own private blend."

"I can't believe she didn't know."

"Oh, she knew. I think it was her way of letting me *know* she knew."

We stopped at the fence, and I turned to him. "Ash, I want to get married."

He raised his eyebrows. "Well, this is a switch."

"I had an—an epiphany, I guess you could say. In the music department at Wal-Mart. It's just that, all of a sudden, it seems silly to wait. I mean, things are moving so fast! You're going to Nashville in just a few weeks, and by the time you come back, I'll be six months pregnant—"

"Wait a minute," he said. "Nobody said that. Where did you get that?"

"Are you listening to me? Everything's changing. I want to put the anchor down now, before things get even choppier. I want . . ."

I felt dizzy with what I wanted. I wanted him shackled hand and foot, my name carved into his forehead in letters three inches high, a chastity belt around his hips to which no one but I had the tiny gold key. I wanted him horribly disfigured, in a painless manner. I wanted him bound up with me in every imaginable way, so close he couldn't breathe in without me breathing out, my love dangling over his head like a yoke, every hour of every day. "What I'm saying is, how long do you think it'll take to line up the license and the judge? Maybe we could do it this weekend. Just the two of us."

"This doesn't sound like you, Lucy," Ash said. "What's up?"

"I've just made up my mind, is all."

"Well, then, I'll knock off early this afternoon and drive into town and see Judge Crumb. Before you have time to come to your senses."

He nodded in the direction of the Buick. "You get anything out of Denny? About last night?"

"Not a word. We bought her a bedspread and some curtains, though."

"It's something to think about, Lucy."

"What is?"

"It's one thing to be taking on a fellow by his ownself. You sure you want one with all sorts of strings attached?"

"I think it's too late."

"Meaning what?"

"Meaning, we were tangled up pretty good before Denny ever showed up."

Ash laughed. "We were, weren't we?"

"Anyway, I remember something you said to me one day up at Willie B.'s, before we ever got . . ."

"Tangled?"

"Uh-huh. You said baggage is how we carry the good stuff."

"You ready, then? All packed up for the long haul?"

"Ready." And we set off toward the house, arms looped around each other's hips, as tight as the strings that pulled us from every direction.

$\mathcal{D}$enny

 Dad went back to work, or to tasting Mrs. Mackey's appetizers, and we drove to Lucy's rent house and picked up Steve Cropper and the shabby cardboard box she was using for a suitcase, then home to hang my new curtains and smooth the new bedspread over my bed. After, Lucy poured us some iced tea and we sat down at the kitchen table to look at the bride magazine together, flipping through the pages exclaiming over what we did and didn't like, and we were still sitting there in the late afternoon, wondering in a lazy way what to do about supper, when Dad got home.

I knew right off something was wrong. He didn't stop the way he usually did to pull off his boots at the front door, or come up the hall singing a slice of some crazy song he'd heard on the radio. I'd managed to keep my mind busy most of the day without having to think too much about what had happened at the Dairy Queen, but I saw now that my promise to Erasmus never had a chance, not the way news traveled in Mooney.

Dad went straight over to the refrigerator and took out a beer. He took a few long gulps, looking out the kitchen window, before he turned and set his gaze on me.

"Why didn't you tell me what happened last night?" he said. "How come I had to hear about it in town?"

"Erasmus made me promise not to tell."

"Well, that was damn foolish of him, Denise, and of you, too. Did you really think I wouldn't find out?"

"About what?" Lucy asked, closing the magazine. "What are you going on about?"

"Tell her," Dad said to me. "I'd like to hear it in your words."

I shrugged. "Those skinheads, the Butler brothers, gave us a hard time in the Dairy Queen. They claimed we had their table, but it wasn't, not really. Anyway, the manager kicked them out. It pissed them off, I guess, but they just left. They didn't really do anything."

"They did do something," Dad said. "They drove out to Eulan Holmes's place in the county and torched his shed and half his cattle pen. He lost two steers, burned to a crisp."

"You mean, the Butlers got caught?" I asked. "The sheriff arrested them?"

"No, they didn't get caught. They never fucking get caught, do they?"

"Then how do you know it was them?"

"Because they've been dicking around like this for weeks! That ex-con Tim Spivey they hang out with? Word is, Spivey told them about some white supremacist group they can join if they just pass the initiation. Word is, they're not in till they— Well, you remember what happened last summer, down in Jasper."

I knew what that meant, even though I'd been in Dallas at the time. Some Aryan Brotherhood guys had tied a man to the back of a pickup truck and dragged him to death; they'd found the body in pieces, scattered up and down the blacktop road.

"I don't believe that," Lucy said. "Things aren't that way around here."

"I'm not so sure," I said. "The way the people at the Dairy Queen acted, it was like Erasmus and me were the circus act, not the Butlers."

"Yeah, old Dorlas had a few words about that for me this afternoon," Dad said. "She wasn't a bit shy about letting me know she didn't appreciate my daughter bringing trouble into her fine establishment." He rolled his bottle between his two palms, back and forth. "You should have told me, Denise," he said. "Right away, the minute you got home."

"Why?" I said. "Those people are just stupid. What could you have done about it?"

"I plan to start by talking to the Butlers. And this Spivey creep, if I can find him."

Lucy pushed back her chair and got to her feet. "Ash, my Lord. Are you out of your mind? These guys, if they're really as hard-core as you say they are, what makes you think they'll back down for you? You can't reason with people like that! Why don't you just let Bill Dudley and the deputies handle it?"

"Did I say I mean to be reasonable?" He took a last drink, then set the empty bottle on the countertop. "Look, I never liked these guys in the first place, not their attitudes or their ugly faces or anything they stand for. And now they've brought my daughter into it. I won't have it."

"So, you'll go out and get yourself killed in the bargain? You'll make us all targets, just like Eulan Holmes's cows?" She shoved the chair against the table, hard enough to rattle the ice cubes in our tea. "Where do you think it stops with people like that? How do you know you won't set them after the whole town?"

"Somebody has to do something," Dad said. "Somebody needs to take a stand."

"Then let the sheriff do it. It doesn't have to be you."

He turned and started for the door. "I thought you had more backbone, Lucy."

"Well, I thought you had more brains!" she shouted after him, but that didn't stop him, it didn't even slow him down. We listened to the truck fire up and spin around in the yard, then tear off up the road.

"Oh, Ash. You asshole," Lucy said, and sat down again and put her head in her arms. I felt like I ought to just crawl in a crack and die. Everything was my fault. Not only had I betrayed my word to Erasmus, my father was liable to set the whole town on fire and get himself lynched in the process. I could picture the news vans arriving from Texarkana, Dallas, maybe even CNN. I imagined myself alongside Lucy at the funeral, her face puffy behind a black veil, her belly swollen with a baby whose father had sacrificed himself over something nobody but him seemed to understand. I could almost see the statue in front of the courthouse: ASH FARRELL, DEFENDER OF THE FREE WORLD. HE GAVE HIS LIFE FOR A DQ DUDE.

"Call the sheriff," I said, and Lucy lifted her head and looked at me. "He'll tell us what to do."

∞

Our worst imaginings didn't come true that night, although Dad did almost end up on the wrong side of the law. A couple of circuits around the courthouse square failed to turn up either the Butlers or Tim Spivey—in fact, people telling the story in town the next day would remark that, even though he was getting more notorious every day, nobody could actually remember ever *seeing* Tim Spivey—and so he'd headed over to the Dairy Queen, where Sheriff Dudley, having spoken to Lucy and knowing the makings of trouble when he saw it, managed to head him off in the parking lot.

The sheriff was a rangy man with a silver crew cut and a laid-back way about him, and he and Mrs. Dudley showed up at the Round-Up with some regularity to dance and hear Dad sing. He was willing to cut Dad a little slack where both the DQ and the Butlers were concerned. But Dad would have to let the law handle it, the sheriff said. He couldn't have his populace up in arms, running around half-cocked and looking for their own brand of justice. For every argument Dad made, Sheriff Dudley pulled out a countering one, and finally got him into the pickup and headed toward home, with a promise to call in half an hour and make sure he'd actually showed up there.

Lucy and I were just finishing up a sad supper, Kraft macaroni and cheese and Jell-O, when Dad pulled in. She seemed bent on ignoring him, didn't even bother looking up from her plate when he came and stood in the kitchen door.

"You called the sheriff on me?" he said. "You ratted me out?"

"Somebody has to be the voice of reason around here. It doesn't look like we can count on you." She got up and set her plate in the sink and turned on the tap.

"Well, I hope you don't think this is the end of it," Dad said. "I hope you don't think I'm just gonna take this thing lying down."

She shut off the faucet suddenly and turned to look at him. "Weren't you supposed to talk to Judge Crumb this afternoon? Or were you too caught up in your big crusade to think about that?"

"I'll do it first thing in the morning. I promise."

"Don't trouble yourself. Not when you've got more important things on your plate." She wiped her hands on a dish towel and tossed it over the back of a chair. "It's a good thing you finished out Denny's room, so you can have the couch tonight," she said, shoving past him out of the kitchen. I kept my head bowed over my plate, and in a minute he sighed a deep sigh and went over to the stove and lifted the lid on the leftover macaroni.

"I just want to do what's right, Denise," he said without turning his head. "Is that so hard to understand?"

"No, sir. Except maybe—"

"Maybe what?"

"Well, maybe Lucy has a point. I mean, what good is calling these guys out gonna do? It'll probably just get them even more worked up than they already are."

"It's a matter of principle, that's why. I don't know why you all can't see that."

"I *can* see it! I can. But did you ever think you might be making things even harder for—well, for Erasmus and his family? It's not your shed they're gonna burn down, or you they—" I couldn't say that I was thinking about the man down in Jasper, couldn't let my mind wrap around that and Erasmus in the same thought.

"Erasmus and his family are my friends."

"So, have you talked to them about this? Have you asked them how they feel?" I remembered Erasmus making me promise not to tell what happened at the Dairy Queen, and I knew what I'd felt in the damp clutch of his hand wasn't anger so much as cold, hard fear.

"I've lived in this town all my life, just about. This isn't the first time something like this has happened, not by a long shot. I just think it's time somebody stood up against it for once."

It was useless to argue with him; his feeling was a righteous thing, like words carved in stone. It was just like him, really, to think he could take the weight of the world on his shoulders; it wasn't much of a stretch to see him in tights and a cape with a big red *S* on his chest. He liked that notion of himself, too, you could tell, which made the whole thing that much more aggravating.

"I'd like to be excused," I said. But Dad was preoccupied now, standing next to the stove with a faraway look on his face, so I left him there, studying on how to save the world.

I'd been worried about talking to Erasmus, wondering how I'd manage to convince him I hadn't gone against him by talking to my dad. Surely, I thought, listening to the phone ring and ring on the other end, he would realize the story would be all over town by now, that I hadn't said a word until Dad heard it somewhere else first.

But, it turned out, I didn't have to explain. A lady's voice answered at last, crying out in a rushed, breathless voice, "Hello?" I asked to speak to Erasmus, please. "Who's calling?" she barked out. I gave my name. There was silence on the other end, then muffled talk, then her voice again, clear as anything I'd ever heard: "Erasmus will not be speaking with you. Don't call here again." And the line went dead in my ear.

⚭

I felt like I had a hole in me, a big jagged thing in the middle of my chest that anyone looking at me could hear the air rushing through, see patches of cloud and blue sky. Any normal person would have seen it. I wasn't living with normal people, though. I was living with Superman, who had other things on his mind—first of which, it looked like, was to convince Lois Lane he was just a normal guy after all. When I went to bed that night, he was still sitting out on the porch, working his way through a six-pack. I woke up a few hours later hearing them arguing in the kitchen. Through my bedroom door I couldn't make out what was being said, just the up and down of their voices. When it got quiet again, I opened my door a crack and saw that the house was dark. The kitchen was empty; and so was the living room. The bedroom door was closed.

In the morning they were all smiles, holding hands and acting googly-eyed over their coffee, never mind that there was nothing for breakfast and the sink was heaped with dirty dishes and I had a hole in me the size of China. They were full of big plans, starting with that night's supper. "How about I run by Willie's and pick up a load of ribs?" Dad said. "Maybe you want to call up Raz and ask him to join us. This'll be better than Dairy Queen any old day."

I stood inside the screen door watching them kissing good-bye in the front yard like I bet Lois and Clark Kent never did. Dad couldn't just smooch and run; he was all over Lucy like she was made of candy, running his lips across her face, nuzzling her ears, pressing his face against the hollow of her neck like he couldn't get enough of that sweetness. I wouldn't have been a bit surprised if they'd turned around and come back in the house and locked the bedroom door behind them, but they managed to pry themselves apart, finally, and without so much as a word or a wave to me, got in their separate vehicles and drove off.

I took out my guitar and tried to call up all the tear-jerking songs I knew, but even those didn't make me feel any better. It didn't really help to know that what I was feeling was the very thing Bobby Bland or Roy Orbison or George Jones had been singing about years before I came along. I guess the first time your heart breaks, it's yours and yours alone, which is why folks go on writing about it, every one of us trying to put words and music to our own particular shade of blue. I fooled around for a little while with a chain of minor chords, a couple of lines that ran along the dark groove my mind was following.

When the phone rang, I just about didn't answer it. I sat on the front step listening to it jangle in the empty hall and tried to think who on my incredibly shrinking list of friends and acquaintances I felt like talking to, and came up blank. I didn't want to get into trouble, though, to find out later I'd missed some important message for Dad or Lucy. Maybe, I daydreamed on my way to pick it up, it was Ed McMahon, calling to say I'd won a million dollars. Maybe it was some nice ordinary family, with rational people for parents, wanting to adopt me.

"Denny?" Air sailed through the hole in me, so strong I thought it would knock me right over. "Look, this has to be quick. I'm out on a job for my dad. If he pushes the redial button on his cell phone, I'm dead."

"My dad found out about what happened when he went into town. I never told. "

"I know that. Jeez, I don't know what I was thinking. I guess maybe I thought it would just die off on its own, you know?"

"Well, it didn't. He's all up in arms. He practically called out the Butler brothers and that Spivey creep."

"My family says I can't see you for a while," Erasmus said. "Until this thing with the Butlers blows over. They think — "

"What?"

"They think it might make things worse for us. Everybody out here's real jumpy, since Mr. Holmes's place got burned. Uncle Isaac's talking about sending Rose and the kids over to his mama's place in Rodessa."

We were quiet for a few seconds, just breathing into the phone. I hadn't had that many friends in my life, and it felt sickening to me that something so random, so trifling, could come between Erasmus and me, separating our families and the place where we lived.

"I don't know what to say," he said finally. "I'm just sorry I got you into this."

"You didn't get me into anything!" I answered back. "I was afraid you were mad at me."

"For what? What did you do?"

"I guess I didn't believe you, about the way things were. You tried to tell me, but I didn't listen."

"I guess I wanted to believe it, too."

"We're having Willie B.'s tonight. Dad said to invite you."

"I can't. My dad'll go ballistic if I even ask."

"I know. I tried to call you, but some lady said I couldn't talk to you."

"That was my aunt Nettie. Somehow she's got it in her head that God died and put her in charge. Tell Ash to be careful, Denny. He shouldn't even be messing with those guys."

"I can't tell him anything. He thinks he's Superman." I thought Erasmus would laugh, but he didn't. "Hey, guess what I was doing when you called?" I said. "Writing a song."

"No way. Can I hear it?"

"Sure. When it's done."

"Maybe you can sing it for me on the porch sometime."

"Okay." I missed him then in a way that felt physical, that seemed to raise his shape and weight in the space in front of me. Then, just that quickly, it was gone, and so was the hole in me. I felt clear, tough, all of a piece again.

"What's it called?" he asked, but before I could answer him, his phone's call-waiting rang, and he had to hang up.

I thought about that question as I walked back out to the porch and sat down to finish the song. It didn't have a title yet, not one I could hear. It was in there, I knew, something fine, waiting to break the surface. I had faith I would find it, in time. One thing I did know, as I watched my fingers shape the chords and heard the strings respond. It would definitely have a part for a fiddle.

24

Lucy

 "It's progress, don't you think?" I said. "This time, I just locked him out of the bedroom instead of packing my stuff and leaving the house."

"Well, it didn't last long, from the looks of you," Peggy said, coming out of the cooler with an armload of sunflowers and mums and gerbera daisies. "You're way too pink and perky-looking for a woman who spent the night tossing and turning alone."

"Oh, I unlocked the door, eventually." She looked up and waggled her eyebrows at me in her trademark way, and I started to laugh. "Peggy, can you keep a secret?'

"Now, Lucy, why in the world would you ask me such a thing? My dearly departed husband, Duane Thaney, God rest his soul, used to say I'd call up the neighbors and gossip about the grocery list if I didn't have anything else to talk about." She waved her hand at me like a surgeon signaling for a scalpel. I took a guess and passed her the clippers, and she snipped a sunflower's fat stem and handed them back. "But I don't figure you've got much of a secret, anyway. Everybody knows Ash paid a visit to Judge Crumb this morning."

"They do? I mean—he did?"

"Yes, ma'am, bright and early. Millie Campbell said he was whistling like a whippoorwill when he came out, too. My guess is they weren't discussing parking tickets. Now, where's that baby's breath?" I reached into the cooler and got her a bunch, and she began to separate it with her swift, sturdy fingers.

"Do you think I'm crazy, Peggy?"

She stopped fussing with the arrangement and looked up at me, her face puzzled. "Why, what for?"

"I haven't known the man six months! Now here I am, pregnant, with his teenage daughter under our roof, watching him get ready to go off to Nashville. In the meantime, he's decided to be the, the Eldridge Cleaver or whoever of Mooney, Texas."

"Eldridge Cleaver was a colored man, I believe."

"Yes, I know." I didn't bother pointing out that it was barely acceptable anymore to use the word "colored"; in this corner of the woods, "colored" was better than a lot of things I might have heard. "My point is, it seems like we find something to butt heads over every day! I just about can't remember what it was like before this summer, when we were just in love and happy. I wonder if we shouldn't wait until things settle down a little bit before we think about getting married."

Peggy laughed. "Sweetie, I hate to tell you, things aren't gonna settle down again. No, ma'am, you're rolling now, and you're gonna keep rolling." She nudged me to give her more elbow room. "Anyway, if you'd stop and take a breath, look around you long enough, you'd find out you *are* in love and happy.

"You know what I think? You spent a long, long time married to a man who never caused a ripple in your little life till the day he died. So now, with Ash, when things get a little dicey, you feel like it's the end of the world. But in real life, in a real marriage, that's how things are between two people. Dicey. Otherwise, I believe you'd bore each other to death. The only thing you and Ash got to figure out is how to kiss and make up a little faster." She cut her eyes at me and smiled. "Not that it doesn't help to lock him out of the bedroom now and then." She took a step backward to inspect the arrangement, then leaned toward it and made a microscopic adjustment to an orange daisy. "I will tell you one thing I think is a mistake, though."

"What's that?"

"You don't really mean to stand up in the judge's chambers, just the two of you? Why, Lucy, this whole town, just about, has got a stake in you and Ash getting married!" I smiled, remembering how, months earlier, a goodly number of them had joined in a pool at the café speculating on how long I'd be able to hold off his advances. I found out later that hardly anyone had bet I'd last a week. "Your mama will be back in just a few days from that Bible Land trip she took with the church group. Don't you think it would make her happy to see you and Ash standing up there with Reverend Honeywell, saying your vows in front of God and everybody?"

"I don't see how my mama has a vote in this." I'd managed to forget she was coming back next week; to tell the truth, I'd forgotten she was coming back at all. "She's going to hit the roof as it is, when she finds out I'm pregnant."

"Oh, she knows."

"She does? How?"

"It's the twentieth century everyplace, Lucy. They've got telephones over there, in Greece or wherever she is, just like they do here. Not to mention computers and fax machines and the good old post office." I tried, and failed, to imagine my mama receiving a fax that announced I was having a baby.

"Well, good. She'll have some time to get used to the idea. All the more reason Ash and I ought to get up in front of the judge, just as soon as we can. Then, by the time she gets home, I'll be good and legal, and she won't be able to squawk about it."

"Forget about your mama, then," Peggy said. "I shoulda known better than to bring her up in the first place. What about the rest of your family? What about your brothers, and Geneva, and Dove? Don't you think they all want the chance to see you two get hitched?"

"You don't fool me for a minute," I said. "This is about you, isn't it?

You want an excuse to curl up your hair and buy a new dress and decorate the church with about five thousand dollars' worth of flowers neither you or I can afford and sit in the front row and cry in your hankie while Ash and I say, 'I do.' And then call up your friends on the phone and talk about it for two weeks afterward. Am I right?"

"Second row, honey. First row is reserved for family."

"You *are* family," I said. "As much grief as you give me, you might as well be. Except that I like you a whole lot more than I like my mama."

Peggy's eyes were watery, but it might just have been her allergies acting up. The Ash and Lucy display in the front window was still in place, though voting had tapered off in recent days. The tally, I'd managed to eke out of her, was something like 487 to 12. I still wondered in the back of my mind who the handful of no voters were.

She snipped a stray blossom from the enormous bouquet and stepped back to admire her handiwork.

"Nice," I said. "Who's it for?"

"Your sister-in-law, as a matter of fact."

"You mean Connie?" I always felt guilty when I thought about Kit's wife, who was solid and quiet and looked after their four children full-time, and who I almost never saw. Had something big happened that I'd missed, something worth commemorating with a fifty-dollar bouquet?

"I mean Geneva. Bailey's wife. Remember her?"

I remembered her, all right, even if I hadn't spoken to her or seen her face in a week. The whole town was bound to know that, too, though no one had said a word. "It's her going-away party at the clinic this afternoon," Peggy said. "This one here's from the other nurses. There's two more in back, from Dr. Crawford and the surgery team over at the hospital."

"I thought her new job didn't start for another week."

"Doesn't," Peggy said. She locked eyes with me, goading me to ask the next, obvious question, but I wouldn't bite.

"What time's the party?" I said instead.

"Two o'clock. I can do the delivery, if you don't want to."

"Don't be silly. I'll do it." *I'm not the one who started this foolishness*, I wanted to say. But it wasn't foolish, as far as Geneva was concerned; the distance she'd put between us was both deep and real.

Peggy looked at the clock over the counter. "Isn't it about time you got on over to the café? Somebody's probably waiting on you." Ash had called and asked me to lunch, probably to fill me in on his visit to Judge Crumb. At the rate we were going, I'd be the last person in town to hear it.

"Waiting to make a first-rate fool out of me, you mean," I said, as I got my purse. "Waiting to strap me down and wreck my life."

"You're already strapped down!" Peggy called after me. "You're already wrecked!"

I clapped my hands over my ears, but I could hear her laughing anyway as I headed for the door.

∞

Ash was waiting for me on the sidewalk in front of the café, holding a take-out bag. He steered me across the street to a shady bench under the Jefferson Davis statue on the courthouse lawn.

"I hope you're in the mood for turkey," he said. "I had to order as quick as I could and hotfoot it out of there. Jesus, this thing has gotten totally out of control."

"What thing would that be, Ash?" I couldn't be sure he wasn't pulling an Eldridge Cleaver on me, riling up the townsfolk to march on the capitol.

"This wedding, that's what! I'd barely set foot out of the judge's chambers when that little blue-haired lady, the clerk—what's her name?"

"Constance Struthers?"

"That's the one. She all but nailed me to the wall and chewed my butt out. She scared me so bad, I hardly heard a thing she said. But the gist of it was—"

"I already know the gist of it," I said, unwrapping my sandwich. "I've been getting an earful all morning from Peggy."

"And Lord knows what I was thinking, walking into the café. They ought to just hang a sign over the door of that place: 'Enter at Your

Own Risk.' I don't think I ever got such a dressing-down from my own stepmom as Carol gave me."

I took a bite of my sandwich. Ash had either forgotten I preferred mustard to mayo or, in his haste to get out of there, he hadn't had a chance to speak up. "Well, you and I've been about the most popular item over there since the day we took up together. Maybe we need to work harder at being less infamous."

"Kinda late for that." He smiled at me and my heart did a long skid, the very kind it had done the first time we'd locked eyes outside the flower shop.

"Are you planning on telling me what the judge said?"

"Are you sure you really want to go through with this? You might not get another chance to save your good name."

"Just spill it. Bottom line."

He peeled the white paper off a second turkey sandwich and took a couple of quick bites.

"Bottom line," he said, swallowing, "this weekend is out of the question. Big deep-sea fishing trip to Port Isabel. Bunch of his old Air Force buddies, get together every year."

"Oh." It was hard to say if what I was feeling was disappointment or relief.

"But any time after Monday, he said, fine. Actually, he said it would be an honor to unite two such esteemed persons in the rite of matrimony. Those were his exact words."

I peeled a piece of crust off my sandwich. "Ash, I've been thinking—"

"Hey, come to think of it, isn't 'esteemed' just another word for infamous?"

"Ash!"

"What?"

"Well, listen. When I said I wanted it to be just us and the judge, I hadn't stopped to think of how everybody else would feel. I mean, maybe we owe it to our friends and our families to let them share it with us. Isn't a wedding really about standing up and, and declaring yourself in public, making it official? Otherwise, what's the point?"

"I thought declaring yourself to God had something to do with it."

"If it's just about God, then what do we need the judge for?" I said. "I'm pretty sure God already knows how I feel."

He reached for my hand. "How do you feel?" His mouth was smiling but his eyes were not. I knew this look, a rarely opened window into his most secret self. The first time I'd seen it was when he'd told me about his earliest years, about a daddy who ran off and a mama who went crazy and gave him up. It didn't surface often, but when it did, I knew better than to kid around.

"Lucky," I said, lacing my fingers through his. "How about you?"

He never got to answer me. A slice of shade fell across our bench, across our joined hands, and Ash and I looked up, away from each other.

The man standing there, blocking our sun, ruining our tender moment, didn't look like much. Short—shrimpy—with an oily, old-fashioned Elvis ducktail, white T-shirt and stiff dungarees, and a two-day beard covering pale pits and pocks. What scared me were his eyes, like blue chrome, the kind of surface that doesn't let light in or out but only mirrors what's in front of it. Even before I saw the tattoos, I knew who he was.

He shifted jerkily from one foot to the other, almost a jig, like he had more pressing things to do and places to be. "Your name Farrell?"

Slowly Ash untangled our hands. "You must be Spivey. Hey, folks around here just about decided you were some kind of tall tale, and now here you are, live and in person. How was Huntsville? The food's pretty bad, I hear. Maybe since they don't figure on too many of the customers getting out to complain about it."

"I did my time," Spivey said, "not that it's any of your damn business. You got some truck with me, mister, you say it to my face. I got no time for Mickey Mousin' around."

"No, you've got more important stuff on your plate, I guess," Ash said. "Like road manager to Tweedledum and Tweedledee. Those are your boys, aren't they? Those skinheads in the big truck you've got running around here torching things and threatening people?"

"If you mean the Butler boys, they's associates of mine, yeah. What of it?"

"Well, you know, it's funny." Ash had picked up the empty take-out bag and was crumpling it in his fist, the veins in the back of his hand bulging like live wires. "Most of the time I'm pretty much a live-and-let-live kind of guy. But I tend to take it personally when it's my friends and family members on the receiving end of the kind of stuff they've been dishing out around here lately. You know what I mean?"

"Not a clue, chief." Spivey's eyes were fixed beyond us, on the plaque at the base of the statue of Jefferson Davis. I knew without looking what it said; every grade-school kid in Mooney had to commit it to memory: *Obstacles may retard, but they cannot long prevent the progress of a movement sanctified by its justice, and sustained by a virtuous people.*

"So, I guess you're saying you don't know anything about the fire at Mr. Holmes's place a couple of days ago. Or the truckload of fireworks the sheriff caught the Butler boys with last week, headed out to a picnic at my partner's, Isaac King's."

"Maybe they wanted in on the celebratin'," Spivey said. "Ever think of that?" His lip curled, but his eyes were as hard and blue as ever.

"My daughter got hassled the other night by the Butlers in the Dairy Queen. I guess you don't know anything about that, either."

"I know she was settin' with a nigger boy. Everbody knows that."

Ash started to his feet, but I lay my hand on his knee and he stayed put.

"The Civil War's over, Mr. Spivey," I said, "even in Texas. Did somebody forget to tell you that, down in Huntsville?"

He switched his eyes to me. "I guess it don't matter to you if your white milk gets a little choc'late syrup stirred in," he said. "Well, wait'll you got yourself a little nigger baby. See how you like it then."

Even at my full five feet three inches, Tim Spivey had only an inch or two on me, and I swear he shrank even more as I stood up.

"What is it you're after with us?" I said. "Because, you know, we've heard all kinds of stories. Maybe you can just tell us yourself. Is this about that group you belong to? The one that tied a man to a pickup and dragged him to death? Maybe you didn't get the word that they convicted those men. They'll die for what they did."

"Sometimes you got to shed a little blood to make things right," he said. "Sometimes you got to wake folks up."

"Well, we're awake, Mr. Spivey. Every damn person in Mooney, Texas, has got their eyes wide open, and every last one of us is looking at you."

Spivey took a step backward, off the curb. He cast a glance toward Ash, like he was hunting for a lifeline.

Ash got lazily to his feet and tossed the wadded-up paper bag into the bed of his pickup. "If I was you, I'd find somebody else's chain to rattle," he advised. "I can tell you from firsthand experience that this is not the one I'd pick."

"This used to be a good little town," Spivey said, backing slowly into the street. "Folks understood how things was s'posed to be. Now it ain't nothin' anymore but bloody hearts."

"Aren't you late for your parole officer or something?" Ash asked. He stretched his arms over his head and cracked his neck.

"Oh, right. A wise guy. Well, let me tell you this, mister. Things is about to go back to the old ways, and someday y'all'll have yours truly to thank for settin' things right. Tear down that old statue of Jeff Davis and put up one of Tim Spivey instead. Yes, sir," he said, giving a quick salute to the likeness of the president of the Confederacy, "mark my words. Y'all ain't seen nothin' yet." He took a few more backward steps, then turned and set off at a jog up Front Street.

People had been filtering out of the café to dawdle on the sidewalk, watching the action. One of them was the sheriff's deputy, Dewey Wentzel. He gestured to Ash that he wanted to talk to him, but Ash ignored him. Those two had been crosswise ever since Dewey arrested Ash and dragged him to jail on a trumped-up assault charge on what was supposed to be our first night together. Unless Dewey produced a warrant or a pair of handcuffs, he wasn't likely to get much out of Ash.

I sat back down on the bench. My knees felt like Jell-O.

"Damn, Lucy," Ash said. "I need to find a way to get you onstage at the Round-Up. That was some performance."

"Are you kidding? Look at me! I'm all-over shakes."

"I take back everything I said the other night about your backbone. Every word."

"Too bad neither one of us has any brains," I said, but Ash didn't smile. I didn't have to ask him what he'd thought of Spivey's parting words, if he thought he was serious. "Don't you think we should tell Dewey what just happened?"

"I think I'll go up and talk to Bill instead. Take it straight to the top." He put out his hand and drew me to my feet. "Want to come?"

"I need to get back. I've got a delivery. Can you do it without me?"

Ash cupped the back of my head with his big, warm hand. "I can't do a thing without you. Don't you know that by now?"

I smiled then, in spite of myself, remembering something Spivey had said. "Just a couple of old bloody hearts."

"Yep. Bloody but unbowed."

"Ash? I'm really scared."

He leaned down and touched his lips to the peak of my hairline. "Don't even think about it. Think about rice and rose petals, okay? I'll leave it with the sheriff. He'll handle it."

❧

Dr. Crawford's front-desk clerk had been eating lunch in the café, so word of our run-in with Tim Spivey was already front-page news by the time I arrived at the clinic with the floral arrangements for Geneva's party. The conference room—what used to be the teachers' lounge, back when this was the elementary school—had been decorated with silver and blue streamers and a glittery banner that said WE'LL MISS U, GEN and a huge sheet cake sat in the middle of the table, replete with blue roses and, in loops of frosting, THANKS & GOOD LUCK.

A few nurses were there already, fooling with a big pile of gifts at one end of the table and the stacks of napkins and paper plates at the other, and they all wanted to hear about what had happened earlier on the courthouse square. I told it as quick as I could as I placed the bouquets along the table at strategic intervals, and by the time the flowers had been set up to everyone's satisfaction—no easy chore, with half a dozen female viewpoints to oblige — and I'd located someone to sign for them, the room had started to fill up with partygoers.

Dr. Crawford's nurse Aurelia came over and patted my tummy. "How you doin', girl?" she said. "How's that little butter bean?"

"Dr. C. says she'll be here for Christmas." I was hoping to make my getaway before the guest of honor arrived, but just then there was a big ruckus as two nurses came in flanking a smiling young man carrying a toolbox and wearing what looked like plumbers' coveralls. Word zipped through the room; the handsome stranger wasn't really a plumber at all, but a stripper from Texarkana. "Oh, baby, I'd let you work on my pipes any old time," Aurelia murmured as the nurses conferred with a handful of others, then hustled him out again, presumably to hole up somewhere until time to spring him on the honoree.

I headed for the exit, making regretful noises at Aurelia, who couldn't believe I didn't plan to stick around for the show. The clinic halls were empty; except for a fill-in receptionist at the front desk, it looked like everybody was at the party.

I let myself out a side door into the parking lot and ran straight into Geneva. She was standing next to a stone bench, puffing on a Marlboro Light, and she didn't look one bit surprised to see me.

"So much for a clean getaway." She tipped back her chin and exhaled twin streams of smoke as fine as angels' hair.

"I didn't want to spoil your party."

"There's a boy in there with a black silk G-string under his coveralls," she said. "You couldn't spoil my party if you tried."

"I thought your new job didn't start till a week from Monday."

"I decided to take a few days in between. Personal time."

I waited for details, but none seemed forthcoming. "Any plans?"

She shrugged. "Go up to Atlanta. See my sister."

"Seems like you and Bailey might head off someplace, take a real vacation. Kick up your heels."

"I think Bailey is glad to be shed of me for a while."

"Y'all are having problems?" *Why didn't I know about this?* I wanted to say, but bit my tongue. I didn't know because Geneva wasn't speaking to me, and when was the last time I'd seen Bailey? I realized I'd been keeping them at arm's length; I hadn't wanted anything dark to impose itself on our household, our fragile happiness. And then Tim Spivey came along and took care of that.

"Get that hangdog look off your face," Geneva said. "God, you're worse than your brother! It isn't your fault, Lucy, or Bailey's, either. Everybody needs a break sometimes, don't you think so? A change of scene? You of all people ought to know."

"I guess so."

"You know, you think this—" She waved her hand in the air, indicating what, I didn't know. "You think it has to do with you, but it doesn't, really."

"How was your appointment with Dr. C., by the way?" she asked, dropping her cigarette to the pavement. "Did Ash get there in time?"

"So it *was* you that told him."

"Well, it was just so pitiful," she said, "both of you acting like a couple of blind people, stumbling around in the dark. Somebody had to point you in the right direction."

I smiled. "You want to come to the wedding?"

She looked right at me for the first time. "I thought y'all were planning to go up in front of the judge."

"I guess you haven't heard the latest. We're taking a national survey." She laughed, a sound that made my heart climb out of my stomach. "It looks like I might be needing a matron of honor, after all."

"Is that so."

"Just think about it, okay? You don't have to answer me now."

"I'll be in up Atlanta till next weekend."

"Atlanta's only forty miles. Anyway, I think we can hold off till next weekend."

She nodded, then looked at her watch. "I'd better go in. There's a couple dozen women in there in serious need of a plumber."

"Have fun."

She looked at me plain for a minute. I knew her face so well: the thrust of her chin, the way she tucked her hair behind her ear as she talked, the flecks of brown like marble chips in her blue eyes. There was so much about her, below the surface, I would never know, but I knew I couldn't stand to lose those small, sharp specifics.

"Sure you won't stick around?" she asked.

"Oh, I've got a plumber at home."

She grinned, and for a moment the old Geneva was there, but before I could pin it down, she'd turned to go.

"Say hello to your sister for me," I called as she headed up the walk, her shoulders square inside her scrubs.

"Keep an eye on Bailey for me," she answered. "Remind him he's not really single. And Lucy?"

"What?"

"Don't get married without me."

⚭

Ash was insulted when he found out about the stripper. "They didn't have to send all the way to Texarkana," he said. "I've already got the coveralls, and a toolbox, too. Hell, I'd've done it for free!"

He was getting dressed for the Round-Up; I'd decided to stay home with Denny, and was sitting on the bed, watching in the bureau mirror as he did up the pearl snaps on his best white shirt.

"You haven't got a black silk G-string, though." I'd known Ash four months, shared a bureau with him nearly that long, and if he so much as owned a pair of underwear, I'd never seen it.

"What are you grinning at?"

"Just thinking about that time you came over to fix my busted pipe."

"*Real* plumbers don't wear G-strings," he said. He fastened the collar of his shirt, then shook his hair loose from it. "Maybe I should have, though. Maybe it would've snapped you out of that mood you were in."

"What mood was that?"

"Jesus, woman! There I was, trying like hell to keep your house from floating off down the road, and you were about to snatch my eyeballs out."

I picked at a loose thread on the woolen blanket. "That was a bad day, I recall."

"Well, it broke my heart to see it. I guess I would have done just about anything to bring you out of it."

"Really? Well, you weren't very persistent."

Ash laughed. "What do you suppose my chances were? Zero, or less than zero?"

"Who knows? Maybe if you'd had a black silk G-string."

He turned away from the mirror to face me. "You know what I really wanted, that night? I wanted to put my arms around you and just hug you, hug you so hard your bones cracked. God, you seemed like you needed that."

I stood up and stepped into the circle of his arms, inhaled his heat and scent: soap, shaving cream, the starch of his shirt. "Ash? Do you think we'll ever be sick to death of each other?"

He picked up his head to look at me. "Now, where is this coming from?"

"I can't stand to think of you being tired of me."

"Oh, baby." He pulled me closer and I held on. "Not in this lifetime."

"Can't you call Dub tonight? Tell him you've got the flu or something?"

"You're not worried about Spivey and those creeps, are you? Because they can't do anything to us, Lucy. Bill won't let them, and I won't, either."

But it wasn't really us I was thinking about, but something bigger, grayer, less fixed. Tim Spivey seemed to me like a grackle sitting on a telephone wire, casting his shadow over the town.

"Did you know Erasmus's family won't let him see Denny?" I said. Ash opened his mouth in surprise, then shut it again. "Now, don't be going off half-cocked. It upsets me, too, but I have to say, I see their point. They're only trying to keep him safe."

"Isaac came out to see me at Mrs. Mackey's this afternoon. He's taking Rose and the kids to stay with his mama for a little while, over in Rodessa."

"I don't blame him."

"He wants me to back off of Spivey and the Butlers. You know what he said to me? 'This ain't your fight, man.'"

"You don't believe that, though, do you?"

He glanced at the clock on the bureau. "First set starts in twenty minutes. I'd better get a move on. You and Denny gonna be okay?"

"The shotgun's in the closet, right? Shells in the medicine chest?"

"Don't be getting into anything over your head, Lucy. Don't take on anything you can't handle."

I wove my arms around his hips and buried my face in his throat and whispered for him to hug me till my bones cracked, but it wasn't enough to wipe out the image of that grackle, its body motionless, its eyes bright and cold, watching from overhead, just watching and waiting, to see what happened next.

∽∘∽

Denny didn't feel like socializing, and after Ash left and we'd cleaned up the supper dishes, she asked to be excused, and went into her room and shut the door. I could hear the soft reverberation of her guitar through the wall as I sat at the table with a cup of tea and the bride magazine, but I couldn't concentrate on a thing. I was relieved when the phone rang, hoping it might be Dove saying she was coming over with a deck of cards or a basket of sewing, but when I picked up the receiver, there was only silence, then, when I said hello a second time, what sounded like a quick exhalation of breath, and a click as the line went dead.

I got up and went to the front door and unlatched the screen. It was the last night of June, sultry and moonless, nothing stirring in the woods but the hum of insect wings. The dogs came running up—Ash had forgotten to feed them before he left—and I dumped some kibble in their bowls and then sat on the step to referee while Booker gobbled his supper and then hovered like a buzzard while Steve Cropper dallied and dawdled over his share. Lightning danced in the south, and it smelled like rain, but nothing would come of it; the storm would move on off toward Louisiana, and in the morning things would be as dusty and dry as they'd been all summer.

A light appeared, weaving through the trees at the end of the road— a single beam that, as it grew nearer, split in two. The dogs ran barking toward it as I got to my feet, listening to the rumble of the approaching engine, thinking lazily that maybe Ash was back, that he'd canceled his show and decided to spend the evening at home after all, when the lights suddenly burst to high beam and the engine's rhythm fell to a mutter.

I stood on the top step, blind in the glare, pinned like a rabbit in a hunter's sights as fear slid its cool, damp hand around my throat. Steve Cropper continued to run in circles yapping his fool head off, but Booker had dropped into a crouch with his ears pinned back.

I don't know how long I stood there—ten seconds, two minutes, it felt like forever and no time at all—before the engine roared up again and the lights swung around into the trees, and with a spurt of dust, red taillights sped off the way they'd come, leaving a stillness that felt like the end of the world.

I backed the three steps to the screen door, eased it open, and stepped inside, fumbling the latch in place. The dogs trotted back into the yard and were nosing around their empty bowls, the interruption forgotten.

I went into the bedroom and dug around in the closet behind the old coats until I found the shotgun. It was a single-pump, the kind Mitchell had owned, and while it was true to say I knew how to load and fire one, it was also true that I'd never much savored the experience. Even so, I took a shell down from the box in the medicine chest and pumped it into the chamber. I thought about rose petals and rice. I thought about Nashville. I thought about Denny, and Erasmus, and my baby, my Sophie, my butter bean. I thought about a grackle on a wire. Then I turned off the porch light and sat down in the swing, the shotgun at my knee, until my back ached and my eyes blurred from watching so hard in the dark, until two more headlights came bumping up the road, and the dogs ran out to meet it with their ears up and their tails wagging, and Ash was home.

25

Denny

 "How do you know it was them?" I was still half asleep, my hair in my face, trying to lace up my high-tops while Lucy stood at the front door tossing her car keys in her hand. "You didn't see the car, right? You couldn't even tell if it *was* a car, or a truck, or what. All you saw was *headlights*. Big deal. Maybe somebody got lost. Maybe they were just looking for a place to turn *around*."

"Be that as it may. Your daddy and I have talked it over, and we don't like the idea of you being out here in this house all alone right now. We'll both feel a whole lot better if you're over at Dove's in the daytime."

"For how long?"

"Today, maybe tomorrow. I don't know. We'll see what happens."

"You don't know if anything's even *gonna* happen!"

"No, but we know it's not happening to you. Not if we can help it."

I sighed and straightened up. Lucy raised her keys and dangled them impatiently; I was making her late. "You should hear yourself," I said. "You sound like a *mom*."

"Get a move on, then, before I smack your butt."

"Can I get a Pop-Tart first? Or are you gonna starve me along with bossing me around?"

"Aunt Dove's got a lot better stuff for breakfast than Pop-Tarts. Come *on*."

"What about my Walkman?"

"You've got thirty seconds, Denny Farrell, and I'm counting. One . . . Two . . ."

"Stop!" I yelled, and ran for my bedroom to grab my tape player and tapes. "You are too corny for words," I said to her as we locked up the house and got into the Buick, but she just clenched her jaw and fired up the engine. There were shadows the color of grape juice under her eyes.

Aunt Dove was out in her garden when we pulled up, pinching back the tomato plants, which looked like giant mutant things from Mars, as tall as trees, some of them, drooping with fruit. "Don't be silly, I'm happy for the comp'ny," she said when Lucy started apologizing for dumping me in her lap, even though they'd already talked it over on the phone that morning. "Look at them marigolds, all wilty-looking. Grab you a bucket, over yonder," she said to me after Lucy drove off. "You can help me deadhead."

The only Dead Heads I'd ever heard of were old hippies who traveled around the country going to rock concerts, but this wasn't even half as much fun as that. It turned out to be just another word for child labor, crawling on my knees between the rows of giant tomatoes, pinching off the faded old blossoms from the flowers planted between and listening to Aunt Dove rattle on about nematodes. Marigolds apparently had some kind of natural poison in them that killed the worms that killed tomato plants, which I suppose was interesting if you weren't fourteen years old and breaking your back under the burning sun before you'd even had breakfast.

Finally, just when I was trying to decide whether to tough it out or faint, she led me inside and sat me down at her long metal kitchen table and cooked me a skillet full of eggs and bacon and biscuits. I ate it almost as fast as it came off the stove, and I have to admit then, I wasn't one bit sorry I'd come. There was something about the way the sun slanted through the window and the old-timey gas stove and icebox and her ugly flowered china plates and the dish towels embroidered with the days of the week that made me feel cheerful, like I'd landed in a place where the outside world couldn't touch me. She poured herself a cup of coffee from a pot on the stove and then sat down beside me while I ate, wanting to know about the mysterious phone call and the headlights and everything that had happened the night before, but I told her the truth, I didn't know anything about it.

"You know, most of the time things 'round here stay pretty quiet, and folks get along good," she said. "But ever now and then some snake slithers out from under his rock and starts stirrin' things up. I remember, Lord, I guess it's been near forty years now, back when Dr. King was ridin' around makin' his speeches and LBJ passed all them laws, thinkin' maybe we'd finally seen the end of it. But it seems like all it does is crawl off someplace for a while and hole up. It always pokes its snout back out again, sooner or later." She stood up to rinse out her cup at the sink. "You want another coupla biscuits? It's just about time for *The Young and the Restless*."

She went to the back of the house to get her knitting, and I wandered into the living room, another time warp, from the gold velour couch and laminated coffee table to the cracked old spines of the books that lined the built-in shelves, more books than I could imagine reading in a lifetime. It wasn't even stuff you *could* read, for the most part, but more like Plato and Jane Austen and somebody named Rumi—who, I learned from reading the back cover, was a Persian poet in the twelfth century—and not a Stephen King or a Jackie Collins in sight.

The one nod to the twentieth century was her big RCA TV and VCR. On top of the set was a picture in a gold frame that showed a skinny redheaded boy, not too much older than me, in jeans and a plaid flannel shirt with a rifle over his shoulders, grinning into the camera. At first I thought it was Bailey, but the harder I looked, the more I saw it couldn't be; the colors of the print were funny and faded, and the boy's jeans and the cut of his hair were out of date, too, way before Bailey's time.

"Who's this?" I asked Dove as she came back into the room, a basket of yarn over her arm.

She followed my gaze, then set her basket on the coffee table and picked up the remote. "My big brother. Garnett."

"I never knew you had a brother," I said. "I always thought it was just Lucy's mama and you." She was studying the buttons on the remote like she'd never seen such a thing before, like she couldn't think how to work it. "Well, where is he now? What happened to him?" Though it was hard to imagine, he would have to be old now, white-haired and wrinkle-skinned, like her.

"He died. Shortly after that pitcher was took, as a matter of fact."

"But he's—" *So young!* I wanted to say. He was not a good-looking boy—whatever thing it was that made Bailey so cute was missing from Garnett's face—but there was something about him, a brightness, that reached out from beyond the edges of the picture, across time itself. *Died, how?* I wanted to know, but all of a sudden the TV came on with a puff of static, and the *Y and R* theme music swelled up, and then there was Victor Newman shooting daggers with his eyes at his old enemy Jack Abbott, and I knew I would never hear another word about Dove's big brother, not that day or ever again.

I couldn't let it go, though. During a station break, when Dove hit the mute button on the remote because, she claimed, the commercials were ten times louder than the regular programs, I got up and started looking around at the other photographs in the room, propped on the shelves and hanging on the walls. Most of the people were strangers to me, though there was one shot of three little kids holding hands on a footbridge with a creek running underneath who I recognized right off. The girl's red hair was in braids and one of her front teeth was missing, and the two boys had crew cuts and matching checked shirts.

"How old was Lucy when her daddy ran off?" It just slipped out; I guess I was thinking out loud, a bad habit of mine.

Dove set her knitting in her lap. She was making a sweater for Sophie, white with pink ducks.

"You got a lot of questions, Miss Denny Farrell." You forgot, most of the time, she was old, but every now and then a sorrowful note crept into her voice that reminded you of everything she'd seen.

"Well, she's fixing to marry my dad," I said. "Don't you think I ought to know about her?"

"You ever asked her?"

I shook my head. "It just now came up."

"She was six," Dove said. "Bailey was eight, Kit was almost ten."

"Was this before, or after?" I pointed with my thumb to the picture of the three little Hatches, who didn't look one bit troubled about anything, smiling at the camera like they had the world in their pockets.

"After. The next summer, if I recall. We was on a car trip up to Fayetteville, to watch the colors change."

"It's funny, don't you think?"

"What's that?"

"How Lucy's daddy left, and so did my dad's."

"Men leave." She shrugged, picked up her knitting again. "Women, too. It's not that uncommon, I'm sorry to say. Not even in a town the size of this 'un."

"Did you know my father's mother? The one who gave him away?"

Dove looked up at me, her needles stopping in mid-stitch. "Lord, child. What a thing to ask an old lady."

"You've lived in Mooney your whole life, right? So you must've at least seen her around town sometime, at the drugstore or on the street or *some*place."

Dove's needles clicked and clicked together. "I reckon I knew Lynette as good as anybody. Which is to say, not that good. She kinda kept to herself, even then. Liked her privacy. Still, like you said, I'd see her now and again, downtown, or at some church gatherin'. Your daddy weren't born Cath'lic, you know. That was the Kellers' doin', the folks that took him in. But Lynette was just as Baptist as the next one, before she done—well, before."

"What did she look like?" I sat down on the arm of the sofa. "Was she pretty?"

"I guess she was 'bout the prettiest thing we'd seen in Mooney in a long time, when she and Frank moved here. When your daddy come along, folks used to goggle over her and that baby in the supermarket like they was some kinda royalty."

"Was she short or tall? What color was her hair?"

"I recollect her as blond more than not, although it does seem to me she faded a bit when the baby came. But she weren't no tall woman, nor skinny, neither. Matter of fact, you favor her a good deal. Give you a coupla years and you'll be right near as good-lookin' as she was. Turnin' heads in the street."

"Did you ever hear her sing?" I asked. "It's the only thing my dad's ever told me about her. That I got my voice from her."

Dove nodded without dropping a stitch. "A coupla years after her and Frank come to town, she joined the choir over at First Baptist. Well, she no more than opened her mouth and the choir director— Billy McCall, his name was—just about fell down on his knees praisin' Jesus. But it weren't the choir Billy was thinkin' on so much as the Dogwood Days festival. He was aimin' to put Lynette front and center at the variety show they had ever year, right there on the courthouse square.

"For weeks that was all folks talked about. Everbody'd heard Lynette singin' at First Baptist, and they couldn't wait to see what Billy and her was workin' up. I guess nobody woulda been surprised if she'd a come out in mink and sequins with a twelve-piece orcherstra. We figgered maybe we had us another Rosemary Clooney on our hands." Dove smiled and went on.

"Come the day of the festival, Billy's fit to be tied—Lynette's nowhere to be found. Then, right at the last minute, the end of the show practically, here she comes, runnin' across the square with her baby—your daddy—in her arms, her hair springin' all around her head and wearing one of her everday cotton housedresses, a little tight in the hips since the baby, and not a thing on her feet but a run-down pair of Keds. Billy was about to have him a spotted cow, right there on the spot, but Lynette, she just hands that baby off to a lady in the front row and climbs up on the stage. Law, I can still see her up there, lookin' like she was standin' in the spotlights of the finest opry house in the world, and then she opened up her mouth and out came that voice, like one of God's right-hand angels.

"It was some old Patsy Cline song her and Billy'd picked, I can't recall which one—'I Fall to Pieces,' maybe—but I don't think nobody cared, we was all just settin' there covered in gooseflesh, listenin' to Lynette sing. Well, down in front, the baby saw his mama up there on that stage just a coupla feet high, and he started to fuss. He was just a little old thing, 'bout a year, and pretty soon he'd worked himself up to a full-blown fit. Without missin' a note, Lynette reached out her arms and took that baby from the lady who was mindin' him and set him on her hip, and right there, in front of God and everbody, he settled right down. Stopped howlin' and just set up there pretty as you please, pattin' his mama's cheek and listenin' while she finished up the song. It was the durnedest thing I ever did see. Like all he ever wanted was to be next to that music, close enough to touch."

Dove lay her knitting in her lap and started rubbing the knuckles of one hand with the fingers of the other. "Later on, when things went south, when Frank took off and Lynette got her mind all tangled up and give your daddy to Christa Keller to raise and got took off to Rusk—well, folks tried to make out that she was a cold thing, a monster, that she never had no tenderness in her heart. But I don't buy that. I was at Dogwood Days, I seen her with that baby on her hip, his fingers on her face, and I heard her sing. There weren't no way she would of give that up if there was a way in the world to hang on. I think that's why she done what she did. Not because she was a monster. But 'cause she just couldn't find no way to hang on."

"I wish I could meet her." I surprised myself saying it out loud, but Dove nodded and said, "Honey, I wish you could, too."

"Why do you think she's never seen my dad?" I asked. "Later on, I mean, after she got out of the, the hospital, and moved back to White Pine. It's not even thirty miles!"

"That ain't my place to say," Dove said, "but I b'lieve it's more your daddy's doin' than your grandma's. Forgiveness ain't never been his strong sweet."

I looked again at the photo on top of the TV, a big-toothed, red-headed boy who hadn't lived to see real love, or his niece and nephews standing on a footbridge in Arkansas, or his little sisters grow up and grow old. It was true that life wasn't fair, but it seemed even more unfair not to try to seal up the chinks between you and the living, to give them a chance to say their say, whatever it was, while you still could.

All of a sudden Dove reached for the remote and switched off the TV. "You know, they's enough foolishness in the world without bringin' it in the house ever day." She folded the tiny sweater and laid it on top of the knitting basket. "What do you say we fix Lucy some lunch and run it downtown? Maybe see how things is comin' along for the Fourth of July?"

We made tomato sandwiches with lots of mayonnaise, the way Lucy liked them, and packed a bag of Fritos and a thermos of tea in a grocery bag and put it in the car. It seemed silly to me to drive six blocks, especially when it took longer to find a parking spot than it did to get there, but Dove loved her big old Lincoln and used any excuse to take it out of the carport and tool around. She was a plucky driver, swinging wide around a pothole on State Street, tooting her horn as somebody nearly backed out of their driveway in front of her, and hollering out, "Look out, now, we're comin' through!" We circled the courthouse twice before a slot opened up in front of the bank, and we nosed in and I ran over to the flower shop and brought Lucy back to the square to share our picnic.

We sat on a bench under a spreading pecan tree on the courthouse lawn, where things were gearing up for the big Fourth of July celebration, three days off. It was a big deal, from the looks of things. Stars and stripes were strung from one side of Main Street to the other and across the courthouse entrance, and on one corner of the square a bunch of men was hammering together a platform that, according to Dove, would hold the speech makers and the little ragtag veterans' band. A wooden fence had been staked out for pony rides, and stacks of folding metal tables waited to be set up for the Jaycees selling plates of catfish and hush puppies and homemade ice cream. There was something kind of pitiful about it, if you asked me, how hard people were trying to make things seem jolly and old-fashioned, like the world was a better place because of a two-bit carnival and a few fireworks. But I kept that thought to myself. This was East Texas, after all, and I was already in enough trouble without people thinking I was a communist.

Lucy went back to work, promising to pick me up at the end of her shift, and Dove decided, since we were here anyway, to run in the bank a minute and see about her Social Security. I collected what was left of our lunch and carried it to a metal can, then wandered over to watch the men building the platform.

One of them, a youngish guy with a blond ponytail, looked up at me and smiled. "Hey," he said. He had so many white teeth, his mouth looked like a pack of Chiclets.

"Hi," I said back. A pickup at the curb said HATCH BROTHERS CONTRACTING on the driver's door. "Do you all work for Bailey?"

"You a little on the green side for him, ain't you?" the ponytailed guy said. He was still smiling, but in what now seemed like a creepy sort of way, when right then I saw the tow truck from Extreme Auto Wholesalers come around the corner. There was no mistaking, with those ears, who was at the wheel. He put the truck in park and rolled down the window, and we looked at each other across that wide stretch of green as soft and trim as a little boy's crew cut.

Dove walked up, snapping her pocketbook shut. "Ain't that your friend? The King boy?"

"Yes, ma'am."

"Well, run on over and say hello. We ain't in any hurry."

"I can't."

"Why not?"

"I'm not supposed to."

"Says who?"

"His family, for starters. And Dad and Lucy won't say it, but I think they'd just as soon I stay away from him, too, with all that's been happening."

"Oh, bosh." She got me by the wrist, and with no warning I found myself being yanked like a dog on a chain by a little old lady no bigger than a minute, right up to the door of the tow truck.

She put her pocketbook under her arm and stuck her hand in the open window. "Howdy-do. Mr. King, ain't it?"

He took her hand and shook it. "Yes, ma'am, it is."

"Well, I'm Dove Munroe. Pleased to make your acquaintance."

"Thank you." He cut his eyes at me.

"We was just havin' ourselves a spot of lunch. Have you had your lunch, Mr. King?"

"No, ma'am, I haven't."

"You like tomatoes?"

He smiled, a smile that took its time making its way all the way around to the back of his ears. Before that I was all right, but when he smiled, missing him felt like a fist in my chest. "Yes, ma'am, I do."

"Come on back to my house, then," she said. "I'll fix you a sandwich that'll make your toes curl."

"You'd better do it," I said. "She won't let up till you do."

"My dad needs his truck back before too long," Erasmus said.

"This won't take thirty minutes," Dove answered. "You foller us on over. That's me there next to the bank, in the Lincoln."

There was something about the sight of Erasmus sitting at Dove's metal table in her sunny kitchen that seemed unreal, and another thing that made perfect sense. For his part, he seemed right at home, rolling up the sleeves of his coveralls and digging into a big plate of sandwiches, polishing off three in about five minutes, washing them down with glass after glass of sweet tea. I don't recall he had much to say, but then Dove did all the talking anyway, chattering away about nothing in particular, sitting at the end of the table cracking pecans for a pie into a big crockery bowl.

Afterward he washed up at the kitchen sink, and she and I together walked him back out through the garden to where the tow truck sat parked at the curb. Her across-the-street neighbor, a fat little lady with bright yellow hair who resembled some kind of fancy-breed chicken, was standing on her front walk, looking fretful. Dove called hello to her and gave her a big wave.

"You all having car trouble over there?" the lady called back.

"Oh, no, ma'am! My Lincoln runs like a top!"

The lady's eyes made a slow trip from the truck with its winch and chain to Erasmus in his coveralls and back again. "Huh," she said, and turned around and went back onto her porch, where I guess she thought the shade would hide her gawking.

"Now, I want you two to come over one evening and sing me a song," Dove said as Erasmus got behind the wheel. "Everbody says y'all sound like a coupla angels."

"Denny, maybe," Erasmus said. "I'm just the backup man."

"You let me be the judge of that. I'd best run on in now, see about my pie. You come back with that fiddle sometime, you hear?" And without waiting for him to say "nice to meet you," or to thank her for the sandwiches, she hurried through the garden and shut the storm door behind her.

"Nice lady," Erasmus said. "Talks your ear off, but nice." Now that we were alone, he didn't seem to know where to look; his eyes roamed from the dashboard to the windshield to the house at the end of the block and back again. "Those were some awesome tomatoes."

"You're lucky she didn't try to send a couple pounds home with you."

"Yeah, I'd have a time explaining that, wouldn't I?"

"Your dad'll probably find out you were here anyway." I nodded toward Mrs. Chicken, who was pretending to inspect the ivy climbing up her porch post.

"This sucks, Denny," Erasmus said. "I mean — It's just so stupid."

"I know."

"I don't care what happens anymore. I don't want it to be this way."

"Lucy and Dad ran into that Spivey guy yesterday in town. Then somebody drove out to our house last night. Nothing happened, they just turned around and left. But now Lucy's scared. She and my dad won't let me stay there by myself."

"What about you?" he said, looking at me straight on. I hadn't had that many opportunities, since I'd first met him, to study Erasmus in broad daylight, to notice the way his hair held so many colors, copper and cinnamon and bronze, or to see the flecks of gold in his eyes, like one of the wise men in the Bible, carrying all those precious metals and spices. "Are you scared?"

"No. Not one bit." It wasn't true, not completely, but this seemed like one of those times my dad was always talking about, where you had to pretend a thing partway in order to make it one hundred percent true.

"You all going to the Fourth of July wingding Sunday evening?"

"I guess so. We haven't really talked about it."

"Meet me there."

"Okay."

He looked surprised. "You will?"

"Well, what did you ask me for, if you didn't think I'd say yes?"

"That little stage, where they do the speeches? It's the same thing every year—the mayor talks awhile, then the band plays 'God Bless America.' I'll look for you in back of there, okay? Right after the fireworks start."

Dove was rolling out her pie crust with an empty Coke bottle on the kitchen counter. I took a seat at the table and started playing with the sugar bowl.

"Good boy," she said without looking up. "Seems smart."

"Too smart for *this* place," I said, not thinking before it came out how snooty it would sound. "He goes to music school in Dallas," I explained. "He has a scholarship."

"He likes you," she said, and I was glad then that her back was turned and she wouldn't see me blush. "Reach up in that cupboard yonder and grab me the Karo syrup, would you?" she said, and like our discussion about Garnett, I knew Dove had said all she had to say.

It wasn't until that night, lying in bed mulling over the events of the day, that I realized I'd misheard her. That what she'd really said was, "He's *like* you."

When I closed my eyes I saw fireworks against the insides of my lids. I saw cinnamon and copper and gold.

$\mathcal{D}enny$

 I walked on tiptoes the next two days, trying not to be good enough or bad enough either way for anyone to notice. Lucky for me, Dad and Lucy were all wrapped up in each other and their wedding plans, when they weren't talking about Nashville — Mr. Amate from the record company had called again — or wondering what to make of what was going on in town. Ever since Tim Spivey had made his appearance, all kinds of crazy things were happening, or if not exactly happening, then getting talked about like they had, around the café and the post office and the other places folks gathered. The sheriff and his deputies were running like fire ants from the scene of one supposed wrongdoing to another, but somehow it never amounted to anything. There was no break-in at the hardware store, no brawl at the working man's beer joint, the Tap, outside town, no big blue truck dragging a body or anything else down Main Street in the middle of the night. No one had really set the big white cross at the Grace Bible Church on fire, though a whole lot of people drove up the highway to Reverend Craig's place near Marietta anyway, leading to an impromptu prayer meeting in the reverend's front yard, where four souls got saved. A bunch of cattle that went missing on the Wilts's farm Friday afternoon turned up in the pasture next door that evening, having trampled down the fence to get to a bale of hay. A little boy was reported kidnapped off the baby-sitter's front porch, before his mother recalled that her husband had picked up the boy to take him to the dentist. People were as jumpy as cats, looking over their shoulders and calling names, but it never seemed to amount to anything, and the sheriff finally had to hike over to the café and beg people to cut him and his men some slack. It was funny, in a way, how Tim Spivey had managed to shake things up without doing a thing other than showing his face in town. I couldn't help picturing him holed up somewhere, laughing up his sleeve at the hubbub he'd caused.

Dad and Lucy argued for two whole days about the Fourth of July, about whether to go or stay away. Lucy didn't see why we couldn't just celebrate at home without all the crowds and the bother, but Dad said it was *Independence* Day, by God, that as Americans we had not just a right but a *duty* to eat greasy food and listen to off-key patriotic music along with all our neighbors. Mostly I thought he was trying to tease her out of her worries, but one time he must have pushed the wrong button. I came in from the yard—it had just gotten dark, and I'd been sitting on the step with the dogs—to hear her in the kitchen shouting, ". . . not another goddamned word about it, Ash Farrell," and I scooted up the hall and looked around the door frame just in time to see her raise up her hand with a big wooden spoon in it, which luckily he was in just the right place and posture to block.

"Do you want me to tear up that piece of paper in the glove box, Lucy?" he yelled, gripping her wrist. "Is that what you're trying to get me to do?" "Go ahead!" she said back. "Go find somebody else to sign on for this job! Somebody with some *backbone*!"

The spoon went clattering onto the countertop. She was crying now, the way you cry when you're a kid, when you don't care what kind of noise you make or how terrible you look; her face was a mess of pink and white splotches, and she wiped her runny nose right on her wrist. "I never asked for this!" she sobbed. "I never asked for any of this!"

I backed out of the doorway, where nobody had seen me, and slipped out the front door and across the yard to the truck. The catch to the glove box was sticky, but I found what I was looking for right on top, a rectangular piece of paper signed by the Cade County clerk that had Dad's and Lucy's names on it and the word "marriage" like a big old flashing neon sign. I didn't know whether to be more shocked that they'd actually done it or that they were inside right now shouting about tearing it up, but in either case I didn't have time to figure it out, because right then the front door banged open and there was Dad coming across the yard toward me, his boots raising dust.

"Y'all got *married*?" I said. "You did it and didn't even tell anybody about it? Not even *me*, right under your very own roof?"

"It's just a license, Denny. Permission, not proof. There's a waiting period. Seventy-two hours." The way he said it made it sound like seventy-two years. He stuck out his hand, but I tucked the paper up close to my chest.

"You're not tearing this up! Not because of some silly fight about the Fourth of July!"

"No, I'm not tearing it up. I'm hiding it. Give Lucy some time to settle down a little."

"Dad? Why don't we just stay home Sunday night? We could go to that firecracker stand up by the Corners, get some bottle rockets and Black Cats and have Fourth of July right here in the yard." As I said it, I pictured the sky behind Erasmus's head erupting in stars, and I couldn't believe what I'd just heard myself let go of.

"Oh, baby girl," he said. "This isn't about the Fourth of July. Not really."

"What's it about, then?"

He looked over the roof of the truck, and for a minute I thought he saw something there, in the trees, but it was only a way he had, of looking back or forward across time, I was never really sure. What if, I wondered suddenly, remembering Lucy's face made ugly with fear and rage, you'd lived your whole life with nothing to lose? How would you feel when you finally found something worth holding on to, watching it shift and slide like water through your hands?

"Tell you what," he said. "Let's put that paper right back where you found it, okay?"

"But what about Lucy?"

"A piece of paper won't make that much difference, one way or the other."

I didn't believe that, not for a minute. But I handed him the paper, and he put it in the glove box and slammed it shut. The cranky old catch clicked but didn't grab, and the door dropped open again, spilling the license, along with a mess of receipts and fishing lures and candy wrappers and loose change, onto the floorboard, which was already ankle deep with cassettes and empty soda cans.

Dad laughed, a hoarse, worn-out sound.

"Perfect," he said. "Now I *know* she'll never find it."

Back in the kitchen, Lucy was standing at the stove, stirring up something in a double boiler. "You know what's wrong with me?" she said. Her eyes were glassy and her smile over-bright. "I need chocolate. I'm thinking brownies. Anybody here want brownies?"

"Sit down a minute, Lucy," Dad said, and reached to take the spoon out of her hand, but she held on.

"No, no, I need to *stir*." Her voice scared me, all high and trembly-sounding, and she didn't seem to notice she was getting chocolate all over the front of her shirt. "Ash, I've been thinking, and I've come up with something."

He made his voice light. "What would that be?"

"Let's let Denny decide."

"Let me decide what?" I was wishing I'd stayed out in the yard, to tell the truth; I was wishing I'd just stayed over at Dove's. Things around here were getting way too thick for me, and I didn't appreciate being put in the middle of it.

"About the Fourth of July. How do you feel about it?" she said. "Would you like to go downtown to the festivities, or do something here at home?"

I glanced at Dad, who nodded, which I took to mean that I should say what I felt, and my heart did a little leap. My motives weren't pure, but I didn't care.

"I want to go."

Lucy stopped her stirring and looked at me, a little crease between her brows. "You do? Really? You're telling the truth, now, not just saying what you think we want to hear?"

Dad laughed. "It's the last thing you want to hear, Luce, so it must be true."

"I really do," I said. "I don't think we should stay home just because of some, some bogeyman."

"All right, then," she said. "We'll go."

"Lucy, we don't—" Dad began, but she cut him off with a look.

"It's decided," she said. "Denny's decided. I don't want to discuss it anymore."

I was the one who smelled the brownies burning, who pulled the pan scorched and smoking out of the oven and threw it in the sink and turned on the water. Dad and Lucy were in the living room, with all the lights off, swaying together in the green glow of the stereo, where Bruce Springsteen was singing about wanting all the time that heaven would allow. Lucy's face was in Dad's neck, and I thought she must still be crying, when all of a sudden Dad swung her in a goofy little dip, and she laughed, way down in her throat. As he pulled her up again, I heard him say, "Come on, now. Give us a kiss."

I threw the ruined brownies, pan and all, in the trash, and went on to bed.

I woke up a few hours later, thirsty, and wandered to the kitchen for a drink of water. A light was on over the stove, and Lucy was sitting at the table wearing Dad's snap-front shirt and digging into a big bowl of Honey Nut Cheerios.

"I never got my brownies," she said, spooning up a mouthful of cereal. "I have to say, this is a pretty poor substitute. You know, I always heard how pregnant women were hungry all the time, but I just didn't realize what it meant. That it meant, well, *all* the time."

"Uh-huh." I was still mostly asleep. I made my way over to the cupboard and got down a glass and filled it from the tap.

"Denny, listen," she said, balancing her spoon on the edge of her bowl. "I'm not really like this, you know. I mean—this is not me, not really." It didn't seem to me like she needed to apologize for eating Cheerios in the middle of the night, so I just shrugged. "It's just such a, a responsibility, you know? I had no idea loving people was such hard work."

"Why?" I said. It seemed to me that loving people ought to be the simplest thing in the world, that instead of sitting around beating yourself up about it, you should just open your arms and run toward it, full tilt, as hard as you could. Who cared, really, whether you fell flat on your face at the other end? Wasn't it less about how it turned out and all about the running?

"Oh, I know you don't know what I'm talking about. But you will someday. Someday you'll be sitting at a kitchen table in the middle of the night, and you'll think of this, and you'll understand exactly what I mean."

She looked up from her cereal and laughed. "Never mind. Go back to bed. This is all a dream. You won't remember a thing in the morning."

∞

The Fourth of July started out with a bank of dark clouds in the east and the air so thick and steamy it felt like you were walking around with a wet blanket over your head. It stormed in the early afternoon, and the wind changed, pushing the clouds on off toward the south, leaving behind a sky the color of a Crayola crayon, that exact shade called Sky Blue.

True to her word, Lucy hadn't said a thing about that evening's festivities, hadn't tried to argue or plead her way out of it, like I'd been afraid she would. Still, it didn't exactly feel like a celebration, driving into town in her Buick; she was too quiet, and Dad, typically, was talking too much to make up for it, rambling on about everything and nothing as we cruised around looking for a parking spot. Lucy finally hit on the idea of parking at the flower shop, and we pulled in alongside Peggy's Pontiac and got our lawn chairs out of the trunk and set off on foot toward the courthouse.

It wasn't even four o'clock, but the party was already in full swing.

I hadn't seen anything like this in Dallas, where I never got to do more than wave a couple of sparklers around in the backyard and watch the Boston Pops with Ma on TV. The streets around the square had been cordoned off for a dunking booth and a fishing game for the kids, stands selling Sno Cones and fresh-squeezed lemonade. On the wooden platform on the courthouse lawn, a group of men in short pants and feathered hats was playing oompah music, which didn't strike me as patriotic in the exact sense, but then I guessed this is what Dad had been talking about in the car, how Independence Day was all about celebrating our many and varied freedoms, including the right to make a god-awful racket with a tuba.

We found Bailey in the Jaycees tent handing out paper plates of catfish fillets and hush puppies and flirting like his life depended on it with the ladies lined up at his booth. Lucy scooted around behind the table and gave him a kiss. "What are you doing in here?" she said. "I thought you were in charge of the pony rides."

"Any old fool can make a horse walk in a circle," he said. "Frying catfish—now *that* takes talent."

"His heart is broken," Lucy said to Dad as we made our way across the courthouse lawn, balancing plates of fish in addition to our lawn chairs. "He won't say it, but I think he can't bear to be around all those little children."

"Well, I can't say I blame him," Dad said, finding us a spot under a shade tree and setting up our chairs. "No more notion how to behave than a bunch of monkeys, most of 'em. That just means I've got good sense, not a broken heart."

Lucy sank into her chair and accepted a plate of fish. "Gosh, Ash. What a terrific father you'll be."

"I *am* a father, may I point out," he said, and nodded at me. "Does this child look like a monkey to you?"

"No." She smiled at me and bit into a hush puppy. "She doesn't look like a child, either, for that matter. She looks like a lovely young lady." Lovely, I knew, was stretching it. But she'd braided my hair for me, and I had on Geneva's flowered peasant blouse and some Whisper

Pink lipstick. I was afraid they might get suspicious, but I'd begun to figure out that sometimes flying right out in the open was a surer thing than trying to sneak under their radar.

"Uh-oh," Dad said, "look out. Here come the Lilac Ladies."

Two old women appeared in front of Lucy's chair, wearing pastel chiffon dresses and carrying shiny patent-leather pocketbooks, like they were on their way to services instead of a fireworks display. One was short and busty, the other tall and all angles, with a nose like a scoop. I smelled Jergens lotion and Listerine.

"Why, Lucy Hatch," the short lady said in a bossy voice, "I mean to have a word with you."

"Hello there, Bernice, Harriett," Lucy said. "How are things over at First Baptist? I'm surprised the place is still standing without my mama to keep things upright."

"That's just what I'm talking about," the first lady said. "What's this we hear about you and your young man sneaking off to get married in front of Judge Crumb? It was all over Sunday school this morning."

"It can't be true," Dad put in, dragging a French fry through ketchup. "She hasn't got a young man. She's got me." He gave the ladies a big smile and popped the French fry in his mouth.

"Now, Lucy, you know your mama has been away on that Bible tour all summer, walking in the steps of the Apostle Paul. Do you really think she deserves to come home and find out her one-and-only daughter has, has *eloped*, like a common—well, like a commoner?"

"I appreciate your concern for my mama, Bernice," Lucy said. "We haven't decided yet about the service. But it's really between Ash and me."

Bernice gasped and clutched her pocketbook. "That's not true! Why, Reverend Honeywell was just saying in his sermon this morning . . . He was saying . . . What was he saying, Harriett?"

"I'm afraid I'm not following you, Bernie," Harriett said, which made Dad start coughing into a handful of napkins.

"He was saying—wait, I've got it!—that a funeral service is *not* for the deceased at all, but for the ones left behind!" She looked around expectantly, then down at the clasp of her pocketbook. "Well, I think that goes for weddings, too, don't you?"

"I surely do," Dad said, pushing out of his chair and getting to his feet. "Weddings are definitely not for the deceased. Anybody want a beer?"

"Sure," I said, just to make him smile. He cocked his thumb and forefinger at me, winked at Lucy, nodded at the church ladies, and strolled off toward the bandstand.

"I promise you," Lucy said, "whatever we decide to do, you all will be the first to know."

"Harriett's granddaughter Mary Margaret got married last February at the VFW hall," Bernice said. "It was a right nice service, but she regrets it now. *She* wishes she'd listened to her mama and gone in for a church wedding."

Lucy shook her head, watching the ladies walk away. "Mary Margaret regrets it, all right," she said to me. "Regrets she didn't pick somebody other than that shiftless Larry Stiles to marry. Like a church wedding could have made a difference."

"I'd like a church wedding," I said, causing Lucy to look at me in surprise, and then smile. "For you all, I mean."

"Is that right? Why?"

"I don't know. I guess I feel it's like Mrs.—like Bernice said. A wedding ought to be about saying what you have to say in front of people. You know, like witnesses."

She nodded slowly, like she was weighing this. "I'm afraid it isn't so simple."

"Why isn't it?"

"Well, for starters, I grew up at First Baptist, but your daddy was raised Catholic."

"So? It's the same God, isn't it? The Baptist God and the Catholic God?"

Dad laughed, hearing that, walking up with a cardboard tray of plastic cups. "No, baby girl, not exactly."

He passed me a cup of beer. I took a sip, wrinkled up my nose, gave it back again. He shrugged and handed Lucy and me the lemonades he'd bought for us, then raised his beer aloft and studied its golden foam. " 'Beer is proof that God loves us and wants us to be happy.' Benjamin Franklin," he said, and drank a toast to himself, to the day, to the God of all of us.

The afternoon seemed to drag on forever, the way midsummer days do. The sun made its leisurely way over the courthouse, and shadows stretched out across the lawn, but still the sky held its light, like it couldn't stand not to wring out every last drop. People came and went all day long; Dove joined us, and Bailey sat down for a little while on a break from frying fish, and Lucy and I tried one of just about everything there was to eat while Dad got quietly, happily drunk in the shade of the bandstand, listening to a bluegrass duo and a barbershop quartet and the Methodist ladies' bell choir's rendition of "The Eyes of Texas."

It wasn't yet full dark when the speech makers finally climbed on to the platform and began their program. The president of the Community Betterment Association did a welcome speech, and the high school football coach stood up and made a pitch for next year's season, which seemed way out of place to me but drew a rousing ovation from the crowd. I looked around at the faces gathered on the lawn while the men spoke. There weren't many that weren't as white as mine. I hadn't seen Erasmus all day. For the first time, the thought entered my head that he might not come.

The First Baptist preacher, Reverend Honeywell, and a pastor from one of the country churches led a prayer for unity, then Sheriff Dudley came forward and begged everyone's cooperation for a safe and peaceful celebration. That got Dad started muttering about where we would be if our forefathers, the ones who'd fought and died for our independence, had settled for peace and safety, until Lucy leaned over and swatted his leg and told him to hush up.

A girl just a little bit older than me in a sailor dress got up and read a piece about growing up in America, where freedom was not a privilege but a right, and the mayor recited Lincoln's speech about fourscore and seven years ago in a slow, pretentious voice, like he'd written the words himself. The veterans' band took the stage, a strag-

gly crew consisting of two trumpets, a trombone, the tuba player from
the oompah band, and a kettle drum. The average age looked to be
about a hundred and ten, but there was something that raised the hairs
on the back of my neck to see those men in their starched uniforms
with their medals shining on their chests as they hoisted their instruments and started to play "The Star-Spangled Banner," to see everybody on the lawn set down their plastic cups and paper plates and
stand up and put their hands over their hearts and sing along.

The first burst came unannounced, red spangles against the dark
purple sky, causing folks to look upward like they couldn't think what
the commotion was. It was followed by twin showers of white streamers trailing toward the ground as everybody sat back and said, "Ah!" in
sudden remembrance of where we were and what we were doing there.
The veterans' band lurched into action; rather, some of them lurched
one way and some of them lurched another, and it took a few bars of
confused bleating for them all to arrive at the same destination, which
might or might not have been "God Bless America."

I stood up and motioned to Lucy that I was going to move toward
the stage, that I wanted to get closer. She'd crawled into Dad's lap, her
legs dangling over the arm of his chair, and she nodded and waved at
me and titled her chin toward the glittering sky.

I made my way toward the platform, working my way through the
crowd. With everybody gazing heavenward, it wasn't hard to slip
unseen behind the wooden riser. I was so close I could make out the
creases in the caps on the old veterans' heads, the rockets and pin-
wheels reflected in the brass of their instruments. The sky was lit up
like a year's worth of Christmas, enough light practically to read by,
but no matter where or how hard I looked, I didn't see Erasmus.

I sat down on the curb. The gutter was a mess, full of cans and cigarette butts and paper. Was *this* what our forefathers had fought and
died for, the right to throw garbage in the street? I tried to concentrate
on the fireworks, but I felt like I had something cold and dull wedged
inside me. I thought about Dallas, my bedroom with its French provincial furniture and posters of Pearl Jam. I never really liked French
provincial in the first place—Ma had picked out the bedroom set—and

who would ever know that Pearl Jam was just a front for the Loretta Lynn records I kept under my bed where nobody, not even Ma, would find them? There didn't seem to be a place for me anywhere, and the one thing I'd learned for sure was that the minute you thought you'd found somebody to stand up alongside you, they flew right on out of your life. It was better to make your own way, not to owe anybody any favors.

I stood up, brushing my hands on the seat of my pants, and just then a silver rocket erupted overhead and I saw a familiar shape, long-boned and big-eared, on the sidewalk across the street, against the window of Showtime Video Rentals. It waved, then ducked out of the light. I looked both ways before I crossed, but the street was empty, everybody who was breathing in Mooney, Texas, was over at the courthouse with their eyes on the sky.

"What are you doing?" I asked as Erasmus gestured to me from the darkened doorway. "You said behind the bandstand. You said when the fireworks started!"

"I know. I didn't count on having to work around those two skinheads."

"The Butlers? Are here?"

"Over behind the laundromat, with their running lights on. I don't know what they're up to, but I didn't feel like being right out in their line of fire. I sneaked around the back way. That's why I'm late."

"We need to tell the sheriff!"

He grabbed my wrist. "Listen, Denny. I like you a lot, you know that. But you don't get it, you really don't get it."

"What are you talking about?"

"The sheriff can't do anything about those guys! You can't arrest people for being mean and stupid."

"They're not just mean and stupid. They're *criminals*. Or trying to be, anyway. The whole town is scared of them."

"Yeah, but why? It's because of what they *might* do, not anything they've really done. It's not against the law to sit in the dark in a pickup truck. They're not even playing the stereo loud. They're not even double-*parked*."

"Well, maybe we should tell my dad."

Erasmus laughed, a short, dry laugh. "Yeah, right. He'll get them *and* us killed in the process. And for what? For nothing."

"It's not nothing," I said. "You know it's not nothing."

He shrugged and looked up as a pinwheel burst over our heads. It was the closest I'd ever stood to Erasmus, and I noticed for the first time how he smelled, like something I'd known when I was little but hadn't thought of since: lemons, soap, clean sheets on a line. I closed my eyes, and saw the tracery of fireworks behind my lids, red and blue, chasing their own tails to the ground.

"Look," he said, "I brought you something."

My eyes popped open. "You did?"

"A lady my dad did some work for makes these. I was out at her house the other day and saw this and it reminded me of you."

He reached into the pocket of his shirt and took something out and put it in my hand. It was too dark to see, so I stepped out of the doorway onto the sidewalk and held the object up to the light. It was a little hand-carved bird, made out of some ordinary wood but in amazing detail, bright beaded eyes and miniature clawed feet and feathered wings.

"She didn't want to let me have it at first," Erasmus said. "But I told her about you, about the bluebird song and the first time I heard you sing, and—well, I guess I convinced her." He'd come out, too, onto the sidewalk; I could finally see his face in the window's light. He reached out and ran a finger down the bird's back. "You know how sometimes you just know something's supposed to be yours when you see it?"

I couldn't find a thing to say or the voice to say it. The band was playing "The Stars and Stripes Forever" with lots of volume, not much tune, and all at once a row of Roman candles shot up, filling the sky with noise and dazzle. I thought of all the stupid things I had craved in my life, the toys and clothes and attention of people who didn't care I was alive—who would guess it could all be replaced in a heartbeat by a lump of wood that fit in the palm of my hand?

"I'll be damned," a voice said, "if it ain't the lovebirds," and automatically my fingers closed tight around the little carved bird, its beak sharp against the skin of my palm.

It had to be a hallucination, the way they were suddenly standing in front of us on the sidewalk, like they'd just materialized there and not walked up the street like normal human beings. I recognized their smell, though, that blend of sweat and beer and something else, a car smell, gasoline or motor oil. I'd been sitting down when we met them in the Dairy Queen and so I hadn't known how big they really were, their shoulders and bellies stretching the seams of their T-shirts, their necks like tree trunks; even their forearms were gigantic, covered with words and pictures that had been scratched into the skin in blue ink: a swastika, a naked woman wearing a ball and chain, "Aryan Nation." One—I never could tell them apart—had a bottle of Lone Star in his hand, which gave him an almost carefree air, but the look in their eyes was a long way from carefree; it was flat and dark and full of purpose.

"Let us alone," I said. "We aren't bothering you."

"Now, that's where you're wrong," the other Butler said. "You're botherin' us a whole lot. You're sure botherin' *me*. They botherin' you, Sean?"

The one with the beer stepped closer and grabbed my arm. His hand was huge and clammy, and I imagined it leaving a print on my skin, one I could scrub and scrub at but that would never come off.

"What's the matter, chickie?" he said, twisting my arm behind my back so tight my shoulder felt like it was about to come out of its socket. "You don't like it rough?"

"Naw, that ain't the problem," his brother said. "It's 'cause she likes her meat nice and dark. Wouldn't know what to do with a white man."

"You guys fuck off," Erasmus said. "Denny, get out of here. Just go." I couldn't believe his voice, the grit in it. I'd never once before heard him curse.

" 'Scuse me, boy, somebody talking to you?" Seth stepped forward and gave Erasmus a shove.

He lost his balance but recovered it, catching himself on the ledge of the video store's front window. "You heard me," he said. "Let her be."

The brothers looked at each other and started laughing, like they thought he was making a joke. The one holding my arm, Sean, tipped back his beer and drained it, then tossed the empty bottle in the air and caught it by the neck, one-handed.

"What'dya think, bro? Maybe we'll have us a chicken dinner tonight, huh? White and dark meat both."

"You better back off right now," I said. "If you do one single thing to us my father will dog you till you die." The fireworks had ended, and the band had quit playing. Any minute, I thought. Any minute the crowd would break up and start drifting back to their cars. Any minute, somebody would come.

"You just relax, chickie. It don't have to hurt." Sean rubbed his huge thumb slowly up and down on the back of my arm, and all of a sudden I tasted every bite of the fried fish and funnel cake and Sno Cone I'd eaten that afternoon, crowding up the back of my throat.

Erasmus moved so fast I didn't see him; one second he was standing against the lighted window, in front of a cardboard blowup of Mel Gibson and Danny Glover, and in the next he came flying at Sean Butler with all his weight, headfirst and shoulders braced, like a football player fighting to cross the goal line. He caught Sean off guard and square in the chest and knocked him off his feet, sending him sprawling backward against a parked car, and they landed together in a heap on the pavement, the beer bottle exploding against the concrete like it had a bomb in it. There was a scream from one of them, a jumble of limbs, and then Seth ran over and grabbed Erasmus by the shirt and threw him across the sidewalk like he was a rubber toy. I heard Erasmus hit the store window, saw the long crack travel up the plate glass, bisecting Mel Gibson's face, as he dropped onto the sidewalk, his limbs at angles, like Pick Up sticks, where they didn't seem to belong. There was blood everywhere, jagged shards of glass scattered across the pavement.

Seth bent over Sean, who rocked and moaned, curled up against a parking meter. "Come on, buddy, come *on*," he said, and jerked his brother to his feet, doubled over and blubbering like a baby, as somebody, a man's voice, yelled, "Hey!" And then everybody in the world, it seemed, everybody except for Erasmus and me, was running.

27

Denny

"Explain to me what goddamned idiotic thing was in your head, Denise!"

We were in Dove's living room, Lucy and Dove on either side of me on the gold couch, Dad roaming around the rug like he was possessed, raking his hands through his hair until his skin stretched so tight it seemed it would split. I'd thought, at the beginning of the summer, that I'd seen the worst there was to see of my father. It wasn't till the night of July fourth that I found out those early outbursts, when I first came to Mooney, had been an ounce in the bucket, that there were all kinds of depths and dark corners to his feelings, doors he never cracked for fear of letting out the wild thing that lived inside, setting it howling and tearing around the universe.

"Just tell me, please, why you thought wandering off on your own in the middle of the goddamned night in downtown Mooney was the wise thing to do!"

"I already *told* you! I wasn't wandering. I was meeting Erasmus. And it wasn't the middle of the night. It was barely nine o'clock." I knew I was pushing it. Dad stopped his pacing and looked at me. "You let me go! I told you I was going off, and you didn't say one word!"

"You said you were going down front to watch the fireworks! You never said a goddamned thing about sneaking off with Raz."

"He was supposed to meet me at the stage! I didn't plan on going off like I did. It's just that, well, he saw the Butlers' truck, and he didn't think it was smart to be out in the open."

"Jesus Christ, where have you *been* this whole week long? Didn't you ever stop to think those guys might be laying for you? You *were* out in the open! Right in their fucking path!"

"Ash, your mouth." That was Dove; she didn't allow bad language in her house, not even in a crisis.

He took a breath, held it, let it out with a rush of noise. "Jesus, Denny. Jesus. Didn't you one time stop to think about what could happen? You don't have any idea what those guys are capable of!"

But it seemed to me that he was the one who didn't know, not truly; it was me who'd stood in the grip of Sean Butler's sweaty hand, had seen the look on Seth Butler's face as he took Erasmus by the shirt and tossed him into a plate-glass window. I reached into my pocket and found the little wooden bird, fingering its pointed beak like a lucky charm.

I stood up. Dad looked stunned, like I was ten months old and it was my very first step. "Where do you think you're going?"

"To the hospital. Who wants to drive?"

"The hell you are! Sit back down. Stay where I tell you to stay, and move when I tell you to move. Goddamn, we don't even know where the Butlers are! How do you know this is over?"

"Sean was hurt pretty bad, I think." It turned out, once the Butlers had run off down the street and Mr. Pate from the hardware store had gotten Erasmus on his feet, that most of the blood had been Sean's, from falling on the broken bottle. Erasmus had been wobbly and disoriented, and there was a bump on the side of his head where it struck the window, so EMS was called—they were right across the street, luckily, at the fireworks—and he'd been taken to County General for what they called evaluation. The only thing he'd said to me as they put him in the back of the ambulance was that his father would murder him, but it looked now like I might beat him to that particular punch.

Dove stood up, patting my knee. "I'll run give the hospital a call."

"Ash, my goodness, would you sit down?" Lucy said as Dove left the room. "You're making things worse with all this hair pulling and stomping around."

"I just wonder if anybody here besides me realizes what almost happened tonight," he said. "Those kids could've been killed!"

"Of course we realize it," Lucy said. "We're all upset. I just don't see what good it does to have a conniption fit about it."

He turned suddenly and faced her. "You're thinking if I'd done what you wanted and stayed home, none of this would have happened. It's my fault, isn't it? Isn't that what you're thinking?"

"Don't put words in my mouth." Her voice was low but firm, and I saw for the first time that she was just as upset as Dad, only holding it inside her, like a small, hard stone. "What difference does it make now whose fault it was? You can't follow Denny around for the rest of her life trying to keep her away from the bad guys. You wish you could, but you can't."

"Damn it! She's fourteen years old, and she's, she's right *out* there—she's got nothing to hide behind! If you expect me just to . . ."

He did sit down then, in a wing-back chair, and tilted his face to the ceiling. Lucy reached across the couch and took my hand. How, I wondered, had it come to this, that the person who shared my blood was behaving like he didn't know me at all, while someone I'd only met a few weeks before had planted herself so deep in my corner?

Dad shoved back his hair with his hands and looked at her. "You don't know how it is," he said. "When you have a child of your own, you'll know."

It was so quiet in the room, I could hear the Big Ben clock ticking on the bookshelf, the murmur of Dove's voice in the kitchen. Outside on the street a car passed, the whoosh of tires on pavement like paper tearing.

Lucy stood up. "How dare you say that to me? After all we — How can you say that to me?" I thought she might cry, or hit something, but all she did was walk out of the room. Somewhere down the hall, a door slammed.

Dove came back, carrying a pot of coffee on a folded towel. She set it down, then left again, returning with a tray of cups and little paper napkins with gold edges, like this was some kind of fancy social event and not a messy family brawl complete with yelling and cursing and slamming doors. She didn't say one word about Lucy, just poured out the coffee and passed the cups around. "You got anything to give this a kick?" Dad asked, but Dove just fired him a look.

"Only kick you need is a kick in the butt. Drink it." He drank. It wasn't smart going up against Aunt Dove under ordinary circumstances, and you didn't stand a chance in her own living room. "They aim to keep Erasmus overnight," she said, handing me a cup of coffee with a big dose of milk and sugar in it. "He might have a concussion."

Liquid sloshed over the rim of my cup and into the saucer. "That's bad, isn't it?"

"Nah, not usually. But they like to watch the first few hours, make sure the brain don't swell."

"I'm not sure the boy *has* a brain," Dad said. The coffee was scalding and bitter and matched his tone. "Seems like anybody with a brain would've had the sense not to drag my daughter out after dark with felons on the street."

"He didn't drag me," I said. "I went on my own. And you know what? I'd do it again. Right this minute."

Dad set down his cup. I braced myself for another tirade, but instead, while I watched, the anger started to leak out of his face, like the air from a tire, until it was flat and beat. It took a lot to make my father ugly, but I had done it.

"Ash, I want you to let Denny sleep here tonight," Dove said. "I think you and Lucy need to go home and rest. Talk this over in the morning, like reasonable folks. None of us is thinkin' good right now. This thing's got everybody wore out."

He rubbed his eyes with the backs of his wrists. "I'm going home and call Marlene, is what I'm gonna do. Her mother started this, let her take care of it. I give up."

"You can't!" I jumped to my feet, my knee bumping the coffee tray and making the spoons clatter. "You can't tell Ma! She'll—she'll take me back to Dallas. Or Chicago! Maybe worse!"

"Well, you should've thought of that before you started gallivanting around the countryside with no more sense than God gave a goose. What am I supposed to do, Denise? I trusted you, and look what it brought me." He raised his hands, palms up, to reveal the answer: *nothing*. One pissed-off fiancée, one worthless daughter, all adding up to a big, fat zero.

"It's always about you, isn't it?" I said. "You, you, you. What about me? It's my life, and you don't even care! All you care about is, is being the boss of everything! Making everybody toe your line. I don't blame Lucy if she doesn't marry you! I hope she doesn't. You're an asshole."

Dad looked at Dove, then me.

"If we were home," he said, "I'd get the strap."

"Get one now, see if I care! I hate you! You knocked up my mom and then you left, like, like I'd never even been born. Well, guess what? Here I am. Hello! See? *Here I am!*" I was yelling now, stamping my feet in rhythm with my words. I knew I looked like an insane person, ranting on a street corner, but I didn't care. I was tired all of a sudden, so tired I wanted to lie down on Dove's quilted satin comforter and close my eyes and sleep for a thousand years.

Lucy appeared in the doorway, taking in the scene, but she didn't come to me the way I thought she would. Her face was a total blank, like she'd never seen any of us before. I was on my own.

"You take Ash home, Lucy Bird," Dove said. "Denny can spend the night here. Y'all three need some time to cool down. Things'll look brighter in the morning."

They left, without saying good night to me or a word to each other. I stayed where I was, listening to the Buick pull out of the driveway, Dove rinsing out the coffee cups in the kitchen. I stared at the photo of Garnett on the TV, his grinning face, full of hope. What, I wondered, was it a tribute to: his stupid trust in the future, or the truth about what really happened instead, the unclaimed life waiting just beyond the frame of that picture, a package that would never be opened?

"Ever notice how the closer you get to something, the harder it is to see?" Dove stood looking over my shoulder, wiping her hands on a tea towel, and for a minute I thought she was going to say something about Garnett, to answer all my questions, but then I saw that Dove had stopped asking those questions a long time ago, that for her, the picture was just a marker, a place to fix her eyes. "I think maybe that's how things are for your daddy sometimes," she said. "That he's too close to the things he cares for to see them clear. All he sees is how they make him feel, and it scares him. Scares him so he don't know what to make of it all."

"Lucy, you mean."

"Not just Lucy. No, ma'am."

"Is that supposed to make everything okay?" I said. "Because, well, no offense, but it doesn't."

"Come to think of it, your daddy ain't the only one might need to take a step back," she said. "Try to see the big pitcher."

But I wasn't about to agree with her, couldn't find it in either my heart or my head to give in; and when she squeezed my shoulder and asked if I wanted to watch a little Letterman or Leno, I turned away from her brother's likeness and asked if she minded if I went on ahead to bed.

❧

I sat down on the edge of the bed in the guest room and switched off the lamp. For a while I listened to Dove moving around on the other side of the door, setting things straight in the kitchen, making her way through the house turning out lights. The water ran for a few minutes in the bathroom and, a little bit later, the bar of light under her bedroom door went dark.

It was a different sort of nighttime quiet than at Dad's house. Every now and then a car drove by, headlights painting a brief, bright slash across the guest room wall, and far away somewhere a string of firecrackers went off, one straggling reminder of the nation's birthday, now almost gone.

Fourth of July in Mooney, the first and last of my life. I tried to imagine myself in Chicago, the inside of an apartment in a city I'd never seen, or back in Dallas, trying to fit myself into the shape of the girl I'd been. For almost fifteen years my life had been a blank piece of paper, and then, for a few weeks, had turned into a oversize, Kodachrome coffee-table wish book. *This*, it seemed to say, *can be yours; and this, and this, and this*. I thought of Lucy and Dad driving home in the dark, far apart on the seat, all the things that had been said and not said hanging between them like a curtain. How, I wondered, would any of us ever get back to where we needed to be with each other? Since I showed up, life in the house on Little Hope had turned into a kind of a nonstop carnival ride, Dad and Lucy and me each in our own little car, careening around, every now and then crashing into each other and shooting off in some other direction, sometimes with a shout of happiness, sometimes fury, and sometimes it wasn't all that easy to tell the difference.

It occurred to me that maybe what was between my father and Lucy wasn't a curtain at all, but me. Hadn't things been sweet and easy with them, before I came? And couldn't things slide back like they had been, if I was gone? Yes, there would be a baby; yes, Dad was going to Nashville. But those things were still ahead; the stuff they were set in wasn't stone, but something soft, possible to mold. With me in their lives, the balance was wrong: weak in the middle, like a broken-down mattress. Without me, maybe there was a chance for them. Maybe the frame would hold.

I got up in the dark and bent to pull on my shoes. I knew what I had to do.

❧

Most of Mooney was already tucked in and dreaming, the houses buttoned up as tight as preachers' collars as I slipped through Dove's front gate and set off up the block. Traffic was light, and I wasn't carrying a thing but the clothes on my back and the carved bird in my pocket, so I made good time, following the striped white line as it led out into the county. I felt good, clear, like something had been lifted off me that I hadn't even known was weighing me down. I felt like I could walk all night.

It was a warm night, the moon ducking in and out through lacy scraps of cloud, and the air smelled of hay and cows and far-off rain. I hiked past a couple of motels, a closed-up Mobile station, more tumbledown shacks with buckled roofs and windows like blind eyes than I could count. A couple of times I crouched in the bar ditch when a car came by, but nobody much was out. I passed farms, barbecue shacks, an empty wooden stand with a cardboard sign that read

STOP

HEAR

PEACH

TOMATO

JESUS ♥ U.

The breeze kicked up a little and I saw lightning in the west, but the sky overhead stayed full of scuttling clouds, coaxing me forward along the paved shoulder till I reached an intersection with a blinking four-way light and a cluster of billboards and highway signs. Mooney, I already knew, was behind me. But straight ahead, twenty-three miles according to the sign, was White Pine.

On the far side of the four-way stop was an all-night grocery, with a Lotto Texas banner out front and ads for Miller Lite and Lay's potato chips taped to the windows. There wasn't much business at this hour, just an old brown beater of a car parked down at one end of the unpaved parking lot and a man in a blue uniform loading crates of milk out of a Lindale Farms Dairy truck. He looked up and jumped a little at the sight of me crunching across the gravel from out of nowhere, it must have seemed.

"Jeez," he said, "I thought you was a ghost, sneakin' up like that. Where in the world'd you come from?"

"Just trying to get to my grandmother's," I said, feeling a little rush of pride at how neatly I skirted his question. "Over near White Pine."

He narrowed his eyes and looked me over. He was a short, squatty guy, not young or old, with greased dark hair and a shadow of a beard. I didn't know firsthand what a psycho killer looked like, but this guy looked purely worn out, ready for home, a glass of beer, and some TV. "Kinda peculiar to be out on your own this time of night, a girl your age, doncha think?"

I shrugged and lied like my life depended on it. "I went with some kids to the fireworks in Mooney, but they took off on me. I've gotta get back to Gran's before she wakes up, or she'll ground me for life. You going that way?" I pointed with my thumb to the west-bound highway sign.

"Sorry. No riders in the truck. Comp'ny policy."

"Thanks anyway." I turned around and started back toward the highway.

"Hey!" He stood watching me with his hands on his hips. "You can't just be meandering up and down the highway in the dark, all alone!" he said. I raised my hands, palms up, as if to say, No choice. "Aw, hell," he said. "I got a stop in Hughes Springs, I can ride you that far. Go on, get in the truck. But don't let anybody see you! I got a boss watches us like a chicken hawk. I can't be gettin' crosswise with him on account of no crazy kid who don't know no better than to stay off the road at night."

I crawled into the cab and waited while the man wheeled his handcart into the store and stocked the case. He stood talking for a few minutes with the lady behind the counter, then made a few marks on a clipboard.

I heard him loading the handcart into the back of the truck, then he came clambering up into the cab and handed me a carton of chocolate milk as he reached to start the engine.

"I was a crazy kid, too, when I was your age," he said.

I thought he might ask me a million questions on the trip up the highway in the dark, but he was quiet, working at a toothpick with his lips and tongue and listening to some right-wing talk-show guy on the radio, talking back under his breath: "You said it, buddy." "Amen to that, pal." The milk was delicious, cold and sweet, the sugar shooting through me like rocket fuel, and as I watched the road fly by under our wheels, I saw that my great plan was full of holes. Never mind that my grandmother had never laid eyes on me, probably didn't even know I existed, that for all intents and purposes she'd written my father and everything to do with him out of her life: How would I ever *find* her? Who knew how many fishing camps there were up and down the rim of the lake? For half a second I let myself think about my bedroom in Dad's house, the yellow comforter, my guitar in the corner. Then I stuck my hand in my pocket and touched the little wooden bird. It didn't do any good to look behind me now.

"Where's this grandma of yours live, anyway?" the driver said, like he'd read my mind, reaching to turn down the radio.

"You know, I'm not real sure."

He swung his head slowly around. "Whadaya mean, you're not sure?"

"I haven't been here that long," I said. "I'm from Dallas. I'm not sure I can find it in the dark." The driver went on watching me out of the corner of his eye. I knew my only chance was to act nonchalant, like I did this kind of thing every day. "If you could just let me out someplace with a phone," I said. "There's somebody I can call. He'll take me to Gran's." *Gran.* I could almost see her, this sweet little lady I'd invented, in an apron with her hair in a bun, sliding a tray of cookies out of the oven. Oatmeal. With raisins.

The driver didn't say anything at first, and I tried to keep my pulse steady, tried not to think about what would happen if he cared enough to unravel my story. "Place up ahead just a coupla miles, called Sid's," he said finally. "They got a phone. Dallas, huh?" He shook his head. "No wonder you such a funny kid."

It was hard to say what the exact nature of Sid's Emporium was. If you could believe the signs plastered across the facade of the long, raw-boarded building, they had the bases covered from jerky, ammunition, dwarf bunnies, and Indian artifacts to fishing tackle, yard art, and peanut brittle, but I admit I might have missed something. The milk-truck driver pulled in next to the diesel pump and shifted into neutral, and I slid down from the cab.

"You run on in now and make that phone call, you hear?" he called out the open window. "Get on back home to Grandma." He was looking all around him, nervouslike, when he said it, like there might be some milk-company spy in the parking lot.

I thanked him for the ride and made my way past a carved wooden Indian wearing a flak jacket and a carbine belt, guarding the entrance. I still had the change in my pocket from the twenty-dollar bill Dad had given me that afternoon, and I'd been thinking I might get something to eat, but besides peanut brittle and jerky, all I saw were a rack of pastries and an old-fashioned metal soda cooler that odds said was full of bait.

The boy behind the cash register followed me with his eyes as I took a package of Ding Dongs off the rack. A baseball game was playing on a radio behind the counter, and next to a card table and a half-full coffeepot on a burner an old man sat on a folding chair, drinking from a Styrofoam cup and looking at a copy of *People*.

"I need to find somebody," I said, laying the Ding Dongs on the counter. "Lynette Farrell. She has a fishing camp somewhere around here. Near White Pine."

"Never heard of her," the boy said. "And I guess I know pret near everybody on the lake. Lived here all my life."

"Are you sure?" I said. "It's—it's her old family place. She's been there a long time. You must have—"

"You mean Evelyn." The old man had looked up from his magazine and was watching me. "She means Evelyn, Trey."

I turned to him in astonishment. "Evelyn?"

"Sure. Her place's just up the road a piece, 'bout a mile, mile and a half. You can't miss it, can you, Trey?" He started cackling, which got the boy laughing, too.

"Sure can't! Just pull in when you see the dinosaur!"

"What dinosaur?" I asked, but they went on like I hadn't said a thing.

"Now, Trey, we had this conversation before. That ain't no dinosaur, it's a copperhead snake!" The two of them snickered. I figured it was a joke I just wasn't meant to get and reached into my pocket to pay for the Ding Dongs as the old man got up to pour himself a refill from the coffeepot.

"You got some business with Evelyn, young lady?" His hand shook slightly as he tilted the pot. On his feet were a pair of scuffed-up ladies' house shoes, the kind that look like they're cut from an old bathrobe.

"Maybe." I didn't even know who this Evelyn was, whether or not she was my grandmother, but I was close, so close now that I was bound and determined to find out.

The old man shuffled back to his chair and eased in, slow, like his bones ached. "Her place been closed up for some-odd years now," he said. "Don't be surprised if she runs you off! Evelyn claims to be reno-vatin', but mostly she just don't want nothing to do with folks."

"A mile and a half?" I scooped my change off the counter.

"Give or take," the boy said. "Like I said. You can't miss the dinosaur!"

I set out again bolstered by sugar and curiosity, but before I'd even left the parking lot, my nerve started to seep away. What I was doing seemed suddenly like a fantasy, the tag end of some crazy dream. Any minute, I thought, I would open my eyes and be back in my bedroom, the sun spilling over the windowsill, Dad whistling in the kitchen; it would be Monday morning, the fifth of July, and the night before would never have happened. I had to remind myself I was wide awake, not dreaming, that I was on my way to find someone named Evelyn, who had something to do with dinosaurs. Who might or might not be related to me by blood, who might or might not chase me off with a shotgun. She didn't owe me a thing, I reminded myself, not a hand-shake or a smile. But I wanted to see her, hear the sound of her voice, that voice she'd passed on, without knowing it, to me. Then, I thought, I could think about what to do next. Then I could move on.

I came to a sign that said, BERTRAM'S FISHING, ALL SEASONS, ALL RATES, then another for a place called Sykes Brothers, but no dinosaur. Had I walked a mile? More? Less? The long night had started to work itself into me, tying itself in knots between my shoulder blades. The moon was gone, and the sky drooped low and wet over the pines. I hadn't been scared one time since I left Mooney, but I felt it coming, walking up my spine like the tip of an icy finger. There was no light or movement to fix my eyes on, hardly a sound. It was like I'd walked off the end of the earth, like if I took one more step into the blue fog, I would start to fall and fall and never stop.

Still, I kept going. There was nothing else to do. I dragged my feet one after the other like my Converse high-tops were concrete boots, my fingers in my pocket working the beak of Erasmus's little wooden bird. I walked, and then the road broke on the right, and I saw the sign.

LEGRANDE'S FISH CAMP, it said in peeling letters, with a crude, grinning cartoon painted alongside the name. What the boy at Sid's had called a dinosaur was nothing but some bad artist's version of a worm. Nailed across the bottom on a sheet of plywood was a big black P.S., no kidding around: CLOSED!

I thought back a couple of nights, standing next to the truck with Dad and Lucy's marriage license in my hand. Their names had been typed into the blanks, stiff and formal-seeming. Lucy's whole name was Lucy Hatch Breward; I guessed she didn't have a middle name. But my father did, even though I'd never heard it before, and now here it was, painted on the sign of a closed-up fish camp: *LeGrande*.

I turned in at the unpaved road. The woods were close on both sides, and the road was so narrow in places that if two cars had been coming from opposite directions, one of them would have had to back up for a quarter of a mile. It twisted and turned awhile, then widened into a clearing. A long, low building sat ahead, unlighted against the backdrop of misty sky and the lake behind, a flat stretch of black giving up a smell of algae and fish and the glow of a dock light across the water. A dog barked, but it sounded far off and not quite real, like a scratchy old record of a dog.

The house, if that's what it was, seemed not so much sleepy as vacant, not a light burning or a single sound but the distant drone of a speedboat out on the lake. In the yard, though, a brand-new Ford pickup truck was parked.

I went up the front steps, tripping a little on the top one, and opened the door to a screened porch. I half expected it to be latched, but it wasn't. I could barely make out the shapes of a porch swing and an easy chair, but it was so dark, if there had been somebody sitting in them I wouldn't have been able to tell.

I felt my way over to the porch swing and sat down. The muscles up and down my legs were tingling, and I loosened the laces on my high-tops. In spite of all I'd eaten that afternoon at the courthouse square, in spite of the chocolate milk and the Ding Dongs, I was hungry, but I didn't think that really explained the hollow in the pit of my stomach. I'd thought it would be a relief, being on my own, responsible for nobody but me. But I wasn't alone; I had Dad and Lucy, Erasmus, Geneva and Bailey and Dove, all crowded up in my chest all of a sudden, making it hard to breathe. I hadn't cried one time, not because of the Butlers or Erasmus or Lucy or my dad, but I felt it now, an old ache at the back of my throat, and I wondered if I would ever get rid of it or if it would always be mine to carry, like the wooden bird in my pocket, a souvenir of what I'd left behind.

There were a couple of moldy-smelling cushions on the swing, and I leaned back and tucked them under my head. In the morning, maybe, like Aunt Dove said, things would look brighter. In the daylight, the pain in my chest would be gone, and I would know how to make my way. But right now, all I wanted was to close my eyes.

❧

When I woke up the sky was full of fog, and I didn't know where I was. Then the night before came rushing up in me, one picture after another: Sean Butler's hand on my arm, Erasmus flying through the air, my father in Dove's living room looking gray and exhausted, saying he'd given up on me.

I sat up, rubbing the back of my neck, thinking I smelled smoke. Then I remembered the sign, LEGRANDE'S FISH CAMP, and sucked in my breath so hard I almost choked.

The figure in the porch chair wore pants and a man's shirt, with pale, wispy hair pinned up at the back of her head. Her features were a blur in the soft white light, and as I watched she raised a cigarette to her mouth and took a drag.

"I could've blown your head off, you know." The voice was mild, blunt. Only then did I notice what was in her lap: a snub-nosed, steel-blue revolver.

I swung my feet to the floor, tucking a strand of hair out of my face. "I fell asleep," I said. "I didn't *mean* to."

She exhaled, two thin streams of smoke rising toward the ceiling, into the fog, then lowered her chin and looked at me.

"What are you doing on my porch?" Her face came into focus, the features smooth, ordinary, a little sharp around the mouth. And her eyes—the darkest eyes I'd ever seen on any human being, except one.

"I'm Denise," I blurted out. "That is, I mean, I'm Denny. Farrell. I'm trying to find my grandmother."

Nothing happened, not for the longest time. The woman smoked and stared, the gun in her lap like a pet cat. When she'd finished her cigarette, she dropped it onto the porch floor and ground it out with the heel of her sneaker.

She stood up, stuffing the revolver into the waistband of her pants.

"Well," the woman, whoever she was, said, and pushed open the front door and stepped inside, leaving the door standing ajar behind her. Not an invitation, exactly, but the only thing I had.

28

Lucy

 I took my foot off the gas and let the Buick coast into the yard, cutting the headlights as we rolled to a stop alongside Ash's truck. It was a muggy night, the moon hidden by low-hanging clouds, the porch light either burned out or forgotten, and the dark that came down on us seemed pure and final.

We'd ridden silently home from Dove's, both of us sheathed in our own little pockets of thought. But I wasn't mad at Ash. I wanted to be, but I couldn't. It was true that he'd sold short my feelings about Denny, but it was also true that he'd been carrying his own feelings for her around for nearly fifteen years, baggage he hadn't asked for and wasn't sure, had never once known, how to handle. How nice it would be, I thought, if love was something you made up your mind to do, if your heart had nothing to say about it. How much easier things would be for him if he could seal Denny up and return her to Marlene like an unopened letter, just go back to being the father he was before, cards on birthdays, maybe visits in the summertime. He couldn't do it, though. The seal had been broken, the letter not only read but taken to heart. I wondered if Ash knew that yet, or if I was better off letting him come to it on his own, the long way.

I reached across the seat and took his hand. Even in the dark, I knew Ash's hand, the broad, strong contours, the ridges of vein and callus. I felt stiffness in all five of his fingers, resistance, but he let his hand be held, and after a minute or so he flexed his fingers and slid them between mine.

"Denny's right," he said.

"About what?"

"She said she wouldn't blame you if you don't marry me. I'm an asshole."

"Ash?"

"What?"

"We have such a long way ahead of us. This is just the beginning, really." He turned my hand over in his and ran his thumb along the palm, and I found myself thinking, *heart line, head line, mount of Venus*. "Don't let what happened tonight get between us."

"You said it yourself. I want to protect her, and I can't. There's too much out there. It just—it never stops."

"But it's her life. You can't keep it from her, even the bad stuff. You just can't."

He was quiet for a long time, stroking the lines in my hand, all those little forks and branches into the unseen future. "How do we do it?" he said. "How do we let them go?" I couldn't tell him. All I could do was sit beside him and hold his hand.

We went inside, finally, and took turns in the bathroom. I climbed into bed and put my head on the pillow, listening to Ash setting out food for the dogs, walking around closing up the house for the night, the familiar nighttime rituals.

I don't know how long I drifted, whether it was twenty seconds or twenty minutes, but I came awake with a jolt and sat up in bed. Ash's side of the blanket was unrumpled, the sheets cool and smooth.

I found him in Denny's room, sitting on the edge of her flowered bedspread. His back was straight and his hands lay, palms turned up and open, on his thighs, like he was waiting for something to come along and fill them. The only light in the room was from the bulb over the stove in the adjacent kitchen, and his face was a mask of shadow.

"Ash? You okay?"

"Just thinking," he said. "About something that happened, oh, I guess twenty years ago now. With Christa, my stepmom. She and I had a big fight about something, I can't for the life of me think what—my hair, my grades, me running around at all hours, the usual. Anyway, I remember it came to blows one night, and she said to me, 'I give up. I guess I'll just send you back to the state.'" He laughed a little, shook his head. "Well, she would never have done such a thing, not in a million years. But all I knew was how it felt to hear those words—like the one thing that always kept me grounded had cut loose. Like there was nothing left in the world for me to hang on to."

"What did you do?"

"Ran away. Got on my little Kawasaki and just took off, toward Arkansas." Ash stood up and stepped over to study the objects on Denny's bureau—her Walkman, a scattering of cassettes, a headband she'd pilfered from me, her pink lipstick. "The bike broke down just this side of Texarkana. I called Bob, senior, my stepdad, to bail me out, but guess who it was showed up to bring me home?"

He picked up the lipstick, turned it over in his hand like some rare archeological find. "We laughed about it afterward, Christa and me," he said. "We laughed about it in the hospital, even, just a few years back, when she was dying. But I can still remember how it felt, riding up the highway in the dark, feeling like everything that ever mattered was behind me."

"There's plenty of time," I said. "Denny hasn't gotten away from you yet."

"I was pretty rough on her tonight."

"You were scared. We all were."

"But how do I know she knows that's what it was?"

"Like Dove said—things will be easier in the morning."

"Maybe." He set the lipstick back on the bureau. "But who ever said it was supposed to be easy?"

"Somebody with no kids." I smiled as he kissed me on the top of the head, then circled my wrist with his fingers and led me back to bed. He lifted the sheet and slid in behind me, his hand making a warm bowl for the small curve of my belly, and the next thing I knew, the curtains were bright with daylight, and the phone was ringing.

Denny

We made our way down a shadowy hallway, big empty rooms on both sides, others stacked full of crates and construction materials, till we came to a kitchen the size of a mess hall. Counters and cabinets lined three walls, along with an industrial-size refrigerator, a couple of deep freezes, and side-by-side aluminum sinks.

The woman turned around and trained her eyes on me like a pair of lasers.

"Are you Lynette Farrell?" My voice shook. It was just dawning on me, a little after the fact, that I really didn't have a clue who I was dealing with.

"My name is Evelyn LeGrande."

"Well, what happened to Lynette Farrell? Wasn't that you?"

Her eyes seemed to look deep into mine, but I realized, as silence unspooled around us, that she was looking through me, and beyond.

"Lynette was my stage name," she said. "And Farrell was the name of my husband, who left me."

"Your *stage* name?"

"Lynette LeGrande," Evelyn said. "'The Nightingale of East Texas.'"

"They really called you that?"

She smiled, tight and scornful. "No, my husband, Frank, called me that. It was a joke, a bad one. I *was* singing, when I met him. It was love at first sight and the end of my career. Where in the name of God did you come from?" She stood looking me over in a way that was creepy but familiar, and I realized it was exactly how I'd felt the first time Dad had sized me up, and that I didn't like it any better on her than I had on him.

"I live in Dallas," I said. "Or, I used to, anyway. My mom got a job in Chicago, at the beginning of the summer. So she brought me here. Well, to Mooney. To stay with my dad."

"But how in the Sam Hill did you end up *here*?"

I opened my mouth to answer her, but the minute I did, all those faces came swimming up, and, to my everlasting shame, my eyes got full. Day number one of my brave new life, and I wasn't doing so hot.

Evelyn leaned against one of the long countertops and crossed her arms over her chest. "If it's a family reunion you're after, you've landed in the wrong spot."

"No, ma'am. I—I just wanted to meet you, is all."

"Oh? And why's that?"

"Well, I got your voice."

Her eyebrows went up, heavy and dark, Dad's all over again, but otherwise Dove had been right—she favored me. "You're a singer, right?" I said. "You used to stand at the kitchen sink in your red pedal pushers and sing like Brenda Lee."

"Now, listen here, young lady—"

"No, you listen," I blurted out, and without skipping a beat, I closed my eyes and opened my mouth and out it came: *"I'm sorry, so sorry . . ."*

I made it through the first verse before recklessness overtook me, and I clamped my mouth shut and opened my eyes again. My heart was pounding.

Evelyn blinked. A light sparked, somewhere way down in the depths of her eyes.

"Pink."

"Excuse me?"

"Those pedal pushers were pink, not red. Jesus, you're a contumacious thing." And then she laughed, one time, sharp and rusty-sounding, like the hinges needed greasing.

"Is that good or bad?"

She uncrossed her arms. "You still haven't answered my question —
how did you wind up here? Did someone send you?"

"No, ma'am. Got a ride on a milk truck, partway. Walked the rest."

"Does anybody know where you are?"

"Not exactly." I saw her frown at my answer. "But it's okay, really!
They won't even miss me."

She looked at me for a long time, until a haze formed over her eyes,
then she turned toward the cabinets. There was nothing to look at but
rows and rows of steel-faced doors, but Evelyn stood there so long I
wondered if she'd forgotten about me. Once upon a time, I knew,
everyone said she was crazy, and I wondered if she still was, if this was
it, how I would know.

"People miss the funniest things," she said finally. "Things you
wouldn't expect them to." I didn't say anything. I wasn't even sure, to
tell you the truth, it was me she was talking to.

She turned around again, and her eyes came back into focus. I could
see how she'd been pretty once, and how, like the saying goes, she'd let
herself go. But I liked her face, even the parts of it that were hard and
distant. I liked knowing my own face might turn out this way, that I
could get old the way she had, proud and strange, saying things like
"contumacious."

"This isn't a place for wayfaring strangers, you know," she said. "It
used to be, when my daddy and brother were running it. But I haven't
had a guest here in six, eight years. And I'm not in the habit of harbor-
ing fugitives. Are you in trouble?"

"I don't — What kind of trouble?"

"You tell me. Boy trouble? Trouble with the law?"

"No!" *Nothing major*, I stuck on, to myself.

"Did your daddy kick you out?"

"No, ma'am. But . . ."

"But what?"

"Well, he's getting married pretty soon, having a new baby. Maybe
even going to Nashville, to make a record. I guess I got to be too much
for him on top of all that."

Slowly Evelyn turned her face to the ceiling. "Jesus," she said. "Jesus, when will You deliver me?" It seemed to be a direct question to the One it was addressed to, so I stayed out of it. "You'd better not be lying to me." This was aimed at me.

"I'm not! I wouldn't."

She crossed the kitchen and opened the big refrigerator. "How long's it been since you had anything to eat?"

"I guess last night. A couple of Ding Dongs at Sid's Emporium."

"I'm surprised they were edible. I don't think they've restocked the shelves over there in the past ten years. You're not allergic to eggs, are you?"

"No, ma'am." I felt like I could eat a dozen. "So, I can stay?"

Evelyn looked at me over her shoulder, one corner of her mouth quirked up. "Let's not be getting too far ahead of ourselves. Breakfast is breakfast. Then we'll talk."

∞

She made her eggs just the way Dad did, with little bits of chopped-up onion and tomato and green pepper. The sun was coming in through the bank of long windows over the sink, flooding the kitchen with light, and I ate two platefuls and drank a big glass of orange juice while Evelyn sat smoking and keeping one squinched-up eye on me, like I might be planning to run off with the silverware. I had a thousand questions bubbling up in me, but I knew it wasn't polite to talk with my mouth full, and anyway, she didn't exactly invite cross-examination, sitting there with her eyes half shut behind a blue veil of cigarette smoke. Luckies were her brand, and she smoked two all the way down to the filter while I filled up my stomach. Afterward I burped as politely as I could into my napkin and pushed back my chair.

"That was so good," I said. "I never had eggs that good." I didn't think I ought to mention Dad's.

"Oh, don't worry," she said, getting up to tip her ashtray into the garbage can. "You'll earn it."

She led me down another dark hall to a bathroom and opened a cupboard full of soap and towels. I knew I could use a shower, but what was the point when all I had to put on were the same old pants and peasant blouse? I took off my top anyway and scrubbed myself at the sink as best I could with a bar of oily white soap, and used a finger's worth of Crest to brush my teeth. My hair looked pretty good, still in its braid, and for a second I thought about sitting at Dad's kitchen table the day before with the sun coming in the window and Lucy's hands at the back of my neck, working with stubborn purpose. She'd tugged too hard, sometimes, sending water to my eyes, but somehow the pain added to the memory, gave it a truer edge. I shook my head to clear it, and pulled my blouse back on.

Evelyn was waiting for me with a big woven basket over one arm. "Now we find out what you're really worth," she said with one of her rusty-sounding laughs, and I followed her back through the big, empty house and out the rear door. The sun was all the way up now, breaking over the trees and spreading a sparkling net across the surface of the lake, where one lonely motorboat puttered, leaving a streak of foam in the blue.

"You fish much?" Evelyn threw this over her shoulder at me as we made our way down a path made of stepping stones shaped like butterflies and lady bugs.

"No, ma'am. Not really." I tripped on a root and nearly stumbled. "Never, to tell you the truth."

"Good Lord," she said. "How old are you?"

"Fifteen on Tuesday. Tomorrow," I added, realizing that in the commotion of the past few days, I'd let my own birthday sneak up and just about pass me by.

"Well, I'd like to know how a child gets to be fifteen years old in the state of Texas without learning how to cast a fishing rod." She walked with purpose, swinging the empty basket from one hand.

"Not much reason to learn in Dallas, I guess."

"Nonsense. Everybody ought to know how to fish. And how to shoot and build a fire and grow their own food. You never know when you might have to do any one of those things." She glanced back at me, never breaking stride. "I'll bet you've never laid hands on a gun in your life." I shook my head. "Well, I don't see how you expect to make your way in the world. How do you plan to look after yourself with no useful skills to speak of?"

"I can sing."

"Ha! Wait and see how far that gets you."

"As far as I want it to," I shot back. I knew I sounded like I was picking a fight, but it didn't seem fair of her to be making fun of me when she didn't even know me.

"I thought that, too, once, when I was your age. It's a good thing I learned how to fish and shoot, is all I can say."

"You aren't one of those, those survivalists, are you?" I'd seen them sometimes on the news, holed up in some cave or on some mountaintop, stockpiling weapons and waiting for Judgment Day.

"Oh, I've figured out how to survive, all right. Nobody else to do it for me."

"You live out here all by yourself?" I asked. She didn't answer me, but her walking slowed so that I had to adjust my pace not to walk up the backs of her heels. Keds, she was wearing, just like the ones Dove said Lynette Farrell had worn all those years ago, the time she'd taken the stage and sung her heart out for Dogwood Days. "It's just that it seems like a lot of space for only one person."

"It is that," Evelyn said. "Lucky for me, I've learned to like it. Here we are."

She reached for the latch on a wooden gate, and we stepped through. I could hardly believe what spread out before my eyes: long, neat rows of tomato towers and bean poles and raised beds of herbs and flowers, bursting green in every direction, as far as I could see. I got dizzy for a minute from all that green, pale sage to the dark, veiny leaves of the impatiens, and the smells, of squash blossoms and rosemary and the rich stew of compost.

I couldn't help it, I said it again: "All this is *yours*?"

"Well, I don't eat it all, of course. I've got a Mexican man, comes by twice a week and takes most of it for his truck stand. But I grow it, yes, ma'am. Every last piece."

"Dove would die," I said, thinking out loud.

Evelyn had bent over to examine a pepper plant. "Who's that?"

"Aunt Dove. She isn't really my aunt. She's Lucy's, Dad's fiancée's. Back in Mooney." Evelyn kept after her task without looking at me. "Dove Munroe. She's a gardener, too. Her whole front yard is a jungle, practically. I never saw anybody with such a green thumb. Till now, I mean." No reply, so I forged ahead. "Maybe you knew her, when you lived there. She told me about the time you sang at Dogwood Days."

Evelyn straightened up but kept her eyes on the plants. "What do you suppose is turning these leaves? I swear, one day it's not enough water, the next it's too much."

"Marigolds are good for nematodes," I said. "That's about all the gardening I know."

"Well, we'll fix that pretty quick. Here." She reached into the pocket of her billowy shirt and handed me a pair of cotton gloves. "The mint bed needs tidying. You do know what mint is, don't you? Pretty plant, but it gets into everything if you don't keep after it."

For a couple of hours she hardly spoke to me, except to give me instructions; mint and weeds look pretty much alike, I found out the hard way, and I never knew there were so many kinds, spear and pepper and lemon and orange. An inch at a time, it seemed, the sun marched across the sky, and once she went up to the house and came back carrying a wide-brimmed hat, which she plunked down on my head, and a canteen of water. The water was cold and tasted like dirt and metal, a strange but not unpleasant taste that caught me by surprise.

"You mean you've never drunk well water, either?" Evelyn said with a shake of her head. "What a life of privation you've had." I said I guessed so, and we went back to work until finally, *finally*, she decided the heat was getting to be too much, and it was time for a break.

Lunch was some kind of smelly, gooey cheese on thick black bread with seeds in it, and a big platter of sliced tomatoes. Evelyn picked at her plate awhile and then lit a cigarette while I polished off all the cheese and bread I could hold. "I'm not usually such a pig," I said, embarrassed by her watching me like she had at breakfast, two eyes behind a smoke screen. "Everything just tastes so good here."

"Better than Dallas, you mean."

"Better than anywhere."

She stubbed out her Lucky and lit a second one from a heavy, silver-plated lighter with the initials "DLR" etched on the side. "Tell me, now, one more time. How did you come to wind up in East Texas? You said your mother brought you here?"

"Yes, ma'am. She got accepted to this training course, see, to be a stockbroker. In Chicago. Where it just so happens this guy she's been dating, Kent, his name is, is working, too. So she brought me to Mooney, to stay with my dad. I hadn't seen him since I was seven. We didn't even know about Lucy, or the baby, any of that. It was all a big surprise for everybody." I watched Evelyn for a reaction but there was nothing but a drawing in on her cigarette. "It was supposed to just be for the summer, but for a while things were going pretty good, and it seemed like I might get to stay with Dad and Lucy and the new baby. We think it's a girl. Sophie. She'll be here for Christmas. Anyway, then all this, this *stuff* started happening, and Dad started getting all tangled up over it, and finally I guess he just couldn't take it anymore."

She tapped her cigarette against the side of the ashtray. "Meaning?"

"Meaning, he said he didn't know what to do with me, and that he was giving up. That he was gonna send me back to Ma." I scraped a few crumbs around on my plate with my fork. "So I ran away. You probably figured that out already."

Evelyn exhaled toward the ceiling, watching the smoke disappear in the blades of the ceiling fan. "The thing I don't quite get is, whatever made you think to come here? You don't know me from Adam. And your daddy hasn't had a thing to do with me in more than thirty years."

"Yes, ma'am," I said, my eyes never leaving her face. "I guess that's what I want to understand."

She stood up, balancing her cigarette in the ashtray and pulling our plates toward her. "Well, I'd like that, too," she said, the words clipped short like she was snipping them with garden shears. "I've been study-ing on it since about 1965, and I don't guess I'm any closer to under-standing it now than I was then. If I ever figure it out, I'll clue you in." She dropped the plates in the sink and turned on the tap, hard, her eyes glued to the window while the water thundered in the metal sink and her Lucky burned itself all the way down to ash.

Then her shoulders sagged, and she reached over and turned off the water. Still, she didn't turn, didn't say a word. I picked up her cigarette and ground out the butt in the ashtray.

"Are you okay?" My voice sounded funny to me, big and loud with all that space to bounce around in.

Her head wagged slowly, side to side. I hopped up from the table and went over and let her lean against me. She surprised me, the sturdiness of her and her readiness to let me take her weight. I'd thought she'd put up more of a fight.

She pointed me down one of the hallways leading off from the kitchen, a different one from the one I'd seen before. We passed a few closed doors, then a pair of big French ones that opened into a kind of study, with a big wood desk and a leather couch and shelves lined with books, more than I'd seen even at Dove's house, and finally her bedroom. It was the size of maybe six of mine, and full of heavy dark furniture, a four-poster bed and an armoire and tables and chests heaped with knickknacks.

She let go of my arm and made her way over to one of the bedside tables and lifted the lid off an enamel box and dumped the contents onto the bed. I watched the bottles roll across the bedspread, a dozen or more little plastic orange-colored vials, watched her fumble around till she found the one she wanted and shake out a couple of pills and wash them down with a glassful of something from a pitcher that sat next to the bed.

She stood for a minute with her eyes closed and her fingertips balanced against the edge of the mattress, then with halting steps crossed to a flowered armchair beside the window and eased herself into it.

"Go on." Her voice had a far-off, rasped-out sound, like it had every cigarette she'd ever smoked down inside it.

"But I— But are you . . ."

She put her head back and shut her eyes. "You've done enough," she said. "Now let me be."

I didn't know what to think. Did she mean she wanted me to leave permanently, get back out of her life for good, or just to let her have her nap? Her hand on the chair's arm trembled a little and then eased. I looked at the bottles of pills strewn across the bedspread, and then around the room, at the heavy carved mirror over the bureau, the pillows piled against the headboard. On the bedside table, along with the pitcher and the glass and a jar of Vicks VapoRub and a box of Kleenex, were a bunch of photographs in silver frames, and I stepped closer and bent to look. Old people, mostly: a man in overalls, a lady in a ruffled hat with a little dog in her lap. And a young woman in a cotton dress and a pair of Keds, squinting into the lens like the sun was in her eyes, with a smiling, black-eyed baby on her hip.

At the window Evelyn breathed in, then out, the pills easing her loose of the grip of her real life and into her dreams. I wondered what it was like there, if she dreamed of the life she'd lost or a whole other one, where everything had turned out the way it was supposed to. And how would that be? I didn't know her much better than I had before I met her, and every peek I'd had, into who she'd been and who she was now, only led to one door and then another, an empty house full of shadowy hallways, not a single one I could see clear to the end of.

I closed the bedroom door behind me and went into the study, where a window looked past a stand of pines to the lake beyond, blue as metal under the July sky. My chest hurt, like something was lodged in there at a wrong angle, up against my heart. The day before was all jumbled up in my head, the Lilac Ladies, the veterans' band, the sky overhead bursting with color and light, Sean Butler's hand on my arm, Erasmus flying through the air like a circus acrobat, Dad storming around Dove's living room, the milk truck, the dinosaur, Evelyn with her little gun and her Luckies. I'd run away, I told her, but all the things I was running from were still with me, etched so deep I couldn't reach them. I'd admired Evelyn and her stubborn ways, her pride and her silence, holding the world at arm's length, but that was before I'd had a look at what it cost her.

I reached into my pants pocket and took out the little wooden bird, turned it over in my hand, stroking the claws and feathers. It was a brave, crazy thing Erasmus had done, and I'd answered him like a gutless wonder, by leaving. But how did you expect to measure yourself in the world without other people to show you what things were worth? It was possible, I guessed, to get old the way Aunt Dove had, without regret; but it was Evelyn I was thinking of, Evelyn in the next room with her stash of pills and all those little portholes into the past on her bedside table, a past she hadn't just lost but had cut herself off from, for reasons I didn't, might not ever, know. Something had beaten her down, disconnected her from ordinary life and its customs and small pleasures, but instead of fighting that thing, she'd caved in to it, hidden herself away. I imagined her now sailing through her multicolored dreams, floating free in a place where her memories couldn't touch her. Or maybe she was onstage at Dogwood Days, with her head thrown back and her throat open and her baby in her arms. I'd wanted something from my grandmother, something whole and warm and absolute, something I barely knew how to name. I saw now that I would never have that thing, but that she might, in her peculiar, broken way, have handed me something else.

I walked slowly back and forth in front of the bookcases, studying the titles on the shelves. Someone loved physics, and astronomy, and the birds and reptiles of the southwest. There were novels, too, one or two I recognized from eighth-grade English. I pulled down a familiar-seeming title and opened the age-stiff spine and heard the pages crackle, watched motes of dust drift upward in the sunlight, like a safe had been cracked.

I wasn't ready to leave this place. We'd been on the brink of something earlier, Evelyn and I, in the kitchen, and in my contumacious way, I believed I might still get a piece of it. Besides, it didn't seem right; taking off while she was sleeping would only add one more name to the list of things I'd let go of too soon. So I stretched out on the leather sofa with a cushion under my head, propping the old book on my knees, and before I knew it I was deep in the world of Gatsby and Daisy and his sad, lost longing for her light.

29

Denny

 When I opened my eyes the room was in shadows, and Evelyn was leaning over me. I wasn't sure at first whether I was awake or had slid one layer deeper into a dream, and I struggled to sit up, knocking *The Great Gatsby* to the floor.

"You aren't easy to get rid of, are you?" she said, her rust-and-gravel voice bringing me back hard into the present. "Just like an old sticker burr. No matter how many times you try to pluck it off, it's hanging on to your pants cuff."

"I just wanted to make sure you were all right."

"Don't be silly. I got too much sun, is all. A little rest, and everybody's restored. Right?"

I didn't feel restored. I felt fuzzy-headed and cotton-mouthed, and a long, long way from home. I didn't know how to say that to my grandmother, though, who in spite of all the property she owned didn't seem to have a home, and so I stood up, stretching the cricks out of my back.

"You've stuck around this long, you might as well get that fishing lesson," she said. "Come on, we'll take the outboard."

We carried the gear down a steep, rocky driveway to the lake, passing a row of shabby cabins, the screens on the porches torn and sagging, the steps caved in. The boat tied to the dock was a beat-up two-tone job, turquoise and white, but the Evinrude motor started on the first try, and I watched with admiration as Evelyn slipped the rope clear of the pilings and guided us out onto the water. It was late afternoon, still plenty hot, but the breeze was steady, and I sat back and watched the scenery, people sitting on a far-off spit of beach, a float where kids were diving, a couple of other boats with their lines already set, little bobbing corks of patience and hope.

We steered into a cove, and Evelyn cut the engine and we drifted in the shade of the pines and water oaks that ringed the shore. I'd been afraid of a lecture about the grand philosophy of fishing, but her approach was more to the point than that: how to bait a hook, how to cast. The bait was some gory-looking stuff in a jar that smelled like death itself, but she swore the fish couldn't resist it, and I managed to pinch my nose shut from the inside and roll a little ball between my thumb and forefinger and get it on the end of my hook. Casting was harder, but Evelyn never got impatient, just showed me one time and then sat back and let me try until I finally got it right. "In Dallas we have grocery stores for this," I said in a grouchy way, but to tell the truth, there was something that pleased me about the sight of our two lines arcing out in opposite directions over the water, the easy way the waves slapped the underside of the boat. A water bug skimmed the surface of the lake, its wings shining in the sun, and I thought, for some reason, just for a second, that the sight of it would break my heart.

"You want something from me." Her voice startled me; we'd been quiet for a long stretch, fifteen, maybe twenty minutes, and anyway, I hadn't expected the first move to come from her. She tapped her cigarette pack against the palm of her hand. "You want to hear what happened to me. How I came to wind up like I did."

"Yes, ma'am, I do," I said as she shook out a Lucky and lit it. "I mean, the story I heard was you went crazy, but you don't seem crazy to me."

"No?" Her smile was tiny.

"Nope. Just—well, hard, kind of. Cold."

She smoked silently, her eyes on the horizon. "You're right," she said finally. "I *am* cold. But you know what? I wasn't always. Not when I met Frank. Your granddaddy."

She glanced at me, tapped her ash into an empty tin can. "I suppose I shouldn't ever have crossed paths with Frank Farrell in the first place. I was just seventeen, had never even been away from home, but when a church friend of my family offered me a chance to study music in Fort Worth, I jumped at it. I was a real serious girl, never had a boyfriend or even a real date, and I thought the big city was a den of iniquity.

"Well, I was right, I just didn't realize how much that would appeal to me. We worked hard in school all week, my roommate and me, but on Friday nights we'd sneak out to nightclubs and sing. It was a lark to us, a break from the classical stuff we studied during the week. I'd taken to calling myself Lynette, and my friend Sherry started going by 'Cheri,' and we'd get up there in our red lipstick and our cheap nylon dresses, and we thought we were hot stuff. Men used to send us drinks and we'd just laugh and send them back. And then, one night, I didn't."

"Didn't what?"

"Send the drink back. It was a Cosmopolitan, cranberry juice and vodka, the prettiest-looking thing I'd ever seen, like a bouquet of tea roses. I took a sip, and I liked it just fine. And by the time I'd turned around to see who'd sent it, there was Frank."

She shook her head. "My, oh, my. My mama died when I was eight, and all the men I knew were like my daddy—hardworking and God-fearing, kept to himself. To me, Frank Farrell was a revelation. I never knew a man could talk so much. And the talk! So smooth you could just about skate on it. He used to take me driving around the city at night in this big Chevy he had, and I'd just put my head back and listen to him talk, and talk . . . It was a kind of gift, really. He could have been on the radio.

"Frank had a job with the Missouri Pacific, and after we'd been seeing each other just a few months, they transferred him to northeast Texas. I didn't give a thought to music school, even though my roommate and some of my teachers tried to talk me out of leaving. One of them, a lady about the age I am now, even cried, but I couldn't be swayed. I was fully and totally under Frank's spell.

"So we got married, by a JP in Fort Worth with Cheri—Sherry— standing up for us, and we moved to Mooney. I was telling myself, then, that it was just the first step, that Frank would get set in his career, we'd go back to the city, I'd still be able to sing someday. I didn't know any better; I figured so long as I had the voice, the chance would always be there. We never talked about kids—it was just something you did in those days, you never thought about it one way or the other. We were doing okay, we had a house and a little money, so when I found out I was pregnant, it just seemed like the next thing, you know?"

She drew on her Lucky and held the smoke a long time, then let it out with a sigh. "I don't know how to tell this next part without— Well, I guess there's no way but straight out." She looked at me and I nodded. I didn't think of myself as too shockable, not anymore, and I didn't want her to keep anything back.

"I admit I always knew Frank saw other women," she said. "He had plenty of girlfriends when he met me, and I was never sure he stopped seeing them even after we got engaged. To be honest, I was relieved when he got the job in Mooney. I thought it would give us a clean start, and how much trouble could he get in, I figured, in a town of less than a thousand people?" I bit my lip, thinking about how I'd heard Dad managed to parcel himself out before he'd met Lucy, but I let Evelyn go on.

"Well, Frank didn't let the move or marriage, either one, slow him down. He was decent enough, or maybe just smart enough, to keep it out from under my nose. But he traveled a lot, for his job, and, well, the opportunities were always there. Frank thrived on the opportunities, I think, more than he did the actual conquests. Although there was one back in Fort Worth, I found out later, he never did give up. Do you know, she had the gall to get herself listed as his 'life partner' in his newspaper obituary? Of course, maybe it was true. She got a lot bigger piece of him than I did, that's for sure.

"Getting pregnant only made things worse. At first I blamed myself, for letting myself get ugly and tired and miserable, and then I blamed the baby for making me that way. I just—oh, I don't know how to say this so it will make any sense, I've been living with it for nearly forty years, and I still can't make it come out right. I just worshiped Frank Farrell. I really and truly revered him. Yes, he was untrue to me, and yes, I didn't know a thing about real, grown-up love, and still, I would have walked on coals to get him to look at me the way he did the first time, over that drink the color of roses.

"It *is* a kind of craziness, don't you think, feeling about somebody that way?" She held her Lucky between two fingers but it had burned itself out. "It just wore me down, till there was nothing left of me to look out for myself anymore, or my baby—it was all just Frank, Frank, Frank.

"He just never could get used to the idea of himself as a family man. All the things he was supposed to do, and feel, those things just weren't in Frank's repertoire, so to speak. At first he resented me for getting him into it, and then I believe he started to hate me for it. We fought—fought like it was going out of style—but there wasn't a thing I could do. It was like trying to change the pull of the moon.

"Finally, he took off. Said he'd had enough, packed a suitcase, and drove away. I was frantic, spent weeks and weeks trying to find him. The railroad wouldn't tell me where he'd gone, or even if he was still in their employ. Things weren't like they are now, where you have all kinds of social services set up to help women who get themselves in a jam. I couldn't even find out if Frank left any money in the bank, or whether or not the house note was paid. And I'd never had to look out for myself before, much less a two-year-old child."

"What about your family?" I asked.

"Well, it was just my daddy and my brothers, and they hadn't cared much for me taking up with Frank in the first place. They'd have been willing, I guess, to track him down and whup him for what he'd done, but they didn't have the first clue how to be of help to me when he left. And I didn't have any female kin, and no real friends close by. We'd only lived in Mooney a couple of years, so we weren't real town folks, you know, and Frank's shenanigans hadn't made us too popular. About the only person who put out a hand to me for the longest time was Christa Keller."

"You mean, you knew Christa Keller?" The way I'd thought of Dad being let go to a foster family, it had seemed random, a quirk of fate; it had never come to mind that his real mother and his foster mother might have chanced to cross paths.

"Sure, I knew her. I met her at one of the band concerts they used to have in the summertime, there on the courthouse square. Our husbands were out of town, and we were out with our babies and we struck up a conversation, sitting on the grass. She was pregnant with her second, I recall. Right off you could see she was taken with my little boy. Well, everybody was, he was such an eyeful, with those big brown eyes and that smile—just like his daddy, could charm the paper off the walls.

"After that, I'd run into her here and there, at the beauty shop, the Food King. I even took her a little gift when her daughter was born. When Frank and I had our first big fight, she came by the hospital to visit me—he'd given me quite a shove, and I had stitches in my head— and she offered to take the baby for a couple of days, until I was back on my feet. I remember I cried, right there in the hospital, it was such a relief."

Evelyn dropped her burned-out cigarette into the tin can. "Later on, after everything was said and done, after I signed the papers giving him up, I couldn't get shed of the notion that that boy was meant to be Christa's, all along. That for some reason he'd been mine to carry, but that I set things right letting him go to her, where he really belonged."

And that's why you keep his picture on your bedside table, I thought but didn't say. "Is it true they took you to Rusk? That place is for criminals."

"Well, I had a gun."

"What?"

"The second time I—well—broke down. There was a gun on the table when they came for me, Frank's old pistol. No bullets, mind you, not in the chamber or anywhere in the house, but somehow they got it in their heads I was armed and dangerous. They *did* take me to Rusk, for three or four days, but they couldn't pin anything on me, and my daddy found a place for me in a hospital down near Beaumont. I was there two whole years, almost. When they let me out, Daddy and my big brother, Mack, brought me back here. And that—" She held up her hands, open and empty, as if what they held told the rest of the story: nothing. Nothing but pills and a truck garden and a run-down fish camp, a house so big your voice could echo from one end to the other, and never anyone to answer you back, unless you believed in ghosts.

"So, are you sane now? Whatever that means?"

"Well, I'm not armed and dangerous, not unless I find intruders napping on my screened porch. And so long as I take my pills, I guess I'm as sane as most folks. Whatever *that* means."

"You never tried to see him—my dad? Not once, in thirty-three years?"

"I signed that away, when I gave him to Christa." She laughed her one-note laugh. "Jesus, you should see your face."

There was a tug on one of the lines, and Evelyn adjusted her position in the bow to check it. "Let me tell you something, miss. Not an hour of my life goes by that I don't think about what I did, whether there was some way to make it come out differently. But it doesn't matter how many times I try to change the ending. There's no going back. I couldn't care for my son, so I gave him to someone who could."

"But what about later, after he was grown? Maybe if you—"

"Look. I made the choice, and I've lived with it. You've got a bite, I think."

I watched the line stretch taut toward the water and thought about what Evelyn had said. It didn't add up, not by any arithmetic I knew. It seemed to me that as long as you were still breathing there was a chance to do things over, that if you didn't like the ending you just backed up and wrote it again. But I was fifteen years old, give or take a few hours, alert to the possibility of reinvention. When I'd baited that hook, I'd never in a million years expected to catch anything. Maybe in my next life I would be a fisherman.

I walked on my knees over to my rod and stood up and took the reel in my hands. Without a word Evelyn eased in behind me, shifting her weight to balance the boat, and then her arms slid around me and her hands cupped mine. They were rough from work and spotted from sun, the fingers knobby and strong. How would it feel, I wondered, making your way through the days knowing nothing you did was essential to another human being? But Evelyn's grip was sure, and I knew she was holding on as tight as she could.

We brought in the little half-pound catfish without a struggle, but it was so pitiful-looking, flopping around in the bottom of the boat, Evelyn picked it up and flung it right back over the side. "Go on, fatten yourself up a little," she said. "We'll come back for you another time."

"Yeah, *catch you later!*" I shouted, and fell all over myself laughing.

Evelyn smiled, the first honest-to-goodness smile I'd seen from her. Wouldn't you know, her front teeth overlapped a little, just like Dad's and mine. You could talk all you wanted about giving up on the world; you could find yourself an old fish camp, let your hair go wild, shut yourself in a room with your pictures and pills. Blood was a chain, a chain you couldn't see, and as long as it was there, it would still, would always, hold you to people, whether you liked it or not.

"Your turn," she said.

"Excuse me?"

"You heard the story of my life. Now let's hear yours. Don't tell me you haven't got one. I wouldn't believe it for a minute."

So I told her, fifteen years condensed into fifteen minutes, as we floated in a speckled mix of sun and shadows and all the catfish in the lake swam under our boat, ignoring our baited hooks.

"So, you've got a decision to make," Evelyn said finally. "East Texas, or Dallas and that music school. Maybe even Chicago. Or Nashville."

I shrugged. "It's not like it's really my choice. Anyway, I'm probably already grounded for the rest of my life."

We hadn't had a bite since that half-grown catfish, so we reeled in the lines and Evelyn started the engine and we roared out of the cove, scaring up a flock of wild ducks that took off ahead of us like an unfurling flag and then split and scattered across the lake. The water had changed color, lost the blue of the day to the dark green of the trees on the banks. The sun had started its downward crawl and the worst heat of the day was past, but we were both red-faced and sweating as we tied up the boat and piled the fishing gear on the dock.

"Do you sing anymore?"

She set down the tackle box and turned to me. "Haven't you gotten a big enough piece of me for one day? Now you want a concert."

"Dad said I got my voice from you."

"He — How could he remember a thing like that? He wasn't two years old."

"I don't know how. But he does."

"Well, that was a long time ago. The old pipes aren't what they used to be." She played with the pack of Luckies in her shirt pocket.

I handed over the little Igloo cooler and the rods, thinking about the tapes I'd swiped from Dad's truck, all those sweet old voices, full of tears and twang. They said nobody sang like that anymore, but I knew it wasn't true.

" 'Searching, I've spent a lifetime, darlin', searching . . . ' "

I started on my own, sweet and low, and after a couple lines Evelyn joined in, a little rough on the first notes but leveling out as we went on, " 'cause I've been searching for someone just like you." We moved through "I Still Miss Someone," "Coat of Many Colors," "Sweet Dreams of You," a whole jukebox's worth of cowgirl heartbreak before Evelyn sat down on the dock and held up her hand and begged to get her wind back.

"Enough," she said, taking out her cigarettes. "Somebody's liable to call the sheriff and report somebody strangling to death out here."

"I bet you'd have your old voice back in no time if you cut out the Luckies."

"That, miss, is not an option." Out on the lake a ski boat flew by, painting a streak of color and noise across the water.

"I only know one song by Brenda Lee," I said. "Do you think you could show me another one?"

"Lord! Does it never stop with you?"

I grinned at her and shook my head, and Evelyn smiled a little and shook hers. She held out her hand, and I gripped it in mine and pulled her to her feet.

"You have a calling," she said.

"Ma'am?" She was making me nervous. Her eyes were funny.

"Don't do like I did," she said, her fingers twined around my wrist.

"Take a hold of it and hold on, no matter what. Don't you let it go for anything."

The dock swayed under our feet in the wake from the ski boat, and Evelyn shut her eyes. She was time-traveling again, but this time she was taking me with her.

"'All alone am I, alone with just a bit of my heart . . . '"

The hair on the back of my neck started to tickle. I was sure we both could see her, a young woman in her pink pedal pushers, moving her hands in a sink full of soapy water, never once thinking the song on the radio might come true. Somewhere off in the trees a car horn honked, but if Evelyn heard it, she didn't let on. The voice was shining and sure, not a speck of grit or a cobweb on it. On the kitchen floor a child played, minding his own business but listening, always listening. Something had started. A chain. I was there. I don't know how I knew that, but I knew. Then, like now, I was there, and I was listening, too.

Lucy

"She said what again, exactly?"

Ash draped his wrists over the steering wheel. "I told you already, Lucy. I told you two times."

Another hot, humid afternoon, just like the day before, and even with all the windows in the Buick rolled down the air felt like damp cotton, like we were swimming in bales of it. I'd put on my best maternity blouse, white with little sprigs of yellow flowers, and left the button undone at the waistband of my skirt, but from the very first minute we'd left town I was sweating, and Ash had rings under the arms of his T-shirt.

The phone call had come late that morning—hours after the first one from Dove, who'd gone in to wake Denny and found her bed empty—and before he even told me who it was or what was said, Ash collapsed at the kitchen table. We'd had the sheriff and my brothers out scouring the county all morning, and I stood in the doorway, petrified, waiting to hear the worst. Never in a million years did I expect what came out of his mouth when he finally raised his head: "She's at my mama's." I'd had to sit down a minute and try to remember who that was.

"Tell me again."

"She said her name—which didn't click, not right at first—and then she said, 'Your daughter's here. I thought you'd want to know.' Then she told me how to get here, and to come at four o'clock. She said they were going fishing."

"Ash." He took his eyes off the windshield and glanced at me. "Come on! There had to be more to it than that. Nobody just picks up the phone after thirty-some years and has a conversation like that! It's like, like some kind of code or something. Are you sure there wasn't anything else? Something you're leaving out?"

"It wasn't a code. And I didn't leave anything out. Did you ever think maybe that's all she had to say?"

"Well, what did she sound like? Was she nice?"

"It was only a couple of sentences, plus the directions."

I looked again at the sign that marked the turn, the road barely visible, a break in a bank of pecans. "I don't get it. She said her name is *LeGrande*?"

Ash set his jaw and put the car back in gear.

"What a coincidence, huh? So is mine."

We bumped and joggled up a single lane of red clay lined with pines and pecans and live oaks, the shade so deep and wet it felt like a live thing, like it was breathing, watching. I recalled the very first conversation I'd had with Ash about his mama, just a few days after I'd met him, and the last, not two weeks later. It was old ground, he said, not one he cared to tread, although I think he visited it often by himself, those nights he'd sit up at the table for hours, sometimes, with a glass of Jack Daniel's and his guitar after I'd gone to bed. I admit I'd thought about her myself, off and on, in the way you think about what you've taken on when there's new life inside you. I wanted to hate her for Ash's sake, but I couldn't; I was beginning to understand the terror she must have felt, that cold black wave of obligation always pulling at you, threatening to drag you under. How did it catch you? I wanted to ask her; why didn't you fight? But I'd never expected to come nose to nose with her, to see my questions, and Ash's, written on her face. Hand it to Denny to turn over a rock nobody else would touch, see what would come swarming out into the daylight.

The road opened at last in a clearing, the house spread out low and ugly and ramshackle, at odds with the dazzle of the lake behind it. Ash switched off the engine and we sat for a minute listening to it cool. No one came out to greet us; a breeze moved through the trees, smelling of fuel and fish, but other than a ski boat out on the lake, nothing stirred. Ash stretched in the seat and eyed the screened porch nervously.

"Relax," I said, pushing open the car door. "She's probably just a nice, normal person. She called you, didn't she? She wants to give you your daughter back."

"I've been thinking about that," Ash said. "Maybe it wouldn't be so bad if—" I cut him off with a look. "You want to knock, or should I?"

"You're the one she's expecting. She might call the cops on me."

He got out of the car and slammed the door. "Look, I just want to say one thing, okay? About this, this Evelyn LeGrande person? If everybody thinks I'm gonna get down on my knees and excuse what she did, well, it won't work. I'm not interested. The only reason I'm here is Denny. The *only* reason."

"Aren't you getting ahead of yourself?" I said. "Denny wanted to meet her grandmother. Why don't we start there and see what happens?"

Ash gave a curt nod and stepped up onto the screened porch and hammered his fist against the door. He hammered and hammered, but no one answered, and the house stayed shut up tight as a drum.

"Shit. She said four o'clock. What time is it?"

"She said they were going fishing, didn't she? Maybe they're—"

He reached through the open car window and applied the heel of his palm to the horn: one long blast, three short ones, two long. It was a good old Detroit horn, suited to all those proud horses that lived under the hood, and its reach was probably half a mile.

All of a sudden, he stopped. He turned his face toward the lake.

"Listen."

"What?"

I didn't hear anything, and then I did—like a far-away radio, tuned to some old-time station. The old tapes Ash carried in the truck came to mind, songs I'd grown up listening to on Aunt Dove's Philco. They didn't make music like that anymore.

It grew louder, swelling, straining toward some bright peak, as a second voice joined the first, layered one over the other like frosting on a cake. Ash walked to the front of the car and stood there, his arms hanging loose at his sides.

"Hear that?" he said. And set off in the direction of the lake, toward the music.

Denny

Evelyn stood looking up the boat ramp, and I shaded my eyes with my hand, squinting into the sun. I couldn't make sense of what I saw, a mismatched image snipped out of one photo and glued onto a different one.

"That's *Dad*."

I turned to Evelyn for some response, but she looked like she always did, poker-faced. The man standing on the ramp could have been a cop or a Bible salesman and not her long-lost son.

"Go," she said to me.

So I went, taking my time, checking him out. The air felt thick, like a storm was coming, even though there wasn't a cloud in the sky. I knew from his eyes that he wasn't about to let me off the hook, not yet. But in spite of everything, I felt a lifting in my chest, all the things I'd carried crowded up in there melting like ice in the sun.

"How did you get here?" I said. "Where's Lucy?"

"It's good to see you, too, Denise. Are you having a nice little vacation, here at the lake, while everybody in Mooney's been turning the county wrong side out, hunting for your ass?"

"It isn't a *vacation*," I said sourly. "I ran *away*."

"I know." He shifted his weight from one foot to the other, the way he did when things got too thick for him. But you could pull his tongue out with pliers before you'd get him to say, *My fault*.

"So, did you bring the strap? Have you called Ma and ratted me out? You might as well tell me now."

He looked off over my shoulder. Evelyn had lit a Lucky and stood at the end of the dock, smoking and watching the ski boat like we weren't even there. I admit I'd thought about it, my dad and my grandmother falling into each other's arms, but I saw right then it wasn't going to happen. There was a lot more than just the length of a boat ramp between them.

"No strap," he said. "And this is no business of your mama's, is it? This is between you and me."

"Yes, sir," I said. "I guess it is."

"Go ahead, then," he said. "Say your piece."

"I don't want to go back to Ma."

He thought about this for a second. "What about music school?" he said. "What about Erasmus?"

"He probably isn't even speaking to me," I said. "I just about got him killed, and took off without even saying thank you."

"Well, I talked to him this morning, when he got home from the hospital," Dad said. "I think he'll be pretty happy to see you. Lord knows why."

"Dad? Look, I know what we did was wrong. Sneaking off like that, getting mixed up with the Butlers. But I can't . . ."

"Can't what?"

"Can't be running around scared all the time, looking for bad guys. You want to keep me in a, a box or something, and I can't do that." I found a loose rock and rolled it under the toe of my sneaker. "I have a calling."

Was it my imagination, or had my father gotten older this summer,

in the handful of weeks I'd known him? The lines around his mouth
and eyes were white against the tan, and his cheekbones—not Evelyn's
or mine, but somebody else's, or just his own—jutted under his skin.
Or maybe I'd just learned to see him clear: not the handsome stranger
I'd first met in his kitchen or the raving beast in Dove's living room the
night before, but his real self, the self that can't be seen until you know
someone truly, dark and light, good and bad.

He smiled then, not all-out, but with a shifting in the muscles of his
face, and with his eyes. "A calling."

"Yes, sir."

"Like the Holy Grail, something like that?"

"Kind of, yeah. *You* know what I mean."

"Jesus help me, I do." Lucy had come to the top of the ramp, and I
raised my hand and she waved back.

"You know I'm going to Nashville in a couple weeks," he said. "You
think you might stick around while I'm gone, keep Lucy company?"

"Yes, sir."

"I can't promise you what'll happen at the end of the summer,
Denise. Your mama has legal custody. You understand what that
means?"

"You can talk to her, though, can't you? *Can't* you?"

"Maybe. We'll see how things go while I'm gone. Anyway, you're
fifteen now. I have to be able to depend on you not to just take off the
first time somebody looks at you cross-eyed."

"You mean I'm on, like, *probation*?"

"Yep. We'll run by the courthouse straight off, get you fitted up with
some nice leg chains."

"Dad?"

"What, baby girl?"

"I wish I hadn't called you an asshole. I mean—well, I'm not all that
sorry about the rest of it, not really. But that part was bad."

He shrugged. "Truth hurts."

"I guess Lucy still wants to marry you anyway."

"Lucky for me, I guess she does."

"When?"

"That's for the three of us to discuss. Dove might have something to say about it, too, once she gets through wearing you out for what you did."

Evelyn had finished her cigarette. I watched her stub it out in the tin can and bend to gather the fishing gear.

"We better get a move on," Dad said. "It's just about suppertime, and Dove's frying chicken."

"But you— You're not gonna come meet her? Not even to say hello to your own—"

He reached out and squeezed my arm, then let go. "Go on now, and say good-bye."

A couple of the rods had gotten tangled, and without saying anything I walked out onto the dock and helped Evelyn straighten them out. I was thinking about the highway that stretched between here and Mooney, thirty miles of two-lane blacktop, the broken white line connecting Evelyn to me, how it had led me to her and how some piece of me would stay behind.

"There now," she said when we'd finished. "I can manage the rest."

"You called him," I said.

Evelyn hoisted one shoulder, looked out at the water.

"Don't be too quick to burn your bridges," she said. "You think you have a chance to build them up again, but you never know."

"Could I come see you again sometime?" I said. "Just, like, a regular visit. No middle-of-the-night business."

Her lips pinched up in the mildest of smiles. "Maybe another time the fish'll be biting." But I saw that whatever piece of Evelyn I'd gotten, the gap had sealed itself again, solid as it had been the night before, when she'd sat on her screened porch smoking a Lucky with a revolver in her lap.

"Well. It was nice meeting you."

She tossed her head, the knot of frizzed hair at the back of her neck slipping a little, and I followed her eyes past my shoulder, to the top of the boat ramp where Dad stood, facing us, his expression hidden in the shade. I wish I could say it happened then, a white-hot spark of connection, all those years of iced-up blood turning liquid in the blink of an eye. And maybe it did; maybe it was just too small for me to see. Dad might have moved his chin an inch, down, then up again, a nearly invisible nod. Evelyn might have returned it. Part of me wanted to believe that so bad. But I knew there was no such thing as a happy ending, only that, every now and then, happiness touches down, like that water bug skimming the surface of the dark green lake, flitting from one surface to the next, brushing it with its bright, beating wings. Sometimes, if you're lucky, if you keep still and make him welcome, he might sit awhile. But you'd better not count on it. Pay attention while you've got him, because he'll be gone before you can blink your eyes.

Then Evelyn turned away, toward the water, and I started up the ramp to my father, thinking about fried chicken, and a bridesmaid's dress the color of tea roses, and a boy with a name like royalty and a fiddle on his shoulder, and home.

Lucy

 I wake with a gasp, my nightgown bunched and sweaty, and push up onto my elbows, still tangled in the cobwebs of a dream. My heart is thumping, but the house is dark and quiet, and Ash's side of the bed is empty, even though we turned in hours ago.

I lie back slowly, still hanging onto the edges of the dream. In it, I was awake, sitting up in this very bed in this very room, and there was a man sitting in the rocking chair in the corner. I didn't know the man, but I seemed to recognize him, his rust-colored hair, his shoulders, the cut of his jaw. He looked, come to think of it, a little like my brother Bailey, and we sat studying each other unself-consciously, in the silence of a sleeping house, at ease in each other's company. If anything passed between us, if anything was said, I don't recall. Then the man got to his feet and stretched his legs and said, "I'll see you later, Mama." And I woke up.

As I swing my feet to the floor, my hand moves to my belly, the modest swell under my nightgown, and I think of Ash standing in the parking lot of the clinic with the photo of the sonogram in his hand saying, *Jude Hatch Farrell,* and a shiver crawls up my spine: amazement, regret, panic, joy. Oh, Sophie; I'd been so sure! But I know—with a sinking, then a soaring—that I was wrong.

I make my way through the dark house, bathroom, living room, kitchen, filled with nothing but hush and moon. We had supper at Aunt Dove's earlier this evening, Ash and Denny and I, then rode by Bailey's to check out his new project, a gazebo in the backyard, complete with a latticed roof and a hammock and an automatic bug zapper, for Geneva. She's always wanted one, he said to me, a wistful note tucked up alongside the pleased, proud one. I'd looked over at him, silhouetted in the backyard floodlights. I don't know if a gazebo will fill the place in Geneva that needs filling. I don't think Bailey knows, either. But then he glanced at me and shrugged and said, "Hey, what the hell," and I thought it was possible to imagine him old, not fifty but eighty, ninety, lying with Geneva in a hammock under the stars. He says they've been talking on the phone every night, like teenagers. He says she's bored at her sister's, that she might come home sooner than she first thought. I told him to tell her she'd better hurry up, or she might miss a wedding.

A sliver of light shines from Denny's door, and I think of knocking, then see the phone cord snaked underneath and decide against it. We had a birthday cake for her tonight, fifteen candles, even though the actual day isn't till tomorrow, and she seems already to have staked her claim to everything that comes with the territory. All that happened to her since last night, whatever she found at her grandmother's, she's keeping it to herself. Still, I managed to eke out of her a promise for tomorrow, to go looking at bridesmaids' dresses. Maybe she'll spill some beans, maybe she won't. This must be one of the hardest things to abide about children, watching them move away from you into provinces that are less and less yours and more and more their own. All you can do is stand there, holding out your hand.

I push open the screen door and step out onto the porch, the boards smooth and dusty under my bare feet. It's a warm night, the sky so black it's nearly purple, spattered with stars. Nobody ever got around to replacing the porch bulb, and so it's a few seconds before I make out Ash on the step, the tilt of his head, the slope of his shoulders, those shoulders I've just seen on someone else, in a dream.

"Hey," he says, and I take a seat beside him, tucking my gown around my knees. I consider for a second telling him about the dream; I imagine myself saying, *I've just seen our son.* But it feels like privileged information somehow, like a secret I've been entrusted with. For the time being, it's between Jude and me.

Ash picks up my hand and folds it into his, and for a long time we're quiet, thinking our own thoughts. In spite of their troubles, I envy Bailey and Geneva sometimes, their history, their pet names and unspoken codes, the fact that they've know each other all their lives. But Ash and I belonged to ourselves first, before we found each other. We have dark corners, both of us, sacred and private ground. And one sweet, shining spot where we meet in the middle. We're there now, I believe, and things feel old between us, and right.

"So, how does it feel to be the father of a fifteen-year-old?"

"You tell me. How does it feel to be her mother?"

"Scary," I say, and Ash laughs.

"Do you know what she told me this afternoon? That she has a 'calling.'"

"Lord help us."

"That's what I said." And we're quiet for another spell. I'm thinking of the person I saw on the dock today with the lake behind her and a cigarette in her hand, the look that passed between her and her son, not a single note of recognition, no warmth or cheer. There's a small, secluded place in Ash where Lynette Farrell used to live, and this stranger, this Evelyn LeGrande, can't fill it. But I know, too, that he's never stopped going there, never stopped asking that last, big *Why?*

"What did the sheriff have to say?" I ask. I know Ash called Bill Dudley when we got home tonight, presumably to talk about Tim Spivey and the Butler brothers.

"Sean Butler turned up at the emergency room, finally, with a big old nasty gash in his arm. Claims he tore it up fixing fence for his granddaddy." Ash turns my hand over in his and runs his thumb slowly across my knuckles. "Bill wants Erasmus to bring charges, but he said he'd have to think about it.

"You know, maybe Denny was right," Ash says. "Maybe I've been trying to keep her in a box. But I'm damned if I know what to do about it."

"Remember what you said to me last week, over at the rent house? That there's always a middle ground?" He nods, but in a way that tells me this isn't one of those times. "Maybe you worry too much. Denny's all right. She's got a lot of spine."

"*That's* what worries me."

"Well, we've got her back. For now." It's hard to believe nearly half the summer is gone, that the scruffy, lost girl I first saw standing in this yard just a few weeks ago has managed to wedge herself so doggedly into our lives, the third point on a triangle that even now is turning itself into a quadrangle, an arrangement for four.

Ash nods. "For now."

A plane passes overhead, red lights blinking on its underbelly, leaving a trail of white vapor across the Milky Way. All those lives moving past, hundreds of miles an hour, toward places I've never seen, can't even dream, choices I'll never make. Meanwhile here, down below, are all the ones I have.

"Do you think they have stars like this in Tennessee?"

He smiles without looking at me, his eyes following the jetliner's contrail. "We'll be finding out ourselves, before too long."

I lay my hand against Ash's back. Between the blades of his shoulders I can feel his heart beat, sturdy and unapologetic, under his skin. He has to work tomorrow; Denny and I have a wedding to plan. But morning is still hours away.

I get to my feet, shake out my gown. "Are your keys in the truck?"

He smiles. "You taking off on me again?"

They're right where I thought they'd be, dangling from the ignition, and I lean in and hit the headlights and twist the radio dial until I find the Louisiana soul station and turn it up, loud, and there in the high beams, bare feet in the red clay, I start to dance. I want to move while I still can, while my step is still light, before I'm all belly and sway; I want to carry this sense of myself, unencumbered, as a touchstone into my new life. *Lucy Hatch*, I sing to the pulse of my heart and the beat of that wild swamp music, even though, in a matter of days now, my name will be Farrell. *Lucy Hatch*. I think of the way Ash held it in his mouth the very first time he said it, like a drop of after-dinner brandy, something sweet and intoxicating. *Lucy Hatch*. I hold out my hands, and he stands and takes them, and together, in a fine swinging, laughing duet, we dance her to the moon.

Denny

It's just a few minutes before midnight, and I'm lying here in the dark, watching the curtains move in the breeze from the air conditioner and waiting for my birthday. I know it's silly, that the little calendar on the digital clock flipping over to the sixth of July won't make that much difference one way or another. But still, I want to see it, to mark it for my own.

There was a cake for me when we got home from Dove's, chocolate, fresh-baked, with fifteen candles. I smelled it right off, as soon as we walked in, but I knew it was supposed to be a surprise so I didn't say anything, just went off to take a shower. Sure enough, when I came out, all the lights were off, and I could hear Dad and Lucy in the kitchen, giggling like maniacs. It was so stupid, but I went along with it. "Hey!" I yelled. "Why's it so dark in here?" I found them at the table with the cake blazing away, and Dad came around and threw his arm over my shoulder and hollered out, "Here comes fifteen!"

Like I said, corny beyond belief. Still, even while I was groaning and rolling my eyes, I felt that place in me that at Evelyn's had been all sad and hollowed out filling up. It's not that I expect things to be all rosy now, like one of those plastic families on TV, where the worst that ever happens is that somebody gets a D in biology. We've got plenty ahead, all of us, and my dad and I have not knocked heads for the last time, you can bet on that. "Contumacious" was the word Evelyn used. I knew without needing a dictionary, just by the tone of her voice, what it means, and where I got it from, too. But this is my family. I've seen the other side, Evelyn's side, and this is better. "Make a wish," Lucy said, but to tell the truth, I stared at all the fire on that cake and it didn't seem like there was anything I wanted that I didn't have.

Well. Maybe one thing.

They took their time cleaning up the kitchen, still laughing and cutting up, then said good night to me, and as soon as their door was shut, I ran for the telephone and dragged it down the hall and into my room. I was nervous, dialing. It was late, and I didn't know what I'd do if that old cranky aunt of Erasmus's answered and told me to bug off.

But she didn't. A man picked up, I guessed his dad. "Mr. King?" I said. "This is Denny Farrell. Sir?" He didn't answer me, but he didn't hang up, either. Then I heard voices on the other end, far-off-sounding, like someone had a hand over the mouthpiece, and Erasmus came on, saying, "Hello? Denny?"

"I know it's late," I said, the words tumbling over each other. "We were having birthday cake, and Dad and Lucy just now went to bed."

"Whose birthday?"

"Mine. Or, it will be, in a couple hours."

"Really? Happy birthday."

"Thanks." Neither one of us spoke for a while. "How's your head?"

"It hurts."

I just about laughed at the way he said it, like he didn't have any idea how that came to be. "Well, what do you expect when you crash into a plate-glass window?"

"I don't even remember it. I remember the guy grabbing me, but nothing after that."

"He threw you against the front of the video store! So hard you broke the window! There was blood all over the place, and you didn't move for the longest time. It was terrible."

"The sheriff was out here earlier," Erasmus said. "He wants to bring those guys up on charges."

"What kind of charges?"

"Assault. Harassment. There are a bunch of different ways it could go. I mean, the whole story is—what do they call it? My word against theirs."

"Circumstantial." I remembered that from civics class, a paper I'd written on famous trials. "But I was there," I said. "I saw everything. It's my word, too."

"Well, that's what I— I didn't know how you'd feel about that."

"About what?"

"Giving a statement. Maybe even going to court, if it goes that far."

"Wow." I hadn't thought about that. I did now, and he was quiet, letting me make up my own mind. "I guess I would if you would."

"You would?"

"No telling what those guys would have done to us. What they might do to somebody else. Anyway, you put yourself out there with them, because of me. I . . ."

"What?"

"I feel like I owe you, for what you did."

"After you took off," he said, real slow, "I didn't know what to think."

"But it wasn't about that, not at all."

"What was it about, then?"

"That night, after you got hurt? I had a fight with Dad. He said he was gonna send me back to my mom. I—well, I panicked, I guess. I thought if nobody wanted me here, I'd better get away. Find a place to think about things. That's all."

"Denny," Erasmus said, "how could you think nobody wanted you here?"

I lay back on the bed and let my eyes travel around the room, the furniture still smelling of honey stain, the flowered bedspread, the guitar standing in the corner, the little carved bluebird standing next to my lipstick on the bedside table. Material things don't equal happiness, they say, but it's true they can be tokens, reminders that someone has made a place in their heart for us, and tried to give us a piece of that, in worldly form.

"So, did you find your grandmother?"

"I found her."

"What was that like?"

"Sad. But, I don't know, kind of good, too. I'm glad I did it. Even if it did get everybody upset at me. I'm sorry about that." If there was anything I'd learned from Evelyn, it was to admit I'd made a mistake, to say I was sorry, and then let it go. I didn't want to look behind me when I was her age and find one bridge after another, scorched and smoking, all the way back as far as I could see.

"Have you still got your bluebird?"

"Right here," I said. "It was in my pocket every minute."

"I didn't know tomorrow was your birthday," he said. "I would've tried to come up with something better than a wooden bird."

"No." I picked up the bird and rolled it in my palm. The wood was cool and smooth to the touch, but I had no doubt that inside was a real, beating heart. "This is all I want."

"So, you want to run into town tomorrow, grab a burger at the Dairy Queen? Ha, ha," he threw in at the last minute, like I might not know he was joking.

"Ha, ha."

"But seriously," he said. "It's your birthday. We ought to do something."

"The last time we did something, we just about got killed."

"Yeah, it's a hard act to follow."

I laughed for real then, and so did he. "Maybe you could come here for supper. Bring your fiddle."

"That would be good." And for a few seconds we just listened to each other breathe. "Can I call you in the morning?"

"Okay. I mean—yes. I want you to."

"Denny?"

"What?"

"I'm glad you came home."

I hung up then, and I've been lying here ever since, watching the curtains wave and waiting for midnight. In some ways it feels like I've been around the world and back, and in some ways, it was like I was never gone. I liked it at Evelyn's, her scrambled eggs, her big, wild garden, the lake. But I feel like this little corner of the world is mine, this room and the house that holds it. There's something that lives in these walls, and if I close my eyes, I can still see every detail, can pick out each thing in it by its familiar place and its smell, varnish, new-laid carpet, laundry soap, chocolate cake, and I say to myself, *I choose this. This is mine.*

All of a sudden the room is full of light, flooding in through the window, and I roll over and put my chin on the sill. I'm not believing what I see. It's Lucy, right out in the front yard with the truck lights on and the doors open, and the radio pouring out loud enough to serenade the countryside, and she's dancing, like some kind of a witch-woman in her nightgown, her arms and her hair all wild, like she's casting a spell. "Oh you worry me to death, Mama, like a dog worries a bone, yes, you love me right and left, Mama . . ." the voice on the radio howls, and she's smiling, moving toward Dad with her arms out, and now he's up and dancing, too. The word "lunatic" comes to mind. I consider calling Erasmus back and saying, Help! — saying, You would not believe this if you saw it with your own eyes. It's a good thing I decided to stick around, is all I can say. That baby is going to need all the help it can get.

"Denise!" Dad yells. "Come on out here! It's a party!"

I can't help but recall the first day I came here, the way I felt seeing them together, like my nose was pressed right up against the glass of something I'd always been hungry for. I wasn't sure I'd ever get inside.

They're laughing now, stomping and swinging their hips, doing the bump while some gutter-voiced black man sings out, "Oh my sweet ginger mama, sweet as sugar pie."

Then I look over at the clock on the night table. The dial says 12:01, the very first minute of my fifteenth year, and just like that, I've made my choice. I jump off the bed and slip Erasmus's little bird in my pocket, and head out to join the dance.